ONLY YOU

McKenzie felt powerless beneath Gavin's stare. And vulnerable. The helpless feeling was unnerving and not to her liking at all.

But that didn't stop her body from reacting. She felt the sun on her back, heating her clothes, sensitizing her skin. Still she didn't look away. And damn him, neither did he.

She heard her father asking questions about the tomb's location, but she couldn't focus on exactly what he said. She knew what was happening. She had grown up in the company of men, had traveled the world. She knew how life worked, that there were needs of the body that couldn't be ignored.

But this wasn't a simple attraction. She wanted Gavin DeFoe, the Earl of Blackwell. Wanted him on a primal, fundamental level that was outside her control.

BEYOND MY DREAMS

Tammy Hilz

ZEBRA BOOKS
KENSINGTON PUBLISHING CORP.
http://www.kensingtonbooks.com

ZEBRA BOOKS are published by

Kensington Publishing Corp.
850 Third Avenue
New York, NY 10022

All Kensington titles, imprints and distributed lines are available at special quantity discounts for bulk purchases for sales promotion, premiums, fund-raising, educational or institutional use.

Special book excerpts or customized printings can also be created to fit specific needs. For details, write or phone the office of the Kensington Special Sales Manager: Kensington Publishing Corp., 850 Third Avenue, New York, NY 10022. Attn. Special Sales Department. Phone: 1-800-221-2647.

Zebra and the Z logo Reg. U.S. Pat. & TM Off.

First Printing: April 2004
10 9 8 7 6 5 4 3 2 1

Printed in the United States of America

For Steve.
For always being there.

Chapter 1

Rosetta, Egypt
April, 1799

A bullet shattered the corner of a sandstone house, inches from Gavin DeFoe's head. Debris flew, slicing his face, but he hardly felt it. He was already running, adrenaline pumping through his limbs. He followed Connor MacLeay down a narrow alleyway of hard-packed earth, leaping over baskets and almost trampling a pair of women mixing bread in earthenware bowls.

He didn't need to look to know he and Connor were still being pursued, but he did. Three French soldiers carrying bayonets were giving chase, and they were gaining. The leader shouted in butchered English for them to stop.

Not bloody likely. Gavin tripped over a mangy dog that was trying to get out of his way and nearly fell. He recovered to the sound of a soldier shouting, *"Percez-les de part á part."* Spear them through.

Gavin spit out a curse. "Connor, take the next alley. We can't lose them this way."

The brawny Scot moved faster than Gavin thought possible, turned right, then slid to a stop and concealed himself in a recessed doorway. Gavin followed, pressed his back to the wall and waited.

"I've 'ad me fill of running," Connor snarled. "Especially from measly French—"

That was all the Scotsman managed before the soldiers ran past. Connor and Gavin slipped from the shadows and pursued, taking them by surprise. With a single swing of his beefy fist, Connor knocked one man unconscious, while Gavin traded punches with a second soldier. Within minutes, the fighting was over and three uniformed men were sprawled bleeding and unconscious on the dusty ground.

Breathing hard, Gavin bent over and placed his hands on his knees for support. Connor wasn't faring much better, but then he'd taken out two of the soldiers. That fact didn't injure Gavin's ego in the least. Connor MacLeay was as big as two men; it seemed only fair that he should fell his share.

"What do ye want tae do with them?" the Scotsman asked as he relieved the three men of their weapons. "They'll report us to Napoleon if we let 'em live."

Gavin straightened, rubbed his hand over his jaw where the soldier had clipped him hard. He didn't like the thought of shooting unarmed men, but this was a time of war. Men died, sometimes in a fair fight, sometimes not. Still, his gut tightened with distaste at the thought of putting a bullet through them, regardless that they'd been perfectly willing to do the same to him.

"They don't know who we are," Gavin said, glancing at the Egyptian robes he and Connor wore. "Or why we're here. They only chased us because we refused to stop and answer their questions."

Connor muttered something in Gaelic, a curse no doubt.

"We'll take their uniforms, however. They may come in handy."

"For who?" Connor grumbled, lowering the cowl of his *galabiya* to reveal a shock of shoulder-length red hair. "It would take a handful of puny Frenchmen tae make one good Scot."

"But I'm English," Gavin said, unbuttoning the first man's coat. "I'm sure I can squeeze into one if necessary."

"Yer an earl, too, which means ye shouldn't be defiling yourself in such a way."

"The French patrols have kept us from our destination for the past week." He couldn't afford to lose any more time. Too much hinged on his ability to carry out his mission.

"Short of shooting our way past the bloody French, I dinna know what else we can try."

Gavin stood, a plan beginning to take shape in his mind. "There's one thing we haven't tried." He held up the uniform. "It's a long shot, but we just may have found a way past them."

As it turned out, they'd only needed one French uniform for what Gavin had in mind. Even if Connor had managed to work himself into a coat and britches, his blazing red hair would have given them away. Resisting the urge to tug on the too tight collar, Gavin half wished he could claim the same excuse. The stink rising off the coarse fabric threatened to turn his stomach. God only knew the last time the soldier he'd taken the uniform from had bathed. He resorted to breathing through his mouth.

"Take it slow, Connor," Gavin said, tightening his fingers on the rifle when a French troop rounded a corner and marched toward them. He kept his head high, his gaze fixed ahead, as if he had every right to walk the dusty streets of Rosetta. Even with Connor disguised in a *galabiya*, the flowing robe the locals wore, anyone who cared to look would know he wasn't a native. If it took two Frenchmen to match the size of the Scotsman, it would take a half-dozen Egyptians.

Eight soldiers. Could he and Connor take them? The odds were slim, made worse because every street in the city was crawling with French patrols, and any disturbance would likely draw more. As they advanced, the sun beat down on Gavin like a living thing, burning through his clothes, suppressing his lungs, drying the sweat before it could gather on his skin. The infernal Egyptian sand didn't need the wind to carry it from one place to another. It hovered in the air, thick and gritty, filling his mouth with every breath he took.

He'd spent far too long in this desolate country, and it might be months more before he would be able to return home to England. *Home.* A chilling thought.

As the patrol passed without incident, Gavin released a breath and whispered, "The next street, turn right. The house we're looking for should be at the end, near some sort of park."

Walking slightly ahead, as if Gavin were escorting him, the Scotsman kept his head bowed and the cowl of his robe pulled low as he followed the directions. The street was deserted, swept clean of life and debris. The beige, sandy ground gave way to beige, sandy walls. Only the blazing sky above provided a change in color, a slate of unforgiving blue that stretched on forever. At the last building, they kept walking and didn't stop until they reached an open area—the park, Gavin assumed, though it was little more than hard-baked ground.

"Are ye sure this is the right place?" Connor asked, heading for the shade of a date palm.

"I'm sure." Though he wasn't sure of anything at the moment. A crumbling stone wall, approximately nine feet tall and covering an area roughly half the size of a London city block, surrounded a mud-brick building. Gavin could see the typical flat roof and small windows, but nothing more. An arched gateway of limestone decorated with carvings of the sun and moon framed a thick wooden door.

"It dinna look like something an excavator would live in," Connor said.

"No, it doesn't." An upper-class businessman perhaps, but not a digger. A muscle pulsed in Gavin's jaw. Had he been set up? Considering the source he'd gathered his information from he wouldn't be surprised. But trap or not, there was no turning back. They'd run out of options. "My robe, if you would."

From beneath his galabiya, Connor produced a bundle of faded blue and white striped fabric. Giving his friend the rifle, Gavin slipped the robe on, concealing his uniform and the loaded pistol at his waist.

"Stay here." With a grim look, he added, "If I don't return within a half hour, you have my permission to rescue me."

"Savin' yer arse is what I live for," the Scotsman said, the corner of his mouth quirking with something that might pass for a smile.

At the gate, Gavin banged on the hard wood with his fist and listened for any noise. He thought he heard a muffled sound, voices perhaps, but he couldn't be sure. Then came the unmistakable crunch of footsteps over gravel. The person on the other side rattled something in Arabic that Gavin didn't understand.

"I'm here to see Willie Tuggle," he said on the off-chance the man could speak English.

"'E's busy. What'd ye want?"

Not only did the man speak English, Gavin thought, but with a thick Cockney accent, too.

"I'm Gavin DeFoe. I have a business proposition to discuss with Mr. Tuggle."

"We 'ave all the business we care tae 'ave."

Gavin clenched his jaw, not about to be turned away by a servant. "Did I mention I'm prepared to pay double the normal rate?"

"Double, ye say?" Gavin could almost hear the man multiplying in his head. "'Old on."

Minutes crawled by. Gavin stayed close to the wall, his attention on the upper end of the street. The French patrols were the heaviest in this section of town. At any second, he expected another patrol to pass, demand to know his business. Though Gavin had black hair and blacker eyes, and his skin was tanned from months of enduring the Egyptian sun, he still couldn't pass for a native. He might not have Connor's imposing bulk, but he still towered over most men.

Finally, he heard footsteps, then the grating of an iron bolt being thrown. The doors swung open and Gavin was admitted by a scrawny fellow wearing baggy, wrinkled pants and tunic that matched his baggy, wrinkled face.

"This way, and mind yer step. People are always trippin' over these infernal rocks." He took off at a quick shuffle through a lush courtyard, the sight of which took Gavin by surprise.

The "infernal steps" were quarried stone that cut a path through carefully tended grass, the deep green so dense it could have been mistaken for an oriental carpet. Date palms and palmettos were strategically placed around the perimeter, leaving room for the red and yellow blooms of jacaranda and poinciana to flourish. In the center, surrounded by perfectly fitted stones was a single, rare lotus flower.

Passing through an archway, Gavin entered the blessed coolness of an open and spacious room. There were more windows and broad doorways than there were mud-colored walls, allowing the constant breeze to pass through.

"Sit," the man mumbled, waving at a stool with legs shaped like the feet of a duck. "Willie'll be with ye shortly."

Then he was gone, leaving Gavin to examine the room and wonder what sort of man this Willie Tuggle was. He had a reputation as an excavator, one of the best according to Rashad, the craftsman who had told him about Tuggle. However, if the man's home was any clue to his talent, he hadn't been well paid for his services. One low-backed couch and a few boxed chairs were scattered in no particular pattern. Rush mats and threadbare cushions dotted the wooden floor. The plain Egyptian furnishings didn't surprise Gavin, but the items interspersed among them made him frown.

A faded oriental screen stood off in one corner, crude oil paintings of an English countryside hung on one wall. A china cabinet was filled with knickknacks and ancient clay vases crowded a hodgepodge of scarred and dented mahogany tables.

Just what kind of excavator was Mr. Tuggle?

Hearing the stomping of feet, Gavin hoped he was about to find out. When a portly man wearing loose-fitting ivory pants, dusty boots and a white linen coat over a matching tunic lumbered through the doorway, his frown intensified. The man had wiry brown hair woven with gray, thick brows that topped brown eyes so pale, they gave the impression of being diluted. But he had the kind of mouth that implied a permanent smile, cheery, that caused most people to smile in return. Gavin didn't.

"Mr. DeFoe!" the man said, his boisterous voice so jolly, Gavin expected him to break into a song. "Welcome."

"Mr. Tuggle?"

"None other," the man beamed and patted the gold pendant of a falcon that lay against his rounded chest, then toyed with the ornate chain of beaded jade and onyx. "Welcome to my humble home."

He crossed to a table holding a plain bottle filled with clear liquid and several glasses. He poured for two. "Kippie said ye have some business to discuss. How wonderful. But I never discuss business without drinkin' a toast."

Handing Gavin a glass, he announced, *"Inshallah!"*

"Which means?" Gavin asked, wincing when he smelled the rough drink. Undoubtedly home brewed.

"If God wills. A good saying, don't you think?" Tuggle threw his drink back and breathed a gusty sigh. Sitting in the only chair in the room and shifting the half-dozen pillows at his back, he motioned for Gavin to take the couch. He did, sitting on the edge, wary.

Tuggle was not what he'd expected. He'd met with several excavators over the last week, and without exception, they had all been sun-tough, work-hardened men who knew their business—and their worth—and had negotiated with firm decisiveness.

Not that I'd been able to negotiate with them at all, Gavin thought, scowling. Napoleon's presence had seen to that.

Considering Tuggle's plump body, flushed complexion and merry eyes, the man would undoubtedly prefer to search for the nearest bottle of gin instead of the buried tomb Gavin had to find.

And he *had* to find King Menes' tomb. Before Napoleon did. Gavin's sovereign, King George, had been adamant that if Gavin failed his mission France would gain enough momentum and allied support to conquer Egypt. A heavy weight for Gavin to bear. *And it'll get heavier if I have to rely on a fop like Tuggle.* But Gavin had an advantage that Napoleon lacked; he prayed it would be enough.

"Now then," his host said. "What kind of business are ye into?"

"I understand you're an excavator, with your own team."

"Ye understand right," he beamed. "We've been in Egypt for the past five years. Had quite a time, I don't mind tellin' ye."

"That's not very long. How much experience do you have?"

"There only be one way to dig, Mr. DeFoe." He chuckled, then sighed with delight. "By using the hands and backs the good Lord gave us. And those we know how to use."

Gavin thought it a safe bet that Tuggle rarely used either. But as long as he had men who did, he'd be satisfied. "Just how many workers do you have?"

"Twenty-five of the bravest, hardest-working men ye'll ever be lucky enough tae meet," Tuggle claimed, sounding suspiciously like a street vendor trying to sell week old fish.

"Like the man who let me in?"

"Kippie?" Tuggle laughed, upsetting his girth. "'E's tougher than he looks. But the others are tougher than 'im, mark my word, Mr. DeFoe. You'll find no finer diggers."

Tension coiled around Gavin's back. If Tuggle's men were anything like Kippie, Gavin had no hope of succeeding in his mission. He didn't trust Tuggle, would walk away if he had the choice, but he didn't. In his pursuit to oust the British from Egypt, Napoleon had commandeered every camel and boat within two hundred miles. And because the French general had teams of scholars searching for Egyptian treasures, namely King Menes's tomb, he had forced every excavator in the area into his employ.

"Are ye after something particular?" Tuggle asked, his attention devoted to Gavin. "Or are ye just gold mining?"

"I'm not here as a tourist. But before I reveal what I'm after, tell me, are you for hire?"

For the first time since entering the room, the cheery glow in Tuggle's cheeks faded. He cleared his throat, eyed the bottle, but drummed his fingers on the arms of the chair instead of reaching for it. A moment passed with him frowning, as if he were torn by some monumental decision. "I could be. Yes, I could. When were you planning to leave?"

"In two days, if possible."

His curly brows shot up. "Oh, my! So soon."

"Is that a problem?" Gavin set his glass aside and eyed the man who'd switched from jovial to apprehensive in the space of a breath.

"No, no." Tuggle hopped from his chair and poured a drink, downed it like water. "I just need a moment to think if ye don't mind."

"Not at all."

"There's so much to plan, ye see, when ye set out for an expedition. Ye can't just pick up and saunter off, ye understand. There are supplies to purchase and gear to pack. Travel plans, those are the hardest."

Gavin sat where he was and watched the man nervously pace the room, his brows dipped in a frown, his hands clenched prayer style at his chest.

"I will acquire the supplies we'll need." Gavin stood. "You only have to gather your men and tools."

"I'm afraid that won't do, Mr. DeFoe." Tuggle stopped his pacing to face Gavin. Cheeriness still glimmered in the excavator's pale brown eyes, but a sudden craftiness gave it a sharper edge.

"Are you for hire or not, Tuggle?" Gavin said tightly. "I don't have time for games."

"Neither do I. I am for hire, given you can meet my, um, requirements."

"I've already offered to double your rate."

"And that's very generous of ye." Tuggle lifted his hands and glanced around the room. "But as ye can see, I have a rather high overhead to maintain. Supporting my men during the slow season puts a damper on my finances."

"I wouldn't call the situation in Egypt now as slow."

"Exactly my point. Considering how Napoleon is running loose and snatching up every available boat and excavation team within reach, I'm afraid double payment won't do."

"What is it you want?" Gavin asked, impatiently.

"One hundred pounds a day."

"Are you—"

"Plus expenses."

Gavin ground his teeth.

"In gold."

If there was one thing Gavin had learned to loathe, it was being in a position that allowed others to take advantage of him, or make a fool of him, but if Tuggle could produce workers, he'd offer the King's crown. "Done. Be ready in two days, Tuggle. You and your men had better not disappoint me."

"Splendid!" Holding up one hand, finger pointed into the air as if something had just occurred to him, he added, "But there's one other matter I should mention."

Gavin narrowed his gaze and felt a sliver of satisfaction when the man's bright complexion paled. "And that is?"

"We must leave tonight."

"Impossible." He headed for the arched doorway. "I haven't found enough feluccas to hire."

"That won't be a problem, Mr. DeFoe. I have me own."

He paused, turned and met the man's fervent gaze; noted the way his freckled hands nervously toyed with his pendant.

Apprehension tightened Gavin's gut. There was more to Tuggle than a jovial smile and contagious laugh. It was obvious the man had an agenda of his own. But what? And what, other than a fortune in gold, would it cost Gavin? He'd learned the hard way that all men, *and women*, had ulterior motives for the things they did. Tuggle was no different. And neither was Gavin. He'd keep an eye on the excavator, however. If Tuggle planned to double cross him, Gavin knew how to handle him. He'd simply give the man to Connor.

"Fine. I'll return with the supplies as soon as I can." Gavin pulled the hood of his galabiya up over his head. "I assume you'll be ready."

"Ye can bet yer first-born son that we'll be waitin' for ye."

Gavin froze in mid-step, shock recoiling through his mind. His breath constricted. He clenched his fists, but it was too late. The trembling started somewhere beneath his heart and spread from there. Fiery and hot, unstoppable.

Tuggle took a step forward, then stopped as if he realized he'd said something wrong. And indeed he had, the one thing that ensured an eruption of Gavin's temper, a cold, vicious thing he struggled with daily to keep under tight rein. An easier task since he'd arrived in Egypt, where there weren't any reminders of the past, or the gaping holes it had left behind.

Wringing his hands, the older man said, "Ye never mentioned where ye'll be wantin' tae dig."

"No, I didn't." Gavin turned, forced himself to walk down the path. He was blind to the swaying date palms, the infusion of jacaranda and poinciana. Instead, he saw blood and broken bones.

"DeFoe," Tuggle said, his tone hesitant. "DeFoe. Now why does your name strike a bell?"

At the gate, Gavin jerked the heavy door open. "Perhaps you've heard of my family."

"Mayhaps. Where about in England do ye hail?"

"Northumberland."

"North . . ." Tuggle's mouth dropped open with a silent gasp.

Gavin felt his lips twitched, and knew from the man's expression that the result resembled nothing close to a grin. "I see you've heard of me."

"You'll be the Earl of Blackwell?"

"I am. And if you know that much, then you might also know I no longer have a first-born son."

Chapter 2

Papyrus reeds flourished along the unused cove south of Rosetta, concealing three well-fitted feluccas. The shallow, single-mast boats were virtually unchanged from those used in ancient times. They had only one deck, open to the elements and no private cabins, unless you counted a screen that could be set up near the stern. Perhaps thirty feet long, the rails were dangerously close to the water's edge. Yet the vessels rarely sank, or so Gavin had been told.

As the sun slipped toward the horizon, the heated air lost some of its bite and began to cool. Life-giving water lapped at the boats in anticipation. Startled by all the activity, a family of hoopoes called out in warning. After a moment, they lowered their hammer-shaped heads into the tall grass to continue their search for insects, evidently deciding Gavin and his crew wasn't a threat. This was a peaceful place. Timeless. If one cared about such things.

Which Gavin didn't. He stood on the bank of the Nile, the fertile black silt dry beneath his boots and scowled as the last of his supplies were being loaded by the workers Tuggle had provided. Gavin had failed to inspect the men before agreeing to the excavator's terms, an oversight that might cost Gavin everything.

Not a man among them was under fifty. A collection

of arthritic bones and shriveled bodies. A breath hissed through Gavin's clenched teeth. No wonder Tuggle had appeared nervous, and why he was nowhere to be seen now. He'd knowingly deceived Gavin. If this were a normal situation, he would have the man charged with fraud and hauled to Marshalsea Prison. But his dilemma was far from normal. If he wanted diggers, he had to take what he could get. And Tuggle knew it.

"So how much is this bunch costing you?" Jacob Mitchell asked as he wiped sweat from his brow with his forearm.

"Shut up, Jake."

The man didn't have the sense to suppress his laugh. "I never thought I'd see a day when someone got the best of you."

Gavin bit out a curse. "As long as you can find King Menes' tomb, I'll have it cleared, even if I have to use Tuggle's body as a shovel."

"I'll find it." Jake shook his head but didn't lose his cocky grin.

Gavin rotated his shoulders to relieve the tension gathering there. "Explorers have been searching for this tomb for hundreds, perhaps thousands, of years. How can you be so certain?"

Jake took a scarab the size of his palm from his pocket and flipped the amulet made of lapis lazuli in the air. Fading sunlight flashed as the artifact spun, blurring the hieroglyphics an ancient artisan had engraved on both sides. "No one has found the tomb because no one has ever had my good luck charm."

Gavin knew Jake wasn't referring to the artifact in his hand that would lead them to King Menes' tomb, but to the woman who sat perched on the front bench seat of the supply wagon. With her sable hair knotted in a bun at her nape, her creamy complexion flushed from the heat, she frantically moved a charcoal pencil over the pad of paper in her lap.

"Sarah's determined to document every part of our trip." The wealth of pride in Jake's voice for his wife was palpable, a living thing for everyone to witness, or feel. But it was a feeling Gavin wanted no part of. He'd come close to having a marriage like Jake's, only to learn his marriage had been an illusion, as deceiving as a desert mirage and just as deadly. The kind of love Jake and Sarah shared was as rare as discovering an undisturbed pharaoh's tomb with all the riches and precious artifacts still intact. It was the kind of love Gavin no longer believed in.

"You've married the only woman worth having," Gavin said, and ground his jaw. He hadn't meant to utter the words out loud.

Jake crossed his arms, his eyes taking on a familiar, possessive glint as he settled in to watch his wife. "And to think you warned me to stay away from her."

"Women aren't to be trusted."

"So you've said, many times. But it's good to hear you admit you were wrong."

"I've admitted no such thing. *Women* aren't to be trusted. Sarah just happens to be an exception."

Turning back to the problem at hand, Gavin's brow creased when he saw two of the older men, Hollister and Smedley, rubbing their lower backs and wincing in pain. "I'd thought us lucky to have found a crew Napoleon had overlooked. Now I realize he hadn't overlooked them, he'd merely been smart enough to leave them behind."

Sighing, Jake ran a hand through his whiskey-blond hair. "How are we supposed to save King George's throne with scrapings from the bottom of the barrel?"

"Don't be fooled by appearances, gentlemen."

Gavin and Jake turned to find Tuggle hurrying up behind them, a nervous smile dimpling his flushed cheeks. Since leaving the man's house, Gavin had kept his anger in check, holding onto it, suppressing it, knowing it would be futile, and dangerous, to let it go. Tuggle hadn't known his comment about Gavin's first-born son would have the power to tear open a wound, so he shouldn't bear the brunt of his anger. But that had been before Gavin had seen the workers. Now that the excavator had arrived, he intended to unleash his temper a bit.

"You demanded an outrageous fee for half-dead men." Gavin stepped close to Tuggle, forcing his gaze up to his. "You're playing a game with me and I feel I should warn you, I don't care for games."

"I have not deceived ye, me lord." Tuggle gripped his pendant as if it were a talisman that would protect him. "They're sturdy, hard-working men, they are. Ye won't be disappointed in 'em."

"I already am."

"Everything's loaded," Connor said, breathing hard since he'd done most of the work. "We should leave before the sun's gone, though we're fools for sailin' at night."

"'Tis the best time," Tuggle insisted.

"Since when?" Jake asked doubtfully. Since Jake had spent half his life in Egypt and probably knew more about the area than Tuggle, Gavin was interested in hearing the answer. Why was the excavator in such a hurry to leave? Was he in trouble? In debt? Planning some sort of trap? He didn't give a damn about the man's problems, but if he intended on betrayal, blood would be spilled, Gavin vowed. Tuggle's.

"We'll avoid the risk of being spotted by Napoleon's soldiers," the older man explained. "They patrol the

Nile like vultures, stopping vessels to search for weapons and artifacts, stealing whatever they find."

Gavin exchanged a look with Jake, and saw that the archaeologist believed him. "Fine, then. Let's board and set sail."

"Mmm." Tuggle fidgeted with his pendant again, his nervous gaze touching all three men before darting to the line of palms that guarded the cove. "We can't leave just yet."

The hairs on the nape of Gavin's neck raised in warning. So this was a trap. He scanned the line of palms. Had Tuggle alerted the French of their location? If he had, the old man wouldn't live long enough to see them captured.

"Why the delay?" Connor demanded, fingering the hilt of the dagger that never left his side . . . unless he intended to use it.

"Your guide hasn't arrived." Tuggle tried one of his jolly smiles and failed miserably.

"What are you talking about?" Gavin asked. "I hired you as our guide."

"Me?" Tuggle forced a laugh. "Oh my, no. I'll be accompanyin' ye, but I'll not be the one tae lead ye. Now if we were on my merchant ship, *Little Bess*, that might be different, but out 'ere in the desert, you'll be wantin' Mac tae see ye safely to, ah, wherever it is yer wantin' tae go."

If he'd wanted to thrash Tuggle within an inch of his life before, it was nothing compared to the urge he now had to wrap his hands around the man's thick neck and squeeze. There had been too many surprises since he'd laid eyes on Tuggle, and Gavin hated surprises even more than he hated playing games.

He headed for his pack, retrieved his rifle, and felt

a sense of control return when Connor and Jake did the same.

"Gentlemen, there's no need for weapons," Tuggle insisted. "Another moment and we'll be able tae leave, please . . . Oh, blimey. Wait, I think I see . . . Yes, there's Mac now! Ye see, everything's fine. Let go men! Time tae board."

Gavin shouldered his rifle and sighted the person emerging from the shadows of palm trees and sycamores. Wearing a *galabiya* with the cowl pulled up over his head and carrying a satchel over one shoulder, he cut through the grass at a leisurely pace. Gavin followed the man's movement, ready to shoot him first if anyone else barged into the open.

"Please, me lord," Tuggle pleaded, his voice high pitched and frantic. "Put yer rifle away. That's Mac yer aimin' at."

"And I'll continue to do so until I'm satisfied Napoleon's men aren't going to follow."

The man continued closing the distance then stopped ten feet from Gavin, studying the scene from the shadow of his hood. Gavin didn't see a weapon and the grove remained quiet but he still wasn't satisfied.

"Show yourself," he ordered.

A pair of slender, work-rough hands reached for the cowl and pushed it back to reveal a tanned, exotic face, framed by an abundance of auburn hair, the rich hue darker than garnets. With growing disbelief, he noted almond-shaped eyes the color of mist, high cheekbones and a firm jaw that was both stubborn and soft. But it was the full, dusty-pink lips that could only belong to a woman that had him growling.

"What nonsense is this?" Gavin demanded of Tuggle. Instead of the excavator answering, the woman spoke in a smoky-smooth voice, "If you shoot me, DeFoe, you might find my men less than cooperative."

"Please, me lord," Tuggle said, moving to stand beside the woman. "This is Mac, me daughter."

"Your daughter?" Gavin scoffed, glancing between the two. Tuggle was big-boned and round, with coarse graying brown hair and skin that was freckled and ruddy from the sun, while the woman, *Mac*, was as fine-boned as any female he'd ever seen. She stood a head taller than her father, nearly matching Gavin in height. She met his gaze with a confident tilt of her strong chin, showing no sign of nerves or fear or that she'd been at all worried that she could have been shot.

"Aye, my very own," Tuggle beamed, regaining some of his courage. "The girl takes after her mother, God rest her soul."

Gavin lowered his rifle, nodded for Connor and Jake to do the same. He glanced around the cove, and was startled to see Tuggle's men had gathered close. Every one of them held a weapon of their own, be it shovel or pick-ax. Kippie was in the lead, his wrinkled face screwed up with intent, his gnarled hands fisted like a professional pugilist. Sarah, Jake's wife, stood on the rim of the scene, her silver eyes narrowed with confusion.

"If you have any more surprises in store, Tuggle," Gavin said. "You'd better tell me about them now. You've tested my patience enough for one day."

The female closed the space between them. He'd been right about her height. She could almost look him in the eye. A disconcerting sensation he wasn't accustomed to.

"You must forgive my father," she said with an amused smile. "He means well."

"I don't like surprises."

"Then you shouldn't be in Egypt." The wind changed direction, teasing him with her scent, something spicy and warm, like cinnamon sprinkled on an open flame. "This is the land of surprises."

He held her gaze, noted that her eyes weren't misty gray. They were the color of polished jade, the rich green soft and drowning. Irritated that he'd noticed, he said in as cold a voice as he could manage, "I didn't hire a woman to lead this expedition."

"Then you're lucky because you've received more than you bargained for."

"You aren't coming."

She tilted her head, her gaze narrowing as if she were trying to puzzle him out. "And why is that?"

"That should be bloody obvious. You're female."

She glanced over her shoulder at Sarah, who was shaking her head in exasperation, her arms crossed over her chest.

"She appears to be of the fairer sex. Is she accompanying you?"

"She's an exception. And she's with me," he said, more possessively than he'd intended. Some might think him insane to distrust all women, but he had his reason. Sarah was the only female who had his trust, and she'd had to nearly die to earn it.

The amused light fled Mac's eyes, and was replaced by a challenge that matched Gavin's will for will. She told him, "If I don't accompany you, neither will my men. Then you'll have to dig up whatever it is you're looking for all by yourself."

"Fine."

"Gavin." Jake cleared his throat and ran a hand through his hair again, a sure sign he was agitated. "Her men may be little better than skeletons, but we need them. And we need her boats."

Gavin glared at his partner and clamped his jaw around a curse because, damn it to hell, Jake was right. He pulled a breath of warm air deep into his lungs, forcing the anger burning through him to cool. He could feel his emotions pulling back, becoming organized and disciplined. Six years ago he'd perfected the ability to control his emotions—he'd had to in order to survive. He wouldn't lose control of them now.

"It would seem I have little choice but to allow you to join us. But I'll warn you now, I won't be responsible for your safety."

"I hadn't thought you would be." Her confident smile back, she held out a hand golden from the sun and waited for him to shake it. When he didn't she arched a russet brow in a silent dare. He gripped her hand, felt her calloused palm, her warm skin, her strong fingers as they wrapped around his own.

His skin tingled from the contact, the response as unwanted as it was persistent. Heat fled up his arm, spread over his chest, the sensation raw and sudden, burning as if he'd been brushed by fire.

"Mackenzie Tuggle," she announced. Then her smile faded, and her expressive green eyes flared with awareness, making him wonder if she had experienced the unpleasant feeling, too. "My friends call me Mac."

"Which one should I call you?" he asked.

"I'll let you decide." Releasing his hand, she stepped around him, taking her disturbing spicy-sweet scent with her.

But he already knew what he would call her, he thought as he watched her divide her men onto the various boats. He'd call her a woman, a bloody, conniving, deceiving *woman*.

* * *

"Are you trying to get us killed?" Mac demanded of her father in a whisper.

Sitting beside her on the felucca's sanded deck, well away from Gavin DeFoe and his friends, Willie Tuggle leaned against the low hull and pursed his lips. She waited for him to answer, but he merely studied the stars and the sliver of moon that had worked its way halfway across the midnight sky, and leisurely drummed his fingers on his rounded belly.

"Pop, don't ignore me," she warned, her voice sounding strangled because she really wanted to pace and rave. She didn't like having things out of her control. And they were definitely out of her control. Her father had committed them to work for a man they didn't know. A man who didn't trust them enough to reveal where they were sailing to! She could order the boats around, she owned them after all, but returning to Rosetta wasn't an option.

"Why didn't you find me when the earl arrived? What did you think you were doing? Negotiating on your own? Pop, you know better."

"I would 'ave made 'im wait tae see ye, but ye were off inspecting the repairs tae *Little Bess*," he whispered solemnly. "We had tae leave Rosetta before Napoleon returned with his troops." His hurt, childlike tone might have been a ploy for another man, but not for Willie Tuggle. Her Pop was good, fun-loving; his only goal to enjoy life as much as possible and to make sure those around him did the same. He had one flaw, however: He didn't always think things through.

Which was why she handled all their business dealings, whether it was to ship cargo on their merchant vessel or to lead excavations through the Egyptian desert. Pop hated to turn anyone down, she understood that, and when Gavin DeFoe offered them a way to escape, he'd grabbed at the chance.

So at dawn, Napoleon would arrive at her home to gather her and her men up to be used like a herd of animals. She didn't want to think about how furious the French General would be when he discovered her gone. If he ever caught up with her . . . She stopped the thought, refusing to consider what Napoleon would do in retaliation for failing to help him discover King Menes' tomb.

But she wasn't sorry to be leaving. She would have left Rosetta on the feluccas days ago if she'd had the money to support her family of twenty-five men for an unknown period of time. But she didn't. Every dime she had was tied up in repairing *Little Bess*. More than five years had passed since they nearly sank off the coast of Alexandria during a freak storm. Without a ship to earn a living, she'd taken her rag-tag crew into the desert.

They'd had a grand time since, digging up tombs, discovering artifacts no one had seen for thousands of years. Until Napoleon. His arrival had changed the rules.

She said, "I would have found a way to reject Napoleon's offer to hire us."

"'Twas no offer, daughter. 'Twas a command, one I could not let ye agree to. We may not live in England any longer, but she's still our country. I could not betray her."

"Pop, I don't want to help the French any more than you do."

"I should think not!"

"Shh!" Mac glanced at the far end of the boat where Gavin sat leaning against the stern, his long legs crossed at the ankle, his hat pulled low over his face. Other than the slow rise and fall of his chest, he didn't move. Yet she wasn't fooled into believing that he was asleep. Twenty paces separated them, but the air hummed with tension. She had the crazed notion that if she reached out and touched the space surrounding him, the air would sizzle, and black lightning would flash. The heated color would be the same as his eyes.

Dark and disturbing, enticing and damning in a single glance. She recognized a wounded man when she saw one, and the earl was definitely wounded, using scowls and gruff warnings as a shield to keep people . . . *or women* . . . away.

But why would he want to? She didn't know how to keep people at arm's length, or contain her feelings. Growing up with a father like Willie and their gregarious crew had seen to that. If there was a problem, she faced it head on, and if it got too big, she fought until she won. She didn't dwell on the past or her troubles. And she didn't know how to stay angry. There was no reason to. And as Willie so often reminded her, "'Tis one life we have, whether we spend it laughing or weeping, so why not laugh?"

Mac recalled the instant she'd seen the earl. She'd just emerged from the row of date palms, worried that Willie had gotten them into more trouble than she could handle. Then she's spotted Gavin and she'd known she hadn't been worried enough.

Tall, menacing, as dark and brooding as any man she'd ever seen. He wore anger and intimidation like a second skin. As she drew closer and got a good look at him, she knew that the hard set of his mouth, his inflexible jaw and the lines bracketing his suspicious eyes weren't caused from laughter, but from a bitter, bitter life.

She glanced at the lady he'd brought along, Sarah, and wondered how she could tolerate him. Perhaps she liked the solemn type, which seemed doubtful considering Sarah was, well, a lady, fragile, cultured, certainly unable to take care of herself in an unforgiving country like Egypt. At the moment, Sarah was wedged between Gavin and his friend, Jake, asleep on a reed mat. Nice and safe, protected by her fearless and overbearing man. Well, Sarah could have the earl. Mac didn't need a man who wanted to dominate her.

She'd always been the leader in her family, the one to take control and solve their problems. She couldn't imagine it any other way.

"What would your mother say if we aided Napoleon?" Willie asked, saving her from her thoughts.

"Mother would have wanted us to stay alive and well."

"We won't be either if that Frenchman gets hold of us. You've heard the rumors. He abuses the native workers, drives them near to death, then refuses to pay when he doesn't find that blasted tomb he's after."

She personally knew some of the crews he'd taken to Saqqara to dig, Egyptian men with homes and families. She hadn't seen any of them since.

"No, yer mother would not be pleased if we were tae fall into his hands."

Her mother, Bess Mackenzie, had been dead nearly twenty years, but every decision Willie made had to pass his wife's moral standards. Mac leaned against the hull, suddenly exhausted. Rosetta was hours behind them but that didn't mean they were out of danger. The French general had soldiers scouring every inch of Egypt, looking for British to fight and new tombs to raid. The man was a plague, swarming over the land like locust, devouring whatever was in his path and leaving nothing behind but destruction.

She'd been a girl the last time she'd lived in England, so her ties to that country were barely knotted, but she prayed King George sent Napoleon back to where he belonged, and quickly. It was her responsibility to keep her father and their crew safe, a task that was becoming more and more difficult with each passing year.

"Ye'd best get some sleep, Mackenzie, girl," Willie said. "Tomorrow will be a trying day."

With that her father closed his eyes, took a deep breath and started to snore. She didn't know how he did it. At that moment she could no more sleep than she could continue sitting still because her thoughts kept going back to one question. As bad as Napoleon was, would Gavin DeFoe, the mysterious Earl of Blackwell, be any better?

Willie had told her very little about the earl. Only that he was reputed to be wealthy, influential, with access to the king's ear. And colder than the North Sea. She needed to know more about him. Such as why he seemed so against her coming along. Mac sighed, wondering if Willie saved them from being at the mercy of one snake, only to have caught another one by its tail? If she were to guess, Gavin DeFoe was as angry and unforgiving as a cobra.

Since sleep was impossible, she pushed to her feet and relieved Hollister from his watch. As the man lumbered away to find a corner, she admitted that she knew one thing for certain.

She had to keep the upper hand, which meant she had to make sure her handsome snake didn't learn that she needed him more than he needed her.

Because if he did, he just might turn and bite her.

Chapter 3

Mac stood watch for the remainder of the night, pacing the crowded deck from bow to stern, careful not to disturb the sleeping crew. Like any good captain, she stayed alert for any change in the surging black water, an approaching crocodile or curious hippo. Both grew large enough in the flowing river to topple their small boat and rip those on board into shredded pulp. The shadowy banks of the Nile didn't escape her attention, either. Whenever she spotted a campfire or heard something she didn't like, she ordered the helmsman to steer clear.

Mac was careful, attentive, her knowledge of the Nile and its dangers evident in her every move.

Gavin knew because he'd watched her throughout the night. She was capable; he'd give her that. But that didn't mean he'd changed his mind about wanting her along. If anything, her confidence presented more of a problem than he'd first thought.

He knew from experience that any woman so self-assured wouldn't hesitate to betray others to get what she wanted.

The sun broke over the horizon at his back, changing the sky from black to pearly gray and pink. Stars vanished and, far to the west, the moon barely clung to life.

As she stood at the bow, her attention on what lay head, the changing light shifted over her hair, the waist-length curls only partially tamed by a colorful string. Loose-fitting pants of creamy white encased her long legs and were tucked into a pair of soft chamois boots that reached her knees. Leather straps crisscrossed her calves. Her blouse was homespun wool, the red, brown and yellow stripes faded from wear. She looked like a gypsy, or a medieval wench surveying her den, and pleased by what she saw.

Gavin pushed to his feet and crossed to her before he realized his intent. All night, he'd had to suppress the urge to finish their conversation. She thought she had him backed into a corner. It was time to set things straight. He needed her men, *not her,* and he only needed them because of his duty to his king.

Except when he saw her profile, the words froze in his throat.

Her eyes were closed, her face lifted toward the dawning sky, a secretive smile tilting the corners of her mouth. She swayed slightly, as if she were listening to music only she could hear. She seemed content, peaceful, and at that moment perhaps the most beautiful woman he'd ever seen.

The thought made him frown.

"Do you know what they call this hour?" she asked, her voice barely above a whisper.

Her eyes were still closed and he hadn't made a sound, yet somehow she'd known he was there. Perhaps she was a gypsy, he thought, with mystical powers that would get her hanged if she were in England.

When he didn't answer, she said, "The Egyptians call the sixth hour 'the straight.'" A small frown creased her brow. "I've yet to figure out why. Perhaps it has something to do with the alignment of the sun and moon, or it could mean the sun god Ra's straight path into the sky. What do you think?"

"I think I don't care."

She blinked her eyes open and looked at him as if he were a newly discovered bug. "How long have you been in Egypt, DeFoe?"

"This trip?" he asked, noting she hadn't referred to him by his title as everyone except his close friends did. "Only a few weeks. But I spent some time here last year."

"Really?"

"That surprises you?"

"Egypt usually has a way of getting beneath people's skin." Her gaze held his, bold and daring, intense. "She hasn't even made a dent in yours."

And just what the hell was he supposed to say to that? He was aware of the walls around him. He's the one who put them there. And he had no intention of letting anything slip past them, either. Not a majestic country or its valuable artifacts, and certainly not a woman who irritated him with her confident stance and expressive, knowing eyes. Eyes bruised from lack of sleep.

"You've been awake all night," he said suddenly, surprising himself. "You should get some rest."

Arching a russet brow, she asked, "And how would you know I haven't slept?"

A muscle pulsed in his jaw as he refused to answer. At first he'd been suspicious about her motive. But after an hour of her patrolling the boat, checking on her crew, he'd stayed awake because he hadn't been able to stop watching her. He'd also been concerned. If they had encountered a problem, he wouldn't leave her to handle it alone.

He might not trust women, but he wouldn't let one come to harm if he could help it. Not ever again.

But he would rather face a hyena than admit that to her.

"You were awake, spying on me." She smiled as if she thought that amusing. "Did you think I would steal your food? Slit your throat while you and your friends were asleep?"

"Had I thought either of those your intent, you wouldn't be on this boat any longer."

"The crew belongs to me. If you harm me, rest assured, they'll retaliate."

"They're old men." He crossed his arms over his chest and tried to glare down at her, a difficult thing to do when she stood nearly as tall as him. "Half your men can hardly stand. Should they try to challenge me, I'm sure I can take care of them."

A jolt of anger, as hot and fast as a spear of lightning, flashed through her eyes. "Let's get one thing clear, DeFoe. My father agreed to provide workers—"

"Which I'm paying an obscene amount for."

"Had you dealt with me instead of Willie, you'd still be in Rosetta without a crew. But my father gave you his word, so you now have diggers." She stepped closer, bringing her face inches from his. Her green eyes crystallized, turning cold and sharp, like chips of malachite fresh from the earth. A flush darkened her cheeks, and a visible tremor shook her body. He could have intensified his scowl, prepared to return whatever argument she was about to make, but just then her cinnamon-spice scent blended with the crisp morning air, the combination throwing him off balance.

His stomach clenched and blood tingled through his veins. He knew what the reaction meant and couldn't believe it. His body was responding to her, her smell, her presence, the flare of life in her expressive green eyes. He suppressed the feeling, not wanting any part of it.

Poking a finger into his chest, she added, "Understand this, if you ever, and I mean *ever,* touch a member of my family in anger, if you so much as hurt their feelings, you'll have to deal with me. And I assure you, you won't be able to *take care* of me as easily as you might think."

He held her righteous gaze, felt the spot on his chest where she'd done her best to poke a hole through skin and bone. Despite the desire that continued to thrum through his body, he felt a smile threaten to ruin his scowl. Mac was not only beautiful, she had an abundance of courage. There wasn't a man alive who would talk to him the way she had. Not even Jake or Connor would dare. Yet this woman, this female guide from hell, had not only stood up to him, she'd threatened to fight back if he hurt one of her family.

The urge to smile faded as an unwanted emotion rushed from behind his walls, taking him by surprise. The sadness he'd suppressed for so long spread through him like a disease, attacking, nipping at him, reminding him of the pain that was as much a part of him as his arm or leg.

He'd once been willing to fight to protect his family, would have gladly died to keep them safe. He'd loved them that much, that desperately and deeply. In the end, he'd been a fool. He hadn't been able to protect anyone, and the sense of betrayal and confusion they'd left behind had made him wish he had died, too.

But when he'd continued to live, when one horrid day had turned into a week, and that into a month, he'd realized the only way to survive without going mad was to close himself off. Stop caring. Move through life because you had to, but keep it at a distance.

He no longer thought about Rachel, or how her pampered fingers would tease the line of his jaw when he returned from a trip out of town, or how her blue eyes could entice . . . and manipulate.

"DeFoe?"

For the last six years his way of living had worked. Focus on the duty at hand, and succeed at any cost. He didn't plan to change his ways, not for anyone.

"Gavin?"

He felt a warm touch on his face, the kind of which he hadn't felt in . . . in . . . too long to remember. He blinked and met a pair of eyes, not liquid blue and deceiving, but green and clear and tinged with concern.

"Are you all right?" Mac asked.

He stared at her, the past and present blurring, one into the other. Her fingers were warm and rough, not the smooth-silky touch he remembered from his wife. For an instant, he wanted to close his eyes and lose himself in the feel of Mac's hand, see if she had the power to cleanse him of his past forever. Realizing the dangerous path his thoughts were taking, he jerked away from her. She couldn't assuage the pain of his past; no one could.

Mac frowned at him, but didn't comment, for which he was grateful.

He heard voices behind him. People stirring. Someone wrenched the lid off a crate, undoubtedly one that contained the store of food. He should help organize the preparation of the morning meal, go over his plan once more with Jake, but he didn't move.

Finally, she broke the awkward silence by saying, "We'll stop soon to give everyone a break. Then I'll need to set a schedule. I don't suppose you're ready to tell me what it is you're looking for."

Grateful for anything that would divert him from

his thoughts, he considered her request. They were away from Rosetta; there was no reason to keep his destination a secret any longer.

He told her, "We're searching for King Menes' tomb."

Her mouth dropped open in shock, but she was quick to snap it shut. Hands on slender hips, she demanded, "Are you out of your mind?"

"I take it you've heard of the pharaoh?"

"Everyone in Egypt has heard of him. Napoleon has a hundred scholars searching for him."

"That's what I understand."

She shook her head in disbelief. "And you're still going to march into Saqqara? Where Napoleon has set up his main camp?"

"I have no intention of going anywhere near Saqqara."

"Then where?" Breathing hard, she fisted her hands, as if she dearly wanted to knock some sense into him.

"Further south, to Abydos."

"I've been to Abydos. Except for the Temple of Osiris, there's nothing there but ruined tombs and an ocean of sand."

"If I'm right, it's also where King Menes is buried."

"Searching there is a waste of time," she insisted. "The evidence found so far indicates Menes is somewhere in Saqqara. Which is why *Napoleon is there!*"

"It's my time to waste. You're being paid quite well for yours."

She tightened her jaw, her expression turning sharp enough to cut through stone. They stood there a moment, their gazes locked in a battle of wills. Then she did something he would never have expected. She smiled. A genuine, full-lipped smile that brought color to her cheeks and a spark of amusement to her eyes. It also twisted his stomach in a way he didn't like.

"Abydos it is, then." Facing the stern, she clapped her hands to draw everyone's attention. "Frewin, a place to dock if you please. We'll take a short stop."

She scanned the shadowed riverbank where a wooden shadoof lifted water from the Nile and fed it into a man-made canal that irrigated nearby fields of maturing flax. The ancient watering system of a counterbalancing sweep, unchanged for thousands of years, provided life to those who lived in the gray, mud-brick huts huddled in the distance.

"Frewin, I see a spot there," she said, pointing to a clear place along the shore.

"Aye, Capt'n," the helmsman shouted with a grin. Barely five feet tall, but possessing the strength of a plow horse, the man turned the boat with ease.

"Kippie, as soon as we land, breakfast is yours. Dried beef and fruit will do. Tonight we'll make camp on land and have a hot meal, but for today, we need to put some distance between us and Rosetta."

"There'll be no dawdling if I has my way, Mackenzie, girl," the spindly man called with a scratchy laugh.

Gavin remained by the bow as Mac issued orders to her men, making sure they were relayed to the two boats following behind. She patted the helmsmen on the back, then assigned another crewman, Smedley, a tall, stick of a man with curly gray hair and a beard to match, to take his place after everyone ate. She spoke with all of her men, making sure they were well, even rubbing a thick, smelly paste into the arthritic hands of one of her men, Hollister, if he wasn't mistaken.

Gavin didn't know what to make of Mackenzie Tuggle. She dressed like a man and acted just as tough, a captain in charge of her troops. There was nothing pampered or soft about her, which troubled him.

He'd never met a woman like her, wasn't sure how to deal with a female who radiated confidence.

And he didn't want to learn.

What he did want was her off his boat.

Because when it came down to it, she was a woman. She would betray him in the end. She wouldn't be able to help herself.

"I'll need to break the men up into three teams," Jake Mitchell announced.

"Well, I don't know if that's such a good idea." Willie removed his hat, dabbed beads of sweat from his brow with a handkerchief, then repositioned the bent, soiled and worn out headgear over his graying brown hair. Pursing his lips, he said, "Perhaps ye should discuss this with—"

"I know this map is rough," Jake interrupted. He took a scarab the size of his palm from his pocket and used it to hold down one edge of the paper that kept flapping in the wind. "I drew it from memory, but I'm certain I have the tombs close to their correct location."

"I'm sure 'tis a fine map, but wouldn't ye rather discuss this with Mac?"

"You're doing fine, Pop." She winked at her father. It rarely bothered her when clients deferred to Willie for advice, as long as she was present, but it always sent her father into a fit of nerves. "Let's hear what Mr. Mitchell has to say."

"Aye, then we can discuss the best strategy." Willie patted his brow once more, then smiled with delight, knowing she would take care of the details.

Jake had gathered her, Willie and Connor around a crate in the center of the felucca, the map spread out between them to formulate their plan. Mac normally would have done this before stepping foot outside her front door, but since she hadn't known where she was going, planning hadn't been possible. Not to mention, there hadn't been time.

"The Temple of Osiris is here." Jake pointed to an area north of Abydos. "I believe we'll find King Menes buried further to the south in the low desert."

Picking up Jake's lapis lazuli scarab, she ran her fingers over the hieroglyphics carved on the flat belly. Interpreting what little she knew of the ancient language, she read, "The rise of Isis, Goddess of Moon shall sit at the feet of Selqet, Guardian after death."

Jake pried the scarab from her fingers and slipped it into his pocket.

Though his smile bordered on his usually pleasant, devil-may-care grin, his blue eyes were guarded. *So, the handsome archaeologist doesn't trust me, either.* She managed to hide her irritation. She wasn't used to having people doubt her. She had built a reputation for being fair and hardworking, determined, which was why Napoleon had been adamant about her joining his excavation.

She crossed her arms over her chest. "What makes you think you'll find Menes there?"

"Just a hunch."

"Does your hunch have something to do with that scarab?"

"It might." The devilish grin turned downright roguish. Mac couldn't help but smile in return because, secretive or not, the man was too handsome to stay irritated with.

"Don't take offense, lass," Connor said, his voice low and rolling. "But Jake-o doesn't like tae share his toys. He 'as a habit of losing 'em."

She'd introduced herself to the brawny Scotsman

after they'd sailed from Rosetta. He hadn't said much since. But she hadn't taken his silence for rudeness. Connor struck her as the type of man who didn't share his thoughts often, or with just anyone. He was bold and brave, a warrior if she'd ever met one. She'd liked him immediately.

Tilting her head back to look up at the Scottish giant, she said, "I think there's a story in there somewhere."

Rubbing a hand over the red stubble of his beard, Connor grunted. It might have been a laugh, though she wasn't sure.

"Not one you'll be hearing from me." Jake glared at the Scotsman, then glanced at the bow, where Gavin and Sarah were in deep conversation, heads bent close. Something dark and consuming wavered in the archaeologist's eyes.

Mac felt her stomach tighten when Sarah waved her fan and said something that made the earl smile. He even managed a chuckle, a feat Mac hadn't thought him capable of. He was too intense for laughter, too bitter about . . . about what she didn't know.

And I'm content to keep it that way. She had problems of her own trying to keep her ragtag family together, happy and out of harm's way.

At that moment, Gavin looked over Sarah's head, his gaze finding Mac's with such force, she took a step back. His eyes were shadowed beneath his hat, but that didn't make them any less compelling, or unsettling. She had the strange sensation that he was warning her to stay away.

If only I could. But as disagreeable as DeFoe might be, he had provided her a way to escape Napoleon. For that reason alone she would endure his peevish behavior.

She tried to look away, but couldn't, which annoyed

her. She was the one in control here, she owned the boats, and the men who worked them were loyal to her. Yet she felt powerless beneath Gavin's stare. And vulnerable. The helpless feeling was unnerving and not to her liking at all.

But that didn't stop her body from reacting. The nerve endings along her neck tingled with awareness, the blood at each pulse-point throbbed. She felt the sun on her back, heating her clothes, sensitizing her skin. Still she didn't look away. And damn him, neither did he.

She heard her father asking questions about the tomb's location, but she couldn't focus on exactly what he said. She knew what was happening. She had grown up in the company of men, had traveled the world. She knew how life worked, that there were needs of the body that couldn't be ignored. She had experienced attraction before, the first time with a man who had a pretty face and an amusing wit. But he had been a passing interest, nothing that disturbed her or consumed her thoughts.

The way Gavin has done.

The tingling low in her stomach, the tightening of her skin signaled more than a passing interest. And it wasn't simple attraction. She wanted Gavin DeFoe, the Earl of Blackwell. Wanted him on a primal, fundamental level that was outside her control. The irony made her want to laugh. Mackenzie Tuggle, the woman who was always in control had none when it came to the one man who couldn't stand her.

If his dislike of her weren't enough, he was also a client and an overbearing nobleman who, it just so happened, belonged to another woman. She had every reason in the world to not give him another thought. *So why can't I push him from my mind? Turn around and ignore him?*

Perhaps it was the way he looked at her, as if he couldn't decide between strangling her or stripping the clothes off her body and making love to her. Not thoughts either of them should be having when he was already spoken for. Yet she found herself glancing at his hands, now folded across his chest and wondered how they would feel. Gentle? The touch firm enough to make her feel protected, loved? Or hard, rough and possessive?

Shuddering, she assumed the latter, imagining a sandstorm would pale in comparison to making love to Gavin DeFoe. Violent and turbulent, consuming. Yes, it would be consuming, she thought. Of both heart and soul.

And too overpowering for a docile *lady* like Lady Sarah.

Not that it mattered to Mac. DeFoe's love life didn't concern her. Period. Really, it didn't. Yet . . .

"What does she see in that man?" she mused.

"What was that, daughter?" Willie asked.

Mac cringed when she realized she'd spoken her thoughts out loud. She drew a deep breath, pulled her gaze away from Gavin to face her father. Only to discover all three men were looking at her, waiting for her answer.

When she didn't say anything, Willie handed her a flask of water. "'Ere, drink this. Ye're all aflush. Now, what man were ye referrin' to?"

She took the flask, but didn't drink, regardless that her mouth was as dry as a mummy's. "Lady Sarah," she finally admitted. "She seems like a nice lady."

"She is," Jake said with affection.

"Then what does she see in DeFoe?"

Jake's blond brow arched beneath his hat. "What do you mean?"

"Well, look at them. They're both cultured, obviously from the same social station, but they don't seem . . . right together."

"They bloody hell better not look right together," he snarled, all pleasantries vanishing.

She glanced from Jake's lethal scowl to Connor's amused grin to Willie's confused frown. She asked, "Isn't Lady Sarah here with DeFoe?"

"Yes," Connor said.

"No," Jake nearly shouted at the same time.

The two men exchanged a glare, then Jake told her. "She's with me."

"But DeFoe," she turned to give a pointed look at the couple, who were now watching, and undoubtedly listening to their conversation, "said she was with him."

"You misunderstood," Jake said, his scowl easing. "We are all traveling together, but Sarah is mine. She's my wife."

"Your wife," Mac repeated, not sure how to interpret the sudden flipping of her stomach.

She was torn between smiling with delight and cursing with dread. She'd never been one to walk away from what she wanted, and her body definitely wanted Gavin DeFoe. But her mind, and her heart, knew better.

The man would hurt her, then he'd trample her. Then he'd leave her behind.

Gavin had heard enough of the conversation to know it shouldn't have taken place. He'd hired Mackenzie Tuggle to dig up a tomb, not dig into his private life.

"She's pretty, don't you think?" Sarah asked, stirring the hot air with her lace fan. "Unconventional to England's standards, but still, there's something exotic about her. And all that auburn hair! It's absolutely gorgeous."

"It's a mess." The string she'd used to tie back the long, dark red mane was fighting a losing battle. Curls had escaped to frame her face, turning her into the sultry gypsy he'd first thought her to be.

"I envy her." Sarah sighed, drawing his attention to her delicate cheekbones and straight nose. He'd seen her eyes turn from silver to smoke, depending on her mood. She had porcelain skin, creamy and smooth, as fragile in appearance as the shell of an egg. At the moment it was tinged pink from the heat. An angel's face, he'd thought more than once. But she was tougher than she looked. Satin and steel, that was their Sarah.

"She's wearing pants," Sarah announced, disgruntled.

"You're dressed the way a woman should be."

Her silver gaze narrowed with annoyance. "You wouldn't say that if you had to don a dress, petticoats and leggings."

Gavin tried to image Mac in a gown with ruffles and stays, something in royal blue velvet to offset her hair, with matching slippers and satin gloves. He tried envisioning her tangled red hair upswept and threaded with a strand of pearls. But the image seemed wrong somehow. Mackenzie Tuggle becoming a lady of society was as likely as a fisherman becoming king.

But she was definitely a woman. Tall and slender with curves right where they belonged. Her clothes were shapeless, but they couldn't disguise the roundness of her breasts, the narrow indention of her waist.

The hips that were perfect for a man to hold onto
while he—

"Gavin, did you hear what they said," Sarah whispered behind her fan, saving him from his
imagination. "Mac thought we were together. Wherever did she get such a notion?"

He couldn't think of an answer. A warning had
begun to buzz through his mind. Mac watched him,
her jade green eyes dark and uncertain. Wary, as well
she should be, he thought.

He held her gaze, feeling as if he'd been caught in a
snare. With each passing second the distance between
them seemed to vanish. He could see the rise and fall
of her chest, the small tremor that ran through her
limbs, the pulse that beat at the base of her throat.

Then her expression changed, as if she finally understood some great secret. Her lips parted in a silent
invitation, softening as if she anticipated being kissed.

The muscles in his body tensed in response. Blood
pulsed through his veins, filled his sex. Gavin clamped
his jaw shut. He would not feel desire for the woman.
He would not!

But he had no doubt that she was interested in him.
She was an open book, he realized, her every thought
there for him to read. So unlike the women he knew
in London, where coyness was a game to be played.
A game Rachel had mastered well. He'd never known
what his wife had been thinking. Perhaps if he had,
his life would be much different today.

"Did I tell you I'm with child?" Sarah asked.

"Really?" Gavin said, wondering how Mac would respond to him now that she knew he was unattached.
She hadn't bothered to make a good impression on
him when they'd first met. But then, he admitted, neither had he.

"Connor's the father," Sarah added with a wistful sigh.

"Is that so." If Mac were smart she'd keep her distance. But if she didn't he would set her straight. His body might be responding to her—what man's wouldn't?—she was attractive in a mysterious, free-spirited way, but that didn't mean he wanted her.

"Jake is just thrilled." Sarah laughed, patting Gavin's arm to gain his attention. "He's hoping for a boy."

"A boy?" He frowned at her. "What are you talking about?"

"Haven't you been listening? I'm having a baby."

"Bloody hell, Sarah." He caught her by the arms and forced her to sit on a crate. "You shouldn't be here. It's too dangerous. How could Jake let you—"

"Jake had nothing to do with this. Connor's the father."

"Connor!"

She smiled, letting her statement sink into his head, as it was meant to.

He had to let a moment pass before his heart returned to its normal beat. "Tell me you aren't with child."

"I'm not."

"Have I been ignoring you?"

"Yes, but you're forgiven." Standing again, she barely reached his chest and was forced to look up at him. As a woman should, he thought.

"But only because you're smitten," Sarah said.

"I most certainly am not," he argued, thoroughly insulted.

She laughed, gripping her side when she couldn't stop. "Oh, yes you are, Gavin DeFoe. And it's about time." Walking away, she added over her shoulder,

"You can't keep running, you know. Someday you'll have to let someone into your life."

Gavin scowled at Sarah's retreating back. *Smitten!* He'd never been smitten in all his thirty-one years. And he certainly wasn't now. Mackenzie Tuggle irritated him, disturbed him. Reaffirmed every reason why he didn't want a woman in his life.

When Sarah reached the group, Jake tucked her into his side and gave her a quick kiss on the mouth. Gavin glanced at Mac, startled to find her unwavering gaze still focused on him. He had the insane urge to hold her as Jake held his wife, see if she fit against him as well.

Gavin turned away and gripped the edge of a crate. He did not want to hold a woman, any woman, and especially not *that* woman.

Chapter 4

Mac knelt and, using the stem of a date palm, drew the outline of Osiris' temple in the rich black silt. The ground was dry here, ready for the floodwaters that would sweep from the Sudan Mountains in the south in two months time, covering the Nile valley with a fresh layer of fertile earth.

All around her, her crew was busy setting up a temporary camp. Kippie had commandeered the food supplies and was preparing his version of English stew. She'd long ago given up trying to introduce him to Egyptian fare; he'd grumbled that the spices were too rich for his old stomach. Willie and the others had agreed, so, though they may live in an exotic country, their meals were always bland and basic.

She'd told Hollister to forgo setting up tents; they'd make do with bedrolls tonight. She wanted an early start in the morning. No one had complained; they had all welcomed the respite from the boat. The feluccas were a convenient and quick way to travel the Nile, but when the deck was crowded with crates and people, with no place to escape for a moment's privacy . . .

She let the thought fade away, knowing the real reason she'd wanted off the boat had nothing to do with needing space. She'd never felt crowded when sailing before, and she'd spent half her life on one type of vessel or another. No, her need for escape was solely because of one man.

With the floppy brim of her hat shielding her eyes, she glanced up and found the reason for her discontent. Gavin DeFoe, Earl of Blackwell. The man was tall, taller than her five-foot-ten, which was a welcome change. She usually towered over men. Jake and Connor stood a handbreadth above her as well, but looking up at them didn't make her stomach dip and her heart flutter against her chest.

The breeze shifted from the south, bringing the soft, dark scent of dusk as the sun sank into the horizon. Gavin patrolled the camp, his restless, unreadable eyes taking in every detail. He nodded when he saw something he approved of and made a comment to whatever crewman necessary when he didn't.

He was arrogant, that one, Mac thought, as mysterious as a pharaoh's tomb. There were undoubtedly all sorts of secret places inside his heart, little chambers where he stored his past as if it was something to hide from the world.

"Don't let him frighten you."

Startled, Mac stood and rounded on the person who'd spoken. The top of Sarah Mitchell's perfectly coiffed head barely reached Mac's shoulders. The woman was petite, frail, as delicate as the china service Mac had purchased on one of her trips to China but had never had the nerve to use. Even now the beautiful cups and teapot were in her home in Egypt locked in her china cabinet and protected by beveled glass doors. The same way Mac had always assumed women of nobility were kept.

At the moment, Mac had never felt more gigantic or unladylike in her life. Not that she wanted to be like Sarah. She couldn't imagine having to wear a dress and corset every day or following rules set by society, *by men*, simply because they thought they knew best. Nor could Mac imagine ever finding a man who would want to share her life the way Jake and Sarah shared each other's.

"Excuse me?" Mac said.

"Gavin. He's not as frightening as he appears."

"I don't think he's frightening at all. Rude. Arrogant. Overbearing."

"Handsome?" Sarah added with a hopeful smile.

Mac shrugged. "If you like the scowling type."

Laughing, Sarah tugged at the high neckline of her gown. "He's only scowling because he doesn't know what to do about you."

"You mean he doesn't treat all women as if we're responsible for the plague?"

"Well . . ." With a flip of her tiny wrist, Sarah snapped open her fan and stirred the loose strands of her chestnut hair. "He does tend to be a bit off-putting, but he's wealthy and titled. Women are constantly throwing themselves at him. For some reason he's decided boorish manners are his only defense."

"It's working."

Sarah was quiet for a moment, her silver gaze sliding from Mac to Gavin and back again. "Last year, when I first met the earl, I had thought him charming. Gavin, Jake and Connor were traveling on the same ship as me to Egypt. As time went on, though, Gavin became cool. Not belligerent, mind you, just distant, making it clear he didn't want to socialize with me."

Mac had no idea why the woman was telling her this, and though she wasn't at all interested in *anything* involving Gavin DeFoe, she couldn't stop listening. "Something must have changed. He's very protective of you now. I had even thought the two of you were . . . uh . . ."

"Were married?" She pressed her lips together as if to stifle a laugh. "I heard you earlier, and Jake has tried to keep me by his side ever since. The jealous man." Stealing a glance at her husband who was sharing a pint of ale with Willie, Sarah added with a playful smile, "Not that I mind."

"You met Jake while you were sailing to Egypt?"

"Oh, no. Long before that. He was my father's partner. The two of them traveled all over Egypt, digging in the sand like little boys looking for buried treasure, while I was locked away in boarding school. I hated Jake for that."

"Hated him? As in—"

"Couldn't stand him," she said matter-of-factly. "In fact, I was sailing to Egypt in disguise. I'd had every intention of returning Queen Tiy, a mummy he had discovered, and all of her artifacts to her tomb in the Valley of the Queens. I was doing it because my father had asked me to; he'd thought the mummy was cursed, but the real reason was that I wanted to ruin Jake."

"Which is why you married him," Mac stated sarcastically.

Sarah tilted her head back to look at Mac with an expression of wonderment and awe. "I suppose what I'm trying to say, is that you never know how life will turn out. I wanted to hurt Jake the way I believed he had hurt me. Instead I fell in love with him, so hard and fast I'd thought I had plunged off a cliff."

With a suspicion already brewing in her mind, Mac asked, "And you're telling me this because . . ."

"Because there's more to Gavin than an ill-mannered nobleman." Snapping the fan shut, she gave

Mac a measured look. "But it will take a strong and persistent woman to discover exactly what."

And she thought Mac might be that woman? She almost laughed out loud, but couldn't quite force the false emotion to surface. "I appreciate your attempt at matchmaking, but it's a waste of time."

"You don't find Gavin attractive?"

"Yes, but—"

"Just average attractive, or more so than any other man you've met?"

Mac shook her head. She wasn't about to tell Sarah the truth, that Gavin affected her in ways she didn't dare dwell on. That she had fantasized about him throughout the night, wondering how his hands would feel on her skin, imagining his firm lips softening once they touched hers.

Instead, she admitted, "If I were interested, I suppose he would be passable."

"There, you see!" Sarah beamed.

"But I'm not interested," Mac said, causing the woman's smile to vanish.

"Not at all?"

Mac tried not to laugh at the woman's crestfallen expression. "Not even a little."

"You're not even a tiny bit smitten with the earl?"

"Sarah, you just said two words that give me every reason *not* to be smitten with him."

"Which are?"

"'The earl.' As in nobility, titled and too lofty for a woman like me."

"The earl is also a man."

Well, hell, she couldn't argue that. And unfortunately he was a man her body was finely attuned to, but she was wise enough to know acting on her body's needs would be foolhardy.

"Whether he realizes it or not," Sarah added stubbornly, "he needs a woman. A good woman."

"Perhaps he does, but he doesn't need me." Of that she was certain because he hadn't shown the slightest interest in her, unless it was to threaten getting rid of her.

"But if you only knew. He's lost so much."

Touched by the woman's persistence, Mac gave Sarah a quick hug and said, "Enough. No more matchmaking."

When she pulled back, she was startled to find Sarah's eyes wide with shock.

She instantly released the smaller woman. "Did I hurt you?"

"No." Swallowing, she shook her head. "I grew up without anyone ever . . . well . . . hugging me, so when someone does, it takes me by surprise."

To keep from reaching out and comforting the woman again, Mac propped her hands on her hips. "I suppose I should tell you then. With my family, you're likely to be hugged without warning. Especially by Kippie."

Frowning, Sarah glanced across the clearing where the wiry man was worrying over the fire. "The leathery old cook?"

"The very one. He may not look like it, but the man is as soft as they come."

Her expression turning wistful, she stated, "You're a lucky woman, Mackenzie. Not only are you allowed to dress in pants, as any sane person should in this country, you have a wonderful family."

Her gaze moving over the camp and her crew, she whispered, "I know."

Wanting to bring closure to the conversation, she knelt and turned her attention to her rough drawing.

She already felt connected to Sarah; if they talked much longer, she just might admit how often she had thought of Gavin over the past day and a half, and how much better she wanted to know him.

"I see I'm not the only artist," Sarah said, kneeling beside her. "That looks similar to the map Jake made."

"It is." She pointed to a series of rectangles. "These are *mastabas,* underground tombs we already know about. Only the very tops are visible, but I know these have been thoroughly searched."

"You mean plundered."

"Yes. They've undoubtedly been empty for a thousand years." Using the stick, she indicated an area she'd left blank. "Your husband believes King Menes will be here."

"There's nothing there."

"Exactly. No visible tomb or *mastabas,* nothing. Digging there will be a huge undertaking. *If* the king is buried there, or anywhere in Abydos, it will take months, perhaps years, to find him."

"You don't have years," an undeniably masculine voice announced, startling both women.

Mac didn't move, but Sarah surged to her feet. "Gavin, we didn't hear you approach."

Because he didn't want us to, Mac thought. The man moves like a ghost. She recalled earlier that morning on the boat, while the crew still slept. She hadn't heard Gavin approach her then, either, but she'd felt him. The air had tingled against her skin, lifting the fine hairs along her arms, alerting her that something unique and disturbing was nearby.

"Mac was explaining the challenges of digging at Abydos," Sarah explained in an overly bright voice.

"We already know what challenges we face," Gavin

said in a gentle tone he'd certainly never used with Mac.

Bracing her hands on her thighs, she stood and turned to meet a pair of raven eyes. She was prepared for the indifference she'd see there, but not for the betraying little jump of her heart that his nearness caused. "Then you know I'm right."

"We're on borrowed time. I'll give you a few weeks to find what we need. Nothing more."

"Perhaps you can run your estates in England with arrogant commands, but you're in Egypt now. You can't simply demand that a tomb appear."

"Are you saying you won't order your men to dig?" The chilling note in his voice warned that she had better not try to betray him. Or control him. *As if I could!*

"I'm saying that if King Menes is there, he's buried beneath five millennia of blowing sand. It will take time to dig him out. And should we search in the wrong place, such as in Abydos instead of Saqqara like Napoleon is doing, we'll never find him."

"Menes isn't in Saqqara."

The certainty in his tone took her back. "How do you know?"

A muscle pulsed in his jaw, the slight movement controlled, restrained and to her ire, utterly enticing. "You'll have to trust me on that."

Mac drew a calming breath, but it didn't help. Heavens the man was annoying . . . and appealing, though she still wasn't certain why. He was irritatingly attractive, with his sin-black hair cut at his nape, his healthy tanned skin, the dark eyes that were as mesmerizing as the sphinx.

The sleeves of his cream linen shirt were rolled back to his elbows, revealing muscled forearms she'd never thought to see on a nobleman. Fitted tan pants were tucked into brown Hessian boots. The clothes were casual, but on him they looked perfectly tailored, perfectly . . . perfect. Nothing about Gavin could be described as an English fop. He was cultured, daring and utterly dynamic.

But there had to be more than good looks to interest Mac.

Like confidence, courage, the ability to stand up to her, challenge her. Traits he possessed in spades. Damn it.

"Well," Sarah said hesitantly. "I think I'll see if Kippie needs any help."

Sarah left, but neither Mac nor Gavin acknowledged her. They were busy behaving like a pair of angry jackals, circling each other in a silent challenge. Which was foolish. He was her paying client. If he wanted to dig in Abydos, then that's where they'd dig. But he had to understand that a few weeks wouldn't be enough. If King Menes was buried in what the ancient Egyptians believed to be the entrance to the underworld, it would take time to find him.

She took a step back, hoping space would dispel the tension burning between them. "Can I ask you something?"

He arched a brow, as if daring her to test him further.

Mac considered walking away. Did the man ever relax his guard? Or was he so suspicious of women that he couldn't react any other way? She wished she knew.

She asked, "Why King Menes?"

"Will knowing my reasons make a difference in your ability to work?"

"Since Napoleon is also searching for the king, I think it makes a difference in keeping my crew safe."

"Fair enough," he said, his voice losing some of its

fighting edge. Kneeling, he picked up her abandoned stick and started to draw in the dirt. "Do you know what a *pshent* is?"

She dropped down beside him. "The crown worn by the pharaohs."

"There are three different designs, depending on who ruled what part of Egypt." He drew a conical shape in the sand, similar to a handbell. "This style was made of white gold and worn by the pharaoh who ruled Upper Egypt. And this one," he said, creating a round crown with a flat top that curved up into a point at the back. "Was made of red gold for whoever controlled Lower Egypt."

"And which are you looking for?"

"Neither. It's believed King Menes was the first pharaoh to rule both upper and lower Egypt. The symbol for the king who accomplished that feat wore a special crown." Using the stick, he sketched a head-piece that combined the red and white gold crowns into one.

"Why is this one so important?" she asked, standing when he did.

"Because Napoleon wants it." Gavin turned and headed for the trail that led through a patch of sesban shrubs and daisies to the thicker grass along the Nile, where their boats were anchored.

Not ready to be dismissed, she followed him. "That seems rather childish, don't you think? Because Napoleon wants the crown, King George doesn't want him to have it?"

"It's more involved than that."

"I'm listening," she said to his back.

He paused to glare at her over his shoulder. "That's all you need to know. Return to camp."

The nerves along her spine clenched. She was the

one who gave the orders; she didn't take them, especially not from a man who showed more anger than common sense. "You shouldn't be so far away from camp. It's getting dark and it isn't safe."

"Which is why you're going to return." With that he started down the path again.

Mac glanced around the area thick with brush and date palms, the tall grass that reached her hips. Shadows stretched over the fertile ground, deceiving the eye with shapes that weren't there. She loved this part of the country, the constant flow of the river, the wild shoreline, the orderly farms that spread into the distance. It was calm and peaceful, a place from another time, undisturbed except for the tension humming from Gavin's body. She started after him.

"So why is this crown so special?" she asked once she caught up with him again.

He rounded on her, his black eyes a dangerous slit. "I told you to return to the others."

"I will after you answer my questions."

"I've told you all you need to know."

She shook her head, a rueful smile playing over her lips. "Napoleon has half his army, every scholar from France and just about every digger in Egypt committed to finding this crown. Why? And why doesn't King George want him to have it?"

A breath hissed through Gavin's clenched teeth. "Do you know anything about Egypt's history?"

She gave him a what-do-you-think smirk.

"Then you know in ancient times, Egypt was considered the center of the world. But even this country was often split, ruled by two different pharaohs."

"Upper and lower Egypt, yes, I know."

"Whenever a pharaoh managed to unite the two and control them both, it was considered an incredible feat. It's only happened a few times in the last five thousand years."

"That still doesn't explain why *this* crown is so special."

Sighing, clearly reluctant to say anything more, he told her, "There is a myth that whoever wears King Menes' crown will have the power to rule the world."

"A myth?" She held his unwavering, unreadable gaze. "All this effort for a legend?"

"I don't question my king," he snarled. "I follow his commands."

"This is insane." Laughing, she held her arms out to her sides. "There are as many myths in Egypt as there are grains of sand."

"And as I follow my king's commands, you will follow mine," he said as if she hadn't spoken. "You will dig where I tell you to or I'll hire someone else."

She saw in his eyes that his last threat was an empty one. If he could've hired another crew, he would have. But he was stuck with Mac and Willie and their aged bunch whether he liked it or not. And he obviously did *not* like it.

"Of course we'll dig wherever you want us to," she said, stepping up to him so they were almost nose to nose. "But it will take longer than the few weeks you've allotted. Your archaeologist friend, Jake, should have told you that."

"The longer it takes us, the more likely Napoleon will learn of our whereabouts."

"And you don't want to get caught." She could certainly understand that. "But that doesn't change facts. Digging up a tomb takes time."

"You have three weeks."

"Bloody hell," she said, matching his stance by placing her fists on her hips. "You are the most unreasonable man I've ever met. I've told you—"

"Enough!" He leaned closer, somehow towering over her more than he should have been able to.

He wasn't going to listen to her, she realized. Nothing she said would get through the barriers he'd set in place. Well, there were others ways to deal with a difficult man. She latched onto the first truly insane idea that came to mind and decided it was time to act.

Clasping his face between her hands, she rose onto her toes and covered his mouth with hers. His body stiffened, his eyes narrowed and his lips turned into harsh, unmoving lines. But she didn't give up.

She threaded her fingers deeper into the cool silk of his hair, nipped his bottom lip with her teeth, then kissed the spot she'd just bitten. He made a sound, a groan or a growl. She wasn't sure which and didn't care, it was a response, and where there was one, more would follow.

She pressed her lips fully to his, adjusted her body closer, felt him move, hesitate, then finally, finally, with a growling sigh, he molded his mouth over hers. Her breath hitched inside her chest with relief. Then again with surprise. The feel of his lips was devastatingly sensual, firm and soft, like liquid fire that didn't scorch . . . but consumed.

His hands locked on her waist, she was sure it was to push her away, but his fingers dug into her skin, squeezing her tighter as he pulled her even closer. Wanting more of that fire, she pressed her body flush to his. Every place they touched, sensations spiraled like rising embers, fanning throughout her stomach and chest, moving to her limbs, lighting fire after fire after fire until she feared she might flame and burn to ash.

Light exploded behind her closed lids. She couldn't feel the ground beneath her feet. She filled her hands with his silky hair and held on. His hips crushed against hers, aligning their bodies into one and proving that not all of his emotions were born of anger. He felt desire as well.

A breath shuddered through her. She wanted to throw her head back and cry out. But she couldn't stop kissing him, couldn't let go. Instinctively, she knew she'd made her first crack in Gavin's protective wall. But now that she had, now that she realized the force of what lay beyond, she wasn't sure she hadn't made a mistake.

Spinning, Gavin was out of control, tumbling as if he'd fallen down a well that had been set ablaze. He shook with startling need, holding onto Mac when he should be pushing her away. Heat seared his body from the inside out, burning the air from his lungs and rational thought from his mind.

He kissed her harder, parted her lips, tasted the cinnamon spice that had haunted his senses since the moment they'd met.

Blood pounded in his ears, filled his groin. Anger tangled with desire, building to a level of trembling need he hadn't felt in years. *Or ever!* And all because of an irritating woman. A beautiful, spirited and fearless woman he wanted no part of. He didn't want to feel desire for her or anyone else; that emotion was better left alone, buried with his past.

But he couldn't stop kissing her, and when she made a helpless sound in the back of her throat, when her fingers curled around handfuls of his hair and her body melted against his, he admitted he didn't want to. He'd denied his needs too long. Now they tore through him, burning, taking.

He shifted his hands from the curve of her waist to her shoulders, feeling her slender torso mold to his touch. Her clothes were a barrier; he wanted them gone, wanted to feel her skin, knowing the sensations would be as wild and untamed as the woman.

He lifted the hem of her shirt, almost blind with his need to touch Mac's body, feel her breasts in his hands. She was pliant and willing, wanting him at that moment as much as he wanted her. Everything about Mac was warm and luscious, the opposite of the women he'd known, especially his wife. Rachel had been prim and proper, the perfect mate.

Gavin froze. *Perfect until I'd found her in bed with another man.* Remembering his wife's deceit, and her last act of betrayal that had destroyed his life, the fire in his veins turned to ice.

He broke the kiss, jerked his hands off Mac's body and stared down at her in dismay. How could he have forgotten?

"Gavin?" Mac's voice trembled and her hands clenched his shirt. "What's wrong?"

He couldn't answer. His memories had swept him back in time, to the night he'd discovered Rachel's beautiful, pure body entwined with another man's, her laughter ringing through their bedchamber, her moans of joy a knife to his heart.

Fury had engulfed him at that moment, his rage so fierce it had frightened him as much as it had her. She'd run from him, taking their three-year-old son Matthew with her. He hadn't trusted himself to pursue her, afraid of the things he would say. Instead, he'd shut himself away in his library where, over bottles of whiskey, he'd cursed himself for being a fool and damned Rachel for stealing the happiness from his life.

Only he soon learned that he'd had more to lose than happiness. Rachel had ordered her driver to take her to the docks, why there he still didn't know. But that's where she was when she'd been set upon by thieves. The coach had been overturned, instantly killing both Rachel and Matthew.

Killing his family, his future, all his hopes and dreams.

"Gavin, what is it?" Mac brushed the hair back from his brow, her fingers rough against his skin. In the fading light, her eyes were as dark as the swirling Nile, powerful and compelling. And filled with concern.

He wanted to believe she was worried, but he couldn't. He couldn't trust Mac anymore than he could trust any woman. He'd made that fatal mistake once; he couldn't do it again. Ever!

"That was . . . interesting," he said, fighting to keep his voice steady, because kissing Mac had been far more than interesting, it had been incredible, thrilling and dangerous. "But I hired you to find King Menes, not to seduce me."

The concern in her dark green eyes turned to wariness, then to cool understanding. She stepped back, crossed her arms over her chest, drawing his attention to the shape of her breasts. Breasts that weren't hindered by a corset, he thought, still able to feel the shape of her body against his.

"My mistake," she said. "I thought you were enjoying it."

The tall grass rustled behind him, but Gavin was too disturbed by Mac to care. "If I'd wanted to kiss you I would have."

She held her hands out to her sides, a tight smile on her flushed face. "As I said, my mistake. I see now that you didn't enjoy it at all. It won't happen again."

He nodded, felt his mouth curl into a scowl. He clenched his hands into fists to rid the feel of her on his skin. Blast it all to hell, he would not allow her to affect him.

"Return to camp, Mac."

"Aren't you coming?"

"After I gather some things from the boat." He turned to leave.

"Gavin," she called.

He paused, but didn't look back. "What is it now?"

"Don't move."

The quiet chill of her voice caused the hair on the nape of his neck to stand on end. "What's wrong?"

"We're being watched."

"By whom?" He reached for his side, belatedly remembering he'd left camp without his pistol. Bloody hell. He searched the dark reeds in front of him. There was a village nearby, but as far as he knew, the people along the river weren't violent. Still, he couldn't see a thing.

"By a mother and her baby. And they're not happy. So whatever you do, stand perfectly still."

Just what the hell was she up to? Trying to make a fool of him, trick him with some made up nonsense? Gavin swung around. "A mother—"

The rest of his statement died on his lips as a massive, two-ton beast crashed through the grass, its huge mouth gaping to reveal ivory tusks.

Gavin didn't have time to register more. The animal released a keening wail.

At the same instant Mac screamed, "Run!"

Chapter 5

Mac spun on her heels and raced up the path. She didn't waste time moving the prickly shrubs aside; she burst through them, the thorny limbs scratching her legs and waist through her clothes. She glanced back, saw Gavin close behind her, his face a mask of fury.

And behind him, the enraged hippopotamus gained on them, her huge head lowered as she charged.

Gavin darted up beside Mac, grabbed her arm and forced her to run faster. She heard the animal snort in rage, imagined she could feel its hot breath on her back. The ground rumbled beneath her feet, the sound echoing the pounding of her heart.

She pushed to stay up with Gavin, only to realize the path he'd chosen would lead them close to camp. She had to stop him.

"We have to split up!" she yelled.

"No." He kept running, his hold a vise on her arm.

"We can't outrun her. She's too fast."

Gavin glanced behind them and cursed. "Go right, through those bushes. I'll draw her attention."

With that he shoved her away from him. Mac stumbled, nearly went down, but caught the base of a palm. As Gavin disappeared through the tall grass, she turned, waved her arms and yelled, "Come on, sweetheart, follow me!"

The hippo hesitated for an instant, then changed
direction and went after Mac. With Gavin out of danger, she started running, batting away the heavy leaves
of date palms, searching the dark for someplace to
hide. She couldn't see much beyond the thick grass
and scattered scrubs. No buildings, no trees to climb,
no nothing. She thought about heading for the Nile
and her boats, but knew she'd be in greater danger if
the animal caught her in the water. And running for
camp was out of the question. She couldn't endanger
her family.

Mac heard the pounding of the animal's heavy feet.
She didn't need to look to know the mother was gaining on her. Mac pushed harder, forcing her legs to
move, but the soil shifted beneath her feet, sucking at
her, slowing her down. The muscles in her thighs
burned, every breath became a knife in her lungs.

But she couldn't stop. She'd seen a man mauled by
a hippo once, a sight she'd never forget. The old
steersman had been in his boat, navigating the river,
minding his own business, when an angry bull attacked, ripping the craft to shreds before tearing the
horrified man in half. No one had ever known why,
other than hippos were territorial and the man must
have encroached on the animal's space.

The same as Mac and Gavin must have done.

She saw a break in the shrubs and headed left, hoping to find a crevice to hide in or something she could
climb. The animal roared in anger and pursued. Mac
ran through the last of the tall grass and found herself
in a moonlit clearing, a farm, she realized, as her
boots churned up loose dirt. The crop already har-
vested. There was nothing before her but a barren
field. Panic tightened her heart. She couldn't run
into the open; the hippo would easily catch her.

She veered right, kept to the edge of the brush. Looking behind her, seeing the animal thirty feet away, a cry escaped her. Mac forced herself to run, made it only a few yards when she gasped, her side knotting with a spasm. She couldn't go on much longer. She had to find a place to hide.

Deciding to head back into the thicket, she darted through a pair of sesban shrubs. It was dark here, the prickly bushes dense. Her boot caught on a root, sending her down hard onto her knees. Her breath left her in a rush. She pushed up, fell again. She gritted her teeth and tried to stand, knowing any second the hippo would be on top of her.

She felt something clamp onto her arm and jerk. She gasped, looked up and saw Gavin's dark face.

"Move!" He hauled her up beside him, wrapped one arm around her waist and forced her to run.

Pain shot up her ankle and her side twisted, but she followed him, turning when he did, her fear pushing her like a hand at her back. But he shouldn't have come after her. Now they were both going to be mauled.

When he headed for the field, she tried to stop, but he wouldn't let her. He forced her to run, faster, harder, her feet barely touching the ground.

The hippo thundered after them, roaring, gaining. Mac glanced back, and would have screamed if she'd been able. The animal was less than five feet away.

"There!" Gavin shouted.

Mac looked to where he pointed. A large dark shadow loomed ahead. Rocks! Or a ruined tomb. She wasn't sure which, and she didn't care. If they could make it . . .

Her legs pumping, her feet feeling like lead, pain spiking through her ankle and calf, she forced herself to keep up. Then Gavin made a leap for the nearest rock, his hold on her arm never slacking as he hauled her up beside him. He didn't stop, but kept climbing, dragging her with him.

Reaching the top, twenty feet off the ground, they both looked back. The mother hippo paced below them, snorting and shaking her huge head. She stomped her feet and let out a terrifying growl of outrage.

Mac bent at the waist, pressing one hand to her trembling knee for support and the other to the pain in her side. Her breath rushed hot through her lungs, and she felt cold, chilled to her bones despite the sweat coating her skin. She'd had many scrapes in her life, but she'd never come so close to dying. Not even when *Little Bess* had been smashed by a storm and in danger of sinking.

"Are you out of your mind!" Gavin shouted at her. It wasn't a question but a reprimand. "Were you try-ing to get yourself killed?"

Straightening, she met his gaze. The night was dark, the quarter moon giving little light, but she didn't need any to see . . . or feel . . . the anger pour-ing from Gavin. It was a living thing, full of vengeance and fury. She didn't blame him; she'd nearly gotten him killed, too.

"I had no choice," she said, once she had her breath under control.

"So you *intended* to be run down by that animal."

She didn't miss his sarcasm, but decided it would be best to ignore it. "Of course not. I was trying to lead it away from camp."

"Bloody hell."

"And from you."

"You were trying to protect me?" he ground out the

words in disbelief, his anger verging on that of the
hippo's, who was still guarding their escape, her stubby
tail twitching in vexation.

"Have you ever run from a hippo before?" she asked.

"Have you?"

"Well, no, but I know what they can do."

He caught her arms, hauled her up to him, then
shook her once like a rag doll. "You were reckless,
Mac. You could have been trampled!"

She heard the terror in his voice, realized just how
much she had frightened him. "I've been in dangerous situations before," she said, trying to calm him. "I
would have found a way out of this one."

"If I hadn't reached you, you'd be dead right now."

Mac shivered, knowing he spoke the truth. For the
first time since she'd become the caretaker of her
family she hadn't been the one to fix the problem or
save the day. It was a humbling realization. But one
she wasn't too proud to admit.

She pressed her hands to Gavin's chest, felt the wild
beating of his heart beneath his sweat-dampened
shirt. "You're right. I'm lucky you came after me. You
saved my life."

She'd meant to break the tension by admitting
she'd made a mistake, but one look at the shock on
Gavin's face and she knew she'd just said something
terribly, horribly wrong.

As Mac's admission sank in, hot pinpricks raced
over Gavin's scalp and down his spine. *I'm lucky you
came after me. You saved my life.*

If he hadn't chased her down Mac would be dead,
just as Rachel and Matthew were dead because he
hadn't gone after them.

He tried to deny the similarities, but couldn't. The
crush of the carriage had broken his wife's body and

son's, taking them from him forever. But Mac was alive because he hadn't let her go off on her own. He'd gone after her.

The way I should have gone after Rachel. But I didn't. I didn't!

The wrenching truth tore through him. He released Mac and stared down at her, saw the confusion in her eyes. She wanted to understand, but he couldn't tell her what he'd never told anyone before. That he was responsible for his family's death.

She moved one hand from his chest to his face, her palm warm against his cheek, a comfort he didn't deserve. He caught her wrist, forced her away.

"Gavin—"

"This proves this trip is too dangerous for you. In the morning, I'm sending you back to Rosetta." He would send her back to England if he could, where she wouldn't have to face the hardships of the desert and brutal sun, or vicious animals that attacked in the night.

Mac ran a hand through her hair, pulling the dark strands away from her face. She'd lost the colorful string she used to tie it with sometime during her escape. She glanced at the ground below, and watched the hippo turn her back on them and lope into the dark. Undoubtedly returning to shore to find her calf.

He waited for Mac to begin arguing with him, as she'd done since the moment they'd met. But this time he wasn't going to let her win.

"We won't have to wait here long," Mac said thoughtfully. "She's probably more worried about her calf right now than us."

"Did you hear what I said?" he asked. "You're returning to Rosetta."

She looked at him, a tolerant smile lifting one corner of her lips. "I heard you."

"I'm relieved you aren't going to argue about it."

She managed a negligent shrug. "There's no need to argue. I don't take orders from you. If you want to go to Abydos—with my men and my boats—I'll be coming, too."

"Like hell you are. It's too dangerous."

"I know how to take care of myself out here. If anyone is in danger, it's you."

"Me!"

"I told you not to move, that we were being watched."

"You said by a mother, not by an irate, two-thousand-pound hippo." Gavin would have walked away to pace off the anger tightening his limbs but, trapped on the rocky mound, he couldn't go anywhere so he directed his anger at her. "You should be in England where it's safe."

"I've been there, thank you. I didn't care for it. And speaking of safe, Lady Sarah is a sweet woman, but *she* is the one who should be in England."

"Jake, Connor and I will protect her."

"Lucky woman."

"But I cannot waste my time and energy trying to protect you."

Her body and voice becoming equally stiff, she said, "Then please don't."

He hadn't meant to phrase his response quite so cruelly, but he didn't regret doing so. Mac had to understand that she was a distraction. He had to focus on locating King Menes' tomb; he couldn't worry about whether she was about to step on a scorpion, or face a hyena, or be run down by an angry beast.

Mac turned away, sat on one of the flatter stones and wrapped her arms around her drawn-up knees. She stared into the dark as he stared at her. The proud tilt of her chin, the curve of her cheek, her full lips that smiled so readily. At the moment they were drawn into a frown.

An echo of the fear he'd felt when she'd attracted the animal's attention ripped through him again. His hands turned sweaty and his heart kicked against his chest. She could have died, and once again he would have borne the guilt of another death.

But I reached her in time.

The thought should have reassured him, but it didn't. He didn't know Mac well, but he knew enough to guess that she thrived on plunging into the unknown, with nothing to protect her but the wind and the sun.

She was wild and adventurous, as free-spirited as a gypsy. He should be repulsed by her lifestyle; she was everything he avoided. But to his disbelief, he found her compelling. Which made her far more dangerous to him than an angry hippo. Even now, he had the unwanted compulsion to sit beside her, draw her to his side, fill his hands with her again, taste the luscious warmth of her mouth.

Yes, she was a threat, one he would not allow. He already felt responsible for her. A situation that couldn't continue.

He had been responsible for Rachel, but he hadn't been able to protect her. He'd loved her, had given her the world. Another error on his part. But he'd learned his lesson. Women were best kept at arm's length. He couldn't trust them. And where Mac was concerned, he obviously couldn't trust himself.

He had only one option, he realized. If she refused to return to Rosetta, he would not—*would not*—be held accountable or feel responsible when she got herself killed.

* * *

Prickly goosefoot heavy with fruit flourished along the bank. Thorny neb-neb trees were spaced with abandon among the sweet smelling acacias, providing shade and an illusion of lushness in a barren land.

Mac watched the landscape drift by, vibrant and mysterious beneath the blazing sun, unable to appreciate the country she'd come to love. She'd ordered the single sails on each boat raised, determined to catch every breath of wind possible to increase their speed. She wanted off the vessel; she couldn't stand much more of the tension that had her by the throat.

Four days had passed since her encounter with the furious hippo, an episode she would have put behind her if not for the strained silence and stern looks Gavin felt compelled to punish her with.

She glanced at him—she couldn't seem to help herself—where he sat at the stern, sharpening a vicious-looking dagger with a whetstone. His attention was solely for his task, and his hat partially covered his eyes, but she knew they would be as sharp and lethal as the blade he honed. A tingle raced over her scalp and her skin burned as if she'd exposed it to the sun. She knew what the tingling meant. It was her body warning her that his dark gaze was now focused on her.

She looked into his coal-black eyes, refusing to give in and look away, though she didn't know why. Except that Gavin was the first man to ever challenge her. Or disapprove of her. The first to try to dominate her. And the first to make her body heat with churning, frustrating need.

To her irritation, Gavin seemed to hold an abundance of "first's" for her.

"Don't let 'im get under yer skin, lass."

Sucking in a surprised breath, she turned to find

the Scotsman behind her at the bow. He stared out
over the Nile, his rugged face set. With his arms
crossed over his chest, his black shirt stretched over a
pair of massive, unmovable shoulders. She hadn't
heard him approach, a trait he seemed to share with
Gavin, and one she wasn't accustomed to. Her crew
was far from quiet, always singing, complaining or
mumbling to themselves, she thought ruefully.

Knowing full well who he was referring to, she asked,
"Are you saying the earl is more bluster than bite?"

A smile tweaked one corner of the big man's mouth
and his green gaze flickered to her. "'E's as sweet as a
bear cub."

She laughed, something she hadn't done in too
many days. "Sweet? Now that's a word I would not
have associated with DeFoe."

"Don't be too hard on 'im, lass. 'E's had a rough
time of it."

"We've all had it rough at one point or another."

"Aye, that is so." In a low, rumbling voice, he added,
"But sometimes tragedy 'appens in a man's life that is
such 'e canna forgive."

Feeling the force of Gavin's gaze on her back, she
glanced over her shoulder at him, met his scowl.
There were tragedies in DeFoe's life? Somehow that
knowledge didn't surprise her.

"What can't Gavin forgive?" she asked, looking at
Connor.

A muscle ticked in his jaw, the hard line covered
with the red stubble of a day's growth of beard. "Now,
that's a story, tae be sure, but 'tis one 'e will have tae
tell ye himself."

She hadn't expected Connor to reveal another
man's past, he wasn't one to gossip, or talk much for
that matter, which made her curious as to why he was

talking to her now. "What about your past, Connor? Do you have something you can't forgive?"

"Aye."

The single word, uttered in a fervent growl, possessed a wealth of meaning. When he didn't expound, she waited a moment, then said, "It's not good to hold onto the past. You can't change it.

"You would have me forget?"

"Of course not. Remember it, learn from it, then go on."

"Ye don't know what yer talking about." He shook his head slowly, disturbing the fiery red hair that brushed his shoulders.

"Then tell me. What happened in your life that is so horrible you can't put it aside? For that matter, why are you tangled up with the earl?"

"'Tis the earl who will help me restore the past."

"I don't understand."

He sighed. "Do ye ken Scotland's terrible history?"

Sitting on one of the crates, she said, "I haven't lived in England for a long time, but I know about Scotland's struggles with England."

That earned her a grunt. "*Struggles?* The Battle of Culloden in '46 verra nearly destroyed us. My grandfather, Laird Duncan MacLeay, was executed, but my father, a lad at the time, escaped. King George II outlawed clans and lairds and the wearing of tartans, but his laws couldn't change what was in our hearts. We still had our clans, and we still followed our lairds."

"If you tell me you hate England because of a battle that happened fifty years ago, I won't believe you. You must know what a waste of effort that would be."

Connor's mouth curled with a scowl, and something sounding like a snarl rumbled from his barreled chest. "My grandfather and men like him followed Bonnie

Prince Charles because it was the honorable thing tae do. Looking back, 'tis easy tae see they were bound tae lose from the start. But my grandfather lost more than just his life and the right for our people tae live as they had for a thousand years, within the protection of our clans."

She watched his green eyes darken as old memories returned and filled him up. His arms were still folded over his chest, but his hands were now fisted, the strength behind them capable of crushing her like an eggshell.

"After the English burned down my home, my father rebuilt it, a grand place called Bachuil Castle. He replanted the fields, divided the few cattle and sheep that hadn't been slaughtered by the English among our clan so they could grow the herds. He gave life back to a people that had been sorely beaten."

"Your father sounds like an extraordinary man."

"Aye, that he is." Connor gazed out over the water as if he sought something in the pearling blue depth. "But he could not replace the one thing stolen from us that we valued most. The Staff of St. Moluag."

She frowned, waited for him to explain; she didn't have to wait long.

"Twelve hundred years ago, as St. Moluag lay dying, he gave his holy scepter to my ancestors, proclaiming it our duty to protect it. My clan has been the Keeper of the Staff of Bachuil ever since. Until it was stolen during the Battle of Culloden."

"And you want it back."

"Aye."

"And Gavin is going to help you."

"The earl has the King's ear. When I learn the name of the wretch who has the staff, DeFoe will see King George orders it returned to me."

"I thought all the disputes from that time were settled. It seems doubtful that Gavin would risk angering the King by dredging up the past now."

"The earl has given his word," Connor said with such conviction, the vow could have been handed down by God himself.

She didn't doubt Connor's loyalty to Gavin, but she didn't fully understand it. How could the Scotsman, who had the strength of a mountain, put his faith in a man who kept himself apart from the world?

But that wasn't true, she realized.

He allowed Connor within his protective circle, and Jake and Sarah. Yet he refused to allow anyone else, specifically Mac, close to him.

Because she threatened him? she wondered. Gavin was more compelling than any man she'd ever met. The anger he exuded was a mask, a poor attempt to camouflage himself in a curious world; she'd understood that from the beginning. He didn't intimidate her or frighten her. Quite the opposite. She found him darkly attractive. Compelling. As mysterious and tempting as a secret tomb waiting to be discovered.

She tensed as a new possibility occurred to her. Did he keep her away because he thought her beneath him? She didn't care for that likelihood. She was as far from nobility as the sun was from the moon, but she was happy with who she was, took pride in what she'd accomplished.

Without intending to, she glanced at Gavin. He'd abandoned sharpening his dagger and was listening to a story her father was reciting, and it must be a grand one, she thought, because Willie's eyes were gleaming and he waved his arms like a bird ready to take flight. As Willie reached a climactic point, Gavin's gaze moved over the ship until it touched on her, held for an interminable moment, then slipped away.

Fingers of heat brushed over her skin, a feather-light touch that was so real she couldn't breathe.

The memory of their kiss by the shore returned as if it had just happened. Her mouth filled with a hint of his taste, her fingers curled around thin air instead of the hard muscles of his arms. The need to kiss him again pushed through her hard and fast. Explosive, unlike anything she'd ever felt before.

Gavin had allowed others to step through his barrier. Perhaps he would allow her through, too. It would require taking the initiative, and possibly igniting the anger that lurked beneath his scowl, but for another of his kisses, for the chance to see if he wanted her as much as she suspected he did, she'd risk awakening a surly dragon.

She smiled at the thought. Egypt was as mysterious as the mythical beast, was it not? Enigmatic and romantic. Equally serene and deadly. Dangerous. Anyone who visited this land knew you could not experience Egypt without experiencing danger.

She had a feeling the same could be said about Gavin DeFoe.

Chapter 6

"Ye lay one finger on me pot of barley stew, and ye'll be eatin' sand for supper," Kippie warned, his face flushing red beneath the layers of wrinkles.

"Your wretched concoction already tastes like sand. The same as everything else you've prepared since we left Rosetta." Suppressing a laugh, Jake held out a small urn filled with exotic spice. "Come now, Kippie. A little curry won't hurt."

Hefting a ladle like a cudgel, the cook ordered, "Ye can keep yer fancy herbs. We're simple men."

"He means we're old men." Hollister lifted a dented metal cup with a gnarled hand as if to toast the fact.

"With old stomachs," Smedley added, his grin as toothless as it was cheery.

"Aye," Frewin agreed. "And our stomachs know what's really important." Having given up his place at the helm since they were camping on land, he was in charge of pouring out helpings of ale from a clay jar.

Lifting his mug to be filled, Willie called, "If we're goin' tae be miserable, let us be so with our hands around a cup 'o good ale, instead of around our ailing bellies!"

The grumpy frown pulling the corners of Kippie's wide mouth gave way to his scratchy, hyena laugh. "'Ere's tae sorry food and fine drink."

As the seasoned men shouted and cheered, Jake sighed and replaced the cap on his urn of spices, clearly defeated.

Gavin watched the debate, secretly hoping Jake wouldn't give up. Kippie was as feisty as they came, handy even, but the old sailor couldn't cook worth a damn. Gavin had been chewing on a piece of Kippie's dried beef for so long, his jaw ached.

"It's no use, Jake," Mac said, entering the camp with an armload of colorful fabric. "Anything stronger than pepper and you'll have a crew of bawling babies on your hands."

Fifty year old bawling babies, Gavin wanted to say, but didn't.

"Don't listen to them," Sarah said, patting Kippie on his bony back. "The last time I was in Egypt, I learned to appreciate whatever I had. Your stew is excellent, just the way it is."

"Lady Sarah," Willie chuckled. "You're a fine woman, but a mute can tell a better lie."

Catching hold of Sarah's hand, Mac led the surprised woman through camp, calling over her shoulder, "Pop, keep an eye on things."

"And where would ye be off tae?"

"Lady Sarah and I are going to have a bath."

The older men didn't pause in their tasks, but Jake, Connor and Gavin tensed in unison.

Sarah tugged her hand back, slowing Mac but only barely. "We are? Where?"

"The river." Mac kept walking, her cheeks pink from the sun, her eyes alive with mischief.

"God help me," Connor said under his breath.

"Hold on." Jake dropped the urn of curry into the dirt, forgotten. "You can't go into the river."

Mac smiled over her shoulder at him, but seeing

the glare on the archaeologist's face, she stopped long enough to say, "We'll be fine." Shifting her bundle to one arm, she pulled a pistol from her waistband and held it up for his inspection. "Nothing will harm us, I promise."

"Nothing such as crocodiles or water snakes," Gavin said dryly, resisting the sudden urge to forbid her from going anywhere. "Or an angry mother hippo."

Mac sent him a dark look, opened her mouth to reply, but Sarah said, "Perhaps he's right. It's not safe. You two were almost killed less than a week ago."

"Do you want a bath?" Mac asked, her throaty, seductive voice spiraling through Gavin. Too easily, he could envision her naked and wet, her slender body gliding through the dark water. Toward him. She'd be smooth and firm in his hands, her body curving to match his. Spiraling heat infused his limbs, tightened his veins. Blood pooled to a point low in his groin, making him unbearably hard.

"Of course," Sarah said. "But the river is so——"

"I know what I'm doing, Sarah." Looking at Jake, Mac promised, "I would never endanger her. I do this all the time. Don't I, Pop?"

"That you do, daughter 'o mine, though why ye can't wait until we return to Rosetta for a bath, I'll never understand."

"Because it could be weeks." Glancing at Gavin, she added with an arrogant smile, "Or months. We'll be in Abydos tomorrow and camped too far away from the river to make use of it. It's now or never."

"Well . . ." Sarah hedged, obviously wanting a bath but frightened by what that entailed.

"If it will make you feel better, Jake can stand guard," Mac announced.

Gavin ground his jaw and ripped his dried beef

in half. He glared at the archaeologist, silently ordering him to refuse, though he knew Jake wouldn't. Nor should he, Gavin rationalized; Sarah had to be protected.

But the thought of Jake watching Mac in the river, soaping all that auburn hair, washing her body, laughing as she cleaned away the dirt and grime of the past few days had him ready to roar like a furious bear. And the fact that he wanted to roar made him even more furious.

"It'll be dark soon," Mac said, glancing at the purpling sky. "We'd better hurry."

Jake collected a rifle and started after the women. "If I see any sign of danger, both of you had better get out when I tell you to."

"Of course," Sarah said, sliding her arm through her husband's.

"Of course," Mac mimicked sweetly. "We're women, we live to obey."

Mac turned her back on her crew's laughter and started out of camp, but not before glancing at Gavin. He tensed, feeling the power of her gaze like a streak of lightning. Quick and electric, with the ability to scorch whatever it touched.

Bloody hell!

He clenched his hands to keep himself seated by the fire. He would *not* go after her. And he didn't give a damn who watched her bathe. Someone added more wood to the fire, sending up a spray of embers and dancing light. The unwanted image of her pulling loose the yellow ribbon in her hair, of her running her fingers through its glossy length had him cursing under his breath in frustration. The woman was a danger to herself and those around her. *And to me*, he realized, not liking that thought.

"She should be in England, where it's safe," he said. "Not bathing in a bloody river."

"I'm thinkin' Jake-o won't leave her behind."

"I was referring to Mac." Gavin glared at the Scotsman, who was watching the trio depart.

Rubbing a hand over his jaw, Connor mused, "England is too tame for a spirited lass such as Mackenzie Tuggle. But Scotland, now, I'm thinkin' she would fit in just fine at Bachuil Castle."

"You can't be serious." Gavin had never before wanted to punch his friend, but he had the insane urge to do so now. And he couldn't imagine why.

"And why not? She may not have the bloodline to match your standards, but I donna care about such things. She's fearless, just what my clan needs."

"I don't give a damn about her bloodline," Gavin growled, realizing he hadn't given her base heritage much thought before now. "But you can't honestly be considering pursuing her."

"But I can." Connor pursed his lips as if giving the idea serious thought. "She's beautiful, is she no?"

"That's beside the point."

The Scotsman watched Gavin with a thoughtful expression, his green eyes dark and hooded. Ripping off a piece of dried beef with his teeth, he said, "You're right. She's more than beautiful and fearless. She's a prize worth having, more so than anything we'll find in this God-forsaken desert."

Gavin struggled to keep his breathing calm. He couldn't believe what he was hearing. Connor intended to turn Mac into the Lady of Bachuil Castle! The idea was laughable . . . and infuriating. Gavin knew it shouldn't bother him, but it did. And not because he couldn't forget kissing Mac. It was . . . it was . . . He wiped his hand over his face. Bloody hell, he didn't know why the thought of Connor and Mac together made his heart race, but it did. It bloody hell did.

At that moment the report of a rifle echoed throughout camp. Gavin lurched to his feet, his heart leaping just as quickly to his throat. His gun was in his pack on the other side of camp. He pulled the dagger from the sheath at his side and started to run.

"Whoa, me lord," Willie called, laughing. "There be no need tae dash off."

He slid to a stop, realized Connor was a step behind him. "But Mac—"

"That's just 'er way of scarin' off whatever's lurkin' about." Turning his attention back to his ale, he said, "She'll be fine. Mark my words. That girl can take care of herself."

"And all of us," Kippie grunted, stirring his stew.

"Ye'd think we were 'er babes," Hollister said. "The way she worries over us."

Gavin rubbed his thumb over the dagger's blade, undecided. Her "family" didn't show the slightest bit of concern, but damn it, he couldn't just sit by and watch old men drink their ale while God knew what was happening by the river. He had to make sure that Mac . . . that everyone was all right.

"Wait here. I'll check on them," he told Connor, not wanting the burly Scotsman's help.

"Jake-o might take offense if ye see 'is wife at her bath."

"I don't give a bloody hell." Stalking into the growing dusk, Gavin followed the faint path that led to an inlet off the main flow of the Nile. He heard the buzz of unseen insects, the rustle of grass as some rodent scurried out of his way. Long before he reached the place where the feluccas were moored, he heard the splashing of water, the muted sound of feminine laughter.

Without thinking, he barged through a stand of reeds and came to an abrupt halt, the barrel of a rifle inches from his face.

"Are you out of your mind!" Jake bit out. "What are you doing here? Never mind. I should shoot you for scaring years off my life."

Gavin pushed the metal cylinder aside with the back of his hand. "Sorry."

"Right. So what are you doing here?" Jake glanced over his shoulder to a shadowed area beyond the boats. Gavin followed his gaze, but the women were out of sight. "As if I don't know."

Gavin didn't know how to answer. What *was* he doing here? Jake didn't need his help. Had he intended to come to Mac's rescue? And if so, from what? Or who? Did he intend to stop Jake from seeing more of her than he should? If that were the case, Gavin admitted he was a fool. Jake was so smitten with his wife, he probably hadn't noticed Mac's allure, or her smoky voice, or the way her body moved and flowed with natural, sultry grace.

To Gavin's ire, he couldn't ignore the truth. He came because he hadn't been able to stop himself. The thought of Mac swimming in the cool black water, naked, possibly in danger, had blinded him to any glimmer of self-control.

"We're coming out," Sarah called with a girlish laugh that made Gavin smile in spite of himself. He remembered a time when he hadn't trusted the petite Lady Pendergrass, her name before she'd married Jake. He'd even warned Jake that she would betray him. And she had, but for a good reason. To right a wrong Jake and her father had allowed. She'd also captured Jake's heart in the process, and Connor's and Gavin's respect.

"You'd better leave," his friend said, taking a proprietary stance between Gavin and the water.

"I'm not going anywhere."

"This is my wife. I'll protect her."

"And I intend to let you." Turning his back to the sounds of someone emerging from the water, he folded his arms over his chest, stared into the building dark and listened.

"Oh, Jake," Sarah said. "You should take a swim. It feels wonderful."

Instead of a reply, Gavin heard what could only be a kiss. A long, passionate, devouring kiss. Sarah's breathless laugh a few seconds later confirmed he'd heard right.

"You can turn around now, Gavin," Sarah said. "I'm properly dressed."

"You call this proper?" Jake demanded.

Gavin turned to find Sarah in the crook of her husband's arm, but that wasn't what caused him to raise his brow. Sarah wasn't wearing one of her prim English gowns, but loose-fitting pants of pale green and an emerald and white-striped top, the sleeves so long they swallowed her hands. She held the pants bunched at the waste to keep them from falling. The clothes were far from a perfect fit. Which meant . . .

"Aren't they wonderful," Sarah beamed. "Mac loaned them to me."

"You look like a desert nymph," Jake said, enthralled. "I'll have to thank her."

Had he ever sounded so fascinated by Rachel, Gavin wondered? He clamped his jaw tight, knowing he had. He'd been crazy about his wife, knew he'd behaved like an enamored lover because that's exactly

what he'd been. But no more, he swore. He was happy
for his friends, but he refused to love a woman so
deeply and completely again. The emotion was too
unreliable and risky. It would only lead to loss and
pain and solitude. And he already had all three of
those in abundance.

"Where's Mac?" Gavin asked, far more abruptly
than he'd meant to.

Glancing toward the water, Sarah said, "She was
right behind me."

"Come along, love." Taking her by the hand, Jake
led Sarah up the path. "Let's get you back to camp. I
want to show you off."

"What about Mac?" she asked.

Looking over his wife's head, an amused grin curved
Jake's mouth. "I'm sure Gavin will take care of her."

The knowing look in his friend's eyes caused Gavin
to take a step after him to prove him wrong. But he
stopped, glanced back toward the water lapping at the
shoreline. Night gathered around the cove, relieved
only by the silvery wash of the rising moon. As much
as he wanted to prove he hadn't come here to see
Mac, he couldn't leave her alone. She thought she
could take care of herself, but he knew better. Their
encounter with the hippo had proven that.

He could still hear Jake's and Sarah's laughter behind him when Mac finally emerged from the shadows.
She walked slowly, leisurely, completely unaware of the
havoc she caused in him. And the kind of anticipation
he was determined to hammer down until he had it
under control. And once under control, he would
douse it as easily as pouring water over flames.

He stood at the head of the path, arms crossed over
his chest, his scowl deepening with each unhurried
step she took. The woman wasn't paying the least bit

of attention to her surroundings. She had yet to see him, and he was less than fifteen feet away.

"Is this how you protect yourself?" he barked, allowing a smile when she jumped in surprise.

Seconds passed before she managed to speak. "What are you doing here?"

"Trying to keep you out of trouble. A difficult task, it seems."

She closed the distance and stood in front of him. "That was very thoughtful of you, but unnecessary."

"I disagree," he said, his stomach clamping when he caught her clean scent, cinnamon and soap and fresh drops of water. "I watched you leave the river. You were careless. Oblivious to the fact that you could have encountered another hippo instead of me."

"Not possible." She pushed a length of wet hair back over her shoulder. Gavin couldn't stop his breath from leaving in a rush. Her damp tunic clung to her chest, outlining the full curve of her breasts. A normal woman would be horrified, but Mac seemed not to care. In the faint moonlight he could see the dark peak of her nipples, pebbled against the thin, sheer fabric. A shudder tore through him.

"The gunshot frightened away the animals," she continued, oblivious to the affect she had on him. "They won't venture back here for some time yet."

"You weren't looking where you were going."

"On the contrary. I was watching the ground. At this time of night, it's the reptiles you have to be cautious of."

"Such as snakes?"

She shrugged.

She shouldn't be here, he thought for the hundredth time. The muscles along his arms flexed as he fought the urge to reach out and touch her. She'd willingly kissed him before, had been disappointed when he'd ended it. Would she kiss him now? As passionately and as completely as she had five days ago? The temptation to find out pulled through him like a living thing. Overwhelming him and making him more determined to put a stop to his attraction to her.

"Connor seems to think you'd make a fair mistress of his clan," he blurted, then wished he had bitten off his tongue instead.

She shook her head as if taken back by the change in subject. "Does he now?"

"You sound surprised that he's taken an interest in you."

"And you sound as if you don't approve."

"It doesn't concern me one way or another."

She took a daring step closer, so close he could feel the heat lifting off her skin. And her scent, God help him, made him want to taste her. "Then why did you bring it up?"

"I shouldn't have. Let's just pretend I didn't."

She tilted her chin in a stubborn angle. "Does it bother you to think Connor might have an interest in me?"

"Of course not."

She placed her hand on his folded arms and pushed down. Her touch was light, but it had the power to force his arms to his sides. She leaned forward and whispered, "You don't lie very well, DeFoe."

"What you and Connor do is your business," he said through gritted teeth.

"I see." She studied him, her eyes wary and seductive. "If I ask you something, will you give me an honest answer?"

He glared at her. "What do you want to know?"

"Do you want to kiss me right now?"

"Absolutely not," he lied.

"I don't think you're telling the truth." With an amused smile, she moved past him so her body brushed his, setting off an explosion of sparks beneath his skin. Gavin let her take two steps before he caught her arm and jerked her around to face him.

He clamped his mouth over hers, cutting off her surprised gasp. Blood throbbed through his veins, a hard beat that pulsed in his ears, his chest, building in strength. Her spicy sweet taste swam inside him like an elixir, hot and hypnotic. He couldn't stop the moan that tore up his throat. He trembled with the need to have her, touch her, strip her of her damp clothes.

Her lips parted beneath his, and he pushed inside, tasting her, absorbing her heat. God help him, how could a woman taste so good! Too impatient to remove her shirt, he cupped her breast, rubbed his palm over the thin fabric until her nipple was taunt, piercing him with shuddering need. With a whimper, Mac's head fell back. He kissed her throat, moved down to her collarbone, and cursed when the fabric prevented him from going lower.

He had to have more of her, needed more.

She burrowed her fingers into his hair, urged him to her breast. Gavin took her in his mouth, laving the full mound, the pearled nipple through the layer of cloth. Shaking, sweating, he worked his hands beneath her tunic, clasped her waist. Touching her bare skin sent a bolt of fire to his erection, making it painful against the constriction of his pants.

She was pliant and thrilling, and his for the taking. His, if he wanted her. Right now, beneath the desert moon. And he did want her, her wildness, her thirst for life, her delight in everything she saw. Yes, he wanted her, as he hadn't wanted anything in a long,

long time. He wanted to bury himself inside her until he couldn't think, couldn't feel.

But numbness with Mac wasn't possible, a faint, rational part of his mind insisted. She would make him feel . . . everything. Need and longing and hope. Temptation and love. All of it. And all at once. Gavin froze, his hands stopping their exploration of her lithe back.

She would make him feel. And that's something he didn't want. Ever. From anyone. *God help me.*

Slowly, he straightened and looked down at her upturned face, her exotic cheekbones and strong jaw, her damp and swollen mouth and had to use every ounce of willpower to keep from kissing her again. He couldn't do this. Couldn't allow himself to feel or need. He'd made a vow after Rachel's and Matthew's deaths that he wouldn't repeat the mistakes he'd made before. He wouldn't be a fool and he wouldn't love.

His body rebelled at the idea of walking away from Mac. His mind tried to convince him that making love to her would only be physical. The same as every other casual affair he'd had over the last six years. He would use her and forget her.

She moaned softly, her hands releasing their hold on his hair to move down his neck to his chest. But he knew he wouldn't be able to forget her; Mac wouldn't let him. She'd get into his blood, confuse his thoughts. With a biting laugh, he realized she already had. But it wasn't too late to stop it.

She blinked her eyes open and looked up at him, her expression glazed and heated. An invitation to kiss her again.

Fighting the need to give in, he gripped her arms and held her at arm's length.

She stared at him, her breath little more than a quiver of sound. "What's wrong?"

"I don't want you."

A frown appeared between her brows. "You have a strange way of showing it."

"Stay away from me, Mac."

She swallowed, glanced around the area as if just realizing what had happened. When she looked at him again, her expression was puzzled. "You want me to stay away from you."

"Yes."

She touched her fingers to her swollen lips. "You came after me, remember?"

"A mistake on my part. It won't happen again." He released her, felt his control stretch, come perilously close to breaking. He turned away and headed back to camp, cursing himself every step of the way.

"Why, Gavin?" she called after him. There wasn't a trace of anger or resentment in her voice, just disappointment and, perhaps, concern. "What are you afraid of?"

You, he realized. *I'm afraid of you and what you make me feel.* But he would get his emotions under control. After Rachel tore his world apart he had put his life in careful working order. And he would do so again.

And careful working order did not include feeling or wanting. And it definitely did not include becoming involved with a woman like Mac.

Chapter 7

"'Tis a bloody wasteland," Connor growled.

"That's why it's called a desert," Jake said, though for once he sounded just as overwhelmed as the Scotsman.

"'Tis useless is what it is." Connor paced in front of the small group like a warrior facing a sworn enemy, knowing he was sorely outnumbered. "We should go home and tell King George the truth. If that damned *pshent* is here, no one will ever find it."

"I hope you're wrong," Gavin said, but the determination that had driven him from England, certain nothing would stop him from finding the double crown, wavered now that he faced the largest and most imposing obstacle yet.

The barren desert of Abydos.

Perhaps he should return home. The task wasn't as arduous as he'd first thought. It was impossible. Only now, as the sand baked beneath his boots and the sun burned through his clothes, did he understand why Mac had been adamant that their expedition might take years to complete.

Situated nine miles from the River Nile, Abydos was a sea of dry rolling sand dunes that crested like sculpted waves. From where he stood, the flat roofs of several mud brick mastabas, ancient burial tombs, were visible, but their entrances were buried deep below the surface. Were any of them that of King Menes?

Farther to the north, the Temple of Osiris had miraculously survived against time. Another tomb had been excavated more than the others, revealing worn limestone walls and a portion of a doorway. He didn't need to enter to know it had been pillaged long ago. A gust of heated wind kicked up a sheet of sand and carried it across the entrance; the desert's way of reclaiming what the ancients had built.

"You three look like you're ready to give up," Mac said, joining them, an amused smile pulling her full mouth.

Gavin tensed before looking at her. During the past day, he'd been busy hiring camels and wagons and purchasing the supplies they needed, so he'd managed to avoid her. But as their caravan headed toward Abydos, his gaze had constantly sought her out. The woman never rested. She continually encouraged her men with a smile, urged them to drink water and keep their heads covered.

He secretly kept waiting for her to show her true self. Demand more money or give some hint that she had an ulterior motive for working for him instead of Napoleon. Perhaps she was spying for the French? Or she planned to steal any artifacts they found and keep them for herself? Could she be so deceitful?

So far, she'd endured the elements as if she loved the heat, didn't mind the blowing dust that coated the skin and dried your mouth and pretty much made life miserable. In fact, she seemed to enjoy the grueling ride through the blazing desert as much as other women enjoyed a carriage ride through Hyde Park.

Gavin felt a scowl spread over his face. Mackenzie

Tuggle could not be as carefree as she appeared. No woman could.

Today she'd donned a pair of cream pants and a cropped tunic shirt that barely reached her hips. She'd wrapped a turban around her head to ward off the sun, but had left her hair loose, so it draped her back like a sheet of silk.

"'Tis a waste of time." Connor looked down at Mac, his tone apologetic. "We should 'ave listened tae ye in Rosetta."

She sighed, pursing her lips as she surveyed the unforgiving land. "It won't be easy. But at least Jake has an idea of where to start our search."

The archaeologist cleared his throat and his dark blue eyes became skeptical beneath the brim of his hat. He shook his head, murmured, "I don't know."

"What do you mean, you don't know?" Gavin demanded, frowning at his partner. "You have the scarab."

Jake took the artifact from his pocket and held the beetle carved lapis lazuli in his hand. "I know I interpreted the hieroglyphics correctly, but now that I'm here . . . I just don't know."

"You'd better explain," Gavin said tightly.

"The scarab refers to King Menes and describes the rise of Isis, Goddess of the Moon, who shall sit at the feet of Selqet, Guardian after Death."

"So what's the problem?"

"I used traditional points of the compass, north, south, east and west. But now I realize I've made a mistake."

"Are you saying we've come to the wrong place to dig?" Gavin asked, his voice a dangerous rumble. "That King Menes might be in Saqqara, as everyone seems to believe?"

"No. I'm certain Abydos is the king's burial site. But

to interpret the exact location of the tomb that this scarab refers to, I'll need to read the placement of the stars."

"Then do it," Gavin snapped, not about to believe they had traveled thousands of miles for nothing.

"I'm an archaeologist, not an astronomer."

"I should 'ave stayed in Scotland," Connor scowled.

"Can I see that?" Mac asked.

Jake handed the artifact to her. As she traced her fingers over the symbols, Gavin felt his chest tighten with . . . with . . . with some emotion he couldn't name. Or won't name, he thought.

He looked at her slender hands, the clipped nails and tanned skin as she studied the symbols. Her hands were strong, every gesture confident and sure.

They were also rough from hard work, he recalled without wanting to. And hot to the touch.

"You can read hieroglyphics?" Jake asked, clearly impressed.

"Some."

"If Jake can't make sense of that, I doubt you can," Gavin said, knowing he sounded uncivil, but he couldn't help himself. He didn't have complete control of his emotions where she was concerned. Her spicy-sweet scent continued to muddle his thinking and the memory of their kiss, the way she felt in his arms was still too fresh. He needed distance, lots of it, but he doubted the entire Egyptian wasteland would be enough.

"I haven't always roamed the desert, DeFoe." She glanced at him, her expression both patient and disappointed. "I grew up on a ship, remember?" She handed the scarab to Jake. "I know a thing or two about the placement of stars."

"That's right," Jake said, pocketing the artifact. "Your father traded cargo on his merchant ship."

Mac smiled, her eyes lighting with pride. "*Little Bess*, named after my mother. The repairs we're making on her should be finished by the time we return home."

Gavin bit back a retort. He didn't like the idea of her sailing from port to port trading cargo any more than he liked the thought of her laboring in the desert. *Someone should be taking care of her.*

"So ye'll be leaving Egypt?" Connor asked. "'Ave ye given thought of doing business in Scotland?"

With a shrewd grin, she said, "There's always a market for fine Scottish whiskey."

"Perhaps we can work out a trade."

Not caring for the gleam in Connor's green eyes, Gavin said, "I'll ask Willie about interpreting the stars."

Mac looked at him, her smile fading. "Of course. He can't read hieroglyphics, but I know he'd love to help you."

Gavin didn't like the questions swirling through Mac's troubled gaze, or the temptation he felt to answer them. He wanted her, and she knew it, but he wasn't going to do anything about it. And he wasn't about to explain why he had to keep her at arm's length. He was here to find King Menes' *pshent*. Not to become involved with a gypsy woman who could never have a place in his life, even if he wanted her to.

"I'll let Pop know you want to speak with him," Mac said. "Now if you will excuse me, there are wagons and camels waiting to be unloaded."

Gavin watched her walk away, her confident gait drawing his gaze to the feminine sway of her hips. Regret tightened like a fist around his chest. He knew he'd hurt Mac the previous night; for that he was sorry. If things were different, perhaps . . . But things weren't different. He was the man he was, and nothing would change that. He'd suffered enough loss and betrayal for one lifetime, he didn't intend to tempt fate again.

Connor slapped Gavin on the back and shook him good-naturedly. "I want tae thank ye."

"For what?"

"I thought the lass might 'ave taken a fondness tae ye," the Scotsman said. "But if she had, you're doing a fine job of changing 'er mind."

Laughing, Connor followed Jake to where Mac was overseeing the unloading of the cargo they'd need for the coming weeks.

The Scotsman could have her, Gavin decided. Maybe then, if she belonged to another man, he'd be able to wipe her from his mind. Glancing toward camp, he spotted her immediately. She took a crate from Kippie and stacked it on a growing pile, then returned to the wagon for another. He'd never seen a woman do physical labor without complaint. Even Sarah, who never fussed about the harsh conditions, left the physical work to the men. But Mac smiled and joked as she lifted and hauled, not caring that her hands were callused or her hair swung about her waist as if she were a common girl.

Only she was common, he reminded himself. Common and poor and born of a different world.

Forget her!

But Gavin was afraid that forgetting Mac was as likely as waking up to find King Menes' *pshent* had appeared in his hands.

"Now where, precisely, is the Moon Goddess supposed tae be?" Willie asked, holding the scarab in one hand and his favorite cup filled with barley ale in the other.

"That's what we're trying to determine," Jake said for the fifth time. "Isis, the Goddess of Moon, is sitting at the feet of Selqet, Guardian after Death."

"Yes, yes, so you've said. But who is Selqet? I've never heard of her. Mac 'ave ye ever heard of her? The Guardian after Death seems a bit mysterious. Could ye be more specific?"

"She protects the canopic jars that hold the king's internal organs," Jake answered with a sigh.

"Well then, there ye go!" Willie announced. "Glad I could be of 'elp."

Mac chewed on her thumbnail, suppressing a laugh.

"Gavin, maybe you'd better try." Jake lowered his head and rubbed his eyes with his finger and thumb.

"It is confusing. The verse doesn't make sense." Sarah was perched on an empty crate on the far side of camp, a drawing pad propped in her lap as she sketched those gathered around the fire, finishing their evening meal of leftover mutton stew.

"I haven't even told him the entire verse," her husband argued.

Sarah arched a brow. "Maybe you should let Mr. Tuggle rest."

"We don't have time to rest," Gavin said, though to Mac the words sounded like the growl of an angry bear. For the last half-hour, he'd sat twenty feet from her on another empty crate, his back to the setting sun, his expression becoming darker and more frustrated by the minute.

Mac didn't blame him entirely; handling her father took extreme patience. But watching everyone try to decipher the scarab without offering her opinion had taken even more.

The harder Jake tried to make Willie understand the inscription, the more confused her father had become. She'd wanted to tell them that William Tuggle was a simple man with a simple mind. As long as he had his friends and his ale—and her, of course—he was happy. Earlier that day she would have told Jake, *and Gavin,* that Willie wouldn't be able to pinpoint the location of the tomb. Not because he didn't know the placement of the stars. He did, better than anyone she'd ever known, but the information was all in his head, arranged in what her father laughingly called Tuggle-jumble.

He could plot a course, steer a ship and reach his destination, but he couldn't tell you how he'd done it.

But Gavin had seemed determined to keep her out of it. Which was fine with her, she decided, irritated all over again. He was paying her to dig. It wasn't her responsibility to decide where. She'd offered to help, but he turned her down.

And she knew why.

Because he couldn't forget that *he* had kissed *her.* And from his scowl and sideways glances, she thought he was fighting the urge to do so again.

That knowledge should have caused her to preen in satisfaction, but instead it disturbed her. She wanted to know why he fought the attraction that was as powerful as a bolt of lightning suspended in mid air. The current between them was constant and real, the force of it promising to scorch them both until they acknowledged its presence.

And did something about it.

But Gavin had made it clear; he wanted no part of her. The why of it didn't matter.

"Let's try once more," Jake said, trying to sound encouraging. "The reference to Isis and Selqet was the ancient Egyptians' way of pointing us in a direction."

"Well," Willie laughed, raising his cup toward the sky that glittered with thousands of tiny bright lights. "They should 'ave been a bit more specific. There be a lot of stars in the heavens. Which one might the moon 'ave been sittin' under, do ye think?"

"Perhaps 'tis time to let the lass 'ave a look," Connor said as he took a sip from his cup, his gaze fixed on Gavin, as if hoping the earl would object.

Gavin drew a deep breath, and his jaw flexed in the firelight. His gaze slid to where she sat leaning against a box filled with shovels and picks. "Well? Do you think you can interpret it?"

His tone annoyed her enough to refuse him, but she wanted to show him that she knew what she was doing, which annoyed her as well. She normally didn't care what people thought of her. But she also wasn't ready to return to Rosetta, and not only because she was still at risk of being at Napoleon's mercy.

She wasn't ready to end her time with Gavin. He might be testy, even rude at times, but he was also enigmatic and bold and incredibly sexy. Traits she couldn't dismiss. But there was something more. Gavin was proud and stubborn, yet someone had wounded him, cleaved a path through his heart that prevented him from allowing anyone else near. Who could have done that to him, Mac wondered? Who had had such power over him?

"If you can't make sense of it," Gavin said, breaking into her thoughts. "There's no reason for us to remain here."

Pushing to her feet, she took the scarab from her father and sat beside Jake, welcoming the warmth of the fire. The carving was old and faint, but enough was visible to allow her to read the symbols. Jake handed her the paper he'd recorded his interpretation on, but she shook her head. She didn't want to use it. The slightest variance could mean the difference between digging in the north near the Temple of Osiris or in the south by the Cenotaph Temple of Seti I, or out in the desert where nothing existed but sand.

"Where did you find this?" she asked Jake.

"In the marketplace in Thebe, believe it or not."

"And you think it dates back to King Menes' time?"

"It's hard to say. It could have been made after he died, but I doubt it. If this is a clue to his tomb, it would have been made while he was alive."

"Well, if it's five thousand years old, it's in excellent condition."

"I'm hoping that it was in a tomb adjoining King Menes. And not in his burial chamber."

"An outer chamber that was plundered after his death?" she asked.

He nodded. "That's my hope."

She turned her attention back to the scarab and read, "The rise of Isis, Goddess of Moon, shall sit at the feet of Selqet, Guardian after Death. Osiris, the God of Life after Death, shall guard the doorway to the first Uniter of the land."

She glanced at Jake. "I assume you believe the 'first Uniter of the land' refers to King Menes."

"He's the first king to rule both upper and lower Egypt."

"But why do you think he's here?" she asked, seeing Gavin stand from the corner of her eye and move closer to them. "Why not in Saqqara?"

Jake turned the scarab over and pointed to several tiny pictures that created a cartouche inscribed on the beetle's back. "This means Abydos. Now keep reading."

Knowing Napoleon would stop at nothing to claim the scarab if he ever learned about it, she turned it over and continued. "Where four points . . ." She pointed to an image of two clasped hands. "What's this?"

"Meet or possibly link."

Feeling Gavin move closer to her, and ignoring the tingle of awareness against her neck, she focused on the last part of the message. "Where the four points meet, the Nile shall guide them."

Frowning, feeling as perplexed as Willie had, she said, "A riddle? Since when did the Egyptians leave riddles about their tombs?"

Jake took the scarab from her fingers and smiled. "King Menes wasn't like any other king. It's believed he created the first written word, hieroglyphics, and is responsible for the style of Egypt's architecture."

She stood, propped her hands on her hips and paced around the fire. "We know Isis is the moon, which creates a path across the sky, so it's a moving target, so to speak. Selqet is the guardian of death, and Osiris is guarding the doorway, wherever that might be."

"And the four points?" Gavin asked.

She stopped, surprised to find herself standing in front of him. She looked into his unreadable eyes, black in the firelight. "The four points of the compass would be my guess."

"We need more than your guess."

Mac decided when she found the damn tomb, she'd not only gloat, she'd demand a thank you from Gavin, knowing the words would choke him.

She rounded on Jake. "Tell me about Selqet."

"Besides guarding the canopic jars, she's the protectress of marriage. She's often shown with extended winged arms and a scorpion on her head."

Mac felt a tingle of anticipation race over her scalp. She glanced at the sky. "Did you say scorpion?"

"Does that mean something to you?" Gavin asked, his voice low.

She didn't have a chance to answer. Jake said, "King Menes is also known as the Scorpion King." He crossed to her, grabbed her by the arms. "Good God, why didn't I see it before? It can't be a coincidence. That has to be it."

"What are you talking about?" Gavin demanded.

Smiling, knowing Jake's thoughts matched her own, she said, "Once the moon reaches the position of Scorpio, we'll know where to dig."

Throwing back his head with a shout, Jake lifted her up and spun her around, then left to do the same to his wife.

"Would you care to explain to the rest of us what you two are talking about?" Gavin said, his teeth clenched as if he were irritated. Or jealous, Mac thought.

"Selqet is represented by the scorpion, or Scorpio, which is about . . ." She pointed toward the stars, hesitated until she found the cluster she was looking for, then said, "There. When Isis, or the moon reaches the position of Scorpio, we should have a better idea of where to start our search."

"Do you really believe it will be that easy?"

Her heart racing, the urge to laugh nearly overwhelming her, she turned to Gavin. She didn't care that he continued to scowl at her, or that he refused to lower the wall he hid behind. She clasped his face in her hands and kissed him. Hard and quick, her excitement too great to care whether he returned the kiss or not.

When she pulled back, his harsh expression could have been carved from stone. She laughed at him and whispered, "Have a little faith in me, Gavin. I promise, I won't let you down."

Not giving him a chance to reply, she spun away and grabbed up a lantern, then raced into the night.

By the time the sun rose, she would be one step closer to finding the walls surrounding King Menes' tomb, and hopefully closer to knocking down the ones standing guard around Gavin.

Gavin stood where he was, every muscle clenching as he watched Jake and Connor hurry after Mac. Willie and the rest of her crew stayed around the fire, talking among themselves, playing dice or finishing their meal. Kippie began playing a bouncing melody on his flute. Hollister joined in with his flageolet, Frewin on his violin and someone kept beat on a small set of drums. Sarah sat frozen on her crate, her expression one of worry as her husband vanished into the dark.

I promise, I won't let you down.

Mac's whispered words echoed in Gavin's mind. He tried to reject them, and the turmoil they made him feel, the temptation to believe her, but he couldn't ignore them. Not completely, anyway. Which scared the hell out of him.

He retrieved his rifle—the foolish woman hadn't even thought to take a weapon with her—and went after them.

Passing Sarah, he paused. "Are you coming?"

She shook her head. "Jake wants me to stay by the fire."

He started to walk away, but he caught a glimpse of what she'd been drawing: Mac sitting with Jake by the fire as they'd studied the scarab. Sarah had captured the glow of wonder in Mac's eyes, the deftness of her slender hands, the wild, silky texture of her hair. Her full lips were parted with a smile that never seemed to leave her face.

Except when she's irritated with me.

His mouth still tingled from her brief kiss, and her taste was like incense in his mind. Elusive and intoxicating.

He shook the feelings away. "I've got to go."

"I think I've drawn her with the wrong man," Sarah said, stopping him with a slight touch on his arm.

He glared down at her, not about to ask what she meant, but that didn't keep Sarah from telling him. "Give her a chance, Gavin."

"You don't know what you're asking."

She held his gaze, her silver eyes soft with understanding. "Yes, I do. I hated Jake, remember? In my mind he was a monster and I had every intention of destroying him."

"Your situation was different. You thought he was the reason your father had abandoned you."

"If I hadn't come to know Jake, I would still think that."

"I can't change the way I am, Sarah," he said.

"She isn't Rachel."

"No, but she's a woman."

Sarah gave him a pitying smile. "You'd better come up with a better argument than that. You are resisting Mac the same way I resisted Jake. I came to my senses. I hope you do the same."

Gavin turned away and stalked into the night. Come to his senses, he thought, suddenly angry. And do what? Allow Mac to get close to him? Prove she wasn't like Rachel? For what purpose? He'd hired Mac to do a job. Once it was over, he'd return to England and she'd continue to dig in the desert or sail the seas on her ship.

They'd never see each other again. Which was how it had to be.

His past had seen to that.

He might have recovered from his wife's betrayal, resolved it through forgiveness or divorce, but losing Matthew had broken whatever hope he'd had of living a normal life. Peace of mind and happiness were beyond his reach now; only a fool would dare strive for something that had never really been his to begin with.

Within minutes, he caught up with the other three. Jake now held the lantern so light washed over Mac as she stood with her head thrown back and her gaze fixed on the sky.

"How much longer?" Jake asked.

She frowned, tilted her head as if needing a different angle. "Not long." Pointing to a cluster of stars, she said, "The moon is just below Sagittarius. Do you see the archer's bow and arrow?"

Gavin looked to where she pointed, but all he saw was a clump of flickering lights.

"Scorpio is next. Half an hour and we'll know."

"Don't you need exact bearings?" Gavin asked, scanning the shadowed expanse of the desert. "Longitude, latitude?"

"It would certainly help," she said. Looking at Jake, she asked, "What was the last part of the riddle?"

Gavin answered first. "Where the four points meet, the Nile shall guide them."

She thought for a moment. "The Egyptians were exact in their building. Everything was to the four points of the compass. North, south, east and west."

"But King Menes was buried in a mastaba nearly five thousands years ago," Jake said. "Long before any pyramids were erected."

"Well, I'm going to assume that King Menes used the four points. The Nile is to the east. Which means, to me at least, that the entrance to his tomb will face the Nile."

"But where?" Connor asked.

She drummed her fingers on her waist, then faced north, where the stone columns of a temple glowed beneath the moon. "Would Osiris' temple have been here during King Menes' time?"

"No," Jake said. "It's believed to have been built around 1300 BC, approximately two thousand years after Menes ruled."

"But he is guarding the doorway," she said to herself. "We're close, I know we are. But there's something missing."

"Like a map," Connor muttered.

She looked at the Scotsman, her brow furrowed, then knelt and smoothed the sand with her hand.

Seeing something scurry in the shadows, not two feet from Mac, Gavin shouted, "Don't move!"

He shouldered the rifle and fired, the stock slamming against his shoulder. Sound exploded, echoing with the force of an avalanche. His heart in his throat, he caught Mac by the arm and jerked her up against him. "What in bloody hell are you doing!"

She looked at him, speechless for once, her eyes wide with surprise. Connor stepped into the circle of light and held up his hand. What remained of a mangled Death Stalker scorpion dangled from his fingers.

"These things are bleedin' ugly," Connor said, tossing the brown scorpion away. "Is their poison verra deadly?"

"Very," Mac said, blowing out a breath.

"Thank God they dinna like Scotland."

"Gavin," she said, her voice low. "You can let go of me now."

Only then did Gavin realize he held her crushed against him, one arm wrapped tight around her waist. He could feel the heat of her skin through their clothes, the pressure of her hands against his chest. He wondered if she could feel the violent beat of his heart.

"That makes twice now that I've saved you," he told her, his voice tight with anger. And fear, he admitted, instant, chilling fear.

"I'm sure the scorpion was only trying to get away from us."

"Because it was frightened, just like the damned hippo that tried to run us down?"

With a weak smile, she called over her shoulder, "Jake, could you bring the lantern over here, please."

Knowing he couldn't toss her over his shoulder and carry her back to camp, Gavin released her. She studied the ground. When nothing moved, she knelt again, and wiped the sand smooth.

Jake held the lamp above her so light spilled down on her auburn hair, the curls around her face stirring with the faint breeze. She drew two parallel lines heading north and south in the sand. "This is the Nile." Then she made a small circle to one side. "Here's our camp. How large do you think Abydos is, Jake?"

The archaeologist scanned the darkness, shrugged. "The exact burial area isn't known, but probably no more than five square miles or so."

"Too big to just pick a place and start digging, but it does narrow it down." She drew a large half-circle around the camp to show the perimeter. "Is there anything else you can tell us about Osiris? Anything peculiar or unusual?"

"Besides being a god?" Jake said, sliding into an

excited tone Gavin knew well. Jake might be an archaeologist, but his true passion was Egyptology. Besides his wife, there was nothing the man loved more than talking about the ancient land, studying shards of pottery and discovering clues about the past.

"He was considered a universal lord," Jake said. "Ruling with his consort and sister, Isis. His brother, Set, was jealous of Osiris' power and plotted to have him killed. When his first plot didn't work, it's said he chopped Osiris into fourteen pieces and scattered him about Egypt. But Isis collected them, sewed them back together, had him mummified and buried here."

Mac ran her fingers through her hair. "Interesting, but I don't think that will help."

"Did the man no 'ave a talisman?" Connor asked. "A good luck charm?"

Jake thought for a moment. "There were numbers sacred to him. Seven, fourteen and twenty-eight."

Gavin saw the instant Mac understood their meaning. A glitter of anticipation filled her eyes, an emerald touched by fire. A slow smile lifted her soft lips. She looked at each of the three men, Gavin last. She held his gaze with a look of promise that drew him in.

"Gentlemen," she said, her smoky voice on the verge of laughter. "I believe the riddle is solved."

Chapter 8

The sun blazed in a sphere of white fire, burning a path across the unforgiving blue sky. A dragon roaring to life, Mac thought. Heat pearled off the land, rising in waves that trembled, causing the human eye to mistake the ocean of sand for a shimmering lake of molten lava. The heat was unbearable, drying each breath in her lungs and sapping her strength.

And it was only morning.

Mac secured her turban around her head, leaving her hair unbound to fall down her shoulders and back. She would braid it later, once everyone was set to their task. She'd allowed everyone to briefly break their fast before ordering their camp moved. Willie and her crew hadn't questioned her, and even Jake and Connor seemed to take it for granted that she knew what she was doing.

But Gavin hadn't been so trusting. He'd demanded to know her plan, and when she'd told him, he had ground out a curse.

She tightened her grip on the copper chisel she held, hoping she hadn't made as huge a mistake as he seemed to think. But she felt certain that Osiris' sacred numbers were the final clue to unraveling the riddle.

Seven, fourteen and twenty-eight.

She had used seven to calculate the distance from the Nile, fourteen and twenty-eight to determine longitude and latitude, her starting point being the moon in Scorpio. It made perfect sense. She hoped.

Because if she were wrong, it would mean weeks of futile digging, and wasting time she didn't have. Gavin was right to worry about Napoleon. Once the French general learned they were excavating in Abydos—and he was sure to learn of it—he would come after them.

"Everything's set, daughter 'o mine," Willie huffed as he joined her at the dig site. "Just give the order tae start."

"I want you to rest, Pop." She took his handkerchief from his pocket and wiped the sweat from his brow. "The day's going to be hotter than usual."

"Nonsense. I'll be fine."

"You're flushed."

"If I am 'tis only a result of celebrating your findin' the right place tae dig." Laughing even as he fought to catch his breath, he added, "I just celebrated a wee bit too much."

"All right then, join the others," she said, already deciding to pull him off the line as soon as possible. He had a keen eye and enjoyed sorting through the wheelbarrows of sand for bits of pottery, clues that would tell her if they were on the right track.

She watched him cross to the area she'd marked with stakes, his gait leisurely, content, as if he were heading off for a pint at his favorite pub instead of a grueling day laboring in the sun. She couldn't help but frown with worry. Willie, Hollister, Kippie, and all the others loved wading through the defiant sand as much as they did sailing the volatile sea, but they were becoming too old to do either. They wouldn't take retirement well; none of them wanted charity. But she couldn't let them continue working much longer.

Yet I have to support them.

Her best hope was to hire a younger crew to man *Little Bess.* With her profits from trade, she should be able to provide a good life for them all. Unless the ship became damaged again, or she lost her cargo to pirates, or . . . She stopped the worrying thoughts. Find King Menes' tomb for Gavin, she told herself, collect his generous payment, then worry about what came next later.

Joining Willie, she picked up a shovel and glanced at Gavin, who stood with his arms folded, his expression as revealing as a hooded cobra's. A clear signal that, should she fail, he was poised to strike.

"Any words of encouragement before we begin?" she asked him.

"Your calculations better be right."

She smiled, undisturbed by his gruff response. He was worried, concerned, perhaps even a little afraid. The emotions swirled deep in his dark eyes, hidden behind layers of distrust, and something else, something she didn't entirely understand. But the troubled emotions were there.

Mac prayed her calculations were right, because if they were, then maybe, just maybe, Gavin would be forced to treat her with something besides suspicion.

She didn't dare hope that he would kiss her again. And she wasn't sure she even wanted him to. The feel of his mouth against hers was too vital and consuming, the reactions he caused in her as hot and raging as the sun burning across the sky.

Don't think about him, she warned herself. She was here to do a job. Nothing more, certainly not to fantasize about a man who kissed her senseless one minute and couldn't stand the sight of her the next.

Exchanging the chisel for a shovel, she gripped it with both hands. She scooped up a spade-full of sand and heaped it into the wheelbarrow. Within the area she'd designated to work, her crew began to dig and, before long, they began to sing a favorite of theirs about battling the sea and fighting the wind, of the pleasures of stout ale and large-breasted women.

Mac sang along with them, filling her wheelbarrow time and again. Her back ached, but it was a good ache that reminded her she was alive. Her hands felt strong inside her gloves, and the muscles in her legs were taut with exertion. She needed to braid her hair; the weight was heavy and hot against her back. But she didn't stop. Her blood warmed in her veins and sweat dripped down her temples. And still she didn't slow.

She couldn't, because she loved feeling her body work and strain, pushing to accomplish something of importance. She felt alive. Whole. Connected to the world in a way she couldn't explain.

She wondered what Gavin DeFoe, the Earl of Blackwell, thought of her toiling in the earth. Would he think her behavior was as low as a common peasant, or would he see her as a woman who wasn't afraid to be independent, to strive for what she wanted?

She paused to glance at him; he stood twenty feet away, taking a break, his sharp gaze focused on her, the message in them clear.

Disgust. His only thought of her was one of disgust.

"Look at her, Gavin," Sarah said, horrified, her pad and charcoal pencils forgotten on the ground. "She's working like a . . . a common laborer."

"That's exactly what she is," he said, through gritted teeth.

"You must put a stop to it."

Gavin rotated his shoulder, stiff from hours of digging. "You think she'll listen to me? I tried to leave her in Rosetta and you see how that turned out."

"She might be hurt," Sarah said, worrying her lower lip.

Finishing his noonday meal, Connor stood beside them. "The lass 'as spunk. She's no afraid to dirty 'er 'ands."

"You still think she has potential to become the next mistress of Bachuil Castle?" Jake asked as he donned his gloves. He, too, had stopped working long enough to eat.

Sending Gavin a hard stare, the Scotsman said, "Perhaps."

"I have to admit," Jake said, picking up his shovel. "I'm surprised by her men. I'd thought they were a lazy lot and too old to do anything besides relive their sailor stories, but look at them. They're amazing. They've already cleared more in a few hours than most men can remove in a day."

"'Tis the lass. She's efficient. She does no allow any waste." Starting down the slope toward her, Connor added over his shoulder, "A fine quality for a laird's wife, I'm thinkin'."

Gavin glared at the Scotsman's retreating back, not certain if the man was serious about his pursuit of Mac or if he was trying to irritate him. During the past two years of their working together, Connor had showed even less interest in women than Gavin had. They were each set on a goal that should have consumed every moment of their time. The only difference between them being that once Connor found his Staff of Bachuil, he would be able to get on with his life, whereas Gavin's had ended six years ago, and he had no hope of starting another.

Connor reached Mac and took the wheelbarrow from her. She protested, but the Scotsman said something that caused her to laugh and raise her hands in mock defeat. The smoky sound of her laughter traveled across the desert, reaching Gavin and causing his chest to tighten. As if she'd known he was watching her, she looked up and their gazes clashed. The smile faded from her lips, and the look in her eyes became intense, determined. Stubborn, even.

Gavin wanted to curse, he wanted to bring her smile back, and hear her throaty laughter. But he didn't deserve the cheerfulness she bestowed on others. Since the day they'd met, he had shown her nothing but his foul temper.

As she lifted her shovel once more and started to dig, Gavin had to fight the overwhelming need to throw her over his shoulder and force her to rest. All day she'd worked harder than anyone else, filling her wheelbarrow with sand, rotating the men to give them breaks from the heat, doling out encouragement with her usual vivacity, along with hugs and pats on the backs. And all the while, the duties and tasks she'd given everyone flowed without interruption.

He imagined she would be the same on her ship, controlling the vessel and the men, and possibly even the sea.

"She's made sure everyone has rested, but she hasn't stopped," Sarah said, glaring at Gavin as if he were to blame. "She even made you take a break."

"She'll stop when she wants to," he said tightly.

But he thought her face was too flushed and her green eyes a shade too bright. With her hair now braided into a thick rope that hung down her dusty white tunic, she seemed every bit the gypsy he'd first thought her to be. But there was nothing untamed about her now. She moved through the dig site in much the same way a lady would move through a society ball, confident and calm, aware of everything that went on around her. But she was doing too much, more than anyone else in the entire camp.

"She shouldn't be here, working like this."

"I quite agree," Sarah said.

Gavin looked at her and frowned, then realized he'd spoken his thoughts out loud again.

"I intend to invite her to England," Sarah announced. "She's originally from London, you know. Do you think she would stay for an extended visit?"

Gavin tried to imagine Mac parading from one social event to another, her tall, lithe body bound in silk and lace, her callused hands covered with delicate white gloves. Wearing satin slippers instead of her rough leather boots, with a plumed hat perched on her head. Her auburn hair would be combed and curled, pinned so ruthlessly that even a strong wind wouldn't be able to budge it.

He couldn't force the image to materialize, though. Not that he thought Mac wouldn't be attractive wearing a polonaise skirt, the hem gathered to reveal a matching petticoat, a white lawn handkerchief tucked into her bodice to conceal any glimpse of her breast. On the contrary, she'd be remarkable, as unique in a crowded ballroom as she was on the desert valley floor.

But Mac wasn't the type to primp and fuss about her looks the way Rachel had, he thought with a scowl. Mac was a simple woman, the snobbery of London society would ruin her. And in a strange way, he didn't want her to change.

I want her as she is, but I can't have her, he thought. He tried to reason out his feelings for her, logically, as if she were a business proposition. They were from two separate realms. He had to remember that, or he'd do something he'd regret. Like making love to her.

His blood heated and pooled in his loins with just the thought of touching Mac, tasting the spicy-sweetness of her skin. He heard Sarah telling Jake to be careful as he left to join the workers, but Gavin couldn't focus on what she said next. Every thought, every part of his body was focused on Mac as she wove her way through the beehive of activity to where her father sifted through piles of sand beneath the shade of a tent.

Could he make love to her, Gavin wondered, and keep it physical, keep his emotions uninvolved? Just a business arrangement? She wanted him, had made it clear both times they'd kissed. They would be spending the next few weeks working side by side. Could he do that without touching her, feeling her warm skin?

If he gave in to his desire and made love to her, could he keep his heart shut away? Just enjoy her body, and allow her to enjoy his?

He decided he could, because his ability to feel was buried in a cemetery at Blackwell Manor . . . alongside his son.

"Do ye think we'll ever reach bottom?" Connor grumbled, his voice a rumble of disgust.

"Keep yer chin up, laddie," Frewin called, filling two buckets with sand and carrying them off. "We've only just started."

"Aye," Smedley agreed. "We could be at this for months before we find a single mud brick. Or we might not find anything at all."

"Bloody hell." Connor wiped sweat from his brow with the back of his arm. "I should'a stayed in Scotland."

Mac didn't look up from her shovel, but she stifled a laugh, sympathizing with the Scotsman. Not everyone loved the desert the way she did, the vast silence in a sweeping land, the mysteries that were locked inside the heat and sun. She glanced to another area a few yards away that she'd staked off and spotted Gavin as if he were the only man there. His shirt was soaked to his back, the muscles in his arms corded as he worked. He loathed the desert, as well, wouldn't be here if not for his King's demand.

She paused a moment, resting her aching hands on the handle of the shovel. A sudden gust kicked up a layer of dust, swirling it high into the air. It was later in the day than she'd realized, the light already beginning to fade.

Gavin shoved a hand through his hair, raking it back from his face, giving her a glimpse of his eyes that were hard and intense. She felt something tug inside her, an invisible magnet that drew her to the man against her will.

Without intending to, she crossed to him, found herself staring into those dark, disturbing eyes. Her mouth went dry.

"Is there something you need?"

The rich timbre of his voice, tinged with amusement, shook her back to reality. "I thought I'd check on your progress."

He sighed, glared at the mound of sand at their feet. Another gust lifted a sheet of grit and blew it up into a choking cloud.

Batting the worst of it away, he said, "We aren't progressing at all. As fast as we dig, the wind covers it up again." He glanced at the sky. "If I were inclined to believe such things, I'd think your Egyptian gods were scheming against us."

She followed his gaze and felt her heart stop midbeat. "No, not this," she whispered, turning in a circle to confirm her worst fear. "Not now."

"What is it?"

She felt Gavin's gaze on her, but couldn't look at him, her attention fixed on the churning clouds high overhead and the wall of black heading toward them.

"I've never seen it rain in the desert before," Gavin said.

"That's not rain. Hollister!" she shouted. "Gather your tools. Everyone, to your tents!"

She turned to run, but Gavin caught her arm. "What the hell is going on?"

"Khamsin." Before the word was completely out of her mouth, the wind strengthened in force, swirling around her body, shooting dust into the sky, where it stayed, thick and heavy.

"I take it that means sand storm."

"Of the worst kind!" she said, raising her voice to be heard. "We have to get everyone back to camp."

Mac started running, helping those who lagged behind. She saw Gavin lift Kippie as easily as a shovel after the older man fell. She pushed herself to run faster, knowing they had little time. The clouds were tumbling over the sky with unbelievable speed, blocking out the sun and throwing eerie gray shadows over the land.

The wind howled at her back, pushed her forward. Stinging sand pelted her hands and face, stung her legs through her clothes. The air became clogged with grit, the dirt so thick she had to cover her mouth and nose to breathe.

Once in camp, she ran to Kippie's campfire, cold now, but his food, pots and pans were being carried away by the storm. She gathered whatever she could, barely able to see and threw everything into a crate and shut the lid. She heard yelling, curses and the cry of the storm.

This khamsin had hit faster than any she had ever seen before. They were known to develop without warning, which was why every Egyptian feared them. She ran to the camels and checked their ropes. The animals grunted, but she wasn't too worried about them; they'd undoubtedly been through this before.

She hurried back into camp, one hand shielding her eyes as wind and dust poured over her. Her hair whipped about her head, her clothes were plastered to her body. She couldn't breathe. She stumbled over something; she had no idea what. Pushing to her feet, she kept going until she saw a tent. Heading for it, she rushed inside and closed the flap behind her.

Coughing, spitting sand out of her mouth and wiping her face, she looked around the dark interior. Empty.

Dusting off her clothes and hair, she collapsed on a pallet, knowing she had no choice but to wait. But as she sat there, listening to the sound of their possessions whirling through the air and crashing, the wind screeching, she began to worry about her family. Had they all made it to their tents? She hadn't seen Pop reach camp. She stood, reaching for the tent flap. She had to check on him, but knew that with the storm still raging, she'd likely become turned around, could even become lost.

Still, she had to do something.

The wind kicked against the sides of the tent, nearly lifting the stakes out of the ground. She held her breath, knowing she'd have to find something to latch onto if that happened or risk flying away like Kippie's pots.

The tent flap jerked and she heard the wind curse. Curse? Someone was out there!

Undoing the ties, she tried to pull one flap aside, but someone burst through the opening, catching her around the waist and throwing her to the ground. A crushing weight landed on top of her, knocking the breath from her lungs. Roaring wind rushed into the tent, filled her ears.

Then the weight was gone. She heard more swearing. Then, thankfully, the wind ceased rushing through the tent as the flap was closed.

"Jesus, bloody hell."

Mac stayed on the ground, frozen. Gavin. Of all the tents he could have sought shelter in, he'd chosen the same one she had.

"I need a light," he said, sounding hoarse and out of breath.

She sat up and gingerly felt around for a candle or lantern. Finding the first, she lit it and held it up. "Are you hurt?"

His head snapped around, his eyes widening with surprise. "You! What are you doing here? I thought you were in your tent."

"I couldn't find it. I hope you don't mind me borrowing yours."

He shook his head, and sand rained down on his shoulders. He brushed the worst away. "Bloody heat, hippos, scorpions and now a damned sand storm. Explain to me why anyone would want to live in this God-forsaken country?"

Her heart sank a little at his vehement tone. She knew he didn't like the desert, and she supposed at the moment she couldn't blame him, but she'd hoped he would see the mystery of the place, the timeless beauty.

Sitting on the pallet, as far from him as she could get, she said, "Don't blame the country. The storm's an act of nature, or perhaps the ancient gods. There's nothing we can do but wait."

"How long?"

She shrugged. "It could be hours. Or days."

Days trapped in a tent with Gavin, she thought, and felt her insides quiver. Nature had nothing to do with this, she decided. It had to be the gods, gods with a peculiar sense of humor.

He sat and looked at her, his face covered with dust, his expression a mask of irritation. "I never should have come here. This entire mission has been a fool's errand."

She'd never heard him sound so defeated; hadn't thought it was possible. She was tempted to reach out and clasp his hand. If he were anyone else, she would have. "Don't give up yet. We've just started."

He shook his head. "What are the odds, Mac, that we're even in the right place?"

"That I can't tell you. But we're here so we may as well try."

He picked up a rag and wet it from a jar of water. Scooting closer, he surprised her by wiping it over her face. Sensations shot through her body, but she managed to hold still. The water was cool on her face, the cloth rough, his strong fingers hot against her skin. She was tempted to turn her face into the palm of his hand, but after his reaction to their kiss, she knew that would be a mistake.

A muscle jumped in his jaw, and his gaze seemed fixed on the movement of his hands instead of her, but she sensed a shift in energy, a power that had nothing to do with the storm.

She shouldn't be alone with him, she told herself. The temptation to repeat their kiss was too great, her attraction to him too reckless.

Go, now! Before you make a fool of yourself! Standing so suddenly that she startled them both, she hurried for the tent flap.

"You aren't going out there," he told her as if he were issuing a command.

"I have to check on Pop. My family—"

"Is fine. I made sure they all made it safely to their tents."

She turned, surprised and grateful all at once. He had seen to her family before he'd taken shelter? Like it or not, her respect for him rose several notches. "Are you sure?"

He nodded and indicated the pallet. "Lay down, get some rest."

Without waiting for her to obey, he stretched out on the ground, put his hands behind his head and closed his eyes. If not for the sizzle of tension that hummed against her skin, she would have thought he'd dropped off to sleep.

With nothing else to do, she lay down on the pallet, her back turned to him. She even closed her eyes, willed herself to relax, but she couldn't. She could feel him, the energy that vibrated in the air. She couldn't hear his breathing for the sandstorm, but she knew every breath he took.

She wondered if he were as aware of her, but re-calling the look in his eyes as he'd watched her work that first day, she knew he wasn't. He'd been appalled by the way she dirtied her hands, wore men's clothes, baked her skin in the sun. And if she'd had any doubt, her present situation confirmed his opinion of her.

They were alone in his tent, trapped by a storm that might rage for days. And he'd made it clear that he had absolutely no intention of touching her. Or repeating his last mistake and kissing her.

Mac ran her palm over the smooth stones, still cool from the passing night, and felt her heart move into her throat. Stones, not bricks made of mud.

"Hollister, keep your team working here," she said, backing away from the area they'd uncovered, a section of wall, three feet deep so far, and four feet wide.

"Aye, boss. There'll be nothin' tae stop us now."

"*Il hamdulillah,*" she whispered in awe.

"Thanks be to God," her crew chorused as they went back to work.

"I can't believe this," Jake said, sounding as stunned as she felt. "Barely a week of digging, and you've found a bloody wall!"

"I'm thinkin' that sandstorm helped us a bit," Connor mused.

"It did. Look what the khamsin revealed," Jake said, clearly in awe of the wall of stone. "Do you know what that means?"

She smiled at him, too excited by all the possibilities to utter a word.

"I don't," Gavin said from behind her, the vibration of his deep voice rolling through her like the toll of a gong. "What does it mean?"

She'd avoided the man as much as possible since the awkward night they'd spent in his tent, but now she turned to look at Gavin, wanting to see if his opinion of her had changed in the slightest. A muscle flexed in the hard line of his jaw. His blue-black eyes were shadowed with concern. But was he as excited by their discovery as she and Jake were? From his expression, she'd have to say he wasn't. But then, she didn't really know Gavin. Perhaps nothing moved him. Not a brilliant sunrise or the discovery of a tomb. Not even his reluctant desire for a woman.

"Stone was rarely used five thousand years ago," Jake explained. "They didn't have the technology for cutting, then transporting huge blocks from the quarries. Mud bricks were the common method. It's still used today. But it decays over time, which is why so many temples are in ruin."

"Finding stone doesn't mean King Menes' tomb wasn't raided during antiquity," Gavin said, more to himself.

"Finding stone," Mac said, drawing his dark eyes to her and feeling her skin tingle from the impact. "Means there's a good chance the roof is still intact. If his sanctuary wasn't pillaged, we might find everything as he left it."

"It also means," Jake cut in, "that if the roof is undamaged, we won't have to spend the next few months digging sand and debris out of the entire tomb."

From Gavin's expression, Mac realized he hadn't thought about that possibility. "Have you considered the likelihood that this is the wrong tomb?"

Mac shrugged. "We won't know until we get inside."

"What's next?"

"We look for a door," she said.

"Which could be on the other side." Gavin arched a brow, his expression far from the disgust she'd witnessed a few days ago. His dark eyes were still intense, still guarded, but they were also filled with interest. For her? Or for their discovery?

"It's possible," Jake mused.

"Are you saying we may have to dig around the entire tomb?"

Skeptical about the change in him, she glanced at the stone wall that was slowly being revealed. A wall no one had seen for thousands of years. "Would that be so bad?"

"We don't have time for that."

"I wouldn't worry," she said, patting his shoulder as she would one of her family. But touching Gavin sent heat sizzling through her hand and up her arm, spreading to her chest in a way touching one of her family never could. Temptation shimmered over her, sharp and insistent and irritating. She should have known better than to touch him.

Stepping back, she willed herself to ignore the desire she felt for the obstinate man, because it was a waste of energy. He felt nothing for her. The sooner she accepted that, the better off she'd be.

"Your luck hasn't run out yet," she told him.

"Now why would you say that?" He watched her as if she were an artifact, and he'd yet to decide her worth.

"You found me when there were no other crews to hire. You reached Abydos without alerting Napoleon, and you've found your tomb, made of stone no less, in record time. Yes, I'd say you have incredible luck."

Something dark and intangible, and slightly dangerous flashed through his eyes. But it vanished as quickly as sand caught by the wind.

"Are you sure there's a way in?" he asked, his tone lacking its customary bite of a challenge.

"*Inshallah*," she said softly. "If God wills, a way inside will be provided."

She left him to join her crew. Over the last few days she'd pushed herself until her muscles ached and her legs trembled, determined to remove the disgust she'd seen in Gavin's eyes. Which angered her. She shouldn't even bother.

Her pride drove her to prove she could succeed. But another part of her pushed her to gain something far more valuable. Gavin's respect.

Just now she had seen . . . something in his eyes. Not respect, not that just yet. But there had been something else, something that hadn't been there before the night in his tent. Whatever she'd seen it had been turbulent and volatile, brewing with the fierceness of a desert storm. Another storm headed straight for her. She had to decide how to act.

Take cover and hide, or face it head on.

Hiding had never been an option for her. Which meant she would defy the storm, and whatever else Gavin intended to unleash upon her.

They found the door late the next day.

Mac stood at the sealed entrance with Gavin at her side. Connor, Jake and Sarah flanked them, with Willie and her crew crowded close behind. No one spoke a word as the sun seeped low over the horizon, turning the nearby cliffs dark with velvety shadows. Vultures circled overhead, silent guards searching for their last meal of the day.

Connor lifted the lamp he held, throwing light over the six-foot wall of dull ivory stone, each chiseled block perfectly squared against its mate. Mac reached out and ran her hand over the smooth surface, felt the grooves made thousands of years before. She tried to imagine the incredible people who had built such an awesome structure. Had they known their creation would become a vital part of history? Or had they hoped the desert would claim the beautiful tomb, hiding it for all eternity?

Mac trailed her fingers up to the stone archway that framed the door, then down to the sealed door itself.

Made from a slab of solid gray granite, she couldn't see any obvious way to open it. There were no hinges, no handles. Nothing. How were they ever going to get inside, part of her mind wondered, while the other part didn't care. Because something else had captured her attention—a symbol engraved on the door's surface.

Proof that they had indeed, found the right tomb.

The image of a scorpion had been chiseled deep into the stone, its tail raised to attack or defend with the sting of deadly poison. The perfect symbol for King Menes, she thought, who must have been both fierce and resilient to keep Egypt united while he protected her from her enemies.

"You did it, Mac," Jake said, his voice barely above a whisper.

"We never would have found it if you hadn't had the scarab," she said quietly, as if they were standing in a chapel instead of beneath an open sky, surrounded by desert.

But this *was* a holy place of sorts, Mac thought. Hallowed ground that should remain undisturbed for all time. Though a part of her wanted to leave the tomb sealed, she couldn't wait to see what lay beyond. Tomorrow she might step where no one had stepped for five millennia, breathe air that was thousands of years old.

Her heart raced with anticipation and her skin felt tight with impatience. Then she realized it wasn't just her own excitement she was feeling.

Energy radiated off of Gavin's skin in waves of tingling heat, like sparks of fire leaping to life. When the impulse to turn her hand and grasp his overcame her, she didn't fight it. This was a moment to be shared, remembered, she decided. He could go back to disliking her tomorrow. She slid her hand into his, shivering when his fingers tightened around hers, a firm band of steel.

"Considering the odds," Gavin said, speaking for the first time since they'd completely cleared the door. "It's amazing we've come this far."

"The ancient Egyptians didn't believe in accidents or coincidence," Mac told him. "They believed everything happened for a reason. Such as Jake buying the scarab."

"And you being able to interpret it by reading the stars," Gavin said, his masculine voice rolling inside her.

Unsure if he'd intended to compliment her, she looked at him and caught her breath. His dark gaze was intense, dizzying, and focused on her.

"Shall we see if your luck is still with you?" she asked.

The semblance of a smile tweaked the corner of his mouth as he held out his free hand. "After you."

Chapter 9

Gavin glared at the solid granite door and bit out a curse. Had it only been a few hours ago that he had stared at it in awe? For most of the night he had tried to open it, but no matter how hard he and Connor had pushed and shoved, it refused to move. He'd even resorted to digging a trench under it, but had met with solid stone.

Now, the sun rode high in the white-blue sky, laying across his back like a heated anvil. Sweat dripped down his temples, and his shirt was soaked to his skin. Mac had ordered her crew to rest, yet she stood before the tomb, arms crossed at her waist, her brows pulled into a frown. Gavin would have joined the others to escape the heat, but he wasn't about to leave her alone. She might be capable and courageous, but she also attracted trouble.

He recalled his vow not to worry about her, or make her his responsibility, which meant he should seek shelter and leave her to fend for herself. But he didn't move, the irrational need to protect her turning his feet to stone.

"Could this be a false door?" she mumbled to herself.

"What do you mean?"

She jumped and spun to face him, one hand pressed to her chest. "I thought you'd left with the others."

"What did you mean by a false door?"

Propping her hands on her hips, she squared her shoulders and looked at the wall as if it were a disobedient child. "I'm beginning to think this is only decoration. That perhaps there's another door, a real one, somewhere else."

Gavin drew a steadying breath. He should have known. Things had gone too well, and reasonably smooth. Until now. "So we keep digging?"

"I don't see what choice we have. Jake knows more about tombs than any of us, but he's never seen anything like this. If he can't figure out how to open it." She paused, tilted her head and frowned at the wall.

"What is it?" he asked.

She leaned close to inspect a block of stone set just outside the archway. "Look at this. All the other stones are the same size, rectangles approximately two feet long and one foot high. This one," she said, touching a smaller stone, "is square."

"You're right, but I don't see how—"

Using both hands, Mac pushed the block and gasped when it slid backwards a few inches. She glanced at him, her eyes wide with shock. She started to say something, but the sound of grinding stone brought them both around to stare at the door as it swung open.

Mac grabbed his arm. "We did it! By the Gods, Gavin, we did it!"

He was still looking into the dark cavern of the tomb with numb disbelief, when Mac launched herself into his arms. He caught her against him, staggering back. He felt her tremors of excitement, and couldn't help but smile at her contagious laughter.

She pulled away to look at him, her eyes going wide with wonder. "I can't believe it. Two miracles in the same day."

He arched a brow at her, not understanding.

"You're smiling."

"You thought I didn't know how?"

"Not at all. I've seen you smile plenty of times with Sarah and the others. But never at me."

"That's because you manage to bring out the worst in me," he admitted, knowing this woman caused his emotions to spike like no other female could.

"Perhaps you're not used to having someone challenge you."

She didn't give him a chance to answer. She rubbed her thumb over his lower lip, sending a flash of lightning straight to his groin. "You should smile more often. You look like a rogue pirate instead of a stuffy earl."

Gavin tightened his hold on her, felt the crush of her unbound breasts against his chest, her flat stomach and firm thighs. He clenched his teeth and drew a steadying breath. He'd toyed with the idea of making love to Mac, keeping it physical. Now was the perfect opportunity to prove that he could. He'd successfully passed the night with her in his tent without touching her. Having her so close without giving in to his need had nearly killed him, but he'd done it.

Now, he would kiss her in celebration of finding a way inside the tomb. He would control his reaction, sate the absurd, unwanted desire he had for her. He'd be done with it, and with her, enabling him to focus on his mission.

He glanced at her lips. They were pink and full and so close he could imagine their taste. Distantly, he felt her hands on his shoulders, heard the rush of her breath, then the soft whisper of his name. Time moved around them, and the sun burned like a living blaze. But all he could focus on was her mouth and how it would taste spicy-sweet when he kissed it.

He bent to take her, but she pulled away, her hands pushing against his shoulders.

"Gavin," she said urgently. "Let go."

The words didn't register.

"They're coming." She twisted out of his arms and looked at him with a puzzled frown. "I think Jake and Connor heard us when the door opened."

Shaking his head to clear the haze of lust, Gavin looked across the slope to see his two partners running toward them. He had to close his eyes and draw a deep breath.

"You've lost your smile," she said, her tone part teasing, part wary.

"With good reason."

With a coy grin, she asked, "You weren't really going to kiss me, were you?"

"And if I were?"

"We've kissed twice before and you ended up growling and ordering me to stay away. I have to wonder why you'd want to again when you obviously don't enjoy it."

"It must have been the excitement of opening the tomb."

She nodded, but he saw her disappointment in her eyes.

Waving at Jake and Gavin, Mac went to meet them, leaving Gavin to stare after her. Which was just as well, he decided. What had he intended to do, anyway? Kiss her until they were both senseless, then make love to her on the burning sand? Not that he would have felt any discomfort. Just the thought of kissing her had blinded him to the sun, the desert, the people less than thirty yards away. Perhaps he'd made a mistake by thinking he could stay in control where Mac was concerned, keep their relationship only physical.

If that were so, then he had to heed his own warning and stay the hell away from her.

Gavin glanced into the tomb, the dark deep emptiness, and felt a similar void spread inside him.

"Stay here," Gavin ordered.

"I most certainly will not," Mac countered, determined to return his glare.

"I have no idea what's inside. It could be dangerous."

"Which is why I should go." Crossing her arms beneath her breasts, she stood in the doorway of the tomb, blocking his path. "I have experience with this type of situation. You don't."

"You're staying here," he warned in a growl that caused the hairs on the nape of her neck to stand on end.

"No, I'm not."

"Perhaps ye should listen tae 'im, lass," Connor said, holding his lamp in one hand and a pick ax and shovel in the other. "Or else none of us will ever get inside."

"It's just for the initial search," Sarah said, trying in her sweet, diplomatic way to diffuse the situation.

Mac ignored everyone else and glared at the man who'd become a constant thorn in her side. He was attempting to be the virile, protective male again. Keeping the weaker sex out of harm's way. She supposed most women would welcome his concern; but it irritated the hell out of Mac.

Watching Gavin clench and unclench his hands, she had no doubt that he was considering removing her, by whatever method necessary. Given his size and strength, he could toss her aside as easily as he could a bucket of sand.

"Fine," she said, the word so sharp it should have sparked against the air. "I'll stay here."

Seeing a victorious smile threaten to form on Gavin's mouth, she added, "For now."

With a parting scowl, he lifted his lamp. "Jake and Connor, you're with me. The rest of you wait here until I return."

Mac stood next to the entrance, her body as stiff as a mummy's; her frown so fierce, the muscles in her face hurt. She watched the men disappear into the dark one by one, the light from their lamps silhouetting their bodies and flickering over the sandy floor.

This is absurd. She could understand Jake going in first; he knew the dangers of entering a new tomb. But Gavin had no idea what to expect. She paced in front of the threshold, her temper and concern escalating with every step. The walls could be weak, in danger of collapsing. The slightest disturbance could cause the ceiling to cave in.

"'Tis no use frettin', daughter 'o mine." Willie wrapped his arm around her shoulder. His touch was warm and affectionate and very much needed. "They'll be fine, ye'll see."

She was tempted to lean against her father, but her anger kept her straight as an arrow. "He hired me to excavate the tomb, not stand safely outside it."

"But ye 'ave found the tomb. Faster than anyone thought possible." He lifted his gold amulet from the folds of his shirt, tilting it so sunlight splintered off the falcon poised for flight. "The Egyptians thought tokens like this brought 'em luck. But you're the luck, daughter."

"If that's so, then I should be with Gavin," she said.

"Ye've 'ad little dealings with men like the earl, Mackenzie. He's the kind who wears his pride like a shield. He canna allow a woman to be put in harm's way."

"I'm not like the helpless females who attend dances and play the pianoforte."

"That don't make no matter tae a man like 'im."

Was that why Gavin had almost kissed her? Because he saw her as he saw all women? Defenseless and weak, and so fragile they couldn't care for themselves? Had he learned nothing about her? "Whether Gavin likes it or not, he needs my help."

"Now daughter—"

"I'm going in." She snatched up a lantern from the ground and lit it, then slid a chisel and pick ax into the belt at her waist. On her way to the door, she collected a shovel.

"But Mackenzie . . ." Willie began, but sputtered to a stop.

At the threshold, she glanced over her shoulder at him and smiled. "Don't frown, Pop. You know I'll be all right."

"'Tis not you I'm worryin' about. 'Tis the earl. He's like tae bring down the roof when he sees ye disobeyed 'im."

He just might, Mac thought, though not from losing his temper. But it was all too possible that he might step where he shouldn't, touch something that would trigger a wall to collapse. He could be hurt or killed because he didn't know the warning signs. She shivered at the thought of him bruised and bleeding or, worse, trapped beneath a pile of crushing stone.

She stepped into the suffocating darkness, refusing to stand by and allow Gavin to become hurt because he was too stubborn to admit she knew what she was doing. Whether he realized it or not, the foolish man needed her.

The God Osiris stared down at Gavin, his expression eternally supreme and patient. Carved from solid granite, he stood eight feet tall, the tips of the chiseled ostrich feathers that adorned his high white miter nearly scraping the ceiling. His body wrapped like a mummy, his freed hands were crossed over his chest and held a crook and flail; the symbols of kingship.

"So Osiris actually is guarding King Menes' tomb," Jake said from beside him, his expression reverent, as if he worshipped the god as faithfully as the ancient Egyptians had.

"I'm thinkin' we're one step closer to getting out of this blasted desert," Connor said, sweat pouring off his face as he held up his lantern. From his scowl, Gavin guessed the Scotsman wasn't the least bit impressed with the ancient god.

Light grazed the area, an antechamber, Jake had called it, and revealed several doorways that led to smaller alcoves. There was utter silence in the room, a stillness Gavin was hesitant to disturb. The dusty hot air dried his lungs and left a taste of another time on his tongue. Looking over the painted walls depicting vignettes of daily life, of harvests and battles, famine and times of food and drink, Gavin imagined he could hear the chanting priests performing their holy rituals, smell the burning incense and spicy sacramental wine.

For the first time in his life, Gavin felt humbled. He'd seen pyramids and tombs before, but never like this. This was like stepping back in time, to a world undisturbed for five thousand years.

"Connor," Jake said, his voice echoing. "Check the rooms on the right. Gavin, you take the ones on the left. Don't disturb anything. The ceiling is still holding, but one wrong move and that could change. If you find a sarcophagus, call me."

"What are ye going tae do while we're searching?" Connor asked, hesitantly looking into the first chamber.

"Interpret these paintings. They might hold a clue." Laughing softly, he added, "I've got to get Sarah in here to sketch these."

"Not until we deem it safe," Gavin reminded him, knowing that if they allowed Sarah in, nothing would keep Mac out. As it was, he couldn't believe he'd won an argument with the green-eyed gypsy.

He stepped into the first room, the hairs raising on his arms as light fell over stacks of decorative boxes, filled with what, he could only guess. Scrolls perhaps, or jewels and cloth, items the pharaoh would have wanted with him in the Afterlife. There were wooden benches with gilded arms, an ivory chest that would demand a fortune, even empty.

But there was no sarcophagus.

The next chamber revealed countless plates and bowls covered with dust. He imagined they had once been filled with bread, fruit and vegetables. Hundreds of sealed pottery jars in every shape and size crowded one corner. Undoubtedly beer and wine to go with the food. But once again, what he searched for wasn't there.

He proceeded to the next room, deeper inside the tomb. Drifts of sand had piled high against the walls and covered the floor, becoming thicker the farther he went. He couldn't hear Jake or Connor behind him. Except for the hiss of the lantern and the soft swish of his boots, there weren't any sounds at all. He became aware of the sweat dripping down his temples, the shadows that leapt from the corners, the utter stillness of the crypt, as if it were holding its breath, listening, waiting to see what he would do next.

His heart thumping against his chest, he entered the third room and froze. His stomach turned over, and his mind went numb. A sarcophagus of black granite in the shape of a mummy rested on a stone slab, an enormous thing, decorated with scenes of gardens and the rising sun, people kneeling in worship with divinities watching over them.

But it was the lid of the coffin that made his heart stop beating. The sarcophagus had been opened, and the mummy was gone.

"Jesus," Gavin whispered. The king couldn't be gone. He couldn't be! But the proof was before him. The mummy, the double crown, everything was gone. Probably for centuries, if not millennia! "Bloody hell."

"It's not King Menes," a female said from behind him.

He whipped around. "I told you to wait outside."

Her green eyes glittered in the flickering light. He expected her to flee, the way everyone did whenever his temper got away from him. The way Rachel had fled because he'd been too enraged to speak to her. But Mac stepped around him and entered the chamber, foolishly undisturbed by the warning in his voice. He didn't want her near him right now. He'd been prepared to find the tomb already plundered, but he hadn't thought his reaction would become so forceful or his emotions so furious. And he was furious.

If this was King Menes' coffin, then his trip had been for nothing. He would have to tell King George he'd failed. Then he would have to return to his empty home at Blackwell Manor and resume his empty life. He wasn't ready for that yet. Not yet.

"I want you out of here," he ordered, not bothering to raise his voice.

"This probably belonged to one of the pharaoh's priests," she said, ignoring him as she traced her fingers over the carvings.

"Mac," he growled. "I won't tell you again."

"A king wouldn't be placed in the open like this," she said as if she hadn't heard him. "He'll be behind a door or at the end of tunneled passageway. Someplace difficult to reach to discourage thieves."

Her words gave him a flicker of hope, but whether she was right or not, he wanted her outside where it was safe.

Pulling his anger back under his control, he told her, "It's dangerous in here. Please, Mac, do as I say and wait outside."

A tolerant smile lifted one corner of her mouth as she stepped within a foot of him. "You're right. It's not safe. Which is why *you* are the one who shouldn't be here."

"Blast it, woman—"

"You hired me to do a job, Gavin, which I'm qualified to perform. You're an earl, an important man who probably has hundreds of people depending on you. You can't afford to be hurt or . . . or killed."

"And you can?" If he weren't holding the lantern and shovel, he'd grab her by the arms and shake her. "What about Willie and the others? Don't they depend on you?"

Her stoic smile faded. "Yes, they do. But they also trust that I know what I'm doing."

Gavin ground out a curse. "Are you always so stubborn?"

"Are you always so overly protective?"

He hadn't always been in the past, not nearly enough, which was why he had to be now. "If infuriating me is your way to convince me to change my mind, you've failed. You're leaving, even if I have to carry you out."

She studied him a moment, her gaze too probing, reaching too deep for his comfort. "Let me help you, Gavin."

The smoky warmth of her voice broke through another layer of his resolve. He couldn't fight his feelings for her and the reminders of his past all at once. They weren't what mattered; he had to focus on finding the *pshent*. "If I agree, you're to stay by my side. No wandering off on your own."

"Agreed." She turned back to the coffin and set her lantern and shovel on the lid. Walking around the confined room, she studied the ground, then knelt and dug in the sand with her hands.

Dropping his tools, he caught her arm and jerked her up. "Did you learn nothing the other night when you tried that? There could be scorpions."

Wincing, she said, "You're hurting me."

He released her immediately and looked down where an imprint of his hand was visible on her sleeve. His stomach clenched. He'd never harmed a woman in his life. *Until Rachel.* After that night, he'd sworn he'd never do so again. "Be careful, Mac, or I will bodily carry you out of here."

She didn't whimper or rub her arm. She pursed her lips, studying him again, so intensely he felt the need to squirm. "There won't be any night crawlers in here. The tomb's been sealed. Though some sand has seeped inside, there isn't much of it, which tells me there aren't many cracks in the walls."

Her theory made sense, but it didn't make him feel any better. There were still too many dangers, and the thought of her becoming hurt . . .

He closed his eyes and drew a calming breath, then watched her kneel once more and rummage through the sand. He didn't argue, but he did stand watch in case she was wrong about the poisonous arachnids.

"Look at these," she said after a few moments. She handed him a handful of chipped pottery.

Gavin studied them in the light. Not pottery, he realized, but ivory, the surfaces smooth and incredibly thin, and carved with pictures. "What do you think it was? A wine vase, like those in the second room?"

"I doubt it," she said, carefully shifting through the drifts of sand. "The craftsmanship is too fine."

"Do you want your shovel?"

"No, I don't want to risk damaging anything."

"If this isn't King Menes' tomb, as you seem to think, then we need to continue searching." Gavin was ready to help her up when she gasped.

"Look! Oh my God, Gavin, look at this!" Pulling a vase out of the sand, she stood and held it out to him. "This one's undamaged. I can't believe it."

Though different from the ones he'd seen before, he recognized the vase for what it was; one of four canopic jars that would have been placed in a special box near the coffin. Except for the heart, the containers would hold the brain and internal organs of the deceased. This one obviously belonged to whoever had been buried here.

"I've never found one so perfect," she whispered, her eyes glittering with unshed tears.

Tears? He frowned at her.

She picked up the broken pieces she'd handed

him. "This must be from another jar. Whoever took the mummy must have broken it, the careless fools."

"I doubt it was a robbery," he told her. "Otherwise the other rooms would have been ransacked, as well."

She gently touched the jar's sealed lid, shaped like a lion's head, then caressed the curved vase, her fingers trembling. Gavin watched her, suddenly as mesmerized by her as she was by the artifact.

The canopic jar was simple in design, not worth anything beyond its historic value, yet from Mac's expression, one might think she was holding a handful of precious gems. Her eyes had a faraway look to them, the green now translucent, as mystical as the sacred tomb. Her face gleamed with sweat, and dirt smudged her chin. Sand caked her nails, yet she didn't seem to care. She possessed none of the qualities he was accustomed to, modesty and elegance, meekness and grace.

Mac was none of those things, yet it didn't matter. At that moment she was the most beautiful, tempting woman he'd ever seen. And he wanted her. More than the first time they'd kissed. And far more than the second. The blood in his veins warmed and pulsed with an urgent beat. As the overwhelming need to touch her took hold, fine tremors erupted in his limbs.

His fingers tightened around the lantern's handle. He wouldn't give in to the need. Not here, not now. Especially when he wasn't sure he could control what he felt for her. The desire was too raw and exposed, too different from anything he'd ever experienced before.

"Leave the jar for later," he said. He had to put some distance between them while he still could. "I want—"

She didn't give him the chance to finish. With a throaty laugh, Mac flung her arms around his neck and kissed him soundly on the mouth. A brief, chaste kiss filled with excitement and delight. Nothing meant to entice.

Gavin tensed, regardless. He placed the lantern on the sarcophagus and his hands went to her waist on their own accord. She was small and firm, her lean body a perfect fit against his. The same as her lips.

Just as he couldn't stop his hands from touching her, he couldn't stop himself from turning her kiss into something else. She gasped, her lips parting beneath his as he devoured her mouth. He drove his tongue inside, tasted her spicy warmth and heard a groan push from deep inside his throat. Crushing her to him, he took the kiss deeper, but it wasn't deep enough. He needed more of her, all of her.

A warning to stop buzzed through his mind. He ignored it. He had to feel her skin, the weight of her breast. Her slender hands threading through his hair.

Not in the tomb, a part of him insisted. Not here. No, not ever! Stay away from her!

He ignored that warning, too.

Pulling back slightly, trembling, he tried to gain control of his body. Slow down. He wanted her, more than he wanted the *pshent*, more than he wanted his next breath.

And from the look in her eyes, she knew it and wanted him too.

Chapter 10

Mac couldn't breathe.

Her mind was a tangle of confusion. She'd been thrilled, ecstatic and amazed by the canopic jar. And in her excitement, she'd kissed Gavin. Again. But it had been an innocent kiss. Quick and chaste. Like a shout of joy.

But seeing the awareness in Gavin's eyes, she knew he hadn't taken it that way. Or was it anger she saw? It was impossible to tell. His face was set, his jaw as rigid as chiseled stone. She had to be mistaken that he desired her. Because if what she saw in his face was passion, it was a dark and dangerous kind she'd never seen before.

"I hadn't meant . . ." she stammered. "For it to . . . the kiss . . ."

"Yes, the kiss."

Before she realized his intention, his mouth closed over hers again, taking, hungry and demanding. Sweeping her up in sensations too fast and turbulent to control. She held on to the canopic jar with one hand and the back of his neck with the other. Her mind reeled, her knees were nonexistent.

Was this his way of punishing her, she wondered with a distant part of her mind. Or did he really want her? He'd become furious the last two times they'd kissed. And she tasted his fury now, hot and driving. Consuming.

His hands moved over her back and down to her buttocks and thighs, molding and shaping, holding her against the ridge of his sex. Her nerve endings spiked, sharp tingles that raced beneath her skin. Mac sucked hot air into her lungs, closed her eyes as desire and need spiraled through her veins.

Liquid fire, she thought, dazed. His touch was burning her to ash.

She felt her tunic shift, then his hands were touching skin. She shivered as she clutched him to her, inhaled his scent, his musky taste. Then he captured one breast. A desperate moan rose from her throat. His hand was hot and rough, erotic as he grazed and lifted, his fingers molding almost painfully to her shape. He thumbed her nipple once, then again. Her mind spun, she couldn't move, couldn't think.

This wasn't punishment, she realized. This was desire and lust and overwhelming need, in degrees she hadn't thought possible. Her decision to help him find the crown—and nothing more—turned to dust. He wanted her, as much as she wanted him. She didn't know what had caused him to change his mind, and she didn't care. She just didn't want him to stop, or take his hands off her, or do anything except what he was doing to her now.

Distantly, she knew Jake and Connor weren't far away. She should stop Gavin, ask him to wait until they were alone. But she couldn't stop kissing him. She wanted to set the canopic jar down, but that would mean taking her lips from his.

She kissed him harder, her mind spinning when a growl rumbled from his chest. She knew what he was feeling, knew what he wanted to—

Gavin jerked away and looked down at her, his eyes dark, his jaw a rigid line. "No."

She stared at him, feeling as if time had just leapt out of place.

"No?" she repeated, barely able to get the word out.

"You heard me."

She shook her head to clear the dizzying buzz in her mind.

"I'm not going to do this with you." He took a step back, then another, and each one felt like a nail being driven into her heart.

Realizing what he was doing, she asked, "Why? Why do you keep doing this?"

"I have my reasons. Now just—"

"Don't you dare tell me to stay away from you *again*."

"I'll take responsibility for things getting out of hand, Mac, but I don't want you."

The words stung, as he'd meant them to. She could still feel the imprint of his hand on her breasts and taste his musky richness on her lips. She glanced down at the ridge in his pants, and felt her body pulse in response. "You want me, Gavin."

"No."

"You do," she said, her voice trembling with need, and sudden, unexpected, out-of-control anger. "Admit it!"

"What I want is to find the *pshent*."

"So you thought to look for it down my throat?"

"Rejoin the others while I finish searching, Mac." He took several breaths, his chest expanding as he struggled with each one. "Just do it, please."

She shook her head, suddenly furious with herself for falling into his trap *again*. She'd been honest with him from the start, about her ability to lead the expedition, and her desire for him. But those were the two things he didn't want from her. Perhaps because he still thought her beneath him or perhaps . . .

She stopped trying to figure him out, because she already knew what held Gavin DeFoe back.

His past. If she knew what had happened to him. Mac stifled a hysterical laugh. She was such a fool. He didn't care about her. He might feel lust for her, but he didn't care enough to become involved with her.

A small voice added that perhaps he'd called a halt because he did care, and he didn't want to hurt her, but Mac shoved that consideration aside.

"Fine," she said. "I'll wait outside. In fact, I'll return to Rosetta and leave you to search on your own."

His dark eyes widened with surprise. Mac felt a surge of satisfaction. Finally, she'd been able to glean an emotion out of him.

"Have you found anything?" Jake asked, startling them when he appeared in the doorway. Oblivious to the tension quivering inside the room, he exclaimed, "Bloody hell. A sarcophagus! Why didn't you call me?"

"Not now, Jake," Gavin said, his heated gaze never leaving hers.

Mac wiped her mouth with the back of her hand. "I think we're finished, DeFoe."

"As long as we understand each other." His voice was low and clipped, a warning she wouldn't forget.

Walking to the doorway, she handed the canopic jar to Jake, who was shaking his head at Gavin. She paused at the threshold and glanced over her shoulder to say, "What I understand, Gavin, is that the walls of a pyramid are nothing compared to the walls you've built around yourself."

When he only looked at her, his expression once more harsh, controlled and unreadable, she added, "I hope you find what you're looking for."

* * *

She didn't leave for Rosetta as she'd threatened.

Gavin had Willie's and Sarah's reasoning abilities to thank for that. But for two days, he had endured Mac's silence. Two long, damnable days. He paced the perimeter of camp, nodding to a few of her crewmen who were taking a break. Mac worked harder than ever, her determination to complete her job almost frantic.

Not only did she stay away from him, she wouldn't look at him. She rarely slept, and only took a break when Connor, Sarah or Willie nagged her into resting. Shadows haunted her eyes, and there were gaunt lines in her face that hadn't been there before.

But more disturbing, and perhaps more important, she no longer smiled. At anyone.

Gavin knew he was to blame, but he didn't know what he could do to change it. If he tried to make amends with her, the temptation to pick up where they'd left off would be too impossible to resist. He knew staying away from her was the right thing to do, but right or wrong, he wanted to kiss her again. He wanted to fill his hands with her breasts, then taste them. He wanted that so badly, a moment didn't pass that he wasn't fighting the need to give in. Right now he wanted to join her where she sat beneath a tent, sorting through the boxes they'd found, and pull her into his arms and claim her. A Neanderthal marking his woman.

But if he did, there would be no stopping again. And that frightened the hell out of him. He'd never lost control with a woman. Not even Rachel had possessed that kind of power over him. She'd been pretty and perfect, a doll he'd loved to watch. But she'd never instilled

blind passion in him. Never had thoughts of her consumed his mind so as to block out everything else;
business, politics, even common sense.

Yes, Rachel had been pretty and perfect, a reflec-
tion of the orderly life he'd created.

While Mackenzie was wild and beautiful and made
him want to grasp for things he knew he shouldn't.

Cursing, he left camp and headed for the mastaba.
Jake and Sarah were inside. Jake was directing Mac's
crew as they sifted through sand, while Sarah recreated
the drawings visible on the walls. Or at least she was
attempting to. There were dozens. Gavin hoped he
wouldn't be in Abydos long enough for her to finish.

Ducking through the doorway, he followed the
voices to a chamber near the rear of the tomb. Jake
stood before a black granite door, his face set in a scowl,
his arms crossed over his chest. Connor was leaning
against one wall, his expression a mask of disgust.

"Problems?" Gavin asked.

"There's no way to open it that I can see," Jake said.

Gavin almost suggested they ask Mac; she'd discovered how to open the main door when everyone else
had given up, but he stopped the words before they
spilled out.

"There must be a secret latch somewhere," Connor
said. "'Tis shaped the same as the main door."

"I know." Jake ground his teeth around a cruse. "But
we've shoved and pried and searched for a hidden
latch, and we've still had no luck."

Gavin studied the thick slab of granite. "Maybe it's
a false door."

The archaeologist looked around at him in surprise.
"Where did you learn about such things?"

Gavin scowled, not wanting to think about her
name, let alone say it out loud.

"Oh, Mac. I should have known," Jake said, his jaw flexing with annoyance. Then he added thoughtfully, "She's an amazing woman."

"I don't believe your wife would appreciate hearing you say so."

"Sarah agrees with me," he declared.

"And I agree with them both," Connor added, inserting his copper chisel into the seam between the door and the wall to pry it loose. The muscles in his massive arms and shoulders flexed and he groaned with the strain, but nothing budged.

"Considering she's only been digging for the last five years, Mac's knowledge of Egyptian history and architecture is remarkable," Jake said. "Imagine going from captaining a ship to leading expeditions in the desert? The woman isn't afraid of anything. She's bold and brazen, willing to grasp the world with both hands and shake it."

"And put herself in danger in the process," Gavin said, not caring for his two friend's fixation on the woman he was trying to forget.

Jake shrugged. "Sometimes a little danger can't be helped."

Needing to change the subject, he asked, "Have you shown her this?"

Jake nodded. "She said the same thing. Only she added that the door is false, or for decoration, because of the stone stela above the door frame."

"But you don't think so."

"I don't *want* to think so." Sighing, Jake sent him a pensive look. "I want to open this door and find King Menes tucked away in a room behind it."

"Considering the clues we had to decipher just to find the tomb, do you really think it will be that easy?"

A strange smile lifted one corner of his friend's mouth. "Nothing worth having is ever easy, now is it?"

Gavin understood the implied meaning. If Mac was willing to take risks for things she deemed important, he should be able to do the same. Refusing to respond, he turned to leave. "Let me know if you find anything."

"One day you're going to have to take a chance, Gavin."

Knowing Jake was referring to Mac and not King Menes, he kept on walking.

He reached the threshold leading outside, believing he'd made his escape, when he heard Connor call after him, "Or is it your intention to spend the rest of your life alone and angry?"

Gavin stepped into the glaring sun, welcomed the blazing heat burning through his clothes. Alone and angry. He might be alone, but that was by choice. But was he still angry? Part of him would always be angry with Rachel for betraying him, for dying and taking their son with her. But he was also angry with himself because he had foolishly believed he had known his wife.

If he had really known what Rachel had been capable of, he would have realized before it was too late that she had been having an affair. That she'd been able to lie so well and so easily. That she hadn't been anything like the pretty and perfect woman he'd believed her to be.

If he hadn't been such a fool, he'd be a whole man right now, with a son he could watch grow up.

Instead, Gavin admitted, he was alone. And he was angry.

* * *

Incense drifted through the open tent, the mixture of red sandalwood and frankincense, juniper berries and dragon's blood blending with the hot, Egyptian air. The exotic smell pulled Mac into another time, allowed her to focus. The camp was quiet. Everyone had found a patch of shade to rest while the sun passed its zenith.

She was glad for the privacy, needed it after the hectic pace she'd set for herself over the past four days. Ever since her last encounter with Gavin. Everyone in camp knew something had happened between them. They were all curious, anxious, wanting to ask questions, but refraining. Thank the Gods.

Jake and the others didn't know her, but Willie and her crew weren't used to seeing her in a foul mood. And she wasn't used to being in one, either. She didn't like the tightness in her chest. She couldn't eat and her hands trembled. She knew of only one way to return to normal: Finish her job so Gavin could sail back to England. Forever.

Rubbing her temples with her fingers, she sighed and forced her thoughts to clear. She'd made a mistake by kissing him, *three times!* And three times he'd ended it by telling her to stay away. She didn't have to be told again. Nothing would cause her to go near Gavin DeFoe, the frustrating, infuriating Earl of Blackwell. Right now she had to concentrate on something else. And she'd found just the thing.

A gold statue of Apep. Her stomach contracted, tingled with excitement. This was part of the puzzle. She was certain of it, because this statue shouldn't have been included in the tomb. Like the scarab that had revealed how to find the entrance, she hoped the ancient god depicted as a snake would help lead the way to finding the king's chamber.

"But how?" she whispered.

"If it answers you, let me know," Jake said.

Startled, Mac looked up from the table. "I didn't hear you come in. Is there something I can do for you?"

Sitting on the stool across from her, he said, "Every time I find a figurine or a cartouche or even part of a bowl, I ask it, who made you? How long ago? Did someone wealthy own you? Someone poor? But they never answer. If your statue starts to talk, I have some questions I'd like to ask it."

She managed a brief smile. "How does Sarah put up with you?"

"Are you kidding? She might have started off hating me, but now . . ." He glanced past the open flap to where his tent sat a few yards away. Sarah worked at a table exactly like Mac's, adding details to one of her drawings. "Now she—"

"Adores you?"

He nodded, his eyes shining with the kind of love Mac had always hoped she would find one day. Honest and open. No secrets, no walls. Just simple, heartfelt devotion that would last a lifetime.

"You're very lucky," she said.

"You don't have to tell me. I know what I've got."

Her throat threatened to close. Tears stung the backs of her eyes. She blinked furiously, refusing to let them fall. If Gavin could control his emotions, so could she. Lifting the statue of Apep she studied it, but the slender body of gold blurred in her hands.

"You've done an incredible job, Mac," Jake said quietly.

Not daring to look at him, she held Apep out to him. "Have you seen this?"

He pushed it aside. "Gavin thinks so, too."

With a deep breath, she met Jake's discerning gaze.

"I think finding a statue of Apep is unusual. It must be a connection to King Menes. If you'll look here—"

"Are you going to talk to him?"

"No. And I'm not going to talk to you, either, unless you change the subject."

"I know he's behaved like an ass where you're concerned, but—"

"You can leave now, Jake."

"—but there's a reason."

"I know. Something terrible happened to him in his past, something he can't forgive."

"He told you?"

"Of course not. Gavin only tells me to stay away from him. Which I'm doing."

"Then how do you know what happened?"

"I don't. Connor mentioned there's something . . . disturbing in Gavin's past that still haunts him."

"To put it mildly," Jake said, looking at something outside the tent.

Mac followed his gaze and saw Gavin striding through camp, tall, self-assured, dangerously handsome. If some dark event from his past still tormented him, most people would never know. But the first day she'd met him, she'd seen the pain his walls hadn't completely concealed. His past lived like a beast inside him, nipping at his soul, torturing him day after day after day.

"I knew before Connor said anything," she admitted. "Whatever Gavin's fighting, the toll it's demanding is in his eyes. Like an open wound that won't heal."

"Then be patient with him."

"Why?" she asked, looking at Jake because she couldn't watch Gavin without remembering the urgent, desperate feel of his touch, or relive his cold announcement that he didn't want her.

"Because you affect him more than any woman ever has."

"And not in a good way," she scoffed, her throat squeezing with the pressure of unshed tears. "He can't stand to be near me."

"You know better than that."

"What I know is that I'm busy. Now if you want to discuss why Apep, a god feared instead of worshipped, would be in a pharaoh's tomb you can stay. Otherwise . . ."

"He was married," Jake announced.

Mac stared at him for a moment as his revelation sank in. "Was? He's divorced?"

"No. He's a widower. Six years now."

"I don't think Gavin would want you telling me this."

"Which is why I am." Jake threaded his fingers together and rested his elbows on the table, as if he intended to pray. "You need to know."

Her nerves twisting tight, she ran her hands through her hair. She should get up and leave. Stop herself from listening to the story of Gavin's troubled life. Learning the details would only make her care about him, more than she already did. She didn't need that, because simply knowing that he would leave soon, and that she'd never have the chance to really understand him, was tearing her apart.

He was troubled, and he was hurting. She'd known that from the moment she'd first seen him standing beside the feluccas outside of Rosetta. But she hadn't known why. *And I have to leave it that way!* Knowing what had happened to him would change everything, make it impossible to stay angry. And she needed her anger. It was the only way she would stop caring about him.

"Her name was Rachel."

"Don't!" Mac put her hands up to stop him.

"She was beautiful, elegant, the star of London society as I understand it."

Everything I will never be, and have no desire to be. "I don't want to know this."

"They had a son."

Mac closed her eyes, told herself to get up, leave the tent. But she couldn't move. The image of a young boy with dark eyes and rebellious black hair filled her mind. He'd have a proud chin, she thought, and a smile as breathtaking as his father's.

"I didn't know Gavin then, so I don't know if their marriage was a happy one or not. But I do know he adored his family, would have given them anything. As a matter of fact, he had returned home early from a business trip with a new carriage and a matching team for Rachel." Jake paused, causing the hairs on the nape of Mac's neck to raise in warning. "Only he discovered her, well, in bed with another man."

Mac stared at Jake, barely able to fathom the words. She could picture Gavin standing in an open doorway, his excitement to shower his wife with his gift splintering apart as he watched her make love with another man.

Mac's breath left in a rush. How could any woman be unfaithful to a man like Gavin? Especially his wife? He may scowl and bark and test Mac's patience, but after knowing him, *she* couldn't imagine even *looking* at another man. Or wanting another man to touch her or kiss her. Even now, she couldn't envision allowing anyone else into her life. Not after experiencing the things Gavin could make her feel. Alive and out of control, lost to everything except the feel of his arms, the taste of his lips.

His wife had to have been insane. Or so spoiled she hadn't realized what she'd had.

"How did she die?" Mac asked, afraid to hear the answer. But she'd heard too much to stop listening now.

"She fled, taking their son with her. Gavin didn't follow her. He was too angry."

Too angry sounded much too tame for the man Mac knew. He would have been furious, heartbroken, shattered. The emotional shock would have been devastating to a man of Gavin's strength and confidence.

"He let her go," Jake continued, his jaw clenched. "I'm sure he would have followed her once he calmed down, but he didn't have the chance. That same night he learned her carriage had been set upon by thieves and overturned."

"Dear God," Mac whispered pressing her hands to her mouth.

"Both of them were killed."

Her throat closed and this time the tears she'd struggled to suppress escaped, streaking a hot path down her cheeks.

"His son's name was Matthew. He was only three."

Mac dropped her face into her hands, felt her tears slip through her fingers. Imagining what Gavin suffered brought an unbearable ache to her chest. She'd known his pain had run deep, that he harbored some wrenching anger, but she'd never imagined anything so brutal.

"So now you understand," Jake said a few moments later.

Mac wiped the tears from her face and drew a deep breath. She hurt for Gavin, ached as if his loss were her own. But her feelings and his past didn't change anything. His body might want her, lust for her, but he refused to let his heart be touched. She might call herself a fool later, when he was gone and all she had left were her memories of him, but she didn't want just his body.

She wanted all of him, his heart, body and soul.

She picked up Apep and stood. "I understand that I have work to do. If you'll excuse me."

Jake pushed to his feet, knocking over his stool. He grabbed her wrist and stopped her from leaving. "Has nothing I've said made a difference to you?"

"It explains why Gavin is so guarded."

"You can break through to him, Mac."

She shook her head. "No, I can't. And even if I did, he would never want a woman as common as I am."

"Damn it, Mac, Gavin doesn't care about status or rules of society."

"Doesn't he?" She stood with her shoulders rigid, determined to remain standing regardless that she was crumbling inside. "Do you really think he'd want a wife like me? I'm hardly beautiful and elegant. Look at my hands," she demanded, holding her empty one out so he could see the calluses and broken nails.

Jake held his own palms out for her to see. His was just as scarred, just as scratched and callused. "You forget, Sarah is from the same world as Gavin. She didn't care about my lack of noble blood, and neither will he."

"It's different for a man, and you know it."

"I hadn't thought you'd let something like social barriers frighten you. Obviously I misjudged you, because I thought you were made of tougher stuff than that."

"Don't you understand? I'll *never* be the star of London society!" she said, clenching her jaw when the full scope of that barrier caused her eyes to well with tears. "Gavin might be attracted to me, the way I am to him."

"The same way I am to Sarah. Mac, you and Gavin—"

"Why do you even care?"

"Because I see what Gavin is doing to himself. And I know how he feels about you, even if he doesn't."

After drawing a deep breath to settle her emotions, Mac cupped Jake's cheek in her hand. "You're a good friend to him. But it would never work, and not just because of our social differences, but because he isn't ready to let go of the past."

She waited for Jake to argue, but he watched her, the fire in his eyes dimming with acceptance.

Her own anger faded, leaving a hollow space beneath her heart. "I realize now that instead of being furious with him for rejecting me, I should thank him. He didn't want to hurt me, and I would have been hurt if he'd allowed our feelings for each other to go any farther."

"But if you tried . . ."

She shook her head, stopping him. "I've got to get back to work. The sooner I find King Menes' chamber, the sooner I can return to a normal life."

"Do you honestly believe that once this expedition is over, you'll just forget him?" Jake asked.

"Forget?" The hollow place inside her spread in a wave of darkness. "No. I'll never forget him, but I have to pretend to try."

Chapter 11

The coiled snake warmed itself by the fire, heedless of the sizzling flames. Light glistened over warm golden skin and flickered in green, hypnotic eyes. It watched those gathered around camp as if daring anyone to come near. And no one did, except for her.

Gavin frowned as Mac scooted close to the snake, her russet brows dipped in concentration, her bottom lip worried between her teeth. He could only guess what was going through her mind. He wanted to ask, wanted to tell her to move away, leave it alone. But since he hadn't spoken a word to her in four days, he found he couldn't say anything now.

Suddenly, she reached out and turned the asp so it faced her fully. His heart kicked against his ribs. A foolish response, but he couldn't help it. He didn't want her touching the snake. It couldn't harm her. But that didn't matter. There was something unnatural about it. Something that made his skin crawl.

Perhaps it was the way it seemed to be aware of everything around it, watching, waiting for something to happen or for someone to make a wrong move. Or perhaps it was Jake's explanation of what it represented that had Gavin feeling wary.

The golden snake was a statue of Apep, the Destroyer,

Demon enemy of the Sun, the Egyptian god of evil and darkness.

"Mac, girl," Willie called, standing safely on the opposite side of the fire, clutching his falcon amulet between his plump hands. "Come away from that statue. 'Tis a vile thing, it is. And ye need tae eat."

"Later, Pop," she said distractedly.

Sitting in the sand, her legs crossed in front of her as if she were a child, her hair loose and curling over her shoulders and back, she studied the snake. *Like a gypsy studying her crystal ball.* He wanted to be appalled; it would make his life so much easier if he found her crass and common. But what he felt for her was a wealth of amazement and respect.

And tenderness, so much that his chest constricted, and when he looked at her he found it difficult to breathe. Mac was more incredible than any woman he'd ever known, beautiful, confident. He couldn't imagine why some man hadn't already fallen under her spell and married her. Given her a house full of children.

The constriction in his chest turned painful and began to burn. He looked away from her, the thought of her with another man more than he could bear.

"You still think Apep holds a clue?" Jake asked, kneeling beside her.

She sighed, clearly frustrated. "Apep ruled the underworld with an army of demons. He represents evil. You told us priests held rituals every year to banish him, and that only by putting their faith in the gods of light would the people be able to defeat Apep. He was never worshipped, *ever,* so why would a pharaoh want him inside his tomb?"

"The statue could have been left by someone else,"

Sarah suggested, looking up from the drawing she was working on in her lap.

"That must be it," Willie exclaimed. "An enemy of the king. Now that the mystery's settled, Mac, come and eat."

"Or, perhaps King Menes wasn't afraid of this god," Gavin said surprising himself and feeling a shock when her green eyes met his.

Mac held his gaze, for endless moments it seemed to Gavin, though it was only a few seconds. A faint smile touched her lips. "Of course. He wasn't afraid of Apep, he intended to use Apep to protect him in the Afterlife."

"A god of the underworld?" Jake said doubtfully.

"Mayhap the lass is on tae something," Connor said, leaning against a crate and smoking a thin cigar. "She is the one who found the tomb."

"I'm not disagreeing with her," Jake said, glaring at the Scotsman over his shoulder. "But why would a pharaoh think an evil god who dwelled in eternal darkness would be of help to him in the Afterlife?"

"Eternal darkness?" Mac whispered to herself as she picked up the statue and cradled it in her hands.

"I would listen to her, Jake," Sarah advised, standing and brushing her skirt. "Her intuition is telling her something and I'd think by now, you'd know to listen when a woman's intuition has something to say."

Pushing to his feet and crossing to his wife, he said, "And I suppose you're going to tell me it's time to call it a night."

"You must have read my mind." Wrapping one arm around his waist, she called out, "Good night, everyone."

"Mac," Jake said. "We'll continue this conversation in the morning."

For a moment, Gavin watched his friends depart arm in arm. Jake and Sarah had been married for almost a year, their love for each other growing so strong it shimmered around them.

He looked away and caught a glimpse of Mac. Her solemn expression as she watched the couple stole his breath. It was obvious that she yearned for what his friends had, binding love, trust and respect.

Mac might find that kind of love one day, but Gavin knew he never would. As if a sudden gust of wind had blown through him, snatching away some vital part of his heart, he felt a wrenching sense of loss.

But what if their situations had been different, if he'd never known Rachel, had never been betrayed? Perhaps he could have had the kind of relationship Jake and Sarah had.

With Mac.

But Rachel *had* betrayed him, and he had lost his son. His life. He didn't think he'd ever be able to open himself up to that like of love . . . or pain . . . again. *But if I could . . .*

Mac looked at him then, her gaze mirroring his regret and sorrow. As if sensing she had revealed too much, she glanced down at the statue. Gavin knew he should leave. Keep the barrier between them standing tall and strong. But he couldn't walk away when . . . He stopped when the truth came rushing in.

When I want to be near her.

Before he realized his full intention, he was kneeling beside her in the sand. She didn't look at him, so he took advantage to observe the straight line of her nose, her rounded chin, the curve of her cheek. Her skin was rosy. He glanced at the slender column of her throat. A perfect place to leave a kiss.

The neckline of her loose-fitting tunic draped to

one side, revealing a glimpse of her chest and part of one shoulder. In spite of the harsh life she'd led, her skin was soft and supple, made for a man's touch.

He clenched his hands, remembering how she'd felt, her heat, the weight of her breasts. When her nipples had pebbled against his palms, he'd thought he'd die from the pleasure. Even now, days later, his body tightened and filled. His breathing turned to a rasp in his throat. Had he ever wanted a woman so much, he wondered? Would he ever be able to think about Mac and not have to bite back a groan of unfilled need?

"They cut a hole in his belly," Mac said, looking up at him.

Wrenched out of his thoughts, he tried to focus on what she'd said, and failed. "Excuse me?"

"Every day Apep would attempt to devour the Sun Boat of Ra as it sailed the heavens."

"The Sun Boat?"

"I'm assuming that means the sun as it makes its way across the sky. Ra is the god of sun, or light." She frowned at him. "Didn't you listen to the story of Apep that Jake told us over dinner?"

"I tried not to. There's something about that statue that I don't like."

She arched a brow and her mouth twitched, almost forming a smile, but not quite. "You sound superstitious. Who would have thought?"

He scowled at her. "What was it you were trying to explain?"

"Set, the true god of the underworld, knew he had to stop Apep from destroying the sun."

He held up a hand to interrupt her. "I thought Apep ruled the underworld."

She sent him a tolerant look. "Depending on his mood, Set could be a good god or a bad god. Apep was truly wicked. His only goal was to destroy light. The Egyptians believed that every day Set battled Apep and cut a hole in his belly so light could escape the darkness."

He wanted to smile at the earnest sound of her voice, as if she believed the story every bit as much as the ancients had. "And you think this has something to do with King Menes."

"Apep dwelled in eternal darkness." Sitting on her knees, she took his wrist and placed the curved statue in his hand. *"Underground."*

He arched a brow, seeing where she was heading. "You think there's another level to the tomb?"

She shrugged, obviously hesitant to answer. "It's a possibility we shouldn't ignore."

Her hand slowly slid away from his, but her warmth had already seeped into his skin. "That could add weeks to our time here."

"Perhaps. Whether we stay is your decision."

Silence lingered between them, awkward and heavy. Finally she stood and took the statue from him. "It's getting late."

"Do you know where to look for the king's chamber?" he asked, standing beside her.

"I have an idea."

"Care to share it with me?"

She started to say something, then stopped. "Not yet."

He nodded. He should leave, he thought. Tomorrow would be another long, hot and grueling day. But he stayed where he was, looking into her eyes that were almost level with his, smelling the warm scent of her skin, and thinking of all the things he wanted to say. Such as how much he respected her, or why he couldn't give her what Jake and Sarah shared. But it wouldn't change anything. The happily-ever-after kind of love wasn't possible for him.

It might be for Mac. And that's what she deserved. But it wouldn't happen for him.

Mac eased into the tomb's main hall, her senses on alert. It was well past midnight, and everyone in camp was tucked in their bedrolls, leaving her to roam the catacomb of rooms on her own. After the chaos over the last few days the tomb was empty and eerily quiet. Her breath was a rasp in the cold night air, her boots a faint scuffing against the sandy floor.

She should be resting along with everyone else; she was weary to the bone, more so emotionally than physically, but sleep had been impossible. Thoughts of Apep and King Menes had plagued her mind. *And Gavin,* she added. Memories of his kiss, and how incredible it could be between them if he ever healed from his past. After tossing and turning on her reed mat for hours, she'd given up and left her tent to work.

For a pharaoh, the rectangle-shaped crypt wasn't large, but with the nearly dozen rooms and narrow halls that branched off each other, she had the sensation of being in a maze. Stepping deeper into the sanctuary, the lamp cut a path through unforgiving darkness, casting light and shadow over painted walls and the timeless face of Osiris. She continued past the Egyptian god, and ignored chamber after chamber, most of which still held ancient treasures. What she was searching for wasn't in any of them.

She shivered. The hairs on her arms stood on end, but she wasn't cold. And it wasn't fear of being alone in the tomb that caused her tremors. Searching through foreboding ruins had never frightened her. She had always felt in awe of the silent stone structures.

And never more so than now. Anticipation tingled over her skin. She was close. She knew it, could feel the possibilities in the air.

Reaching the rear of the tomb, she held the lamp up to the carved stela over the false door. A king wearing the double crown was seated on a throne and flanked by priests. The headless bodies of his enemies lay in a row at his feet. Off in the lower right corner was a curving line. A snake, she wondered? Apep? It could be a clue, or it could be nothing but a twisting line.

"You loved riddles, didn't you, King Menes?" she whispered, reaching up to trace her fingers over the stone slab. "These symbols held special meaning to you."

She held her breath, listened to the utter stillness of the room, hoping to grasp some understanding of the message he'd left behind. Other than the hiss of the lamp, there wasn't a sound. She sighed and stepped back, no closer to knowing where the king's chamber was located than she'd been that morning.

She imagined the dead pharaoh sitting besides Apep in the Afterlife, laughing at her and boasting that she'd never solve his riddle, and she would never, ever find him.

She moved away from the door and ran her hand over the cold stone wall, careful not to disturb the murals. She paused beneath one of King Menes wearing the double-crowned *pshent*. Standing over a defeated enemy, preparing to behead him with a mace, the Scorpion King seemed as powerful as a god, as arrogant and bold.

She imagined Napoleon would see himself just as

Take A Trip Into A Timeless World of Passion and Adventure with Kensington Choice Historical Romances!
—Absolutely FREE!

Enjoy the passion and adventure of another time with Kensington Choice Historical Romances. They are the finest novels of their kind, written by today's best-selling romance authors. Each Kensington Choice Historical Romance transports you to distant lands in a bygone age. Experience the adventure and share the delight as proud men and spirited women discover the wonder and passion of true love.

Get 4 FREE Books!

We created our convenient Home Subscription Service so you'll be sure to have the hottest new romances delivered each month right to your doorstep—usually before they are available in book stores. Just to show you how convenient the Zebra Home Subscription Service is, we would like to send you 4 FREE Kensington Choice Historical Romances. The books are worth up to $24.96, but you only pay $1.99 for shipping and handling. There's no obligation to buy additional books—ever!

Save Up To 30% With Home Delivery!

Accept your FREE books and each month we'll deliver 4 brand new titles as soon as they are published. They'll be yours to examine FREE for 10 days. Then if you decide to keep the books, you'll pay the preferred subscriber's price (up to 30% off the cover price!), plus shipping and handling. Remember, you are under no obligation to buy any of these books at any time! If you are not delighted with them, simply return them and owe nothing. But if you enjoy Kensington Choice Historical Romances as much as we think you will, pay the special preferred subscriber rate and save over $8.00 off the cover price!

We have **4 FREE BOOKS** for you as your
introduction to
KENSINGTON CHOICE!
To get your FREE BOOKS, worth up to $24.96, mail
the card below or call TOLL-FREE 1-800-770-1963.
Visit our website at www.kensingtonbooks.com.

Get 4 FREE Kensington Choice Historical Romances!

♡ YES! Please send me my 4 FREE KENSINGTON CHOICE HISTORICAL ROMANCES (without obligation to purchase other books). I only pay $1.99 for shipping and handling. Unless you hear from me after I receive my 4 FREE BOOKS, you may send me 4 new novels—as soon as they are published—to preview each month FREE for 10 days. If I am not satisfied, I may return them and owe nothing. Otherwise, I will pay the money-saving preferred subscriber's price (over $8.00 off the cover price), plus shipping and handling. I may return any shipment within 10 days and owe nothing, and I may cancel any time I wish. In any case the 4 FREE books will be mine to keep.

KN044A

Name_____

Address_____ Apt._____

City_____ State_____ Zip_____

Telephone (____)_____

Signature_____

(If under 18, parent or guardian must sign)

Offer limited to one per household and not to current subscribers. Terms, offer and prices subject to change. Orders subject to acceptance by Kensington Book Club. Offer Valid in the U.S. only.

powerful if he ever possessed the crown. And in his madness to rule, he would destroy anyone in his way. Which was why she had to help Gavin find the *pshent* first.

Moving further down the wall, her lamp flickered, almost fluttering out. Her heart skipped against her chest. She wasn't afraid of anything in the dark tomb, but she didn't want to have to feel her way to the entrance. Holding up the lamp, she checked the wick. It was fine, and she knew the base was full of fuel because she'd filled it before leaving her tent.

Deciding it was nothing, she continued through the tomb. But barely a few steps later, the lamp sputtered again. Mac held her breath and watched the flame struggle to survive. Then she felt a change in the room, a shift of energy. As if the beginnings of a storm were gathering within the stone walls.

She glanced up at the painting of King Menes, and knew it wasn't him. It was another man, one who was just as powerful, just as arrogant and bold. Gavin.

Without turning to face him, she asked, "Are you trying to frighten me by sneaking up behind me?"

"It's no less than you deserve," he said, his voice a low vibration in the empty chamber.

"You should be asleep," she said.

"So should you."

"Yes, well," she muttered. Holding up the lantern she continued deeper into the tomb and did her best to ignore him. "I couldn't sleep, and you're to blame."

"Am I now?"

She realized he might misinterpret her statement and think she'd been kept awake because she couldn't forget their kisses, which was irritatingly true, but she didn't want him to know that.

She quickly told him, "You were right when you said

Menes wasn't afraid of Apep. A king who calls himself the Scorpion King wouldn't be afraid of anything. I think he decided to align himself with Apep and use his demons to keep his enemies away from him in the Afterlife."

"But you don't really have anything to base that on."

"No," she said, wishing he would leave. Their last encounter was still too fresh in her mind.

"You're grasping at straws, Mac," he said, sounding closer. "Leave this until morning."

"I wanted to search alone, without everyone underfoot," she said, hoping he'd take the hint and go. He wanted distance between them, and she was doing her damnedest to give him what he wanted. But the last four days had been the hardest of her life. At any given time of day, all she had to do was look up and there he was, tall and handsome, a testament of everything she wanted. *But will never have.*

Hearing the shift of sand, sensing that he was moving toward her, she took a steadying breath and turned to face him. Lamplight fell over the hard planes of his face. There was nothing pretty about Gavin, but he was breathtaking just the same. Rough, dark stubble covered his jaw, and his mouth formed a stern line of annoyance. Those full lips looked relentless now, but she knew how they felt when they softened, how he could use them to make her come apart inside.

The light reached his eyes, and she felt her knees go weak. Dark and penetrating, and strangely languorous, as if he wanted to reprimand her *and* take her into his arms.

Not again, she told herself. She'd made it clear that she didn't just desire him, but that she cared about him. And he'd made it just as clear that he wasn't interested.

"You should go," she told him, tilting her chin in an attempt to hold on to what little dignity she had left.

His eyes took on the hard, stubborn glint. "I don't want you in here alone."

"I'm fine, Gavin. It might be dark outside, but it's always dark in here."

"I'd prefer it if you'd—"

"I don't care what you'd prefer. I'm doing my job, which should please you." She didn't like the surliness in her voice, but she couldn't help it. Did he intentionally want to make this more difficult for her? Or was he oblivious to the fact that just by looking at him she felt her willpower crumble? Maybe he didn't know how he affected her because he didn't feel the same. He appeared calm and stoic. As if he'd never kissed her, held her, wanted her.

She discarded that last thought. Gavin *had* wanted her, and the emotions darkening his eyes weren't stubbornness or anger, but possessive fire. He wanted her still, but he was fighting it, and making them both miserable in the process.

"If you insist on working," he said tightly, "I'll stay with you."

"I'd rather you didn't. The entrance to the king's—"

She heard the faint scrape of sand again and tensed. Neither of them had moved. She held up her lamp, flooding the area behind Gavin with light. Who was joining her now? Kippie with a midnight snack, or Jake and Sarah with Connor in tow?

She saw a dozen tools leaning against a far wall. A stack of empty crates that would eventually be filled with artifacts to be shipped back to England. Nothing, or no one else, though.

"What's wrong?" he asked.

"Shh. I heard something."

He started to turn, when out of the corner of her eye Mac saw something move. She glanced at a shadowed corner five feet from where Gavin stood. Her heart lurched against her chest and her mouth went dry.

"Gavin," she whispered, her blood turning to ice. "Don't move."

His dark eyes locked with hers, but this time he did what she said and stayed still. "What is it?"

"A cobra." At least eight feet long, she guessed, as the asp uncoiled its body until the upper half stood as tall as her waist, bringing it within reach of Gavin. Watching them with terrible black eyes, it extended its hood to display a pattern of black and white bands. Its tongue flicked through its mouth, tasting the air.

"A . . ." Gavin's body straightened with a new kind of tension.

"Do you have your pistol?" Sweat prickled her scalp.

"No," he growled so low and harsh, the word could have been a curse.

"All right then," she said, taking a slow step toward him. "Close your eyes."

"What!"

"Do it. Cobra's spit poison."

"Mac—"

"It can blind you."

"I'm not closing my goddamn eyes and letting you fight that thing alone."

She glanced at Gavin and knew from the rigid set of his jaw that he wouldn't stand aside while she faced something so deadly. The snake was too close to him, swaying with deadly, mesmerizing grace. If it attacked now, Gavin would be bitten and nothing she did would stop it.

She took another step closer to him, and gasped when the snake feigned a strike, coming within a foot of Gavin's hand. She froze, and goose bumps skimmed her arms as the snake hissed in warning.

"Gavin, stay still." *Please don't move. Please.* She was still too far away to help.

"I'm not going anywhere," he said, sounding unnaturally calm.

She risked a glance at him, noted his rigid stance, his fisted *empty* hands, and knew he was preparing to confront the cobra head on. He wasn't trembling the way she was, but moving slowly, putting himself between her and the snake.

"Gavin, don't," she warned. "Let me take care of it."

"The way you took care of the hippo and that scorpion?"

She took another step, then stopped when the cobra slithered to the left, cutting off their exit. Her heart thundering against her chest, she whispered, "Have you ever come up against an angry cobra before?"

"It doesn't matter. I'm not letting you near it."

"Damn it, Gavin. I know what I'm doing. And stop looking at it. If it spits its poison, it will blind you. Permanently."

She had fought a cobra, but only once. And once had been enough. She'd been in Rosetta less than a year when she'd returned home from an expedition to find a ten-foot monster had taken up residence in their garden.

And it hadn't wanted to leave.

She had her crew to help her corner the asp and net it, but it had taken five of them to accomplish the feat. Now, it was only her and Gavin, without a gun or a net or enough space to even leap out of the way should it strike.

And the longer they stood there, the more certain she was that the cobra would attack.

"All right," she said. "Here's what I want you to do. When I reach your side, get behind me."

He made a sound that might have been a laugh or a growl.

"Once you're behind me, I'll taunt the snake with the lamp."

"You bloody hell will not."

"Gavin—"

"No!" he said in a near shout.

With a hiss, the cobra lunged for them. Gavin leapt back, shoving her out of the way. Gavin hadn't been quick enough, though. The snake's fangs struck his boot, leaving a two-inch gash on the leather surface.

"Did it go through?" Mac demanded, terrified. "Did it bite you?"

"I'm all right."

She pulled him against her until the cold wall was at their backs. She wanted to run her hands over him, make sure he was all right. But the snake was in front of them, blocking their exit. Keeping hold of Gavin's arm so he wouldn't move, she held the lamp out to her right and illuminated a thick, limestone wall. There would be no escape that way.

"There's only one way out of here, Gavin."

"Through him." He held his arm across her waist, trying to keep her behind him. A gallant move on his part, but one that terrified her. She'd come inside the tomb to escape thoughts of Gavin, and instead she might get him killed.

But she knew the desert and its dangers better than he did, and she wasn't about to let him be hurt. Before he realized her intention, she stepped around him so she stood in front of him.

He caught her waist, bringing her to a standstill.

His breath a hot rasp against her neck, he demanded, "What in hell's name are you doing?"

"I'm going to draw its attention. There are shovels and pick axes next to the wall—"

"Behind the cobra, where they can't do us any good."

"If I can distract him, you might be able to get past him."

"It's too dangerous—"

"It's the only way. If we don't make a move quickly—" Before she could finish the statement, the cobra feigned another charge, then pulled back and hissed. His mouth gaped open, ready to bite. Mac could see its fangs, small glistening white hooks that dripped with venom. She shivered.

Focusing on the snake, she took a step away from Gavin. "I'm going to—"

The cobra lunged, surprising her. She stumbled back against Gavin, felt the snake strike the lamp, almost knocking it from her grip.

Gavin tried to pull her behind him. "Jesus, Mac," he growled, his voice far from his earlier calm. "Stay back."

She didn't have a chance to answer. The cobra, his head swaying, his eyes black glass, opened his jaw wide, giving Mac enough of a warning to turn and shout, "Close your eyes!"

She shut her eyes, and slapped her free hand over Gavin's, felt the spray of poison hit her shoulder and back. She didn't hesitate, knowing the cobra would strike again. She pushed away from Gavin, edging along the wall, toward the cobra, using the lamp as a shield as she forced the snake back.

It struck at her again, hitting the metal lantern with such force, the vibration shook her arm. The handle dug into her hand. "The next time the snake—" Before she could tell Gavin what to do, the cobra uncoiled his body another foot, bringing itself almost eye level with her.

Fear turned her blood to ice. She couldn't draw a breath; her lungs constricted with the need to scream. *Don't panic. Don't!*

She heard Gavin move, but she couldn't look away from the cobra to see what he was doing. The small, black eyes were fastened on her. Venom dripped from its fangs. She could see its powerful jaws, extended wide, the frightening flare of his hood, his writhing black skin.

She decided not to wait for it to attack; but provoke it, hopefully force it back, so she could get away from the wall and into the opening and out the front door!

Waving the lamp in front of the cobra's face, she lunged forward, coming close to hitting it. It swayed back, lowering its head close to the ground. Its body coiled and wound around itself, slithered toward her instead of away. Then it rose up again, taller and closer than before.

"Oh, God," she whispered, hearing the fear in her voice, and tasting the hot, metallic taste in her mouth.

"Mac, stop what you're doing."

She ignored Gavin, kept the lamp in front of the cobra's face. It struck, the attack so forceful, her arm was knocked aside. The snake hissed and released a stream of venom. Mac ducked, closed her eyes as the spray landed on her clothes.

"Damn it, Mac, stop antagonizing it!"

"I can't hold it off much longer!"

She heard running feet, the clang of metal. Then a vicious roar. The cobra turned away from her, hissed and started to strike, but Gavin swung a shovel, catching the snake just below its head. The cobra flew backward, hit a pile of rocks. It instantly recoiled its body, using its long, powerful tail to slither over the floor, toward Gavin.

Mac leapt out of the way as Gavin brought the shovel down on the snake's head again, pinning it. Its body, as thick as her arm, thrashed in the air, winding around the wooden handle, before latching onto Gavin's leg and squeezing. Venom spewed from its mouth.

Seeing a pick ax on the ground, she snatched it up.

"Mac, stay back," Gavin shouted, straining to keep the viper pinned, but as it struggled, its head was slowly slipping free.

Mac fell to her knees beside the snake, raised the pick ax and brought it down with all her strength, burying the metal tip into the cobra's neck. She felt the snap of the spinal cord, and scurried back, out of the way, expecting the snake to go still. But it lurched in a mad thrashing, knotting itself, then uncoiling, whipping its tail in a frenzy she thought would never end. Gavin cursed, trying to hold the snake down. And then, suddenly, the slippery black body went slack and collapsed to the ground.

Breathing hard, she sat where she'd fallen, ready to scurry out of the way should the cobra move. She watched it, afraid to look away, certain it was only waiting for them to relax their guard. Seconds passed with nothing happening. Finally, she looked up at Gavin, who was breathing just as hard as she was and looking every bit as stunned.

He tossed the shovel aside and swiped one hand through his tousled black hair. She expected him to curse or leave, or lean against the wall and draw a thankful breath. But he surprised her instead by reaching down and jerking her up to her feet. "This country is too dangerous for you! When I leave, you're coming to England with me."

She stared at him, too shocked to reply.

"There will be no arguments, Mac." He shook her, as if not sure his yelling was getting through to her. "You're not staying here!"

"Gavin!"

"I'm waking everyone. We're leaving. Today."

"But we haven't—"

He didn't give her a chance to finish. He picked up the snake's limp body and stormed from the tomb, to wake everyone, she was sure. So they could pack and return to Rosetta. No, to England, she amended, if Gavin had his way.

When I leave, you're coming to England with me.

She didn't dare believe that he wanted her with him. He was reacting out of fear. He'd never faced a cobra before; his emotional outburst was normal. Once he calmed down, he would once again insist she stay out of his way.

Her legs no longer able to support her, she slid down the cold rough wall, glad for the support at her back. She needed a moment, then she would go after Gavin, assure him that there was no need to return to Rosetta. Or was there? Her days would be easier to endure if Gavin weren't constantly nearby, reminding her of how much she needed him. How desperately she wanted to help him heal from his past. But whether they were in Egypt or in England, he would never allow her to do those things. He didn't want her in his life, and she couldn't continue standing on the outside of it. It wasn't her way. If she wanted something, she went after it. Or she had until she'd met Gavin.

She sighed, deciding she wouldn't even try to convince him to stay. It would be better to cut their ties now, before she fell in love with him.

More than I already have.

She bowed her head, lacking the strength to move. Of all the men she'd met, why had she fallen in love with Gavin? A man who had closed himself off from his feelings, refusing to allow anyone close? But she knew the answer to her questions. There was more to Gavin than a stern, angry man. He cared about Jake and Sarah and Connor, more than he would probably admit.

And he cares about me. And that frightened him. She understood that. *But am I going to do anything about it?* Fight to break through his walls completely? She'd already caused his gruff surface to crack. Could she bring his walls down the rest of the way?

If she didn't try, she would regret it for the rest of her life. But if she decided to try, she had to accept that she might fail.

She sat where she was in the dim tomb, considering her options. Love Gavin or leave him alone. Either choice would bring her heartache.

Lost in her thoughts, she ran her hand over the smooth limestone wall beside her. The one that had blocked her and Gavin's escape. Moments passed with her staring at one particular square before she realized what she was looking at.

She sat up straight, her troubling thoughts clearing as she registered what she was seeing.

"By the Gods," she whispered.

Carved into the smooth limestone rock was the body of a coiled snake. Not a cobra. But one just as menacing and just as feared.

The Egyptian god, Apep.

A weak, hysterical laugh escaped Mac. She'd found Apep. But more importantly, she'd found the way to King Menes' tomb.

Chapter 12

Gavin stormed across the dark work area littered with wheelbarrows and shovels, past tents covering tables loaded with gilded boxes and vases. He didn't see any of it. He clenched his hands around the snake's cold body. Tremors raced up his arms, spreading in a sickening wave through his chest and stomach. It wasn't just anger that was making him ill. It was the fear. A suffocating surge of blinding, terrifying fear.

Mac could have died.

He couldn't get that one thought out of his head. If he hadn't seen her leave camp, if he hadn't followed her to the tomb, she would have been alone when the cobra cornered her. With no way to escape. A chill slid down his spine.

He couldn't recall ever feeling the riot of emotions tearing through him now. Not even when he'd found his wife in bed with a young soldier she'd met at a ball. He'd been shocked, stunned, furious enough to want to tear the house apart. But he hadn't felt the terrible, shaking fear that had hold of him now.

He drew a deep breath, but the control he used to ruthlessly govern his life failed him. Then he realized he *had* felt this way once before, the moment the constables told him Rachel and Matthew had been found.

And were dead. Dead because he hadn't stopped
Rachel from fleeing, nor had he gone after her.

But I can stop Mac from endangering herself ever again.
He'd known her for three weeks, and three times she'd
almost lost her life. He wasn't about to allow a fourth.

Reaching the fire in the center of camp, he tossed
the snake onto the coals, and watched to make sure
the lifeless body would burn. He didn't feel a sense of
satisfaction when the flames licked at the slick black
skin, because if he stayed in Egypt, there would be
another danger to face, and another. And next time,
he might not be there to save Mac.

"Gavin," she said from behind him.

Not yet, he wanted to shout. He couldn't look at her
when his heart was still racing with so much fear he
could taste it.

"There's something I have to show you," she whispered, her voice shaking, with excitement, he
realized, not with the horror of the past few moments.

"Not now, Mac. Go to your tent." He struggled
against the unbearable need to turn around and
gather her in his arms. He wanted to make sure she
was all right, that she hadn't been bitten, that the
venom the snake had showered her with hadn't somehow poisoned her. But he couldn't touch her now,
not yet, because if he did, he was afraid he might
never let her go.

"Gavin, come back to the tomb with me. There's—"

He rounded on her, the emotions he'd been trying
to suppress breaking free. Grabbing her by the upper
arms, he hauled her up against him. "You're not stepping one foot in there again, do you understand!
Never!"

She sucked in a breath, her face draining of color.
"Shh, you'll wake everyone."

"I have every intention of waking everyone, Mac. We're leaving. And I'm taking you away from this Godforsaken land."

She shook her head so the firelight sparked through her hair like burning embers. "No, Gavin, listen to me. I found it."

"I don't want to hear anything about King Menes. You're not going back inside."

"But I found the entrance to his tomb."

"I don't care."

"Yes, you do." She gripped his shirt in her hands. "Come with me. Bring your gun, and I'll get mine. But don't wake everyone up yet. Please."

He saw the imploring sheen in her eyes, felt the tremors that shook through her limbs. He had to refuse, it was the only sane thing to do.

"You could have died in there," he told her, feeling something inside his chest break.

She bowed her head for an instant, then looked at him with the same wrenching emotion he felt.

"You could have died, too," she admitted, sounding angry with herself. "And it would have been my fault."

"You aren't responsible for me. I'm not one of your ragtag crew."

"You might not be a part of my crew, but you're my client," she said softly. "That means I care about what happens to you."

They had a relationship that went beyond business, Gavin thought with dread. Right now he wanted to wrap his arms around her, felt himself falling apart inside with the need to hold her against him.

There would be no turning back if he did. He already cared about her, more than he had about anyone in a long, long time.

"No, Mac." He let his hands fall to his sides and took a step back. "You aren't going into the tomb."

She propped her hands on her slender hips. Temper sparked in her eyes. "I know you're unsettled—"

"*Unsettled* doesn't begin to describe what I'm feeling right now," he said, almost choking on the words.

"Cobras don't travel in packs. There won't be another one in the tomb, I promise. Now, please, get your pistol and come with me."

"It's too dangerous."

She considered him for a moment. "It won't be if you're with me, Gavin. So you'd better get your gun because I'm going back inside."

"No, you're not."

"I found the entrance." She stepped closer, so close he could see the fire reflected in her emerald green eyes, feel the warmth radiating off her skin. She took his hand in hers. "I intend to open it, and I want you to help me."

Tell her "no!" Gavin knew staying away from the tomb was the sensible thing to do, just as staying away from Mac would allow him to keep his walls in place. But the eager look in her eyes, the feel of her hand holding his, blurred sensible with sensation. He should turn his back on her and walk away. But he couldn't, and while that unnerved him, the thought that he might not *ever* be able to walk away from her unnerved him more.

"Bloody hell, woman," Gavin swore, grinding his teeth. He didn't get a chance to say more. With a confident smile, she reached up, kissed his cheek then turned and hurried to her tent.

To get her gun, he was sure.

She walked with the arrogance of a warrior, he thought, confident, self-assured. But it was her fearless confidence that would get her killed.

Another woman would have screamed in terror, then fainted into a heap when faced with a spitting cobra. But not his Mac. She had tried to use herself as a shield to protect him.

But she was the one who needed to be protected.

He would speak with Willie. There were other places where they could earn a living, a land that snakes and scorpions didn't call home. Someplace safe.

Like England.

The coiled snake stared at them in challenge.

Her heart hammering with anticipation, Mac sat back on her heels and gripped her pick ax in her hands. Gavin knelt beside her, holding a chisel and mallet as if they were a sword and shield. They both had pistols tucked into the waistbands of their pants. They'd brought extra lanterns, flooding the tomb with light. But Gavin still scowled at every shadow, and Mac knew better than to make a sudden move. He would likely tackle her to the ground, thinking she was in danger.

She bit back a smile and recalled his declaration the first day they'd met. *"I'll warn you now, I won't be responsible for your safety."* Sometime between Rosetta and Abydos, the man had begun to care about her. He may not like the idea, but he definitely cared.

"This is it?" he asked doubtfully.

She traced her finger over the faint carving of Apep in the smooth limestone wall. "Other than the statue, this is the only place I've seen this god. It has to mean there's something behind it."

"Or it could mean nothing. There are paintings all over this tomb."

She met his skeptical gaze. "Were you always such a pessimist?"

Something hard flashed through his eyes, and she knew he had glimpsed into his past. "Not always."

Wanting to ask him about his wife and son, but knowing now wasn't the time, she said, "When we find King Menes, I'll gladly accept your apology for doubting me."

Turning to the wall, she swung her pick ax and smiled when she made her first crack in the stone. Within moments, chips of limestone flew and the dust grew thick in the air. As a hollow began to take shape, Gavin took the ax from her. His swings were stronger, biting deeper into the rock. He swung again and again, harder each time, as if taking some long-stored anger out on the wall.

Sharp chips of flying stone sailed in every direction. Mac gasped when one cut her cheek. She brought the scarf she'd wrapped around her neck up to her face. It came away spotted with blood.

She ignored the sting and watched Gavin work. He struck the wall over and over again, never slowing. The muscles in his arms and back flexed beneath his damp shirt. His bare forearms were covered with silt, and his face was a mask of determination. Mac wanted to watch him forever. Whether he was scowling at her or smiling, or simply observing her with his guarded eyes. There was so much more to him than the unapproachable man he pretended to be. And she wanted to learn it all. *But will I have the chance?*

Would she be able to break through his walls the way he was breaking through King Menes?

A crumble of rocks brought Mac out of her thoughts. She scooted closer to help Gavin move the smaller debris aside. A cloud of dust hovered above the floor. She batted it away until the air cleared and revealed a hole the size of a fig. Holding up the lantern, she looked inside, gasped in surprise, then turned to Gavin.

"There's nothing behind it," she whispered, unable to believe her eyes. She'd dragged Gavin back inside the tomb hoping to find King Menes' crypt. But the entire time she'd feared they would find nothing but a wall of sand behind the stone.

"It's hard to believe that his sarcophagus might be somewhere in there," he said, his voice raw. He took a drink from his water bottle.

Picking up the ax, smiling, she said, "We're going to find out."

For the next hour Mac worked with Gavin, clearing stone, coughing, and wiping dirt and sweat from her eyes. Faster than she would have thought possible, all traces of Apep vanished.

Gavin picked up a lantern so light flooded the narrow opening they'd revealed. After a moment, he looked over his shoulder at her and smiled, a roguish twist of his lips that made her want to kiss him. She didn't, but just barely.

Instead, she said, "I'm ready for your apology."

"We haven't found the king, or the *pshent,* yet," he said dryly, but the corner of his mouth twitched as if he were fighting the urge to kiss her.

"Don't tell me you still have doubts."

He didn't reply, but he didn't have to. His thoughts were transparent; he couldn't believe any of this was happening.

"I'm going in first," he told her.

Gathering a lantern, she frowned at him. "Why?"

"Because I'm a man, and I'm bigger, which means I get to go first."

She shook her head. "What ever did I do before you arrived to keep me out of danger?"

"God only knows."

Holding his lantern in front of him, Gavin ducked into the tunnel. If he had his way, Mac would wait for him in her tent while he explored the crawl space. Anything could be at the other end. A dead-end, a room full of slithering, hissing snakes, a caved-in ceiling. But telling her to stay behind would be a waste of breath.

Inching forward, he scraped his broad shoulders on the narrow opening, ripping his shirt and his skin. "Bloody hell!"

"Gavin?"

He felt her hand on his leg, a touch of concern, he was sure, but his stomach clenched in response. He muttered a curse. Now, of all times, he should not be affected by her. *But I am, no matter how much I don't want to be, I am.*

"Are you all right?" she asked.

No, he almost growled. The walls closed around him so he could barely move. The air was stale and hot. And he had no idea what might lie ahead. The walls on either side of him were of the same limestone they'd chiseled through. But would they hold? Or with one wrong move, would they collapse on top of him, *and Mac,* killing them instantly?

"Mac," he said, breathing hard. "I think you should wait until I find whatever is at the end."

"You're not leaving me behind."

"Damn it, woman."

"I'll wait a few minutes to give you a chance to see what's in there, Gavin, then I'm following you."

"Jesus, bloody hell." Using his forearms, he crawled deeper into the tunnel. "I knew I should have left you in Rosetta."

"If you had," she called after him with a husky

laugh. "You wouldn't be moments away from finding King Menes. Just think about how furious Napoleon will be when he learns King George has the *pshent*."

He started to smile at her arrogance, but just then he bumped the ceiling with his head. A cloud of dust rained down on him in a thick white sheet, covering his head and neck, pounding down on his shoulders. The lamp sputtered and Gavin's lungs filled with grit. He closed his eyes, waiting to hear a rumble, then feel the crushing weight of collapsing rock.

But the shower of sand and dirt slowed, then finally, the air settled. Gavin wiped his eyes and willed his heart to stop pounding in his throat.

"Try not bringing the walls down on us," Mac said, from behind him. Much too close behind him.

"Mac—"

"Get moving, DeFoe. I've waited as long as I'm going to."

He heard amusement in her voice. *Amusement!* He couldn't believe it. They could have both been crushed to death, and the woman was all but snickering. Not frightened, unnerved or even shaking. She was bloody hell *amused*.

"Tell me something, Mac," he said, inching forward. "Are you afraid of anything?"

Grunting with the effort to maneuver, she said, "Of course I am."

"Of what? I'd like to know."

He waited for her answer, listened to the scuffle of their bodies, the ragged sound of his breath. "Mac?"

"I'm afraid . . ." she said, her voice echoing softly. "I worry that someday I won't be able to take care of my family. I worry about what will happen to them."

"A single woman shouldn't have to take care of two dozen capable men."

She mumbled something he couldn't make out, then said, "If Willie, Kippie or Hollister, or any of the others, were to arrive at your door, asking for employment, would you hire them?"

Until he'd seen her crew at work, he wouldn't have thought them capable of anything besides drinking ale and telling stories. Yet they worked with more tenacity than men half their age.

But she didn't give him a chance to tell her that. "You wouldn't have spared them a second glance." The edginess leaving her voice, she added, "Don't feel guilty. You're not alone. They're old men, and I'm all they have."

And they're all you have, he wanted to say. It had been clear from the moment he'd met her that she didn't resent the responsibility of caring for her hodge-podge family, as most people would have. She loved every one of them. *And would endanger herself to provide for them,* he thought with a scowl.

As the tunnel began a downward pitch, he told her, "You wouldn't have to worry about their fending for themselves if you lived a safer life."

She scoffed at that. "How many people in London never leave their homes, yet die of consumption?"

"I'd wager the number is far less than those who die in Egypt from the sting of a Deathstalker."

"It's a chance we all take, Gavin. But I do everything I can to take care of them and keep them safe."

"Who takes care of you?" he asked, feeling his chest tighten, and knowing it had nothing to do with the confined space. "Who keeps you safe?"

"Oh, that would be me, too." She grunted as if she'd struck something. "And I'm doing a fine job, so there's no need to become my knight in shining armor and rescue me."

But that was exactly what he wanted to do. Rescue her, take her away from the dust and the brutal sun. Away from the dangers that threatened from beneath every rock and crevice. He wanted her in London, where he'd know she'd be safe.

In London doing what? he asked himself. There were few positions available for women, and fewer for a woman as capable as Mac. He couldn't imagine her as a nanny or a servant, a costermonger selling fruit or vegetables, or God forbid, a barmaid in a shanty ale-house. He would sooner give her one of his overseer houses at Blackwell Manor to live in.

He stopped, not sure where the idea had come from. But the idea took hold and grew. Her crew could farm a parcel of land, raise enough food to feed them all. They wouldn't have to test the restless seas or the barren desert ever again. They would all be safe and well cared for. *And all I'd have to do to see her is cross my land.* The image was too easy to envision, and caused both panic and a sense of overwhelming pleasure.

"Is something wrong?" she asked.

Yes, I want more than just to ensure your safety. I want to do the one thing I swore I'd never do—I want to see you every day, talk to you. Make you mine.

He closed his eyes, drew a steadying breath. He was in a bloody tunnel. He could be crushed at any moment. He couldn't think about making Mac a part of his life. Either permanent or temporary. It went against every vow he'd made after Rachel's and Matthew's deaths. Something had to be affecting his common sense. He wanted to believe the stale air was responsible for his crazed thoughts, but he couldn't lie to himself any longer. He cared about Mac.

"Gavin?"

He clenched his jaw, not trusting himself to speak.

Holding the lantern up with one hand, he pulled himself forward a few inches, then stopped, his eyes going wide. "Bloody hell."

"What is it?"

He'd reached the end of the tunnel, and all he could do was stare.

"Gavin, you'd better tell me what's going on," she snapped.

"We found it," he finally said, crawling the rest of the way out of the tunnel.

He took Mac's lantern from her and helped her out. She stood next to him, her face white with dust and her eyes glittering like jewels.

"The king's chamber," she whispered in awe. Taking her lamp, she held it up and moved into the small room. "It's the king's chamber."

Just as in the main tomb, vignettes covered every wall. A three-foot boat of woven reeds, complete with central cabin, oars and wood-carved slaves to tend it, rested on a stand. In the corners and along the walls, gilded chests were piled as high as Gavin's waist. They would all be filled with gold and jewels, cloth and food, things King Menes would need in the Afterlife. The *pshent* might be in one of them. Gavin would search them all, but right now his complete attention was on the massive granite sarcophagus dominating the center of the room . . . and the woman standing beside it.

Mac ran her hand over the lid, her fingers trembling. Joining her, he glanced down at the rough carving of a man's head, his face stern and his eyes hard and flat. The features of a warrior, Gavin thought. Or a king. With his arms crossed over his chest, he held a crook and flail in each hand, the sign of a divine kingship. And below them . . .

Her fingers hovering over a symbol engraved in the stone, she whispered, "I can't believe it."

Neither could he. A carved scorpion the size of his hand, and below that a coiled snake. The signs for King Menes and Apep.

"If there was any doubt before, I think this takes care of them," he said.

She looked around the crowded room. "I've never seen a tomb like this one. They couldn't have carried all of this, let alone the sarcophagus through that tunnel."

"They must have built the tomb around him after his death."

She laughed softly, the sound filled with awe. "King Menes outwitted them all."

"Until you," Gavin said. He expected her to preen from his compliment, but her expression grew solemn as she looked at the sarcophagus.

Rubbing her palms nervously down her pants, she asked, "Do you think we can open it?"

"I'm not leaving until we try."

Returning his smile, she took their lamps and set them on a nearby chest. "All right, but I should warn you, pharaohs have been known to have as many as four shrines encasing their sarcophagus. And then there's the coffin itself. We may not be able to remove them all without help. Especially this first one." Frowning, she added, "It looks . . . extremely heavy."

"Connor won't fit through the tunnel, and Jake will undoubtedly want Sarah to draw everything exactly the way it is before we touch anything, so—"

"So we open it now."

He looked at her, stunned that he had even considered asking for her help in moving the granite lid. He never would have allowed a woman to subject herself to such a difficult, physical task before. But Mac had already proved she could work as hard as any man. There was nothing soft or pampered about her. Her face was smudged with dust, her hair was littered with bits of rock, and her clothes were filthy and worn. Yet he didn't care. In fact, he couldn't imagine her any other way.

And he couldn't imagine anyone else he'd rather be with right now than Mac.

"Are you ready?" she asked, looking at him as if she were trying to read his thoughts.

He was relieved she couldn't, because they would undoubtedly confuse her as much as they confused him.

"We'll push on the same corner and try to work the lid off," he told her as he positioned his hands near the carved head.

She did the same, then looked at him with her contagious smile that he had come to miss. "Now!"

Together they pushed. Gavin gritted his teeth, tightened every muscle down his back, dug in with his feet. He pushed, straining as hard as he could, Mac doing the same alongside him. Her face was flushed, her eyes squeezed closed. But the lid didn't move.

"Gavin!"

"Keep pushing!" He drew another breath, renewed his efforts. "Come on, damn you. Move!"

A strangled cry tore from Mac's throat. Afraid she had hurt herself, Gavin opened his mouth to tell her to stop, when the lid slid back an inch.

In unison, Gavin and Mac stopped to stare at it. Her eyes glittering with excitement, she nodded and they started pushing again. With a grating sound that echoed like thunder in the cramped room, the lid moved, one inch at a time, until they could see a wooden lid underneath.

Breathing hard, Gavin stopped and touched Mac's arm. "Rest a moment. Then we'll start on the other end."

Wiping grit off her hands, she said, "I'm fine."

Before he could argue, she leaned against the edge with the carved feet and looked at him over her shoulder. "Well, are you going to help me?"

Placing his hands beside hers, Gavin wondered if he'd ever get used to her daring nature. He didn't think so, but now that he knew her, he doubted that he would be able to tolerate a woman who fainted at the sight of a mouse. *A specialty of Rachel's,* he recalled without wanting to.

"Are you going to help me or stare at me, DeFoe?" Mac asked, one russet brow cocked with amusement.

"I thought you might need to rest."

"You sure it's me you're worried about?"

I'm worried about us both, he realized. Her safety, and his heart.

"Now," he said and pushed, surprised when the lid slid from its resting place.

Sweat dripped down his face. His shirt was soaked, and each breath hurt his lungs, but he didn't stop. And neither did Mac. She worked just as hard as he did, until she was just as sweaty and exhausted. Every time he suggested they rest, she refused. He didn't blame her. They could see the wooden coffin inside the sarcophagus, carved similar to the granite lid, but in exquisite detail.

When the lid was halfway off and ready to fall, Gavin moved to the head and nodded for Mac to push. Pulled by weight and gravity, the lid slid off the granite base and fell to the floor with a solid thud that shook the ground.

Panting, too breathless to speak, Gavin looked at Mac instead of King Menes' coffin. Some distant part of him wondered if he'd lost his mind. He should be lifting the coffin's lid, find out once and for all if the *pshent* was inside, but all he could do was stare at Mac, his gaze going from her stunned expression to her soaked tunic. The gauzy fabric clung to her body, outlined the fullness of her breasts and hardened nipples. Every breath she took stretched the damp cloth tighter against her skin. Her hands were shaking, from fatigue, he was sure. Stray curls of cinnamon dark hair had escaped her braid and were now adhered to her face and neck. There was a cut on her cheek, a trace of dried blood still visible. The sight caused his gut to clench.

Crossing to her, he cupped the side of her face in his palm, rubbed his thumb over the gash. She caught hold of his wrist and watched him with wary green eyes that darkened to smoke. He wanted to say something, tell her how much she amazed him, how much she frightened him.

And how much he cared about her.

The words formed in his mind, but he couldn't force them from his mouth. He wanted to curse in frustration. He'd guarded his thoughts and emotions for too long to reveal them now. As he had done time and again, he told himself it would be a mistake to tell her how he felt. They would go their separate ways . . . after he convinced her to leave Egypt. They lived in separate worlds . . . He stopped the reminders because at the moment he didn't give a damn about any of them. If nothing else, she deserved to know how special she was. He could tell her that, at least.

"Mac, I want you to know—"

She dropped his hand and faced the open sarcophagus. "It will be morning soon. If we want to see what's inside the coffin before Jake finds us and starts ranting about touching things, we need to hurry."

He watched her move to one end of the sarcophagus and grip the bottom of the wooden coffin's lid. She glanced at him, a warning clear in her eyes—she wouldn't allow either of them to repeat their past mistakes. No revealing conversations, no soul-shattering kisses.

He didn't blame her. He'd put her through enough already.

Moving to the head of the coffin, he gripped the lid and prepared to lift it, but the entire time his attention was on her. Perhaps he couldn't give her the life she deserved, perhaps he couldn't make love to her the way he desperately wanted to, but he could let her know that she had made a difference in his life.

Before their job was finished, and they went their separate ways, the least he could do was let her know that he cared.

Chapter 13

King Menes had been wrapped for the dead.

Strips of linen soaked in salt bound his head and the length of his body. The fabric was yellowed and brittle, so fragile, Mac didn't dare breathe on it, let alone touch it. Gold wristbands inset with gems adorned both wrists where they crossed over his chest. A simple gold-link collar surrounded his neck, and a corselet of beads and lapis lazuli draped his waist. Rings of every size and design were on each finger and every toe.

Even in death it was obvious that he had been a king. She could only imagine what he had been like in life.

Especially if he had been wearing the *pshent*, the double-crown of red and white gold that even now embellished his skeletal head.

Mac stared at the crown and the king, unable to move and unwilling to break the solemn quiet. She'd found him. She hadn't thought it possible, even if she'd had all the time in the world. Searching in Abydos instead of Saqqara, with no idea where to start, knowing that *if* the tomb existed, it would be buried beneath an ocean of sand.

But here he was.

A laugh bubbled up in her throat, but she pressed

a hand to her mouth to stop it from escaping. Only suppressing the emotion brought tears to her eyes. King Menes had rested in this place for five thousand years, undisturbed. Until now, and only because she'd solved his riddles.

Gavin reached inside the coffin and gripped the *pshent*. Mac caught his wrist to stop him, but she pulled back, realizing he was only doing what they had set out to do. Find King Menes' *pshent* so they could give it to King George.

But suddenly it felt wrong. All wrong.

With the crown balanced between his palms, Gavin looked at her, frowned. "Are you all right?"

She nodded and had to swallow before answering, "Yes."

"Then why are you about to cry?" he asked, so softly that the gentle sound of his voice nearly caused the tears to spill down her cheeks.

"I wish I'd never found him," she blurted.

Gavin arched a brow, not needing to voice his question that was clear in his eyes.

"King Menes has been here for five thousand years," she explained, feeling foolish. "This is where he should stay."

"What is it that compels women to return mummies to their tombs?"

"If you're referring to Sarah taking Queen Tiy back to her tomb after Jake discovered her, I agree with her."

Gavin pressed the crown into her hands. "Your job is to dig up the past."

"I know," she whispered around the sudden knot in her chest. The crown pulled at her arms, the smooth gold cool against her hand. "But this time, it feels different."

"I can't leave it here," Gavin said, sounding both apologetic and angry.

"I know."

"This is why I came to Egypt."

Unable to look at him, she focused on the *pshent* instead, the dome-shaped bell inset against the scrolled outer crown. "And now that you have it, you'll be able to leave."

"Yes."

She thought he wanted to say more. When he didn't, she turned away and tried to concentrate on the *pshent* instead of the man who had tied her heart in knots. He had vowed only an hour before that he wouldn't leave her in Egypt. She didn't believe he meant that he wanted her in England with him, but she wondered if he now regretting his rash vow. Not that it mattered. She wouldn't let him force her to leave her home. She belonged either in the desert or on the sea, not among the cramped buildings and soot-choked skies of London.

But whether Gavin left the crown or took it with him, their time together was almost at an end. She would never know the real Gavin, the one without a wall built of anger and guilt. She'd never have the chance to . . .

Mac's thoughts came to a sudden halt when she saw something inside the crown. Turning it over, she held it up to the lamp and gasped. "Gavin, look at this!"

She pointed at a single row of hieroglyphics engraved along the gold headpiece.

"Can you make them out?" he asked, taking the crown and holding it so she could get a better look.

"I think so." Squinting, she read, "Master of this crown is . . . is the God who rules the world."

"Bloody hell," Gavin said.

"So the rumor about why Napoleon wants this is true."

"Which makes it imperative that he never gets his hands on it." Tucking the crown in his arm, Gavin headed for the tunnel. At the opening he paused to help her, but Mac didn't move.

She stayed by the sarcophagus, her thoughts racing as fast as her heart. "We can't take it."

"We bloody hell can." He held out one hand to her. "Come on, Mac."

She shook her head. "This is wrong. We shouldn't have found the tomb. If it hadn't been for Jake's scarab, we never would have learned the coordinates. King Menes would have been safe from us *and* Napoleon."

Gavin set the *pshent* on a nearby chest and crossed to her. "You said yourself that the Egyptians didn't believe in luck, that they believed everything happened for a reason. Jake buying a scarab on a whim, my coming to Egypt, hiring you, a woman."

She shook her head, regardless that she agreed with everything he said.

"You being able to read the stars," he added, standing so close she felt the warmth of his breath on her cheek.

She faced the mummified remains of King Menes, his body covered with his noble regalia and ran her hands through her hair. For days she'd imagined the king laughing at her, certain she'd never find him. Now she couldn't help wondering if he were sick at heart because she had.

"We were supposed to find the *pshent*, Mac."

"I'm not so sure."

"Well, I am."

"Look at him, Gavin," she insisted, holding her

hands out over the coffin. "He's been here for five thousand years."

"A long enough stay in the Afterlife." He caught her arm and forced her toward the tunnel.

"At least let me cover him up."

"Bloody hell, woman," Gavin growled, and stopped long enough to help her lift the lid to the coffin and replace it.

When he started for the tunnel again, she said, "If we seal the tomb, cover our tracks—"

"And leave the crown behind for Napoleon to discover? No."

"He won't find it if we're careful."

Gavin stared down at her, breathing hard, his eyes drilling into her even harder. "What is this really about?"

"I know it doesn't make sense. I've worked twenty hours a day trying to find this room, and now that I have, I want to leave it the way it is."

"Exactly my point. What is your real purpose here? Are you honestly concerned about a man who's been dead for five millennia? Or are you planning to return and dig up the treasures for yourself?"

Her mouth dropped open in shock, and it took a moment for her to catch her breath again. "I think you know me better than that."

"I don't think I know you at all."

"I don't care about money. At least not the kind you're alluding to."

"Are you sure? The money you can earn by selling these artifacts would support your family in luxury for the rest of their lives."

Several scathing replies ran through her mind, but she didn't say any of them. Instead, she reached back with her hand and slapped him so hard, his head

jerked to the side. She tried to hit him again, but he
caught both her wrists and forced them behind her
back.

"Let go of me!"

"Mac."

"Now, Gavin." She struggled, but he only tightened
his hold. "I've had enough of you, DeFoe. I'm not a
thief, and I won't stand here and be accused of being
one."

"Mac, listen to me." He backed her up until she was
against the wall.

"Go to hell."

"I will, as soon as you hear what I have to say."

She stared up into the hard set of his black eyes, saw
a muscle pulse in his jaw. She wanted to hate him,
right at that moment, she wanted to hate him with
her entire soul, but the thought of doing so nearly
broke her heart.

"I'm sorry," he said, surprising her.

She closed her eyes, turned her head away and
willed herself to not be affected by his apology.

"I know you're not a thief." He hesitated, drew a
steadying breath. "But I've been angry and suspicious
for so long, that I—"

"Naturally assume the worse?"

"Yes. There are things I don't know about you."

"You mean secrets?" she asked. "I'm not the one
hiding behind secrets, Gavin, or clinging to a painful
past. I'm exactly the person you see. I'm not a lady or
an aristocrat. I'm just a woman who's trying to survive
the best way I know how."

Mac felt his body tense, heard the rhythm of his
breathing change. He released one of her wrists and
cupped her face. "Look at me."

She did, against her better judgment, saw his gaze

focus on her mouth and knew he wanted to kiss her. Her stomach twisted and her skin warmed in response. *Not again!* her mind screamed.

Before she could stop him, his mouth covered hers in a gentle kiss. A buzzing started in her mind and her knees began to shake. She wanted to open her mouth, return his kiss, hold onto it and make it last and last and last. But her common sense knew better. She'd been through this before. She couldn't allow it to happen again.

She jerked her head away. "Stop! I'm not going through this again."

Breathing hard, fighting the betraying sensations spiraling through her body, she glared up at him. "You've kissed me three times and three times you've told me to stay away from you. I don't need to hear it a fourth."

"You won't," he said, releasing her other hand to move his to her lower back. She felt each of his fingers against her spine, molding her to him. "I promise, you won't."

She wanted to believe him, even as she wanted to walk away. She felt too much for this hard, complicated man. She wanted to help him, learn everything there was to know about him, even though knowing would rip her apart.

"You accused me of being a thief, Gavin."

"I didn't mean it. None of it. I'm not even sure where it came from, except that I want you so badly, it frightens me."

His admission shook the thin grasp she had on her anger. "The idea of us together is insane."

"I know."

"Nothing can come of it."

He closed his eyes briefly, then looked at her with

such misery, she thought he had changed his mind again. But he said, "I know."

"Then why?" she asked, barely able to speak because the touch of his fingers kneading her back and the warm, masculine scent of his skin were making her dizzy.

"Because I want you." He placed a feather-light kiss on her temple, then moved his lips down to her cheek, shocking her with his tenderness. Their kisses before had been heated, almost violent. She didn't know if she could withstand gentle.

"I wish I didn't, Mac," he whispered against her ear. "I wish I could think straight when you're near me, keep my life nice and orderly, the way it was before I met you. But knowing you has ruined all of that."

"You make me sound like a disease."

He caught her by the waist and lifted her against him, bringing her eye level with the intensity of his gaze, a swirl of dark power that stole her breath. "I've tried to deny what I feel for you, Mac, God knows I've tried, but I can't ignore it any longer."

Responding to the harsh edge of his voice, she warned him, "You're going to regret this later."

"Perhaps." His pupils dilated, turning all that dark power into dangerous seduction. "But if I don't kiss you right now, I'll regret that even more."

He didn't give her a chance to respond. His mouth was on hers, arousing and urgent, his tongue plunging deep inside. When he urged her to, she wrapped her legs around his waist, felt his swollen sex against hers. A foreign sound tore from her throat, and her head dropped back.

Sensations spiraled inside her, as hot and intense as the burning sun. She tried to hold on to her thoughts, keep what was happening in perspective, but her logic and feelings became intertwined, like blood mixing with water until they were one. She'd wanted him for too long, forever it seemed, had been denied time and again. Now it took nothing more than his touch for her desire to spike to full flame. For her mind to turn to ash.

She could feel the hardness of his body, smell the scent of desperate need on his skin, but it wasn't enough. She needed to touch him, taste him, feel every part of him. And she wanted him to do the same to her. They had to shed their clothes, but that meant letting go of him, and that she couldn't do.

Without breaking their kiss or releasing her, Gavin tossed her pistol aside, loosened her belt and dropped it to the floor. He slipped one hand beneath her tunic, found the sensitive skin at her waist. Mac sucked in a breath, her eyes going wide, her skin tightening as she anticipated what would come next.

He didn't make her wait long. He found her breast, the touch so expected, yet so startling, she bucked against him, gasping deep in her throat. He thumbed her nipple again and again, drawing circles around it until lightning tore through her body and she thought she would scream.

He lifted her in his palm, molded her, teased her with the tips of his fingers. Mac knew she was coming apart inside, knew she couldn't wait any longer. She wanted him, needed him, now.

As if he'd read her mind, he murmured against her neck, "Mac . . . I can't . . ."

He didn't finish. Instead he pushed the waistband of her pants down, releasing her only long enough for her to shed them completely. Then he untied his own, freed himself, but he didn't give her time to look and explore. Lifting her against the wall, he cupped his hands beneath her parted thighs and braced himself between them.

His breath washed over her hair, hot and forceful. A shudder of excitement tore through him. She pulled back to look at his face, saw his thin grasp of control in the lines bracketing his eyes, in the firm set of his jaw. He was holding back, but only barely.

"I want you," he ground out, as if he were giving her one last chance to call a halt.

Don't stop. Please. Not this time!

He adjusted her slightly so he could lower her onto the hot tip of his sex. Heat against burning heat. Mac couldn't breathe. He pushed into her, stretching her flesh almost to the point of pain. He eased in and out, setting a rhythm, going deeper each time.

She clenched his shirt in her fists and held on even as she felt herself fly apart. She couldn't take much more, yet she knew she'd die if he stopped. "Gavin . . ."

"It's all right, love. Just . . ." He pushed again, growling as he buried himself so deeply, flesh met flesh. A garbled moan rumbled from his chest. Resting his forehead against hers, he said, "It's all right. Just relax."

Relax? she wanted to cry. She could fall into a million pieces, shatter like hand-blown glass. But she could *not* relax.

He trembled against her, so fiercely, Mac felt the vibrations clear to her soul. She tightened around him, tried to pull him completely inside her. With a shudder and a vicious shout, Gavin thrust inside her, forcing a gasp from her lungs. Her vision blurred as he filled the empty part of her, scraped raw the ache of desire.

She held onto him as he drove into her, hammering her with sensations that were ruthless and intense. Her muscles pulled tight, her mind was a haze of sensation. Vengeful, violent, inconceivable sensations that were beyond her imagination. She strained to hold them tighter, take them deeper. *Take Gavin deeper.*

"Come for me, Mac, God help me . . ."

He no sooner ground out the words than light and heat exploded through her body. She tensed into an arch, held on as he bucked against her. She was out of control, limp in his arms, helpless as shuddering sensations flooded her in a gushing wave. Tears welled and fell down her cheeks. Her chest squeezed with an agony of emotion. A tide of profound wonder and contentment. And love. So much love she thought her heart would break.

Gavin moaned her name the same instant he buried himself fully inside her. He did it again and again, his arms a vise that had the strength to hold her forever. She held on, her heart tearing as she lived through the power of his release.

Moments passed with him holding her against the wall, his head resting in the crook of her neck. Their ragged breaths echoed throughout the room, King Menes' chamber, she remembered dully. She'd forgotten where she was, who she was during the last incredible moments. She didn't want to remember now, didn't want to move . . . unless it was to make love to Gavin again.

Moving her hand beneath the collar of his shirt, she felt the warm slickness of his chest, the thudding beat of his heart. She wanted to stay like this forever, with their bodies wrapped around each other, the scent of their passion thick in the air. But they didn't have forever, she thought, closing her eyes and circling his neck with her arms. She'd known that from the beginning. She couldn't regret it now. Couldn't allow herself to want more.

But I do.

Gavin eased himself from her, but her body was reluctant to give him up. When she finally stood on her own, her legs trembled like papyrus reeds during a storm. Without a word, he found her pants and helped her dress. She waited for him to say something, exactly what, she wasn't sure, but . . . something.

His eyes were indiscernible dark spheres, his mouth a grim line. A new, strange kind of tension hummed off his skin. Did he regret making love to her? She didn't want to think so. But if not that, then what was bothering him?

"Gavin?"

"We need to get back." He collected both lanterns, handed her one, then retrieved the *pshent.* "Everyone should be up by now."

"Gavin—"

He stopped her with a kiss, a firm, sweeping touch of his lips that told her he didn't regret what they'd done. He just didn't know what to do next.

She would have smiled at his dilemma if she'd been able. But the truth was, she didn't know either.

Chapter 14

"My God, you did it!" Jake shouted.

Gavin set the *pshent* on a wobbly table and stepped back so everyone else could take a look. Jake fell to his knees before the crown, as if in prayer. Sarah, who was wearing another of Mac's outfits, was already putting pencil to paper. Connor arched a brow and nodded with quiet respect.

Willie and Kippie, Hollister, Smedley, Frewin and the others all crowded around, slapped each other on the back and declared it was time for a toast. It didn't matter that the sun had barely crested the horizon.

Everyone was there, laughing and smiling, demanding to hear the details. Everyone except for Mac.

Though she was only a few yards away, inside her tent, Gavin felt her absence. The spicy-sweet scent of her skin still filled his mind. The satin smoothness of her breasts still lingered in the palm of his hand. She should be sharing the victorious moment along with everyone else—it wouldn't have happened if not for her—but she'd mumbled that she had things to take care of and had hurried away without a backward glance.

Every instinct told him to go after her. But common sense stopped him. What would he do? Or say? He'd made love to her, backed her up against a wall in a five-thousand-year-old tomb and had taken her as if she were a whore.

She'd deserved better than that, he thought, furious with himself. He'd wanted to make love to her almost from the moment he first saw her. He wanted her still, the deep, pulsing thrum of his body urging him to find her now, show her how it could be between them.

But there couldn't *be* anything between them.

He knew it, and so did she.

"Why didn't you wake me when you'd found the tunnel?" Jake demanded.

Pulled back to the moment, Gavin murmured, "We weren't sure it was safe."

"You've got to show me where the sarcophagus is."

"I'm going to stay here and copy this in detail," Sarah said.

"Don't forget the hieroglyphics on the inside," Jake told her, gathering a lantern. "I can't believe the bloody rumor is true. 'Master of this crown is the God who rules the world.' If word of this reaches Napoleon, we'll never get out of Egypt alive."

Gavin knew Jake was right, but at the moment the French general was the least of his problems.

"Come on, man," Jake said, tugging on his arm. "Show me this find of yours."

Gavin knew his friend meant King Menes' tomb. But his gaze strayed to the tent across camp, and knew his "find" was somewhere inside.

"What is it yer about, daughter of mine?" Willie Tuggle lowered his great bulk onto a stool, careful not to spill the ale from his cup.

"Packing," she said, placing a handful of pick axes into a crate with the others she'd already collected.

"I can see that." He took a sip of his drink and furrowed his graying brows. "But why would ye be doin' such a thing?"

"Because we've found what we came after." Closing the lid with more force than necessary, she added, "Gavin will want to return to Rosetta now."

"There's much tae go through still. Are ye sure he's wantin' tae leave so soon?"

"I'm sure," she said around the growing tightness in her chest. Willing herself to ignore it, she turned her attention to the dozen shovels that needed to be boxed next.

Gavin didn't care about the canopic jars or the king's coffin, or the cache of jewels and relics that filled the chests they'd found. His only goal had been to find the *pshent* and give it to King George. He'd completed half of his task. Nothing would deter him from completing the rest.

Not even me, she thought, hating that she was feeling sorry for herself. It wasn't like her to wallow in self-pity. It was a place she didn't like, but she was at a loss as to how to get out of it.

There was one shining spot to her misery, however. Gavin had decided to leave King Menes' tomb intact— except for the crown, of course. They would take selected items from the outer rooms, but he had already given orders to seal the tunnel to the secret chamber. Before they left Abydos, her men would cover all traces of the main door. She should be happy about that.

And I would be if he weren't leaving me behind, too, she thought, unnerved by the strange sense of abandonment. She'd known making love to Gavin would be powerful, more incredible than anything she had imagined. But it had been more than that.

It had changed her. Touching him, holding him, becoming a part of him made her want things she'd never considered possible before. She had a ragtag family of men she loved, but not the way she loved Gavin. She'd never imagined such feelings for a man could exist. A painful, overwhelming need to be a part of him forever. She'd known she was halfway in love with him before, but she'd foolishly thought she'd be able to stop herself from falling the rest of the way. She realized too late that that sort of control was beyond her. She loved him, with all her heart, with every breath she took.

"Where 'ave ye gone off tae, Mackenzie, girl?"

Hearing her father's voice, she blinked and realized she was standing before a crate, staring at nothing, her hands filled with shovels.

Shaking thoughts of Gavin and the things she wanted from him away, she said, "You shouldn't drink so much, Pop. It's too hot today."

"Blast me hide! 'Tis the ale that keeps me on me feet."

Kneeling to arrange the shovels, she looked at her father and heard Gavin's furious words. *Are you planning to return and dig up the treasures for yourself? The money you can earn by selling these artifacts would support your family in luxury for the rest of their lives.*

It had never occurred to her to be so dishonest, but seeing how much her father had aged, and knowing he couldn't endure another trip into the desert, the idea was tempting. The fee Gavin had paid her to bring him to Abydos would take care of them for the coming year, but she still had to worry about the year after that, and the one after that. Her family would continue to grow older, and every year fewer of them would be able to work. What would she do then?

But even her worry about her family couldn't assuage the pain building around her heart. Gavin would leave soon. And she would stay behind. She would have her family, her desert, and her ship. And her memories of Gavin.

Cramming more shovels into the crate, she told herself she would have to be content with that.

She pushed to her feet. "You should rest, Pop. The trip back will be difficult."

"Hold on there, daughter. I want a word with ye."

"Maybe later. There are things I need to see to." *Like putting my thoughts back in order, gather a semblance of control over my emotions.*

"Now see here, Mackenzie. I know yer used to runnin' things, but I'm yer father, and there be somethin' I want tae discuss with ye."

"Pop—"

"Yer just like your dear mother, God rest her soul," Willie said with a sad smile.

Mac closed her eyes. She needed to be alone, gather the stubborn strength she used to pull her through each day. Strength she was sorely lacking right now. "You've told me this story before, Pop. If we could wait until later."

"Yer goin' tae hear me out."

Never having heard her father use an authoritative tone, *ever*, Mac arched a brow. "All right. I'm listening."

"We all know ye got yer looks from yer mother," he said, fingering his thinning brown hair. "Lucky for ye, I always said. Ye got her stubbornness, too. Nothing would stop that woman if she set her mind tae something."

"You've told me this before."

"Aye, but what I 'aven't told ye is that yer mother was of noble birth."

"What?"

"Aye, from a small town in the south of England, near Dover. Her father was a baron, owned a fine estate, he did. He 'ad five daughters, Bess being the youngest. And the wildest, I'm thinkin'."

Her grandfather was an English baron? The thought was too bizarre to believe. She glanced at her father's cup of ale and decided she had to put a stop to his drinking. The man was losing his mind.

"I already had me ship, then, and was in her village, delivering a shipment of goods tae her father. That's when I met her. Mackenzie, girl," he said with a sigh. "It was love at first sight for the both of us. We met in secret every chance we could steal, both of us knowin' it was foolhardy. I would be leavin' tae another port, and Bess, she couldn't go with me, and I couldn't expect her tae wait. She was a baron's daughter, after all. Used tae a fine house and fancy clothes. I wanted tae marry her more than I wanted my next breath, but what could I give her except a hard life at sea?"

Realizing he wasn't hallucinating, Mac knelt beside him and took his hand. "Why haven't you told me any of this before?"

"'Cause it didn't matter none." He laughed softly. "Ye see, Bess had her own ideas of how things should be. She knew if she told her father she was in love with the captain of a merchant ship, he would send her to an abbey or marry her off tae any man of worth who would have her."

"I take it Mama didn't tell her father."

A sparkle of mischief and love brightened Willie's eyes. "No, she did not. That woman, God love her, stowed away on me ship without me knowing. I was near to Wales before I found her. I gave the order tae turn around and take her home."

Setting his ale aside so he could rub his chest, he admitted, "But I proved tae be a weak man. Before we reached Dover, I realized I couldn't let her go. I sailed to London and married her instead. And there wasn't a day that either of us regretted it."

Mac reached up and kissed him on the cheek. "I'm glad you told me, Pop."

He looked at her with rheumy eyes that were filled with concern. "I see what ye feel for the earl. Ye look at 'im the same way my Bess looked at me. Ye love 'im, don't ye now."

"Yes," she said, feeling as miserable as she sounded.

"And what are ye goin' tae do about it?"

"What do you suggest? Stow away on his ship, perhaps?"

"You're your mother's daughter to the bone. I'm suggestin' ye go after what ye want."

"It's not that simple, Pop."

"Life isn't about *simple*. Ye've never given up on anything, Mackenzie." He tilted her face up and kissed her forehead. "Don't start now."

"My mother having noble blood won't make a difference to Gavin."

"I don't give a camel's arse if your blood will make a difference or not. Yer missin' the point of me story. If ye love him enough, and he loves ye the same way, nothing else will matter."

"Oh Pop."

"We aren't leaving yet," he announced suddenly, pushing to his feet with a groan.

She frowned at him. "What are you talking about?"

"Two days, Lord Blackwell said, for Jake and Lady Sarah to finish drawing the tomb. And for the boys tae cover up the entrance. We can't 'ave anyone findin' the tomb after we leave."

"Two days?"

Looking quite pleased with himself, he added with a wink, "Ye 'ave more than just yer mother in ye, girl. If yer any daughter of mine, ye'll make use of the time."

Sunlight blazed over the camp, baking the earth, the tents, the camels sleeping nearby. Heat rolled off the land in shimmering waves, distorting the desert to the east and laying low the mountain cliffs to the west like a furnace of burning coal. Despite the sweltering heat, Mac's crew worked tirelessly to crate the few items Jake had selected to take with them to England. *"A paltry few items,"* as Jake had put it.

The archaeologist had stared at Gavin in disbelief when he'd announced that, except for the crown, they would leave King Menes's chamber untouched. But he hadn't argued, for which Gavin was grateful. He didn't want to examine his reasons for abandoning the incredible find too closely.

Because every reason would come back to Mac, and the look of respect and remorse on her face when she'd held the crown.

Gavin glanced at the *pshent*, sitting on a table three feet away, near the smoking fire. The white gold conical centerpiece glowed bright enough to hurt his eyes, while the red scrolled outer crown seemed to absorb the light, darkening to the shade of blood. Since finding it early that morning, he hadn't permitted it out of his sight. He wasn't worried about anyone stealing it; it was the fact that he couldn't believe they'd actually found it that made him reluctant to let it out of his reach.

"Just wanted tae let ye know we're makin' fine progress."

Gavin turned, surprised to find Willie Tuggle behind him, wiping sweat from his brow with a limp handkerchief. He hadn't heard the man's approach, which said a lot about his state of mind. Willie's labored breathing could generally be heard throughout camp at any given time of the day. And when he slept, Gavin didn't worry about desert foxes or lions sneaking into camp. The horrid noise Willie made would frighten the bravest and the hungriest of them away.

"That Scotsman of yours, he's a fine worker. Had me doubts about 'im at first," Willie said, then blew out a breath as if he were exhausted.

Concerned, Gavin told him, "There are some wheelbarrows of sand that still need to be sifted through." *In a tent, and out of the heat, where you need to be.* "Perhaps you could finish that up for me."

"Aye, that I'll do." He didn't move, but watched his crew haul and carry and hammer crates closed. "That Scotsman, though, he's seems a bit on the anxious side, as though he wants tae get out of Egypt."

Connor had his reasons for wanting leave, Gavin thought, but didn't explain. His friend had unfinished business to attend to in England. And Gavin still owed him a debt of gratitude in that regard that had yet to be paid.

"But 'e's a good man."

"Yes, he is," Gavin said, not sure where Willie was heading with his conversation, but if he'd learned anything about the man over the past weeks, he was certain it was going somewhere.

"Now some men come to Egypt and find they can't leave. Take myself, for instance. I'm a man of the sea. Sailing the ocean, fighting storms and blustering winds, that has always been my idea of home. But 'ere I am in the middle of a bloody desert." He chuckled, his pudgy hands holding his belly. "And I couldn't be happier. 'Tis the same with Mac."

Mac. Gavin didn't want to think about her, had worked hard to keep her out of his thoughts, because if he thought about her, he'd go to her, and make love to her and the rest of the world could be damned.

But recalling Mac's fear about her family, and knowing she would eventually be their only source of support, he heard himself ask, "Have you ever thought about moving back to England?"

"On occasion, but whenever it's put tae a vote, we always decide tae stay here."

"Regardless of the dangers?" Gavin said, hearing the stir of frustration in his voice.

Willie met Gavin's narrowed gaze with an insightful lift of one gray brow. "There are dangers tae be sure, but isn't that the case no matter where ye live?"

Gavin realized this might be the opportunity he needed. If he could convince the father to leave Egypt, then the daughter would follow. As matter-of-factly, and as gently as he could, he said, "You realize you can't make another trip into the desert."

"I'm an old man. There's no arguing that me body's no longer what it used tae be."

"Then you also know your crewmen aren't going to be able to keep up this kind of work much longer."

Pursing his lips, he said, "What are ye gettin' at?"

"When none of you can earn a living, Mac will be responsible for caring for all of you. She can't do it on her own."

"She won't 'ave tae."

"She will, unless you have a cache of money you haven't told her about."

Willie frowned up at Gavin for a moment, his yellowed eyes troubled. "If ye don't mind me askin', what concern is it of yer's?"

Gavin ran his hand through his hair, wanting to curse. He hadn't wanted Mac to be his concern, he'd tried his damnedest to keep his distance, but for all his efforts, he had come to care about her, so much he couldn't stand the thought of her worrying, or suffering, or having to support her family alone.

But more than that, *he* wanted to be the one to take care of *her*.

He'd given considerable thought to her living on his property, but he knew her well enough to know she'd view that as charity, and her pride would force her to refuse. Besides, having her close enough to visit whenever he wanted would take their relationship to another level, a deeper one that might destroy her pride altogether if he tried to make her his mistress.

Willie cleared his throat, bringing Gavin out of his thoughts. Scowling, he said, "I've come to . . . care about . . . all of you. I was just wondering if you've given thought to the future."

"Aye, that I 'ave. *Little Bess,* me merchant ship, should be good as new when we return to Rosetta. I intend tae hire a younger crew tae man her."

"And who will captain her?"

"Why, Mac, of course. She loves the sea as much as the sand." His bushy brows shooting up his forehead, he pointed across camp. "See what I mean? Can't keep the girl from exploring one part of the world or another."

Gavin looked to where he pointed and felt the muscles along his spine tense. Mac, wearing sage-colored pants and tunic, was leading a camel by a rope into the desert. Blankets, shovels, a lantern and several bulging sacks were strapped to the animal's back.

"Where in bloody hell is she going?" Gavin demanded, drawing the attention of everyone within shouting distance.

"Can't say for sure. But when I told 'er we'd be staying another two days, she said there was a pottery field, or some such thing, she wanted tae 'ave a look at."

"Damn! Of all the bloody, stupid . . ." Gavin took a step after her, stopped and ran his hand through his hair. "The woman is determined to get herself killed."

"Aye, she's determined, she is. But I don't be thinkin' she'll get 'erself killed. She knows her way around the desert."

"You wouldn't be so confident if you'd seen her attacked by a cobra."

"Attacked, was she?" He pursed his lips as if he were impressed instead of horrified. "Well, I think I'll see tae those wheelbarrows ye mentioned."

Gavin scowled at Willie's departing back. It was obvious the old man wasn't concerned about his daughter. And Gavin knew he shouldn't be, but blast it to hell, he was, and he wasn't about to let her leave camp alone.

Snatching up his rifle, he gave the *pshent* a departing glance, then started after her.

Mac felt him gaining on her long before she heard the crunch of his boots in the sand or his muttered curses scorching the air. She allowed a smile, but only because he couldn't see it. Those curses were for her benefit, she was sure. She'd left camp again, alone, and for that he would be furious with her, regardless that this time she was well armed. And not with just a rifle. He would rant and rave and tell her how irresponsible she was. And she'd let him, so long as he kept following her.

The sun hovered above the distant cliffs, a blinding disk guiding her toward her destination. The place where she would take a stand and possibly change the course of her life. Or at the very least, grasp another day.

"Are you determined to get yourself killed, or is this your way of trying to irritate me?"

The question, asked with rumbling anger, made her heart jerk against her chest. She glanced over her shoulder, saw he was nearly on top of her and stopped. "Neither."

"You left camp alone."

"I'm not alone," she said, running her hand down the camel's neck.

Scowling, his eyes hard beneath the shadow of his hat, he said, "And you're unarmed."

Stepping around the animal, she pulled a rifle from the holder and showed it to him. "As you can see, I'm prepared."

"Damn it, Mac," he growled, stepping so close she could see his pulse beating at the base of his neck and smell the warmth of his skin. "After everything that's happened, why do you keep taking risks?"

Wanting to wipe the worried frown from his brow, but knowing it was too soon to touch him, she said, "Sometimes you have to take risks to get what you want."

"What could you possible want in the middle of the desert?"

You, she thought, but didn't dare say it. "I'll be fine, Gavin. I have everything I need to see me through the night."

"You are *not* staying out here all night alone."

Suppressing the tingle of anticipation along her spine, she shrugged, gathered the camel's reins and started walking. "Come with me if you like. But I'm going."

Hearing his vicious curse, she flinched, but kept on walking. A moment later, he was at her side, his long strides eating up the desert.

"Tell me something, Mac. What is out here that's worth risking your life for?"

You, she wanted to say again, but pressed her lips together to keep from revealing too much and scaring him off. Sneaking a glance at him, seeing the firm set of his jaw and wishing she could kiss him there, she said, "You'll see."

Chapter 15

Gavin didn't know if he'd done the rational thing by coming after Mac, or if he'd made an enormous mistake. Anger burned through his veins, but it wasn't the explosive kind of anger. This was different. He wanted to shake her, then hold her tight until he was certain nothing would harm her. Ever. A dangerous thought he hadn't been able to shake, regardless that he'd tried and tried.

He followed her over one rolling sand dune after another, heading toward the limestone cliffs in the distance. She didn't speak, and neither did he. He'd already reprimanded her, and she hadn't been fazed in the least. And to be honest, he hadn't expected her to be. She was too headstrong to be intimidated by him. A trait that would have annoyed him a few weeks ago, yet he found it was another of her qualities that amazed him.

But an inner voice warned that he should force her to return to camp, that being alone with her was madness. He still didn't know what to do about her. She couldn't stay in Egypt, and she would refuse his offer of a house to live in if he suggested it. So where did that leave them? He wanted to make love to her again, and again, the need so desperate his arms trembled with the urge to touch her. But if he did, the sliver of control he still possessed would crumble, and if that were to happen, walking away from her would be impossible.

"Oh, my God, Gavin," she whispered, catching his arm and stopping him. "Look!"

He did, stunned to find himself on the peak of a sand dune. Below him, the earth swelled like the waves of the ocean, cresting and dipping until they splashed against the base of the cliffs. Littering the sand were millions upon millions of pottery shards. Broken, jagged bits scattered like stones.

"I'd heard of this place, but I'd had no idea it was so . . . so enormous." She pressed her hands to her mouth and shook her head.

"What is it?" he asked, not understanding why broken pots would astonish her.

"Pilgrims used to come here to worship Osiris, God of the Dead. After they prayed to him, they'd leave vessels of wine as an offering."

Gavin bent to pick up a rust colored shard, turned it over in his hand. It was made of clay, and plain in design, a poor man's jar. And there were more just like it, for as far as he could see.

"Why here?" he asked. "Why wouldn't they have brought their offering to Osiris' temple in Abydos?"

She scanned the area, her eyes bright in the dying sun. "Some believe an ancient city is buried here beneath the sand. Perhaps it was another temple to Osiris, the first one maybe. When the desert reclaimed it, the people continued coming here to pray."

Tossing the shard away, he said, "Now you've seen it. If we leave now, we'll reach camp by dark."

"I'm staying."

He looked into the swirling green of her eyes, and knew he'd have to carry her kicking and fighting if he wanted to rejoin the others. And damn his soul, he wasn't sure he wanted to. "There's nothing here, Mac."

"There is. You just have to know where to look." From the soft tone of her voice and the warming of her gaze, he knew she wasn't referring to the pottery field. But to them, and what could be between them.

Before he could respond, she started unpacking her supplies. "I have to build a fire before it gets dark."

Gavin helped, knowing he was making a huge error, but for the life of him, he was unable to stop. An hour later, when everything was ready and a stew was simmering over the fire, Mac gathered a shovel, an empty sack and a lantern.

"Now what do you think you're doing?" Gavin asked, already knowing the answer.

"I want to search the past," she said quietly, looking at him as if she could see through skin and bone to what he kept hidden inside.

"There are plenty of shards to look at here. There's no need to wander off."

"I won't be far."

She turned and left, leaving Gavin to stare after her in frustration. He shouldn't follow her; he shouldn't even be alone with her. He wanted her too much to resist her, and if he didn't keep his hands to himself, he'd end up hurting her. No matter what happened, he didn't want to hurt her.

Hefting his rifle and a water bottle, he started out, only to have his chest tighten at the sight of her. She walked through shifting sand as if she'd been born in the desert, her gait easy and confident. The fading sun swallowed her in golden light, shimmering against her auburn hair and sliding over the unruly braid draping her back. She was a desert nymph, sleek and graceful. A chameleon that changed to blend with its surroundings. Watching her now, she seemed an illusion, almost magical. As if what he was seeing couldn't possibly be real.

Perhaps she wasn't real, he thought. Perhaps there was another part of her, a plotting, conniving part she'd yet to reveal. He wanted to believe that was the case because it was easier to distrust her, safer to the guarded life he'd created. And safer to his heart.

Mac knelt suddenly, dropping her shovel and sack to dig in the sand with her hands. By the time he reached her, she was pulling a wine vase from the ground. The clay surface was scored, by blowing sand he thought, the handle missing and the spout chipped. But otherwise it was intact.

She sat back on her heels, and when she looked up at him, her eyes were wide with wonder. "It's beautiful."

He knelt, took the vase from her to examine. There were no carvings or even a trace of paint. It was plain and basic. The markets in any town in Egypt would offer better, yet seeing the awe shinning in Mac's eyes, he might as well be holding a handful of gold.

"It's a clay pot," he said, knowing it would irritate her.

"It has been sitting right here, untouched, in this exact spot for thousands of years. Someone made this, used it in their everyday life before leaving it for Osiris."

Touched by the sincerity in her voice, trying to see the relic through her eyes, he asked, "Why do you care so much about a simple vase?"

"The past is important."

"Sometimes it's best to forget the past."

She held his gaze. Hers was steady and clear. "And sometimes it's best to learn from it."

Gavin handed her the vase and started to rise, but Mac caught his arm and said, "Tell me about yours."

"There's nothing to tell," he said in a tone that would have stopped any sane person from pursuing this line of questioning. But this was Mac he was dealing with; he should have known better.

"You were married once."

"And now I'm not."

She sighed, but didn't give up. "You had a son."

Not about to discuss that forbidden subject, he shook off her hold and stood. "Keep the rifle with you. I'll check on dinner."

He stalked away, anger and loss driving each step. He half expected her to call after him, or chase him down. But he didn't hear a sound beyond the soft whistle of breeze and the crunch of his boots against sand. The muscles in his back tightened, but he forced himself to keep walking, regardless that every step became harder and harder. He was not going to discuss his past with her, damn it. Rachel and Matthew were a tragedy he would bear alone.

Yet he stopped on the crest of a sand dune, his breath coming hard as indecision tore through him. Glancing over his shoulder he saw her sitting where he'd left her among the litter of broken shards, the vase in her hands, her tools forgotten at her side. She wasn't looking at him, but at the setting sun, her expression solemn, and so sad, he almost couldn't bear to look at her. What did she know about his family? Had she heard the rumors?

In London, he still endured the pitying glances, as well as the suspicious ones, and knew what people whispered. Had Rachel died in an accident, or had the Earl of Blackwell killed her in a fit of rage?

With a muttered curse, he crossed to her, demanded, "What do you know about them?"

She turned her emerald green eyes to him. "Only

that you lost them both, and that you're suffering because of it."

"As I should be," he said with a growl.

"Their deaths weren't your fault."

"No?" he barked, rougher than he'd intended. But after years of never speaking about the night that tore his life apart he found trying to now was more difficult than he'd thought possible. "And what do you know of their deaths or of fault? My wife and son died violently and painfully while I sat in my study drinking myself into oblivion."

She didn't flinch in revulsion as he expected, but said, "You can't blame yourself."

"I most certainly can. If not for me they would both be alive. Instead they're buried in the hard, cold ground. My son was only three years old, Mac, and I didn't protect him."

As the blurred image of Matthew swam from his memory emotions crumbled, pressed against his heart, so tight and heavy he couldn't breathe.

"Tell me what happened," she pleaded softly.

"They died," he said around the pressure in his throat. "That's all that matters."

"Gavin," she said with quiet patience. "Tell me."

He closed his eyes for a moment, spinning back to the night six years before when he'd thought he'd owned the world. He'd believed in perfection then, in his control over fate. Nothing could touch him if he didn't want to be touched. But he'd deceived himself, just as Rachel had deceived him.

"Yes, I was married, and yes, I had a son."

"What were they like?"

"Rachel had pale blond hair and bluebird eyes with a voice to match. Matthew was a miniature of me, his hair as black and thick as midnight."

"I'm sorry, Gavin," Mac said with honesty instead of pity, for which he was grateful.

"So am I," he said. "More sorry than you can know."

"You miss them."

"Every day of my life. Or at least Matthew. Rachel?" He shook his head, unable to voice his gnarled feelings for the woman who had betrayed him.

"You loved her."

"Once, I suppose I did." He shrugged, feeling a fraction of his anger slip away as resignation took hold. "I don't really remember."

But he was certain that what he'd felt for Rachel didn't compare to his feelings for Mac. He'd never burned for the sight of his wife, had never yearned to touch her, or to taste her porcelain skin. He'd enjoyed looking at her, listening to her laugh or play the pianoforte. But lust for her? Need her? With a sense of regret, he realized that kind of urgency had never been between them.

Now, he wondered if Rachel had known their marriage had lacked fire, and needing it, had looked for it elsewhere.

Placing the clay vase in her sack, Mac stood and brushed the sand from her pants. "Time might have dulled your memory, but you loved her. You wouldn't have married her otherwise. That's not the kind of man you are."

Hefting his rifle, he took the bag. "It's a moot point in any case. What happened is over and done with."

"Is it?" she asked. "You discount your emotions so easily." She touched his chest with one finger, right over his heart. "But they're still here, hurting and burning. Until you forgive her."

"Forgive her for sleeping with another man?" Gavin

snapped. "Forgive her for taking my son and killing him?"

"Yes." She flattened her hand over his heart. "And forgive yourself for not being there to save them."

He sucked in a breath. No one, *no one,* had ever said those words to him. Words that constantly circled in the back of his mind, burrowing into his soul. Festering like a disease that had no cure.

He stepped away, but Mac slid her hand up and caught his neck in her palm. Her voice sharp, almost angry, she said, "Don't turn away from me, Gavin. I know what happened, and I know you're not to blame for their deaths."

"You don't have any idea what really happened."

"Jake told me."

"Then I'll deal with Jake later."

"He cares about you." When Gavin tried to turn away, she gripped his shirt with both hands. "And so do I."

He stared down at her. The last rays of sun slid beyond the cliffs behind her. Shadows gathered, a sheet of black that closed out the world. But he could see her face, the earnest plea in her eyes for him to listen. Talk to her. He didn't want to. Didn't want to admit that what he felt, the blame he bore for killing his family, had become a living thing inside him, preventing him from hoping for a normal life. Rachel might have betrayed him, but she hadn't deserved to die for her crime. And Matthew . . . Matthew had been innocent, yet he'd died because Gavin had failed him.

The hideous truth was that he'd failed them all.

"It was a tragic accident," Mac said, shaking him to gain his attention. "But you aren't to blame."

Others had told him the same during the weeks

and months that followed, but he hadn't listened. He'd known better, had known that if he'd pursued Rachel, she and Matthew would be alive today.

"I appreciate your faith in me, Mac, but it's misplaced. I killed my family as surely as I'm standing here now."

"No, you didn't. Your wife cheated on you, broke her vows of marriage."

"Thank you for the reminder, but it's not something that I've forgotten."

"You were furious with her," Mac continued, releasing him with a shove of frustration. "So furious that she was frightened of you. So she took your son and ran."

"You seem to have all the facts."

"You didn't go after her, Gavin," Mac said, standing up to him the way no one else ever had before. "Not because you didn't care, but because you did. You were angry, and knew you had to calm down before you confronted her again. You did the right thing."

"I allowed my family to be attacked by thieves, Mac! I allowed them to die."

A tremor tore through her, and her eyes blazed with exasperation. "You did no such thing. You loved them. Now it's time to forgive her . . . and yourself."

"Why are you doing this?"

She smiled, a soft, sad tilt of her lips. "Because I love you."

"Jesus, bloody hell," he ground out, pacing in a circle before glaring down at her. "You do *not* love me."

"I know about love, Gavin." Picking up her lantern, she started back to camp, but paused long enough to say, "Whether you like it or not, I know I love you."

* * *

"I know about love."

Mac's declaration wove through Gavin's mind, creating knots that wound tighter and tighter as the night wore on. He tried to ignore them, and what they meant, but, staring at the stew she'd prepared and unable to eat any of it, he realized he couldn't.

She loved him.

The weight of that knowledge made him want to race into the desert, away from her, away from the things she made him feel. The temptation, the need. He didn't want love in his life. Didn't trust the emotion. It had ruined him once, and he'd sworn never to let it touch him again.

But it had, and now he had to deal with the consequences.

"Mac," he began, setting his supper aside. "We need to talk."

She made a faint noise of acknowledgment but continued to study the handful of clay shards she'd laid out near the fire.

"About what you said earlier."

Her attention fixed on trying to connect the fragments, she said, "I'm listening."

Drawing a steadying breath, he plunged ahead. "You said you loved me."

"So I did."

"You're mistaken. What you feel is a result of what happened between us after we found the *pshent.*"

She glanced up, arched a brow. "What happened? Oh, you mean when we made love."

His body tightened, deep inside his gut. She made it sound so simple, yet what they'd done hadn't been merely sex. Sex was enjoyable, a craving that needed to be filled. What he'd shared with Mac had been overpowering, shattering, and so incredible he wanted to repeat that moment again and again. Regardless that doing so would only hurt them both in the end.

"You're a woman," he said, his voice cool and distant to his own ears. "It's natural that you misinterpreted your feelings."

Abandoning the pieces of clay, she turned her green eyes to him. "And what are my feelings?"

"You enjoyed what we shared. It was new to you."

She scoffed. "I may not be as experienced as you, Gavin, but I'm not naïve. And if you'll recall, I wasn't a virgin when we made love."

A scowl crossed his face and a rumble of sudden anger churned inside his chest. He'd been so blinded by the rush of being inside her that he hadn't given a thought to the fact that it hadn't been her first time. The realization was so jolting, and so disturbing, he wanted to shout in rage, especially when he looked at Mac again.

She had the nerve to laugh, her eyes sparkling with mischief in the firelight. "You look like a jungle cat who's had his territory invaded."

And that's the way he felt, he realized, and clenched his hands to stop himself from claiming Mac so no one else could. *Ever.*

"I made a mistake once." She sobered, her expression turning thoughtful. "I know the difference between lust and love. And I know the difference between the love I have for my family, and what I feel for you."

"Stop," he told her, standing to pace the camp.

"Do my feelings frighten you?" she asked.

Everything about you frightens me, he wanted to shout.

When he didn't respond, she continued, "I don't expect you to confess that you love me. Or even feel a glimmer of what I do. But it's not my way to hide my emotions."

Pulling the stopper from a jar of water, she poured some into a large bowl. "But, if it makes you uncomfortable, I won't say it again."

Gavin ground out a curse. That's exactly what he wanted, the way it had to be, but it didn't make him feel any better. "I never meant to hurt you."

"I know." She dipped a folded cloth into the water, then washed her face and neck, lifting her dark mane of hair to reach her nape. "I wanted you, Gavin. I don't regret it, and you shouldn't either."

Gavin watched her uneasily. She was too calm and rational for his liking. Most women he knew would demand he do the right thing and offer marriage. Yet Mac talked about their lovemaking as if it had been as meaningful as sharing a good meal.

Grasping the hem of her shirt, she started to lift it, but paused. "Perhaps you should turn around."

"Why?"

"I'm going to bathe."

Heat flushed through his body, tightened his gut, filled his sex with explosive heat. "Not here, you're not."

"I do this every night before bed. Since I don't have a tent, and it would irritate you if I left camp, I have to bathe here. Now turn around."

Before he could move, she whisked off her tunic. Gavin turned his back to her but not before seeing pale breasts tipped with coral pink nipples. Hearing the splash of water as she soaked her cloth, imagining her rubbing the wet fabric over her bare skin, his blood began to thrum painfully through his veins.

"I'll be finished in a moment," she said on a sigh.

But not soon enough, he thought. His body pulsed

with the need to turn around and take her, reach once more for the only glimpse of heaven he'd ever known. When he heard her stand and slip into her top, his insides began to tremble. Or was she removing her pants? God help him. She was teasing him, testing his will. He knew it, and knew he couldn't give in to the desire that burned in his blood like fire.

"You know, Gavin, not all women are the same."

He knew it, because he'd never wanted another woman the way he wanted Mac right now.

"Most are faithful," she said, her voice as soft as the tinkling of water.

And loyal and caring, he added despite the blaze consuming his mind, but none more so than Mac. Or compelling and beautiful, seductive and tempting. She was like no woman he'd ever known.

Every breath became an effort and his pulse pounded at his temple. Sweat coated his skin. His body demanded he turn, grasp the only thing, the only *person*, he'd ever wanted during the last six miserable years of his life.

"Your wife hurt you, Gavin, but that shouldn't stop you from loving someone else."

"Mac, of all the bloody—"

"I don't mean me," she said quickly, almost cheerfully. "We're too different. I belong in Egypt or on my ship. You have responsibilities in London. And I would hardly fit in with your peers."

She was using the same arguments he'd already thought of, only he didn't like hearing them from her. But it was the truth. They couldn't exist in each other's worlds. Which gave him every reason to do the honorable thing and end their relationship now.

"You're a good man, Gavin. I just wish—"

"Bloody hell, Mac," he barked, his throat tight. "I'm not going to discuss this. Now get dressed."

"I already am."

He turned around, only to have his breath leave on a strangled hiss. She'd shed her tunic and pants and had wrapped herself in a blanket of thin colorful wool. The upper portion of her chest, shoulders and arms were bare, but the rest of her was covered, though he hardly noticed. Her skin glowed like satin in the flickering light. Catching a hint of her cinnamon-sweet scent, he swayed. His gaze strayed to the pulse beating at the base of her throat, and his mouth went dry as he thought about kissing there. She would be cool and damp and incredible.

Her eyes warm and dark, she held the bowl of water out to him. "It's your turn."

"I know what you're trying to do. It's not going to work."

"I won't look," she said as if he hadn't spoken.

Forcing the water into his hands, she sat across the fire with her back to him and began to unbraid her hair. She combed her fingers through the silken length, removing the tangles with the same dexterity as she was removing the last shred of his control.

"We can't do this," he insisted.

She didn't pretend to misunderstand him, but looked over her shoulder. Her eyes were intense and determined. "You want to make love to me, Gavin."

"I don't want to mislead you."

"And I want you."

"That's enough, Mac."

"Do you regret making love to me?"

"Jesus, bloody hell."

"Or is it because I'm not from nobility?" she demanded with a stubborn tilt of her chin.

"Damn it," he shouted and threw the bowl of water into the desert. "I'm trying to protect you!"

"You can't protect me or Jake or Connor." She stood to face him, one hand clenched at her side, the other at the top of her blanket to hold it in place. "Or Rachel. We're all responsible for our own actions."

"I should have stopped her."

Sighing, Mac said, "Perhaps, but at the time you thought you were doing the right thing by letting her go."

He bowed his head, not wanting to admit she was right. He *had* thought he'd done the right thing by staying behind. Reeling from the blow of finding his wife with another man, he hadn't been able to speak to her rationally, demand an answer to the question that haunted him still.

"I'll never know why she betrayed me," he said, revealing his deepest fear.

"It's been six years, Gavin. Does it matter?"

"Yes, it does. If I knew I might be able to make sense of it all."

"Perhaps she made a mistake."

"Or perhaps I never really knew her."

"Perhaps," Mac said softly. "I for one believe she was a fool for turning to another man when she had you."

Gavin looked at her. Was it time to do as Mac said, forgive Rachel and himself for what happened? Bury the past and his anger once and for all? He wanted to; the weight of both was destroying him. But he'd carried both for so long, he was afraid they were a permanent part of him now.

"Let me help you."

"I don't want to hurt you," he told her again.

Drawing a shuddering breath, she whispered, "If

you don't kiss me right now, I'll be hurt far worse than if you never touch me again."

"Mac," he said, shaking his head.

"You're going to leave me, Gavin. I know that." She stepped closer, breaking through the last of his barriers. "But we have now. Please, give us now."

Chapter 16

Mac knew the instant Gavin made his decision and nearly fell to her knees in relief. His eyes flashed with black lightning. His jaw clenched and his hands were on her waist, jerking her toward him. She would have smiled or sighed but his mouth was on hers, demanding, biting.

She clasped his shoulders as he explored her back with his hands, then her bottom, skimming over her hips through the blanket. The sensations he stirred were raw and teasing and not nearly enough to soothe her. She wanted his hands on her, wanted to feel him skin to skin. The blanket had to go, but she couldn't release his shoulders long enough to shed it.

Standing on tiptoe, she leaned into the hard contours of his body, the erection that pressed against her core. Shuddered when he ground himself into her softness and kissed the sensitive vein along her neck.

Her head fell back. Staring at the millions of stars crowding the sky, she felt herself coming apart, quickly and completely. She loved Gavin, wanted him, with every part of her soul, but all they had was now. *Don't think about tomorrow.* The stars blurred as her eyes filled with tears. She blinked them back and held him tighter. *I have him now.*

Stepping out of his hold, she met his fierce gaze.

"Have you changed your mind?" he asked, his voice low and rough.

"No."

He ran his hands up and down her arms. "It would serve me right, for everything I've put you through."

"Denying you would mean denying myself." Undoing the knot that held the blanket, she held out the ends and let it fall to the ground. "And I think we've both been punished enough."

"Mac," he breathed, his gaze burning down the length of her naked body.

Her breasts filled and grew heavy. She needed his hands on her, lifting her, molding her against his palms. Her nipples pebbled against the cool night air. Her stomach muscles tensed and her nerves pulsed deep inside her core, persistent flicks of demanding, aching need. She felt empty, hollow with loss. God help her, she wanted him inside her, felt herself grow moist and ready. But she didn't want to hurry. If all they had was now, she wanted it to last.

She hadn't had the chance to see him the last time they made love; she intended to correct that. Gavin reached for her, but she brushed his hands aside. "No touching. Not yet."

His gaze narrowed, and she saw a muscle pulse in his jaw, but he didn't argue.

Under his hawk-like stare, she unlaced the front of his shirt then lifted it over his head and tossed it aside. His chest was of flesh and bone, but the carved lines were perfection, as if the finest craftsman had honed him with a blade. Firelight danced over the width of his shoulders, shimmered against the swirl of dark hair shielding his chest. She grazed her hand down his sides, skimming his ribs to the line of dark hair that disappeared below his pants.

His stomach muscles jumped beneath her touch. His voice sounding strangled, he said, "I thought you said no touching."

"That only applies to you." She ran the back of her fingers over his waist. He was hot and hard, smooth to the touch. And for tonight, he was all hers.

"That hardly seems fair."

"This has nothing to do with being fair." She raked her tongue over his left nipple, closed her eyes to cherish the salty taste of him. "And everything to do with desire."

She flicked the right one and felt a small thrill when he shivered. "And pleasure." Pressing a kiss to the center of his chest, she whispered, "And need."

She trailed her fingers over his rib cage to his waist. Gavin sucked in a breath when she unfastened his pants and pushed them down his hips, freeing him at last.

The ground dipped beneath her feet. He was solid and hard, the thick length of him pulsing with life. Her body tensed, became a rope wound so tight she was on the verge of snapping.

She'd wanted to take her time, touch him, learn every inch of him, but she now knew going slowly wasn't possible. He was too beautiful and her body ached as it never had before. The constant thrumming of her blood turned into a roar in her ears. Her breath rasped against her lungs.

"Gavin . . ." She slid her palms up his back, down to his hips, gathering her nerve to take what she wanted. Closing her hand around the length of him, she almost jumped back when he bucked in response. A breath hissed out though his gritted teeth. Muscles knotted and rippled along his arms and chest. His hands flexed at his sides, clenched and flexed in a frantic rhythm.

She stroked him again and again, watched him

tremble, absorbed the vibrations racing into her hand and up to her chest, before spiraling down to feed the throbbing pulse between her thighs. She wanted him there, inside her, wanted him so badly she couldn't think beyond that one thing.

"Touch me, Gavin, please."

He didn't give her the chance to finish. He lifted her in his arms, his mouth finding hers with desperate accuracy. His tongue plunged inside, sweeping her with his taste, pushing her desire to the edge. He knelt, laid her down on the blanket she'd used moments before, then stretched out by her side.

He kneaded both her breasts at once, his hands so rough and erotic she arched her back and whimpered deep in her throat. It was agony and ecstasy, all at once, his hands on her body, the explosive sensations, the knowledge that more was to come.

Threading her fingers into his hair, she dragged his head down for a kiss, only like no kiss she'd ever known. He consumed her, tasted, nipped and bit, twisted everything she felt into something new and tighter and devastatingly surreal.

His hand slid down her stomach to her hip, her thigh, his fingers coaxing her to relax and tense in turns. He teased the inside of her leg with his fingers, moving higher and higher until Mac couldn't breathe. He circled her core, dipped low, brushed her sex and moved away. She squirmed against him, wanting more, God, wanting so much more.

"Look at me, Mac," he said, his voice harsh.

She did at the same moment his hand closed over her flesh. Gasping, she jerked in response.

"Shh," he murmured in her ear, adding pressure as he massaged her tender nub. Heat pounded through her limbs. Sensations bombarded her and she was helpless to stop them or control them. Gavin changed the rhythm, sweeping her up so fast and furiously she wasn't prepared for the lightning that exploded in her mind or for the sound of her scream when she found her release.

She would have thought time had stopped, but her heart raced against her chest. Her skin tingled and her blood burned hot through her veins. Tremors rippled through her, aftershocks of pure pleasure.

Go slow, her mind warned, but her body refused to obey. She needed him, so much she hurt, and heaven help her, she had the insane urge to cry. She'd loved countless people during her life, her Pop and crew, but she'd never loved anyone the way she loved Gavin. *But he's not meant to be mine.* She'd never realized that loving someone could bring so much pleasure—and so much pain.

He kissed the curve of her throat, the bend of her shoulder, the touch of his lips gentle and searing. Bliss and agony intertwined into a blinding haze. At that moment she knew she'd never experience anything so powerful again. Or so right. She'd promised never to repeat the words, but what she felt for him was too overwhelming to contain. Though she knew she shouldn't, she couldn't stop herself from whispering, "I love you."

Blood rushed through Gavin's mind, a swirling fog of heat and need. He'd been so close to turning his back on Mac, holding his ground and keeping his hands to himself. And he would have succeeded if she hadn't shown him the one quality that attracted him to her the most; her ability to know what she wanted and reach for it.

She wasn't afraid of life, or of being hurt. Two things he'd excelled at since Rachel's and Matthew's deaths.

He'd stopped living that day, and hadn't started again until he'd met a green-eyed gypsy named Mackenzie Tuggle.

Kissing her after her plea to "give them now" had been like stepping into heaven after spending a lifetime in hell. She was sweet and open, honest and everything he needed. And God, the way she responded to him.

But now the fog that clouded all common sense cleared because of three simple words. *"I love you."*

He raised up on one elbow, looked down at her flushed face, her kiss-swollen lips. He tightened his grip on her waist, his fingers curling with the longing to touch her breast again. Roll her hardened nipple between his finger and thumb. Taste her cinnamon skin. Instead he held her gaze and felt his protective instincts circle like a vulture searching for prey. A small voice whispered in the back of his mind telling him to stop, now, before walking away became impossible.

Out of habit, he tried to tell her he was sorry, but as Mac watched him with trusting green eyes, waiting for him to make a choice, the words died in his throat. The choice had already been made, he realized, and no matter how right his common sense might be, he wanted Mac.

He would have to walk away tomorrow. But for now, tomorrow didn't exist.

He kissed her lightly on the lips, then again, but deeper, and again, until she closed her eyes and sighed into his mouth. Wrapped her arms around his neck. He covered her body with his, entwined their legs and shuddered, fought to stay in control. Their bodies fit in complete, earth-shattering perfection.

Or almost complete, he thought. She lifted one leg, cupped it around his hip, opening herself to him. He found her, the heat and wetness of her making his mind spin. He pushed inside, easing into her inch by inch, feeling her body stretch to accept him. She shifted to take him deeper, but in doing so her inner muscles clamped down.

A guttural moan tore from Gavin's throat. She tightened around him again, stripping all of his restraint. With an uncontrollable shudder, he drove inside her, a forceful thrust that embedded him skin to skin. Panting, he forced himself not to move. If he did, it would be over. He focused on breathing, the pounding rhythm of his heart. He felt her hands on his back, urgent and kneading, heard her whispered plea not to stop.

"Don't move," he managed to say.

God help him . . . and her . . . he wanted to go slowly, make love to her the way he'd imagined night after night. Not rush like a randy schoolboy bedding a chambermaid. She tilted her hips, and he slid even deeper.

Slow wasn't to be.

He kissed her, or perhaps she kissed him, he wasn't sure and didn't care. Their mouths were as entwined as their bodies, taking and tasting, consuming whatever they touched. He withdrew from her, flexed his hips, buried himself to the hilt. And nearly exploded from the tight fit. He thrust into her again and again, each time moving faster and faster. Whimpering with each stroke, she matched his pace. He shook with the effort to stay in control, to wait, to make their moment last.

"Gavin!" Gasping a ragged breath, she gripped his shoulders and arched her back.

He drove into her, felt her tremors build and grow then finally crest. He watched her cheeks flush, her eyes darken to smoke. She cried his name and tears slid down her temples, then his vision blurred and he couldn't see anything at all. He could only feel; Mac climaxing around him, holding him tight. He threw his head back, strained against her as the fury he tried to control broke free. The storm rolled through him, a pounding, shuddering release that was more powerful than anything he'd ever known. He felt numbed by it, humbled, overwhelmed and in need of more.

The spasms slowed, and he had no idea how much time passed before his mind cleared. Thoughts gradually returned, and with them his other senses stirred to life. He felt the heat from the fire, heard the whistle of wind and a desert fox cry in the distance. But still he didn't move.

He had Mac in his arms, her scent in his mind and right or wrong, there was no other place he wanted to be. Because he had every intention of making love to her again.

Tomorrow was still hours away.

Chapter 17

The felucca's bow cut through the River Nile with the efficiency of a sword parting reeds. The dark water rippled and churned as the three boats sped past banks of palms and sesban shrubs, clustered gray mud-brick huts. They were sailing too fast, Mac thought, frowning as soot-dark clouds tumbled across the sky. The air smelled of rain, but that was impossible. It never rained in the desert.

But it wasn't the possibility of a freak storm that had her on edge. A biting wind from the south filled the sheets, pushing hard toward Rosetta.

Toward home.

Normally she would be excited at the prospect of seeing Rosetta again, but her trip to Abydos had been anything but normal. She glanced toward the stern, where Gavin stood speaking to Smedley who manned the rudder.

Her blood warmed at the sight of Gavin, tall and lean in his fawn-colored pants and cream shirt, his face and arms tanned from working in the sun. She now knew the rough feel of his hands when they moved over her body, knew the musky taste of his skin. The sound of his breathing when he slept. He'd been her lover for the last four days. Four incredible, heartbreakingly beautiful days. She wanted more, wanted a lifetime, but she wasn't foolish enough to think she'd get what she wanted. She'd bargained for "now" and now was all she had.

A sudden gust tore over the deck, pushing her off balance and reminding her that the time she and Gavin had stolen was almost at an end. If they managed to pass Saqqara without alerting Napoleon, they would have one more day together, two if she were lucky.

As if he'd heard her troubling thoughts, Gavin turned his dark gaze to her. His eyes were less guarded now, she realized, easier to read. His desire for her was clear and sharp, there for anyone to see if they cared to look. But there was remorse, as well. He knew, as did she, that they would have to say their good-byes soon. If only she could think of a way for them to stay together. Stow away on his ship as her mother had with Pop, tell Gavin she had noble blood in her veins after all. But neither would work. He was the Earth and she was the Moon. One couldn't exist in the other's world.

He crossed the rocking deck with ease, stopping so close she could feel the heat lifting off his skin, inhale the scent she had come to love.

"There's been no sign of Napoleon," he said, toying with the braid draping her chest.

His slight touch sent tingles racing over her skin. "I wish I knew if that was a good sign or bad."

"I'll take it as a good one." Tugging on her braid to draw her closer, he bent and brushed his lips across her temple and whispered, "I want to make love to you."

Mac drew a shaky breath. Her Pop was napping near the stern, Connor was at the bow on the lookout for French patrols and Jake and Sarah were adding details to their drawings. She and Gavin were in plain view of them all, yet she couldn't make herself care. Every minute with Gavin, every touch, was precious.

He'd made love to her early that morning, long before the sun stole over the horizon. Her body still hummed with the aftereffects, and her blood began to warm and pulse, in preparation for loving him again. Perhaps the constant ache never faded because she knew their time was so short. But she didn't think so. She just wanted Gavin. Wanted, needed, loved. It was that simple. And that complicated.

"After we reach Rosetta," he said, trailing the tip of her braid along her jaw. "It could be several days before I find passage to England."

"That would be unfortunate," she lied.

"I may have to impose on you and your father's hospitality a while longer."

She gripped his wrist, giving in to the desperate need to touch him. "We may have to renegotiate our contract, but I'm sure we can come to some agreement."

He didn't smile as she'd expected. "It could be dangerous. With Napoleon—"

"I've evaded the French general before. You shouldn't worry about us."

"You . . ." He stiffened, folded his arms across his chest and scowled at her. "What do you mean, you've evaded the French general before?"

Since their relationship had changed, she realized it was pointless to keep her reason for leaving Rosetta a secret. But she still didn't want to tell him, knowing the protective beast would raise his snarling head again. "It was nothing."

"Only a fool would call any kind of involvement with Napoleon 'nothing.'"

She tried to turn away, but he caught her arm and

demanded, "Tell me what happened, or I'll pry it out of your father."

She glanced at Willie sleeping on a pad of blankets. His face was pale, with a pasty tint she didn't like. The last thing he needed was to be badgered by Gavin.

"Fine," she said, turning back to him. "You already know that Napoleon has hired every crew he can find to dig up Egypt. Actually, 'hired' is too ambiguous for what he's done. The Egyptians who work for him don't do so voluntarily."

"I'm aware of that. There wasn't a crew left to be hired, which is what ultimately led me to Willie. Did Napoleon try to hire you, as well?"

"Not try. He did."

"Is that so?" Gavin said on a dangerous hiss.

"Actually, we were to report to him the day after we left with you."

A muscle pulsed in his jaw and a steel edge sharpened his gaze, reminding her of the man she'd first met. In a deceivingly gentle voice, he asked, "And when you didn't report to him, what do you think he did?"

She shrugged. "It doesn't matter. Pop and I had already agreed that we wouldn't help him find the *pshent.*"

"And so you think he forgot all about you and went on his way?"

"He had more than enough workers."

"Why didn't you tell me about this before?"

Not caring for the scolding tone, she crossed her arms over her chest and returned his scowl. "It didn't concern you."

"It most certainly did. He could have sent patrols searching for you."

"He didn't."

"How can you be so sure?"

"He's obsessed with Saqqara. He wouldn't concern himself with one missing crew."

"That doesn't explain why you didn't tell me."

"As I said. It didn't concern you."

Catching hold of her braid again, he wrapped the length around his fist. "Be honest, Mac. You didn't tell me because you didn't want me to know you needed me as much, if not more than I needed you."

She tilted her chin, determined to be as obstinate as he was being, but she couldn't do it. The frustrating man had come too close to the truth. She allowed a mischievous smile. "You're absolutely right. I did need you then."

"Not telling me was a foolish risk."

Ignoring his reprimand, she took hold of his shirt-front, and drew him close until her breasts brushed his chest. "And I need you now."

A growl rumbled from deep inside his throat. "You can't change the subject that easily. Napoleon could still be a threat to you."

"If he is, I'll deal with him."

"Damn it, Mac."

"Kiss me, Gavin."

He glared down at her for a moment, then said, "Everyone will see."

"Kiss me."

Thrusting his hand into her hair, he pressed his lips to hers in a searing kiss that left her wanting more. Then he said, "Whether you like it or not, I'm going to protect you for as long as I'm able."

And how long will that be, she wanted to ask. One day? Two? Ten? It wouldn't be enough. Not nearly enough.

* * *

"This is the last place I should leave the crown." Gavin held the *pshent* in the crook of his arm, reluctant to give it up.

"There's no place safer," Mac said, tugging the crown away from him and placing it in a bucket. Holding the rope tied to the handle, she lowered it down into the well.

"I was referring to it being here, in your home." He leaned over the mud brick wall encasing the dark hole and fisted his hands in frustration. "Though in a bloody water well is no better."

"Should anyone try to pillage my home, which is unlikely considering how many people live here, they'd never think to search for valuables outside. And since you and I are the only ones who know that it's here, our hiding place couldn't be any safer."

She had a point, but that didn't mean he liked it. Ever since she'd told him about her involvement with Napoleon he'd wanted to hide her away, in a place as dark and safe as the well. She thought she could take care of herself, and in many ways she had proven she could. But not against someone like the French general, who was as ruthless as he was determined.

"It seems I have no other choice at the moment." He glanced around the deserted courtyard, noting the date palms and palmettos as he had the first time he'd visited her home. The poinciana's red blooms were struggling to reach for the sun. And in the center of the lush garden Mac had created, a single lotus flower drew the eye with the power of a fallen star.

Half of her crew had stayed behind to secure the feluccas, while others had gone into town for supplies. Willie and Kippie had hurried off to check on the repairs being made to *Little Bess*. Everything was quiet, peaceful, yet he couldn't shake his unease.

He told her, "Still, I want the crown away from you by tomorrow."

"You shouldn't worry so much," she said, releasing the rope after it stretched taut.

"And you should worry more." Then, more to himself than her, he said, "Once I've secured passage to England, I'll move the *pshent.*"

Mac didn't respond and kept her gaze fastened on the well, but he saw the slight tensing of her shoulders. He lifted his hand to touch her, assure her that everything would work out for the best. But that would be a lie. As soon as he located a ship, he would leave, and would probably never see her again. He'd known this moment was coming, had prepared himself to walk away from her. But the reality didn't seem right. He had to leave; staying wasn't possible. They both knew that, so why the hell did he feel like a wretch?

"Mac."

"Do you think Connor, Jake and Sarah have had any luck finding a ship?" She faced him, her eyes overly bright and her smile strained.

A hollow ache tightened his chest. From the moment he'd met her, Mac had been unafraid to face anything, yet she seemed unwilling to discuss what would happen next. "You know I wish I could stay."

Her smile wavered. "And I wish I could go. But neither can be."

He pulled her to him, buried his face in the silkiness of her hair. "Damn it, Mac."

She kissed him lightly on his mouth, then looked at him as if nothing else mattered in the world. "We bargained for now, Gavin. Make love to me now."

He heard the plea in her voice, as if this might be their last time together. He swore it wouldn't be. He would return to Egypt. He had to, because he didn't want to lose her, or the incredible things he felt for her. He never thought he'd trust another woman again, but somehow, over the past few weeks, he'd come to trust Mac . . . with his life, his soul. His heart. But he didn't simply trust her, he realized with startling awareness. He loved her. The kind of love he hadn't thought himself capable of.

The kind of love that could complete him.

Or completely destroy him.

He lifted her in his arms, earning a surprised gasp and a smile. Crossing the sunny courtyard, he carried her into the cool shadows of the house, savoring the weight of her in his arms, the pressure of her breasts against his chest, the possessive feel of her hands around his neck.

"It's broad daylight, you know," she said and kissed the line of his jaw.

"If you're suggesting we wait until nightfall, I'm afraid you're out of luck."

"What if Jake or Connor return with news?"

He reached her room, a small space crowded with bits of pottery and urns, treasures she'd collected over the years, and kicked the door closed. "They can wait."

"What about Pop and Kippie?" she said, stretching like a spoiled cat after he laid her on the soft covers of her bed. "They'll want to tell me about the repairs to *Little Bess.*"

He captured one taut breast, felt her nipple hardened beneath his palm. "No one's coming through your door until I've made love to you. Several times."

She laughed, a deep smoky sound that coiled through his body like heat. She was bewitching him, he decided, weaving a spell around his mind and heart until all he could think about was her.

"The first time I saw you," he said. "I thought you were a gypsy."

She ran her fingers through his hair and smiled her secretive, knowing smile. "Do you think me one still?"

"I have to wonder if you haven't worked some kind of magic on me."

"This is Egypt. The air is full of magic."

Pushing the panels of her shirt aside, he exposed her breasts, the satiny soft skin, the rose-tipped nipples that begged for his kiss. He gave in to the need, filled his mouth with her sweet taste and shuddered in relief. He swore he heard her purr.

He filled his hands with her, touched every part he could reach. Tasted every inch he exposed. Within moments their clothes were gone. He didn't recall removing them, but now they were skin to skin, heat to heat. His body covering hers, fitting as if they'd been carved from the same piece of stone.

Then, with a deep, soul-shattering moan, he was inside her. His mind spun for an instant, and he thought his body would crumble from the sheer force of ecstasy flowing through his veins. Passion and desire bled into something bigger, something he couldn't name. But he knew its source.

This is what it feels like to be with a woman you love. A bond that went beyond physical. A linking of lives and souls so rare, the beauty of it shook him.

Her eyes glazed and her mouth parted as she moved against him, urged him closer, as if calling him home.

"My God." Threading his fingers with hers, he moved their joined hands above her head. She was exposed to him, completely open, giving herself to him without fear or doubt.

She loved him. And God help him, he was falling deeper and deeper in love with her, too.

The realization should frighten him, he thought with a distant part of his mind. And perhaps tomorrow it would. But right now, feeling her wet heat, her trembles, seeing every emotion he felt reflected in her eyes, loving her didn't frighten him at all.

Chapter 18

The herd of goats appeared from nowhere, nearly knocking Mac off her feet. She sidestepped the ones in the lead, then flattened herself against the wall of a house as the stragglers darted past. A boy of ten or twelve trailed the skittish animals, his attention more on kicking a stone than on his task of herding.

She quickly checked to make sure the hood of her *galabiya* was secured around her head. Already she'd passed three groups of French soldiers racing through the streets. She'd managed to blend in with the crowd and escape notice, but if Gavin learned she'd left her house to visit the market, she knew he would become furious. If she ran into any trouble, he just might become violent.

Muttering under her breath, she shook her head. He still didn't understand that she could take care of herself. And though his continued skepticism chafed her pride, she caught herself smiling. In a strange way, it was comforting to have someone worrying about her.

Which was why she'd had to leave the house without his knowledge.

He'd made love to her, for hours, in the glorious sunlight where every touch and kiss had seared a memory in her mind. They would undoubtedly still be locked away in her room if Jake, Connor and Sarah hadn't returned with news that they'd found a ship. A ship that would sail in two days.

Two days. Mac closed her eyes as an echo of the despair she'd felt at that moment filled her with cold, leaving her hollow inside, shivery and panicked. The need to race to the harbor, where Gavin and his friends were even now buying passage and making the final arrangements to load their cargo nearly overwhelmed her. She even took a step toward the harbor, but caught her mistake. She couldn't beg him to stay, or ask him to take her with him. That wasn't their agreement.

Drawing a deep breath, forcing her nerves to calm, she glanced down at the basket in her hands. It was filled with the ingredients for the meal she would make everyone tonight. Everyone except her Pop and crew. Nothing in the world would budge them from their traditional English diets.

But for Gavin, she wanted to make a special meal to celebrate their last nights together. *Sanyet batates,* a spicy Egyptian stew prepared with lamb, vegetables and a healthy amount of *habahan.* She had mashed fava beans and *shammy* bread to eat it with, and *torshi,* a bright pink vegetable that was prettier than it was tasty. And wine from the Delta, a northern region of Egypt. She'd had the fine wines from France, but nothing compared to those made in the Delta, where each bottle was as sweet and pure as honey.

Emerging from an alley, she turned on to her street, and was surprised to find it empty in the middle of the day. Normally there would be women returning home from shopping, their baskets full, men laden with bales of flax or carts and drivers going about their business. But there was no one, not even a member of her crew sitting out front, smoking a pipe. Though she hadn't really expected to see them. After weeks in the desert, they would finish their chores then head for their favorite pub on the edge of town.

But the vacant street didn't hold her attention for long. Her thoughts circled back to Gavin, as they had since the day she'd met him. Who would have thought the scowling, angry man she'd been so leery of would be the same man to capture her heart?

Capture it and break it, she thought. *But I have no one to blame except myself.* She'd known she was in love with him when she'd led him to the pottery field. She'd known she would make love to him, just as she'd known she was destined to lose him.

Her goal to make every moment she spent with him count hadn't changed. And neither had Gavin's, she thought with a frown. Regardless of what they shared, or how deeply he cared about her, nothing would stop him from returning to England. They'd avoided discussing his plans, but she knew him well enough to know he intended to present the crown to King George. She imagined he would then return to his life at his grand estate, attend balls and teas. Now that he had put his guilt and anger aside about his deceased wife and son, perhaps he might even begin searching for the next Lady Blackwell.

Everything inside her rebelled at the idea of Gavin marrying someone else, smiling, laughing, making love. Having children.

Reaching the wooden gate that led to her courtyard, she shoved open the heavy doors and stomped inside, but she came to a halt and sighed, irritated that she had allowed herself to become irritated.

"Don't do this to yourself," she whispered.

Gavin was destined to leave, and he might remarry

one day. Those were things she couldn't control. They only had two days left. She refused to let anything, including her fears, spoil them.

She was halfway through the lush garden when she hesitated, realizing something wasn't right. The palmettos and date palms swayed in the heated breeze. But that wasn't what caught her attention. The once lush jacaranda and poincianas lay flattened on the ground, crushed as if they'd been trampled. Something, or someone had snapped her precious lotus flower in half, then stomped it into the earth. Rocks were overturned, and the sand was kicked up, as if horses had been turned loose to run.

She started toward the house, her nerves humming in warning. She wanted to run, but common sense forced her to move slowly, listen for any sounds out of place. Hearing nothing unusual, she touched the hilt of the dagger at her waist with one hand and pushed the front door open with the other. She gasped, her heart leaping to her throat. Her fingers went numb, and the basket of food dropped to the floor.

"Dear God." She drew her dagger and moved quietly into the room, her eyes darting from one scene of wreckage to another.

The low-backed couch lay on its side. Two box chairs had been hacked into splinters. Rush mats had been kicked aside, and the faded oriental screen still stood upright, but the fabric had been slashed beyond repair. Circling the room, Mac saw Pop's favorite oil painting of an English countryside. She picked up the picture by the snapped frame and blinked in disbelief. Her mother had painted this picture, she thought with a sense of helplessness, as a reminder of where she and Pop had met. Long, ugly slashes crisscrossed the canvas, destroying the picture. Mac dropped it and moved on, her boots crunching the shattered china knickknacks and broken clay vases.

"Who did this?" She pressed one hand to her brow. "Dear God, who could have done this?"

She didn't have a chance to think of an answer. At that moment she spotted someone, a man, lying on the floor, partially hidden behind the couch. She leapt over the debris and knelt. Sheathing her dagger, she took the man by the shoulder and gently turned him over.

Kippie's head lolled to the side, revealing a wicked gash at his temple. Blood streaked part of his face and pooled on the floor. A bruise already purpled his right eye. His lips were split and caked with drying blood.

She felt the side of his neck for a pulse, her fingers trembling so badly she couldn't find it. "Kippie, please, say something. Tell me you're all right."

He didn't move, and she didn't feel a beat. Tears blurred her vision and she couldn't breathe. "Kippie, don't you dare die on me. Please," she begged, her voice whisper thin. "Please wake up."

Still nothing. Removing her cloak, she used the hood to wipe blood from his face. The gash on his temple was wide, but since the bleeding had slowed, she didn't think it was too deep. She tried to find his pulse again, praying as she did, then sobbed when she felt it, slow and faint.

"Kippie," she said, examining his arms and chest for broken bones and whispering a prayer of thanks when she didn't find any. "Can you hear me?"

His eyes moved behind his closed lids, but he didn't answer.

She glanced into the ravaged room behind her, terrified and furious. Who had done this, and why? And were they still here? She had to get him out of there, find some place safe where she could care for him. "Kippie, wake up. Talk to me! Please, wake up."

"Blimey," he said, the words hoarse and slurred. He brought a hand up to his brow. "Stop all your shoutin' so a man can think."

She stared at him, tears running down her face. "Kippie, how badly are you hurt?"

"Can't rightly tell," he said weakly. "Someone's usin' my head as a drum."

"Who did this to you?" She helped him into a sitting position and had to catch him by the shoulders when he nearly toppled sideways to the floor.

"Leave me be, girl. I can sit up on my own."

"Of course you can," she lied as she propped him against the side of the couch. "I'm just frightened is all. Now tell me. What happened?"

"I need a drink."

"Later, tell me now."

"I need a drink, girl. And yer gonna need one too, after I finish tellin' ye what happened."

Mac hesitated only a second before dashing to her father's room where she knew he kept a flask hidden. She didn't let herself stop and consider the destruction to his room, or any of the others she passed. Every one of them had been ransacked, completely destroyed. She couldn't think about them now. She had to focus on Kippie.

Handing him the flask, she bit down on her bottom lip as she waited for him to down a drink that would settle his nerves. "I thank God ye weren't here, Mackenzie. If ye had been, it would've been bad."

She glanced from his bruised and bleeding face to her pillaged home. "And this isn't?"

"Not as bad as it could 'ave been. Though it isn't over."

"You think whoever did this will come back?" Tensing, she searched the room, her hand going back to her dagger once more.

He looked at her through one bloodshot eye; the other was swollen shut. "No, they won't be back."

"How can you be so sure?"

"'Cause he gave me a message tae give tae ye."

"He?" she asked, feeling a cold, cold chill creep up her spine.

"Aye. The bloody French general himself was here."

Mac sat back on her heels, knew the blood had drained from her face because the room spun and for the first time in her life, she thought she might faint. "Napoleon was here?"

"'E knows about the *pshent*. Don't ask me how he found out about it. Maybe one of the boys said something he shouldn't 'ave down at the pub, but—"

"It doesn't matter how he found out," Mac interrupted, her thoughts racing furiously. She had to find Gavin. If Napoleon knew she had found the *pshent*, it stood to reason he would also know that Gavin was involved. If so, she was certain the French general would go after him next.

Her heart pounding, she pushed to her feet. She had to reach the harbor before he left. She couldn't wait for him to return. For all she knew, French soldiers might be watching her house, preparing an ambush.

"I have to find Gavin, Kippie. Will you be all right?"

He caught her wrist and forced her to kneel. "That's not the all of it, Mackenzie."

Afraid to take a breath or speak, she nodded for him to continue.

"He wanted tae know where the *pshent* was." Kippie sent a scowl around the room. "Didn't believe us when we said we had no bloomin' idea. That was a smart idea ye had, hidin' the crown so no one else would know its whereabouts."

"We? You said we. Is someone else hurt?" The words died as she remembered that Pop had been with Kippie, inspecting *Little Bess*. "Pop!" she called out, frantic. "Pop, answer me. Where are you?"

"'E ain't 'ere." Kippie held up his other hand. The gold pendant of a falcon on a beaded chain of jade and onyx dangled from his fist. "'E's gone."

"Is . . . is he all right?" she said, trying to stay calm, but fear bubbled up through her body. She reached for the amulet, afraid to touch it. Pop never took it off. "Was he hurt?"

"No worse than me, I'd guess."

"Where is he?"

"Napoleon 'as him."

The breath left Mac's lungs in a rush. She doubled over as if she'd been punched in the gut. Sinking to her knees, she fought back tears, tried to think straight. But she couldn't. She couldn't! Napoleon had her father! Dear God. What was she going to do? *Pop* . . .

"That blasted Frenchman only left me alive so I could give ye a message," Kippie said, swigging another drink of whiskey, then squeezing his eyes closed and wincing in pain. Hissing out a breath, he told her, "Said he'd be willing tae make a trade. If ye bring the *pshent* tae his palace in France, Tuileries 'e called it, 'e'd give yer father back tae ye."

"Tuileries. Why there? Why would he leave Egypt now?"

Kippie laughed, the sound raw and bitter. "Could 'ave something tae do with the rumors I heard about the British Navy closin' in tae retake the ports in Alexandria and Rosetta."

Standing, Mac paced, tried to think of a plan, but

she already knew what she had to do. "Will you be all right on your own for a while, Kippie?"

"Where are ye goin'?"

"I have to warn Gavin."

"Why?"

"I still have the crown." She glanced out the front doors to the well. "Or at least I think I do. We need a plan before we face Napoleon to make an exchange."

"After everything Lord Blackwell went through to find the *pshent*, do ye think he'll just let ye hand it tae Napoleon?"

Mac stared at her old friend, unable to answer. She wanted to say yes, that Gavin, the man she loved, would sacrifice the crown, sacrifice anything, the same as she would, to save her father.

But would he? Did he care about her enough? She wanted to believe he would. But to her despair, she wasn't sure.

The harbor teemed with people, donkey-driven carts, crates of goods being loaded onto ships or waiting for transfer to a distant town further up the Nile. The smells of rotting food, dead fish and too many bodies made breathing a sickening effort. As rancid as they were, Mac barely noticed. Her heart raced against her chest, her hands were sweaty and cold, and a tremor born of fear ran through her limbs.

Never in her life had she been so frightened, or felt so helpless. She darted through the crowd, frantic to reach Gavin in time. *He has to be all right. Please God, let him be safe.* If he had been captured or hurt . . . She couldn't finish the thought. As soon as she found him, he would help her plan a way to rescue her father. She'd never asked for help before; she'd never needed to, but she'd never faced a threat like this. Everything she did, she did to keep her father safe and happy. And now she'd failed. Pop was in greater danger than any of them had ever imagined. If the voyage to France didn't kill him, Napoleon just might.

She raced through the crowd, darting around the people blocking her way until, finally, she saw the mud brick building where Gavin was to meet the captain of the ship he'd bought passage on. She stepped inside and had to pause a moment to let her eyes adjust to the dark interior.

Blinking, she eased forward when she heard voices. As her vision cleared, she realized she was in an outer office, and the voices, Jake and Connor if she weren't mistaken, were coming from another room to her left. She couldn't see them, only a bookcase crowded with ledgers and scrolls. Hurrying toward the doorway, she started to call out when something they said stopped her in her tracks.

"Everything's set then," Connor said, his voice a low rumble in the other room. "We leave tonight at dusk."

Tonight? Mac staggered back a step, her hand going to her mouth in shock. *They can't leave tonight!* She needed their help.

"Gavin," Sarah said with a remorseful sigh. "What about Mac? She'll be devastated when she hears we're leaving so soon."

"I know," he said. The two words were abrupt, even irritated. "But it can't be helped."

"Why don't you ask her to come with you?" This came from Jake. "Consider it a holiday."

"She won't leave Egypt," Gavin said.

"But if you ask," Sarah began.

"Enough! All of you." Mac could envision Gavin

pacing and glaring at his friends. "My relationship with Mac is none of your concern."

"We donna want tae see the lass hurt," Connor said.

"Neither do I, but we have no choice but to leave tonight. If we delay, who knows when we'll be able to leave or who will control this port after the British Navy confronts the French."

"We wouldn't really be in any danger if we stayed longer," Sarah said. "Jake and I could use the time to document the artifacts we brought from King Menes' tomb."

"Considering how many French patrols are swarming into Rosetta, I'm surprised we haven't been captured or killed already," Gavin said, the truth of his statement enough to stop any further arguments. "We can't risk a delay. As it is, we barely have enough time to get everything loaded before we sail."

"Connor and I can take the crown to London. Give you some time to settle things here," Jake offered.

"And break my word to the King? You know me better than that."

"But to leave Mac behind—" Sarah tried again.

"What Mac and I had belongs in the desert, not in England," Gavin said in such a harsh tone, Mac shivered.

What they'd "*had.*" With a sick feeling in the pit of her stomach, she realized he'd already put his feelings for her in the past. The room spun and she thought she might be sick. She had to get out of there. Not needing to hear any more, she quietly retraced her steps, slipped out of the office and into the busy street. Tears flooded her eyes, and her body was tight with gut-wrenching pain as she stood there, unsure of what to do.

He's leaving tonight. Did he even plan to say good-bye?

It didn't matter, she decided as she moved blindly

through the harbor. Taking the crown to England was all that mattered to Gavin; he wouldn't stay long enough to help her rescue her father.

But if I tell him, perhaps it would make a difference.

She laughed at her own foolishness. In order for Gavin to save Pop, he'd have to relinquish the *pshent* to Napoleon. And that he would never do.

Which meant she had no one to rely on but herself. A cold chill ran through her limbs as she considered the overwhelming odds of successfully negotiating with Napoleon and escaping alive.

Hurrying her steps, she pushed through the crowd. She had no more time to waste. Gavin meant to sail by dusk, which meant she had to leave before then.

She had to hurry, because if he learned what she intended to do, he would try to stop her. And she had no intention of giving him the chance to try.

Gavin stood outside the mud brick wall and stared at the oak doors to Mac's home. The wind blew warm against his skin. It smelled of the sun and sand, a crisp dry scent he'd always hated. Or had, until he'd met Mac and she'd shown him how magical the desert could be.

He would miss that smell, he realized, and the heat and the blazing sun, but not as much as he would miss the woman.

Dreading what he had to do, he briefly closed his eyes, felt his heart hammer against his chest. They'd both known this moment would come, but he'd thought, he'd hoped, they'd have a little more time.

He pushed the door open. They couldn't have lived a lifetime in two days, but he'd wanted them regardless. Now fate had stolen even that. The British Royal Navy was sailing into the Mediterranean Sea in a strategic move to overtake Napoleon's ships. War was inevitable. Perhaps his friends were right; he should take Mac and her crew with him. They wouldn't be safe in Rosetta. He could easily imagine her response. Her chin would tilt at a stubborn angle, and she would undoubtedly tell him she could take care of herself.

He shook his head, wanting to curse. Facing Napoleon might be easier than forcing Mac to leave.

Then stay. He wanted to, more than he'd thought possible. Yet giving the crown to King George wasn't a duty he could dismiss. But that didn't mean he had to remain in England. There was nothing, and no one, to keep him there. And there was every reason to return to Egypt. But what to do about Mac in the meantime?

If she refused to travel with him, then he had to convince her to leave Rosetta until the fighting was over. He didn't like that idea any better. She needed him.

And I need to be with her.

Even if he could leave her on her own, which went against everything he believed in, he wasn't ready to say good-bye. Even temporarily. Because he loved her.

He stopped at the outer gate, stunned by his realization.

He loved her; she made him feel things he hadn't dreamed possible. Did he really want to walk away from what they had, without knowing how deep their feeling for each other could go?

Knowing he didn't, that he wanted Mac more than he'd wanted anything in too long to remember, he entered the garden and called, "Mac, I need—"

The words froze in his throat. His heartbeat leaped into a frantic rhythm. Instinctively, he pulled his pistol from his belt beneath his robes.

"Bloody hell," he ground out as he backed up against a wall. The colorful plants had been ripped from the ground and trampled. The once neatly groomed walkway of sandy dirt had been kicked up, as if there had been a fight. His heart in his throat he moved into the house, already knowing what he'd see. Looking through the doorway he saw furniture overturned and smashed to pieces. Trinkets and paintings, vases and chairs all lay in ruin.

He wanted to call out, but didn't dare. When everything remained silent, he eased further into the room, searching every shadow and corner as he went. When he reached the couch, he spotted a stain on the sanded wood floor and knelt. A deadly chill raised the hair at his nape when he realized what it was. Blood, dried blood.

"Dear God, Mac." Fear pushed through him so fast and so viciously he was momentarily blinded. He couldn't breathe. He'd made her promise not to leave the house without him. And now she might be hurt, or worse. She might be . . . He couldn't finish the thought.

"God, please, let her be all right."

Hearing something creak behind him, Gavin whirled around, pistol aimed and ready to fire.

"Hold on now!" Kippie shouted, then hissed and pressed his palms to his head.

"Jesus," Gavin said, sagging in relief. When the old man began to sway, Gavin caught his arm and held him upright. "You've been hurt."

"Ain't nothin'." But he didn't protest when Gavin righted the couch and helped him sit.

Kneeling before the old sailor, Gavin demanded, "What happened?"

"Got ambushed, that's what. I should 'ave seen it

comin' but I didn't." He sighed, the sound more weary than Gavin had thought the energetic man capable of producing. "Guess I'm gettin' old."

"Where's Mac, Kippie?" Gavin asked, glancing at the bloodstain on the floor and feeling his own blood drain from his face.

"That be mine," he said, following his gaze. Then he tapped the side of his head where someone had haphazardly wrapped a white bandage around it. "They done this."

"Who?" Gavin asked, gently probing the man's swollen black eye, only to have his hand swatted away.

"Napoleon Bonaparte, that's who. Ye were right tae worry about that bugger. He knows ye 'ave the crown."

Gavin thought he'd been afraid before, but it didn't compare to the ice that ran through him now. "Does Mac know?"

Kippie looked away, pursed his lips without answering.

Gavin frowned. "Where is she?

The old man blew out a deep breath.

The nerves along his spine tingling, he gripped Kippie by his bony upper arms and demanded, "Talk to me. Does she know Napoleon was here?"

"She knows."

"And? Where is she?"

Kippie looked at Gavin with his one good eye. "Gone."

"She fled the city?" Even as he said it, he knew she wouldn't have left one of her family behind, wounded at that. "Where did she go?"

"I can't be tellin' ye that."

Gavin didn't know what kind of game Kippie was playing, but he wasn't going to tolerate it. Barely resisting the urge to shake the old man, he growled, "Damn it, tell me where she is."

The sailor studied Gavin for a moment, his expression changing from a scowl to a thoughtful frown. "If I tell ye, ye have tae promise me one thing."

"Name it."

With a shrewd glint in his eyes, he said, "Ye take me with ye when ye leave Egypt."

He couldn't believe the old man would want to leave Mac and Willie, but at the moment he'd promise anything. "Done. Now where is she?"

"I suppose she's on *Little Bess* about now."

"Her ship?"

"Yep."

"She's sailing away from Egypt and she left you behind?"

"Thought I was too hurt to make the trip, the fool girl. I done told her she won't make it without me, but did she listen?" He sniffed. "She did not."

"Where, Kippie? Where is she sailing to?"

"Tae France, ye halfwit. Where else do ye think?"

"Why in God's name would she . . ." As the realization sank in, Gavin couldn't form another word.

"Ah," Kippie said, nodding. "I see ye understand which way the wind blows. I told her she was makin' a mistake, givin' the *pshent* to Napoleon. But she didn't listen."

Gavin couldn't believe it, refused to believe it. *Mac is going to give the* pshent *to Napoleon?* He shook his head, tried to tell Kippie that she wouldn't deceive him, but he couldn't utter the words. He rose and blindly walked outside to the well in her garden.

Pulling the rope, he drew up the bucket, praying that his worst fear wasn't about to come true, that Mac, the woman he loved, hadn't betrayed him.

When the rusty pail finally came into view, he stared at it, willing the image before him to change. "Mac, what have you done?"

But he knew. He already knew.

Because the bucket was empty and she was gone.

Chapter 19

"I'm not likin' this." Hollister ran his big palm over the gray stubble on his chin, his expression set in a sneer.

"Aye." Frewin nodded, glaring at the soot gray clouds rolling over the city. "There be a bad smell here. Like something up and died."

"Nah, that'd be greed and deceit yer smellin'," Smedley mused, then spit over the rail of the ship. "Paris didn't stink like this before they executed Louis XVI. That's what 'appens when ye have a Revolution."

"Aye, yet get schemers like Napoleon runnin' the country," Frewin agreed.

Mac paced the deck of *Little Bess* and tried to ignore her crew's grumbling comments. They were nervous, and more than leery of her plan. She didn't blame them. She didn't like what she had to do any more than they did, but she had no choice.

Just like she'd had no choice when she'd taken King Menes' *pshent* from the well.

A chill skittered over her spine, as it did every time she thought about Gavin and his reaction when he learned what she'd done. She could easily imagine his fury, and knew he would feel betrayed.

Any caring, any glimmer of love he might have felt

for her would have been destroyed the moment he realized she had taken the crown.

But I had to. Yet no matter how many times she told herself she'd made the right choice, the pain in her heart never lessened. She'd betrayed Gavin's trust, taken the crown without first asking for his help. Even now, she wished she could go back to that day at the harbor and tell him Napoleon had demanded the crown for her father's life.

But if somehow, fate or life, or the Gods were able to spin her back through time, giving her the chance to relive that moment, she knew she'd make the same choice. She had no doubt Gavin would have helped her rescue Pop, but would he have given up the crown to gain Willie's freedom?

She didn't know, and the risk had been too great to take. So she'd taken the *pshent* and fled. And for two weeks, she'd lived with the fear that she might never see her father again, and the certainty that she'd never see Gavin.

"'Tis near dusk," Hollister said, joining her at the bow. "Are ye sure ye don't want tae wait until morning?"

"And let Pop spend another night at Napoleon's mercy?" She shivered and ran her hands over her arms. Despite the humid night air, she hadn't been warm since she'd left Egypt.

"I don't mind tellin' ye," Smedley said, straightening his lanky body. "I don't like this plan of yours."

"So you've said," she answered tightly. "Every day we've been at sea."

"Then maybe ye should listen," the old sailor suggested. "There 'as tae be another way."

"There isn't." She looked at her crew, their aged faces possessing more lines than they had only a few days ago. "If there was another way to save Pop, I'd gladly try it."

Smedley scowled. "But tae go tae Napoleon alone, without us tae help ye."

"No. We've been through this." She crossed to the starboard side of the ship. At the rope ladder, she lifted the satchel containing the *pshent* and prepared to climb down.

"Ye've always known what tae do, Mackenzie," Hollister said, catching her arm and forcing to halt her descent to the dinghy waiting below. "But this time yer wrong."

She looked up, fear and worry tempting her to snap at her friends. But one look at their faces stopped her. All three men were given to laughter, a glint of joy always lighting their eyes. Now they wore matching frowns. Anxiety darkened their gazes and deepened the creases at their temples.

She looked beyond the three men and saw the rest of her crew gathered close, their expressions grim. A knot of tears tightened her throat. Every one of them were her family. She loved them as much as she loved her father. She'd already failed to protect Pop; she would not risk their lives any more than she already had.

"If I'm not back by morning," she said, "you're to sail for London."

"Bloody hell, we will," Frewin growled, pacing the deck on his stocky legs. "We'll not leave ye here."

"You will." She gave each of them a faint smile. "Promise me."

"No, Mackenzie," Frewin said with an adamant shake of his head. "Ye ask too much."

Mac sighed. She didn't have time to argue with them. "I'm the captain of this ship, and I expect my orders to be obeyed."

"Yer orders usually make sense," Smedley grumbled.

"I can't do this if I have to worry about all of you. Please," she pleaded, briefly closing her eyes when they clouded with tears. "Promise me you'll leave if I'm not back with the dawn."

All three of them opened their mouths to argue, but she shook her head, stopping them. "This is the way it has to be."

Smedley muttered a curse, Hollister ran his weathered hand through his hair and Frewin pursed his lips as if he were in deep thought.

"Wish me luck," she said.

"Yer gonna need it, girl," Hollister said reluctantly. "All we got and more tae spare."

"This isn't gonna work." Frewin stepped toward the ladder, looking as if he intended to bodily lift Mac up and lock her in the hold. "Yer risking yer life, girl. Willie wouldn't want that."

"I know what I'm doing," she assured them, but her heart pounded against her chest.

Had she truly known what she was doing, Willie's life wouldn't be in jeopardy now. She'd been careless, arrogantly believing she could handle any situation.

Gavin had been right, she realized. She'd thought she could manage Napoleon. Now her overconfidence was demanding she pay a price.

Not only did it require she give up King Menes' crown for her father's freedom, but she also had to deceive the man she loved.

She started down the ladder again. Once in the dinghy, she gripped the satchel in her lap and stared unseeing at the distance shore as her two crewmen manned the oars.

I know what I'm doing, she repeated to herself, desperately wanting to believe it. But she was afraid that this time, she might be wrong.

Not only was she going to lose the *pshent*, she might not be able to save her father. She might even lose her own life.

Dying didn't frighten her so much. She risked her life every time she went into the desert, or stepped onto her ship.

But the thought of dying, knowing that Gavin must surely hate her, was more than she could bear.

The three-story façade of bleached stone stared down at her, daring her to walk between the rows of granite pillars that guarded the palace like stoic armed guards.

Mac's heart raced out of control; she could scarcely breathe. She'd never seen Tuileries Palace before. Passing through the arched entryway, her boots echoing against the marbled floor like the blast of a gun, she would have preferred to keep it that way.

A servant appeared from a side hallway. He didn't bow, but she hadn't expected him to. She wore her *galabiya*, the pants and tunic of soft cream wool, and her hair was tied back with a strip of leather. She could have dressed like a lady, she supposed, tried to appeal to Napoleon's chivalrous nature—assuming he had one.

But if she couldn't act the malleable lady for Gavin, she certainly wouldn't try for the general. Besides, she was here to rescue her father; what she wore didn't matter.

She gave the servant her name and told him Napoleon was expecting her. Ignoring his skeptical smirk, she held the satchel tighter and followed him through a series of passageways and adjoining rooms. The halls were adorned with life-sized portraits, the walls trimmed with gilt. Furnishings from the finest craftsman filled every room. But all she saw was a cold and foreboding prison that held her father.

Reaching a long assembly room lined with mirrors and crystal chandeliers, Mac came to an abrupt halt. She hadn't known what to expect when facing Napoleon, but she'd thought she would see him in a private office.

This room teemed with people. Dozens of men were dressed in military uniforms, others in fine silks and satins. Powder-faced women wore gowns with plunging necklines, revealing a shocking amount of their breasts. Jewels encased their throats and dangled from their ears.

She hesitated, even took a step in retreat. She might have noble blood, but in her heart she was Mackenzie Tuggle, the daughter of a sea captain. She didn't belong here. Now more than ever, she realized the differences between her and Gavin. She pushed thoughts of him aside with a muttered curse. She couldn't think about him now.

Gripping the satchel with both hands, she fought down the overwhelming need to flee. Pop was somewhere inside this horrible place, and she wasn't leaving without him.

Ignoring the shocked stares and disapproving comments, she made her way down the center of the room, searching for the Frenchman who held her father.

Suddenly, the crowd parted, and there he was. Sitting in a high-backed, red velvet chair as if it were a throne, Napoleon sipped from a golden chalice while listening intently to a man dressed in military garb. Her heart beat furiously and blood pulsed at her temples. As she approached the two men, she realized she'd never been more alone in her life. Or in more danger. But there was no turning back.

She stopped three feet away from the general and waited for him to notice her.

It took only a moment, and when he did, his small brown eyes widened and a gleeful smile split his mouth. Then he did something she hadn't expected. He threw his head back and laughed.

The buzz of conversation quieted as quickly as if a door had slammed shut, locking everyone out. But the milling crowd was still there; she felt their curious gazes drilling into her back.

"Well, this is a lovely surprise," Napoleon said in flowing English. His eyes sparkled with delight.

"Where's my father?" Mac asked, relieved her voice didn't tremble.

"You've arrived just in time," he said, ignoring her question. "My supporters are here to celebrate my return."

She bit her tongue to stop herself from asking if his "supporters" knew he'd fled Egypt and had left his army behind, abandoned. Sailing from Rosetta, she'd had to evade the French and British fleets preparing for battle. From what she'd seen of the Royal Navy, she doubted there was anything left of the French by now.

"I've done what you asked," she said. "Now, where's my father?"

"You have King Menes' *pshent?*" Napoleon's gaze flickered to her satchel.

She opened it and lifted the crown so he could see. Gasps echoed throughout the room. Mac knew how they felt; she experienced that same sense of awe every time she looked at it. Only now that she was about to hand it over to a monster, she felt ill.

Napoleon reached for it, but she stepped back. "My father."

He leaned back in his chair and chuckled, a small, humorless sound that made her skin crawl. "You want to see your father, and you shall."

He snapped his fingers once. Before Mac knew what was happening, two guards caught her by the arms, while a third took the *pshent* from her and handed it to the General.

"You made a bargain."

"So I did." He arched a brow. "But there is a rule I follow when making bargains. There is no need to honor them when dealing with spies."

"I'm no spy." Mac struggled to free herself, but the guards jerked her arms painfully behind her back.

"Ah, but I think you are. And what I think is all that matters, yes."

"You have the crown. Release my father and we'll go."

"I think not." He pursed his lips, then nodded to the guards. "The mademoiselle wishes to see her papa. Take her to him."

"You can't do this!"

"But I can. To show you how generous I can be, I shall allow the two of you to share a cell. That is until your trial."

A trial, in France? Dear God. She tried to twist out of the men's hold, but this time they wrenched her arms back until her shoulders burned and she cried out.

Gasping for breath, she told him, "You can't just lock us away. There are people who won't stand for it."

But even as she said the words, she knew she was on her own. Her crew would sail to England as she'd ordered them to. And even if they didn't, none of them had the power or contacts to negotiate their release.

"The world will thank me for ridding it of two desert rats such as you and your worthless sire." Napoleon stood and lifted the *pshent* with both hands.

An endless moment passed as he held it high so everyone in the room could see him. Then, with exaggerated solemnity, he lowered it onto his head. He closed his eyes a moment, a frightening smile twisting his lips.

As she watched, he seemed to transform, becoming bolder, taller, more menacing. Invincible.

Dear God, what have I done?

As if he'd heard her, Napoleon met Mac's horrified gaze. "Yes, I shall rid the world of the likes of you. Now that I wear the crown that once belonged to the greatest king who ever ruled, no one will be able to stop me."

"I'm callin' a halt to this insanity right now," Captain Muldrow growled.

"I've paid you well." Gavin checked his pistol, his fingers cold against the steel barrel.

"We're in bleedin' France." Snarling so he revealed his yellowed teeth, the burly captain muttered, "A lot of good your gold will do me if I'm too dead to spend it."

"If you and your ship aren't here when I return," Gavin warned, his voice no louder than the hiss from the nearby lantern. "I promise you'll have no further use of money, or a ship, or anything else, for that matter."

"Everyone's armed," Jake said, joining them where they waited on the starboard side of the ship. "We'll be ready to leave as soon as we hear from Connor."

"We've waited long enough." Gavin secured his pistol in his waistband. "I'm going to find her myself."

"And then what?" Kippie scowled, obviously still irritated that Gavin wouldn't allow him to accompany them. "How you gonna get Willie out of the palace?"

"That's not your concern," Gavin said. But so far, none of them had devised a feasible plan. Storming Tuileries Palace with a handful of men would be suicide. Napoleon wanted the *pshent*, and the Frenchman could have it as far as Gavin was concerned. He could always return with an army provided by King George and get it back.

But first he had to find Mac and stop her from trying to deal with the General herself.

Because no matter what it took, he had every intention of getting his hands on Mac again. First so he could kiss her, and second so he could wring the life out of her for not trusting him.

A scuffling noise from below the *Nightingale*'s railing drew his attention. A moment later, Connor's shaggy red head appeared, then the rest of him as he scaled the ladder.

"Have you learned anything," Sarah asked, clinging to Jake as if she were afraid to let him out of her sight. Gavin didn't blame her; they were in enemy territory.

"Plenty," Connor said, catching his breath. "And none of it you'll be likin'."

"You found out where she is?" Gavin asked, afraid to hope. For the past six hours, they'd been searching for her ship, without any luck.

"Aye." Connor turned toward the rail just as another head appeared. This one belonged to Hollister, who was soon followed by Smedley, then Frewin. He waited, his heart thundering against his chest, hoping beyond reason that Mac would be next, that the fear that had him by the throat would finally loosen its hold.

Once the three men were on deck, they stared at him with a mixture of suspicion and hope. Gavin looked over the rail, praying he would see Mac. But there was only a single crewman from the *Nightingale* in the dinghy below.

He rounded on them. "Where is she?"

"She's, ah, not with us." Frewin shifted uneasily, his gaze dropping to his scuffed boots.

"Then where has she gone?"

"Ah . . ." The three men exchanged worried looks.

"I should string each one of you up for bringing Mac here."

Hollister's head came up, his mouth curling with a snarl. "Do ye think we wanted tae let our girl face Napoleon?"

"If we didn't bring her, she would have found another way," Smedley complained. "Nothin' stops that girl once her mind's made up."

Frewin added, "And Willie is one of us. Did ye expect us tae let 'im rot in a cell? In France, of all the miserable places?"

"I would have expected you to come to me." Gavin studied each man's wary gaze. "I would have helped you."

"Ye would have given up the crown?" Frewin challenged.

"Yes." Gavin bit the word out, furious that they would doubt him.

"Ye say that now." Smedley crossed his arms over his narrow chest. "But how would we 'ave known?"

"I suppose you'll never know for sure." But Gavin knew the truth. The instant he'd realized what Mac had done, he would have given up anything, his title, his home, whatever necessary to have her back. To have the chance to help her and her family.

Since the moment he'd met her, he'd battled the overwhelming need to protect her, keep her safe. Now she was in the hands of the most devious, manipulative man Gavin had ever known. And all because she hadn't trusted him enough to come to him first. That knowledge tore through him. She'd said she loved him, but she obviously hadn't loved him enough to believe in him.

"Enough of this," he barked, causing everyone to flinch. "Where's Mac? I want to see her."

Frewin coughed, Smedley pursed his lips and Hollister blew out a weary breath, before saying, "She's at Tuileries Palace. From what we've heard, she's locked away with Willie."

Gavin's vision blurred. Blood pounded at his temple, the base of his skull. He gripped the railing as fear poured through him. "How long?"

"Two days. She ordered us tae sail tae London if she didn't return at dawn on the first day." Smedley shook his head. "We told her we'd leave. A lie tae be sure. There was no way we'd abandon her and Willie."

"You were right," Gavin told them. "We aren't leaving without them.

"How are we gonna get 'em?" Kippie demanded. "We still don't know how we're gonna get into the palace."

"We do," Hollister said with a slow grin.

"Aye," Smedley agreed with a matching smile.

"I've heard their idea," Connor broke in. "It probably won't work."

"'Ave a little faith," Frewin said, rubbing his beefy hands together.

"Let's hear it," Gavin said.

As the three men revealed their plan, Gavin shook his head in disbelief. Connor was right; it probably wouldn't work. But good or bad, it was all they had.

* * *

Carriages crowded the wide, graveled drive by the time they arrived. Blazing torches lined the front garden and stood like a regiment of soldiers down the awesome length of Tuileries Palace. Light and laughter poured from every window and door. Music floated on the air.

The coachmen and attendants took no notice of Gavin, Jake, Connor and the others as they passed. Nor did the armed guards patrolling the grounds. The muscles in his shoulders and back knotting with tension, Gavin walked to the main entrance as if he had every right to.

Offering a slight bow to the doorman, he said in perfect French, "We are here to relieve the musicians."

The doorman's fine brows dipped with a frown. "There must be some mistake. I am not aware of the need for a second orchestra."

Gavin shrugged. "We were hired to play tonight. The General does not wish a lapse in the music."

"I have heard no such thing." His mouth pursed with distaste as he scanned the group, his gaze pausing the longest on Connor.

Kippie and Hollister had been in charge of gathering the proper clothing for them to wear. Gavin wasn't sure where they'd found them, and he hadn't asked, but Connor's coat had been made for a man half his size.

The doorman complained, "You certainly do not look like musicians."

"We have already been paid." Gavin shrugged again and turned to his cohorts, waving for them to depart. "We will leave if you wish. It matters not to me. But if Napoleon sends his men to demand the return of my fee, I will tell him who sent me away."

"Wait!" The doorman cleared his throat, reconsidering. "You may enter. Follow André down this hallway to the musician's alcove. Make sure you do not interfere with the guests. Tonight is special for the General, and he will become enraged should anything spoil it. Do I make myself clear?"

Gavin nodded, and ushered Jake, Connor and the men he'd selected from Mac's crew into the building. They all carried instruments, Kippie's wooden flute, Hollister's flageolet, a violin and small drums, but they also carried daggers and pistols. And a special surprise Gavin had arranged for Napoleon and his guards.

At the alcove, they gathered behind the orchestra who were playing a minuet. Gavin scanned the crowd of dancers. Whatever Napoleon's reason for holding a ball, it had brought every nobleman within a day's ride to the celebration. People crowded the dance floor, huddled in groups along the walls. Dozens of couples strolled on the terrace beyond a set of glass-paned doors.

"Blimey," Smedley murmured as he nervously ran a hand down the front of his coat. "Let's find Mac and Willie and get the 'ell out of 'ere. If we 'ave tae play for these folks, we're dead men."

"You assured us you could play something besides ale-house songs." Connor gripped the neck of the flageolet as if he intended to strangle it.

"We might have over-exaggerated a bit," Frewin admitted, holding the drums as if they were weapons.

"We won't be here long enough for it to matter," Gavin told him, searching the crowd for Napoleon. He wanted to make sure the general was distracted before he began his search for Mac and her father. There would be guards to deal with, he was certain, but he wasn't too concerned with them.

"Bloody hell," Jake hissed under his breath. "Look, there, to the left, at the end of the room."

Gavin followed Jake's appalled gaze . . . and felt a deadly chill run down his back.

Positioned on a dais so he could observe the entire room, Napoleon reclined on a gilded chair of red velvet. Like a king, Gavin thought, since France was now without one. Wearing his military uniform, white trousers and black, knee-high boots, he commanded the room, just as he commanded his troops. And if he had his way, he would one day command the entire world.

Should anyone doubt his authority, the double crown of red and white gold adorning his head might convince them.

"So he took the *pshent*, then locked up the lass." Connor growled deep in his throat. "The bloody, low-life, cutthroat—"

"Enough," Gavin said quietly. "Everyone knows what they have to do. Fan out, and take care not to draw attention."

Gavin had been to the palace once before. He'd shared what knowledge he had of the layout with his men, but he didn't know every passageway, and only God above knew how many secret chambers a place this size could hold.

As the orchestra finished their piece, the dancers, laughing and fanning their faces, left the dance floor, revealing a part of the room he hadn't noticed before now. He started to turn away, but paused, his heart stopping mid-beat. Denial roared through his mind, obliterating everything else.

"Bleedin' hell," Frewin whispered in horror.

To the right of Napoleon's chair, Mac and Willie stood sword straight, their backs tied to wooden poles.

Thick ropes bound their feet, and their arms were pulled at sharp angles and tied behind them. Leather straps held their heads back, so their necks were arched, their gazes forced up to the ceiling.

Rage, as primitive as it was explosive, shook through Gavin. He had to reach her, get her the hell out of here.

A man and women walked up to Mac, circled her, looking her over as if she were a horse at auction. The woman leaned close and said something that caused a muscle to flex in Mac's jaw. He could see the anger darkening her green eyes to smoke, knew that even helpless, she would try to fight.

He glanced at Willie, and was glad she couldn't see the pain glazing her father's eyes. The old man trembled. Sweat dripped from his pale face. If Gavin were to guess, the only thing keeping him upright were the ropes.

"We've got tae get them out of there," Hollister said, heading for the door to the ballroom.

"We will," Gavin said, following the man.

Connor caught his arm. "No."

"Let go of me, Connor," Gavin warned.

"What do ye mean, 'No?'" Hollister paused, glanced at both men.

"We cannae go down there now." Lowering his voice when the men in the orchestra turned to see what the commotion was about, he added, "None of us would stand a chance of escaping."

"He's right," Jake said. "We have to stay with our plan."

"I don't like it," Hollister said, his rough voice breaking as he looked back to Mac and Willie.

Neither did Gavin. He didn't want to wait. He'd waited once before and it had cost him everything.

But charging into Napoleon's domain would get them all killed.

Mac was in pain, and Willie might not make it through the night. But he had to wait. Bloody hell, he had to.

He followed his men through the door and slipped into a corridor, praying that this time, waiting was the right thing to do.

Chapter 20

The single torch flickered light over walls that were wet and slick and black with slime. The constant sound of dripping water echoed throughout the dungeon, a hollow sound, forlorn and destitute. A mood Mac felt clear to her soul.

She'd faced countless hardships during her life; starvation, shipwrecks, pirates, the loss of her mother. She'd faced every obstacle with the certainty that she would overcome it. She'd even come to believe that as long as she worked hard, nothing would ever stop her or hold her down.

But now, for the first time in her life, she knew that wasn't so.

Napoleon was gloating over the idea of her standing trial as a spy. She had given up arguing that she hadn't done anything against him. She'd never agreed to work for him in the first place; he'd given a command and had expected her to obey. But none of that mattered. If he had his way, she and Willie would stand trial tomorrow, with only one verdict expected. Guilty.

She recalled stories of how Louis XVI and his queen, Marie Antoinette, had faced the guillotine with courage and grace. She wondered if she'd be so strong.

Not likely, she thought. She pressed her hand to Willie's fevered brow, careful to keep the thick metal cuff and chains binding her wrists from hitting him. Her heart sank, and fear of tomorrow gave way to the present. He lay on a pallet of old straw, his arms limp, his face so pallid it frightened her to look at him. She'd never seen her father so weak. When they'd put her in his cell two days ago, she'd been horrified by his condition. Wracked with tremors and hallucinations, she'd demanded a physician be brought to see him.

To her surprise, one had arrived a few hours later. A small, frail man who'd stood two feet away from Willie as he looked him over from head to toe, without touching him once. She'd asked if he could help her father. Instead of answering, he'd rapped his cane on the door. As he left, he told the guards that if they intended to behead Willie, they'd better do so quickly.

The memory boiled through her. Helpless. She was completely helpless to save her father. Tears burned her eyes, but she refused to shed them. She'd fought her way out of dangerous situations before. She could do so again.

"Think," she demanded of herself. "Think of a way out of here."

But every idea that came to her was useless. Her crew was in London by now. She had no friends in France. Napoleon wanted her dead. Even if she managed to escape, Willie couldn't walk, and she couldn't carry him. The spectacle Napoleon made of them during the ball had drained the last of his strength. He needed decent food and medical care. He needed to get out of here!

"Daughter 'o mine," Willie said in a hoarse whisper.

She caught his cold, clammy hand and pressed it to her face. "I'm here."

"Aye, yer 'ere, ye fool girl. Exactly where ye shouldn't be."

"No more talking. You need to rest."

"I expect I'll be havin' a nice rest sooner than either of us expected."

"We're going to get out of here." She rubbed his hand, desperately trying to warm it.

"Don't worry about me, girl," he said, coughing. He coughed again, then again, the fit so severe, he nearly came off the pallet. Finally, the attack eased and he looked at her through glassy eyes. "Get out of 'ere, daughter. Now."

"We're going to leave together."

"I'll not be goin' with ye."

"But Pop—"

"You've done your duty tae me, Mackenzie. I love ye. After I lost Bess, I'd not have survived if not for ye."

"We took care of each other."

"Aye, that we did." His breath wheezed in his lungs as he struggled to speak. "But now I want ye tae do your Pop a favor."

"Anything."

"Leave me 'ere." He rubbed his thumb over her cheek, making her aware that they were wet with tears. "Find a way out."

She shook her head. "Not without you."

"Ye'll go. If ye love me at all, ye'll go."

"Pop . . ."

He pulled her down so he could kiss her brow. "Make me proud, Mackenzie. Get out of 'ere and show that fool Napoleon he'll never best a Tuggle."

She started to argue, but he turned his face away toward the wall. *I won't leave him behind.*

But even as she made her vow, she was terribly afraid that his next labored breath might be his last. And that she was the one who would be left behind.

* * *

Her decision was made.

It hadn't been easy, but now that she'd made it, she wouldn't change her mind. There were no windows in her cell, but she guessed dawn was less than an hour away. Soon they would be brought to Napoleon to stand trial. She doubted he would wait to execute them. But even if he did postpone putting them to death, she knew Willie wouldn't survive much longer in the dank, wet cell. He had lapsed into a dazed half-sleep, muttering things from a time before she had been born, before he'd lost his precious wife.

Mac had to get him out, or die trying.

Her thoughts went to the rest of her family. If she didn't make it, they would never know what happened to her and Willie. Who would take care of them? How would they manage? She pushed the unanswered questions to the back of her mind, only to have thoughts of Gavin take their place.

Gavin.

Moving to the thick door, she closed her eyes and rested her head against the rough surface. If only she could see him, explain why she'd taken the *pshent* and fled. Or did he already know the circumstances that had caused her to betray him? Did he understand, or did he hate her, as he'd hated his wife?

She would never know. Straightening, she told herself that right now it didn't matter. Saving Pop was all that counted.

First she had to get him out of the cell. She had a plan, weak though it was.

She knocked on the door. "Guard? Guard, I need to speak with you."

"Quiet!" a voice snarled in stilted English.

"Please, I think there's something wrong with my father."

"Not for long," he said with a laugh. "And not for you, either, I think."

"I need help. He . . . I think he might be dead," she said with a shiver, hating that she had to speak the lie. "Please, come look at him."

She heard grumbling, then the rattle of metal. A moment later a key grated in the lock and her door swung open. She would have sighed in relief for having completed the first part of her plan, but couldn't. Not only was her heart beating in her throat, but the guard was as big and solid as Connor.

He crossed to the pallet where Willie lay unmoving. As he bent to take a closer look, Mac raised both her hands high, prepared to bring the cuff of her wrist chains down on his head.

Just as she swung, a thunderous explosion shook the air. The walls vibrated and the floor shifted. Gasping, both she and the guard looked at each other. He rushed into the hall. Mac ran after him. Dust rained down from the ceiling and billowed into a gritty mist.

Muttering something in French, the guard pushed her back inside the cell and slammed the door shut. She lunged for it, beating her hands against the wood.

"Come back!" She shouted for him over and over. What was happening? Was the palace under attack? She heard people running and shouting on the floors above.

She tugged on the door, but it didn't budge. She pressed her hands to her stomach. How would they ever get out of their cell now? And what had happened? Were the French trying to overthrow Napoleon as they had Louis XVI?

Another explosion rocked the building. Dirt

streamed down on her head. She threw herself over Willie to protect him, and knew that whatever was going on, they were in danger of being buried alive.

She went back to the door, yanked on the handle. "Let us out!"

To her shock, she heard a key turn in the lock. She didn't wait for the guard to open the door; she jerked it opened herself. The torches in the hallway had been doused, and the lamp behind her struggled to stay lit, but she saw the outline of the guard filling the portal.

"We can't stay down here," she told him. "Please, take us someplace safe."

"I intend to."

The floor rocked again, but this time it wasn't because of an explosion. She knew that voice, she heard it every night in her dreams.

"Gavin?" she whispered, stunned.

"Surprised to see me?"

She heard the cold distance in his voice, but she didn't let it stop her from flinging herself into his arms. He was here! She couldn't believe it. Hadn't even dared hope that he would come after her.

He caught her by the waist and held her away. "We have to hurry."

Her heart skipped at his dismissal, but she knew he was right. She went to Willie to take one of his arms, only to be pushed aside. Jake and Connor crowded into the tiny room and lifted her father between them.

"It's good to see you, Mac," Jake said, throwing her a smile as Gavin unlocked the chains on Willie's wrists.

"Aye, lass, that it is." Connor nodded once, then left with Jake and Willie.

Gavin removed her chains as well, then caught her hand and followed them. He drew a pistol from his waistband, his gaze searching every shadowed corner as they moved through the pitch-dark dungeon. She couldn't see, could hardly breathe from all the lingering dust and had no idea where they were going. And she didn't care. Gavin was here! She couldn't believe it.

Stumbling down the dark corridor after him, a dozen questions raced through her mind. How had he found her? Was he responsible for the explosions? Did he hate her? She bit the questions back and ran.

Gripping her hand like a vise, he led her through one passageway after another, then up a set of stone stairs. She braced her free hand on the wall to keep from falling. How could he tell where they were going? She couldn't see anything.

They rounded a corner when he came to a sudden stop. Faint light leaked from beneath a door at the end of the hallway. She heard the pounding of running feet and muted shouts, the echoing sounds seeming to come from everywhere at once.

"Where are we?" she asked.

"Shh!"

She looked past Gavin, her eyes going wide. She spun around. "Where are the others?"

"Bloody hell," he growled, facing the stairwell behind them, then searching the hall.

"We lost them?" she cried, her voice strangled with fear.

"They'll make it out."

She pressed a hand to her brow. "How can you be sure? How did you even get in here?"

"Later." He tugged her hand, leading her down the hall.

She followed him without another word, wishing

he'd brought a pistol for her when she saw his glint in the growing light. She knew they'd need that and more before this was over.

At the door, Gavin eased it open, looked inside, then nodded to her that it was clear. He pulled her into another hallway, this one lit by a dozen wall sconces.

"Do you know where you're going?"

"Not exactly."

She bit down on her lip, her instincts screaming that they were heading in the wrong direction. "Maybe we should retrace our steps, find where Connor and Jake went."

"There should be another exit up ahead."

Before she could ask how he knew, an explosion echoed through the walls. Mac flinched, grabbed Gavin's arm. He paused, a grim, dangerous smile twisting his lips. It sharpened the angles of his face, made him seem reckless and wild. Two things she'd never seen in him before.

As he led her down another corridor, she heard approaching footsteps. Gavin pulled her into an alcove, and she held her breath as a group of armed soldiers ran passed.

She started to leave, but Gavin stopped her with a hand on her waist. She closed her eyes as heat sped through her body. God, how she'd missed his touch. Missed him. His seductive voice, his hard-won smiles, the changing moods that flowed through his eyes. She wanted to throw her arms around his neck, breathe in his scent, feel him around her if only for a moment.

As if reading her mind, he glared at her, then snatched his hand away.

Confused, she tried to straighten her thoughts. "Are you responsible for the explosions?"

"In part," he answered in the same clipped tone he'd used since he'd appeared in her cell.

"In part?"

"It was my idea." He glanced into the hallway, but didn't make any attempt to leave. "But your men carried it out."

"My . . . *my* men?" she whispered in disbelief. "I ordered them to leave if I didn't return. Are you saying they're still here?"

He shot her an exasperated glance. "For once they didn't follow your orders, but used their own heads."

"What is that supposed to mean?"

"That they shouldn't have allowed you to leave Rosetta."

"I suppose I should have let my father die."

"You should have come to me."

She sucked in a breath, stunned by the wounded sound of his voice. Then he looked at her and she knew she'd hurt him deeply, possibly beyond repair. Had she been wrong not to trust him?

She started to explain why she hadn't told him about Willie's capture, but Gavin narrowed his gaze, as if daring her to offer some poor excuse for her actions. The muscles in her throat stopped working and all she could manage to say was, "I'm sorry."

His jaw flexed and his eyes were spheres of onyx in the dim light. She thought he wanted to say something, perhaps yell at her, but he did something worse. He looked away, dismissing her. Mac recoiled as if she'd been struck.

"It's clear," he said. "Let's . . . bloody hell." He suddenly pressed her back against the wall. A second later, she heard another group of people hurrying toward them. They weren't running as the others had, but talking in frantic voices. Once again, Mac held her breath until they passed, then she let it out slowly, sagging with exhaustion. The palace was full of soldiers; how would they ever manage to escape out without being caught?

Just when she thought it was clear, Gavin turned and jerked her against him, kissing her before she had time to think. His mouth was hard, demanding, his hands bruising on her back. She felt the anger in him, a madness that ran through his veins.

She pushed against his chest, tried to demand he stop, but he deepened the kiss, his hand burrowing into her loose hair to hold her still. She'd wanted his kiss, had thought never to feel it again, but not like this.

He tensed and pulled away just enough for her to see the warning in his eyes. Then she heard the voice coming from the hallway, speaking in French. If she were to guess, she thought the man was demanding to know what they were doing.

Gavin answered him, his tone just as curt. The other man responded with a cynical laugh, then snapped something that caused Gavin to nod. The Frenchman left, his footsteps pinging against the stone floor. Long after they faded, Gavin continued to hold her, his back to the alcove's opening, shielding her like a wall of strength.

He looked down at her, his expression a mixture of anger and need.

She wanted to kiss him again, desperately, until the anger disappeared and only need remained. If they survived this, that's exactly what she intended to do.

"I think they're gone," he said.

"What did you tell him?"

"A man has to take his pleasure where he can."

"Even while the palace is under attack?"

He shrugged.

"I didn't know you spoke French."

The anger flared. "There are many things you don't know about me. Such as I would have done anything to help you."

"Gavin, I—"

"I don't care to hear your excuses." He released her, stepped back. "You didn't trust me enough to come to me. That's all I need to know."

"But I did come to you."

He scowled a warning for her to be quiet. He looked around the corner again, then pulled her out into the bright hallway. She followed him, as wary of being caught as she was of the anger simmering off Gavin.

"There," he said, stopping by a narrow set of stairs leading down to a plain oak door. "Our way out."

"A way out for some," a male voice drawled behind them. "But not for you, I'm afraid, monsieur."

Gavin whirled around, pistol raised. Mac turned as well, her breath ending on a gasp.

Napoleon stood ten feet away in the same military uniform he'd worn at the ball. Holding a sword in one hand, he smiled, a cruel twist of his lips that she was fast becoming familiar with. He also wore the *pshent,* perched on his head as if he were a king. He clearly thought himself one, she realized. And intended to conquer the world, just as King Menes had done five thousand years ago.

"I don't know who you are, monsieur," Napoleon said, taking a slow step toward them. "But that is my prisoner and I would have her returned to her cell. She is to stand trial very soon. Something I do not wish her to miss."

"I'm afraid you're going to be disappointed. She's leaving with me."

"And you are?" Napoleon asked, stepping so close the tip of his sword hovered a foot from Gavin's chest.

"The Earl of Blackwell."

"Ah, the man who found the *pshent.*" He touched the crown with affection. "You may leave, Lord Blackwell, as my appreciation for finding this for me."

"I didn't find it for you."

"Nevertheless, it is mine. And so is the woman." He angled his body in line with the sword, raised his free arm for balance. A stance of attack. "Now release her."

"After I've gone to so much trouble to free her?" Gavin raised his pistol, took aim at the general's heart. "I think not."

"The palace is surrounded, monsieur." A shrewd gleam flashed through the general's eyes. "There is no escape."

"We'll take our chances."

"When I call the guards, they will be here before you open that door."

Gavin clicked back the hammer on his pistol. "But you'll be dead before they arrive."

The general's face darkened with fury. "You do have the advantage. Go then. But know I shall be behind you." Pointing the tip of his sword at Mac, he added, "And know this, as well. She will be mine."

"You are too late, General," Gavin said, moving toward Napoleon, keeping the pistol trained on the man's heart. "She has already been claimed."

Taking the crown from the general's head, Gavin added, "And so has this."

Gasping in outrage, Napoleon shouted, "I will see you both beheaded before the night is out!"

Mac rushed down the stairs and out the door, Gavin close on her heels. They raced across an open courtyard to the shouts of fury. She didn't need to understand French to know Napoleon was calling his guards. Mac ran with all her heart, the cool night wind crisp and wonderful against her face.

She was out of the castle! She prayed her father was, too.

They darted past a hedgerow and onto a path that led to a cluster of trees. That's when she saw the horses, several of them with riders. She tried to slide to a stop. "Who—"

Gavin jerked her forward. "They're ours. Move!"

She did, pushing her tired body as hard as she could. The shouting behind them grew louder, the sounds of running feet and barking dogs filling the air. They were so close. She could see Hollister now, with Willie in the saddle in front of him. Connor and Jake, Frewin and Smedley!

A few more minutes were all they needed. She reached her horse, leaped into the saddle. Gavin tossed the *pshent* to Frewin, then caught the reins to his mount.

A shot rang out, and then another. Gavin jerked sideways, his cry of pain cut off as another gun was fired.

"Gavin!" she screamed, reaching for him.

He staggered, but kept himself from falling. Raising his hand, he slapped her horse on the rump and shouted, "Go!"

Her horse bolted across the yard and out the gate. She heard the other horses behind her. Hollister flew past with Willie. Then Jake, Connor, Frewin and Smedley. She looked behind her for Gavin. He wasn't there!

She sawed back on the reins and wheeled the animal around. "Gavin!"

He had yet to mount his horse, and she watched in horror as he slowly slid to the ground.

Chapter 21

"No!" Mac kicked her horse into a run. Gavin was on his back, his arms limp at his sides.

"Please, please . . ." she whispered, racing toward him. She glanced toward the palace, saw French soldiers converging at the door where she and Gavin had escaped, their bayonets visible in the pre-dawn light. Panic closed her throat. She leaned over the horse's neck, urging him faster, then leaped from his back before he slid to a stop. She knelt beside Gavin. His eyes were closed; she couldn't tell if he was breathing.

"Gavin, move, please wake up!" She gripped his shoulders to lift him, but gasped in horror. His shirt was warm and wet with blood. So much blood, her stomach turned with fear. She felt the vein along his neck for a pulse, and nearly crumbled with relief when she found one.

Hearing a commotion, she glanced up, saw soldiers rushing through the gardens. They would be on her within minutes. *Dear God!*

"Gavin, open your eyes." She tried to help him up, but he was as heavy as stone. She couldn't budge him, let alone lift him onto a horse. Her voice choking on a sob, she pleaded, "Help me, Gavin. I'm not leaving without you."

She heard pounding hooves and flinched, expecting

to be grabbed and jerked away from Gavin. But it was Connor who dropped down beside her and lifted Gavin as if he were a child. "Go!"

She caught the reins to his horse and held the animal still while he mounted, positioning Gavin, who was still unconscious, in front of him.

"Go!" Connor shouted again.

This time she obeyed him, leaping into her saddle just as the soldiers cleared the hedgerow. She kicked the animal in the sides. The frantic shouts escalated and the dawn exploded with gunfire. But she was far down the graveled drive and through the gate, racing after Connor.

They were free, she realized, as the sound of gunshots faded behind her. The sun flooded the horizon in gold, and tears streaked down her cheeks. They were free. She would have given up anything, paid anything to save her father, but she hadn't bargained on paying with Gavin's life.

Fleeing into the deathly still morning, she feared his life was the price the Gods were going to demand she pay.

Catching up to Jake and her men, they raced through the empty streets toward the harbor, pushing the horses until their necks and flanks were lathered with sweat. The sun hovered low in the sky, a beautiful orange disk that promised a perfect day at sea. She glanced behind her again, expecting to see Napoleon's soldiers. Except for a few merchants on their way to market, the road was deserted.

Mac stayed close to Connor, her gaze drawn again and again to Gavin. Blood soaked his chest and dripped down his sleeve, the vile red color glistening in the soft morning light. Too much blood. Everything inside her shook. He had to hold on. He was too stubborn and demanding to die this way.

He can't die, not while trying to save me.

She squeezed her eyes closed. He needed medical care, and so did Pop. Once she had them on her ship, she'd be able to help them both. Gavin first, she decided, already making a list of things she'd need. She had to stop the bleeding, see how badly he'd been shot.

Willie needed a tonic to ease the fever, decent food, clean water and rest. She prayed that was all he'd need, that whatever ailed him wasn't more serious than she could handle. Because she couldn't lose him, either.

Heaven help her, she thought, nearly choking on a sob. She might lose both men she loved. *Please, God, anything but that.*

The dreary row of buildings made of wood and grime that lined the harbor outside of Paris came into view. She could smell the Seine River now, and knew *Little Bess* wasn't far.

Reaching a fork in the street fronting the harbor, Hollister veered right. She started to follow, but Connor and Jake took the path to the left.

She reined to a stop. "Connor! Wait!"

They kept going. She kicked her mount to pursue them, only to hear someone shout her name.

She looked back over her shoulder. Frewin waved one arm. With the other, he held the *pshent* snug against his body. "*Little Bess* is this way, Mac."

"I know, but . . ." She glanced at Connor and Jake and shouted for them to stop, but either they couldn't hear her or were ignoring her. Where were they going? "Connor!"

Frewin rode up beside her. As if reading her mind,

he said, "Their ship is further up river. Hurry, Mac. Willie needs ye."

Her heart pounded against her chest. This couldn't be happening. She was being torn in two. Both men needed her. Gavin more urgently than her father, she believed. But she couldn't ignore Pop's condition. She could go to Gavin, quickly tended his wound, then return to *Little Bess*.

At that moment, Jake and Connor took a corner and disappeared from sight.

"Come on girl," Frewin said. "The lads will take care of the earl."

"Gavin needs me, Frewin. He could bleed to death."

"And Napoleon's on our trail, or I'm not English. We've got tae set sail, Mackenzie. Now!"

She knew he was right. They didn't have time to delay. But to leave Gavin without seeing him. She didn't even know if he was still alive.

Wheeling her mount around, Mac raced toward her father . . . and away from the man she loved.

"Raise sail," Mac told Smedley, who was acting as first mate in place of her father.

"Aye, Cap'n." The agile sailor moved over the deck, shouting, "Hands lay aloft to set tops'ls! And you, mate, bring the sheets home."

Mac performed a cursory check to ensure that everything was under control. It was. The anchor was raised, decks were cleared, ropes secured. Her crew had been prepared for her return. Hollister and Frewin were just now getting Pop settled in his cabin and already her crew had *Little Bess* heading up the river toward the English Channel.

There had been no sign of Napoleon, which surprised her. She hadn't thought the crazed general would give up so easily. Perhaps the explosions Gavin set off had done more than just startle everyone.

Her fear for Gavin drew her toward the stern. She gripped the railing in her hands, urging the three-mast ship following her to come closer. Gavin was on that ship, the *Nightingale*, the vessel Gavin had virtually commandeered to reach France.

"Please," she whispered. "Please hold on."

Once they were away from France and in the relative safety of the English Channel, she'd signal to come alongside the *Nightingale*. She had to see Gavin. She couldn't wait until they reached London to know if he was alive. *He has to be.* She couldn't believe otherwise.

"What should I be doing with this?" Frewin asked, holding out the red and white double crown.

The *pshent* was as beautiful as the first time she'd seen it, an incredible sight that took her breath away. She wished she'd never lain eyes on it.

If she'd never found the artifact, Napoleon wouldn't have held Willie for ransom, she wouldn't have had to rescue him, and Gavin . . . Gavin wouldn't have been shot.

"Put it away, Frewin," she said.

"Mac," Kippie called, joining them.

She turned and her concern immediately shifted to surprise at seeing the older man, his eyes still bruised, a cut healing on his temple. "What are you doing here? Never mind."

It was obvious to her now that Kippie had told Gavin what she'd done, and where she'd gone.

"It's Willie," Kippie said.

"I'm coming."

"'E's talkin' out of 'is 'ead. And the fever, well, I think ye better have a look."

She rushed down to the lower deck and to her father's cabin. He lay on his bunk, tossing his head from side to side, muttering feverishly. Hollister had already stripped him of his soiled clothes and had covered him with a blanket. She opened the porthole window to allow the sea air to flow in. If anything would cure her Pop, it would be the briny scent of the sea.

"I need my bag of medicines, Hollister."

"Consider it done." She heard him running down the corridor to her room.

Taking a rag, she dipped it into a bowl of water that someone had had the foresight to bring. She sponged Willie's face, wiping away the dirt and sweat. He was pale, frighteningly so. His breathing was shallow and rattling in his lungs, and coming much too fast.

She felt his brow and trembled, tears springing to her eyes. He was so hot. Burning from the inside. Her meager supply of medicines wouldn't be enough. She had to get him to a doctor.

Hollister returned, handing her the bag. Mac took out the bottle that held a mixture of calendula, peppermint and horehound. It had worked in the past, for minor illnesses. But nothing as severe as what Pop suffered now. It might dull the fever and the cough. But she knew it wasn't strong enough to cure him. She could only hope that it would ease his fever until they reached England.

With Hollister's help, they managed to lift his head. She poured small amounts of the syrup into Willie's mouth, making sure he swallowed it all. Satisfied he'd had enough, she set the medicine aside and began to bathe his face, arms and chest with cool water.

"Will he make it?" Hollister asked, his voice as grim as she'd ever heard it.

"He will," she swore, squeezing her friend's hand.

"We'll hire the best doctor in London. He'll be fine, you'll see."

"Mac . . . Mackenzie girl," Willie called in a breathless voice. "Is that you?"

"I'm here, Pop." She ran her hand over his heated brow.

"Where are we?" He blinked his eyes open. They were glazed and full of fever.

"On board *Little Bess*. On our way to London."

His bottom lip trembled. "*Little Bess?* We're out of that prison? Napoleon—"

"You're safe now, Pop."

"I was dreamin'." He closed his eyes, a contented smile curving his mouth. "Yer mother was talkin' tae me. As pretty as the day I met her, she was."

"Shh, sleep now. We'll talk later."

"She's in Egypt. Yer mother's been in Egypt all this time. She's waitin' for us."

"We'll see her soon, Pop," Mac said, and bit down on her lip. The need to cry pushed against her chest, cutting off her breath. "After we see a doctor in London, we'll sail straight for home."

"No, no! Too late." He shook his head and tried to rise, only to fall back onto the bed. His breath wheezed in his lungs, the hollow sound more terrifying than anything she'd ever heard.

"Shh," she said, stroking his face to calm him. "Easy now. Easy."

"To Egypt, Mac. Ye cannot delay."

"You need a doctor first."

He caught both her hands and forced her to lean close. His eyes softened for an instant, as if the fever had vanished. Though she knew it hadn't. She could feel the heat rising off his skin, feel the burn where his hand gripped hers.

"I'm beyond a doctor, daughter 'o mine," he said with a regretful smile.

"No, no—"

"I am, and I think in your heart, ye know it."

She shook her head, tried to argue, but her throat closed around the words.

"'Twas a brave thing ye did, daughter, comin' after me. Ye shouldn't 'ave. We both know me old body is givin' out."

"Shh, please, don't say anything more."

"I've been talkin' tae Bess. She's waitin' for me."

"Pop—"

"Don't take me to London, daughter. I beg ye. Take me home."

Mac stared into her father's brown eyes and felt an invisible fist tighten around her heart. After everything they'd been through, was she still destined to lose him? *Please, no! No!*

"Pop, I can't . . ."

"Yer strong, Mackenzie. Ye can do anything."

But could she sail away from London and the best hope of saving her father? He needed the care of a doctor, now. What was she supposed to do? Grant his last wish? If she did, she'd lose him for sure.

She glanced out the porthole window. She couldn't see it, but she knew the *Nightingale* was close to her starboard side. There was another reason she needed to sail for London. If she didn't, it would be months before she would see Gavin again, learn if he had survived his injury.

He still didn't know why she'd left Egypt without telling him. Or why she'd taken the *pshent*. Though that seemed trivial at the moment.

Something crumbled inside her. Hope and despair collided, taking her dreams and desires and shredding them beyond repair. She'd made a promise to herself that nothing would ever come before her family. But that was before she'd fallen in love with Gavin. She hadn't known it was possible to love a man as much as she loved him. She needed to see him, ached with the longing to board the other ship so she could take care of him. But she couldn't. Pop came first; he had to.

Her heart twisted, the pain so unbearable, she thought it a miracle that it didn't kill her.

"Hollister," she said, her voice breaking. "Have Frewin set a course for Egypt."

"We're going home?" Willie asked, sighing with relief.

"Yes," she said, kissing her father's brow. "We're going home."

A line of fire streaked across Gavin's left shoulder, and continued to burn like a white-hot poker down his chest, spreading into his gut. The *Nightingale*'s deck rocked beneath his feet, the swaying making his head spin and his stomach heave. If it weren't for Connor supporting him, he'd surely fall flat on his face.

"Yer a pathetic sight for an earl." The Scotsman made a sound of disgust. "Best ye go below."

"No," he said, his voice a raw croak.

He was hot. Burning and shivering at once. Warm air blew over the ship's stern, but it did little to dry the sweat dripping from his face and body. His skin felt stretched taut over his bones, his limbs weak as a helpless babe's. He gritted his teeth to keep from moaning; the throbbing ache where the bullet was still lodged in his shoulder was becoming more than he could bear.

Yet he couldn't go below. Not yet. Because he couldn't believe what he was seeing. Mac, the woman he'd fallen in love with, the woman he'd raced to France to save, was running away from him. Again.

"I'm not surprised you're being stubborn," Sarah said, joining him at the rail. "You hardly know how to be anything else. But you're frightening us all. Please, Gavin, let Connor help you to your cabin."

He shook his head, his gaze fastened on the three-mast ship skimming the waves. Every sail on *Little Bess* was full of wind, hurtling the sleek vessel on an easterly course.

East instead of west.

Toward Egypt and away from him.

He'd already ordered Captain Muldrow to turn his ship and give chase, but the captain had refused, and Gavin's friends had agreed. Now, barely able to stand, all he could do was watch the other ship sail further and further out of his grasp.

Mac was running away from him. Why?

She'd known he'd been shot. He could still hear her frantically calling his name, feel her cool hands against his neck and face. She had come back for him after he'd collapsed. But she was leaving him now. Why? For the same reason that had sent Rachel fleeing into the night? Did Mac fear facing his anger? Did she not know that he was angry with her because she'd endangered herself, and not because she'd taken the *pshent*?

Or did she not care whether he lived or died? Had her vow of loving him been a lie? The pain in his shoulder paled as that horrible possibility sank in.

"She must have a good reason for not coming to London," Sarah said, trying to sound encouraging and failing.

"And what would that be?" Gavin heard himself ask.

"She has the *pshent*," Jake said, joining them.

"Jacob Mitchell! I'm sure that's not the reason she isn't coming to England," Sarah said in Mac's defense.

"What other reason could there be?" Gavin said, more to himself than to his friends.

When no one offered an answer, Sarah touched the bandage she'd temporarily placed over his wound. Her mouth thinned with disapproval. The linen was soaked with his blood again.

"Please, Gavin," she pleaded.

"Soon," he conceded, but only because he knew he wouldn't be able to stand for much longer. "Give me a moment."

"If I let go of ye," Connor argued, "you'll be meetin' the deck with your face."

Gavin gave the Scotsman what he hoped was a glare, and thought he might have succeeded when the man muttered a curse and left with the others.

Once alone, Gavin returned his gaze to the departing ship, and couldn't help but wonder what Mac was doing, what she was thinking.

He'd thought he understood the way her mind worked, why she felt the need to be in control, that driving force to take care of her family. But he didn't understand this.

Unless she doesn't love me. Then her fleeing makes perfect sense.

He'd regained consciousness shortly after Captain Muldrow had set sail down the Seine River, and had remained in his cabin long enough to endure Sarah's frantic effort to stop his wound from bleeding. Despite the haze of pain her prodding had caused, he'd been desperate to see Mac, learn for himself that she was safe. Nothing else had mattered, not his friends, his wound, his life.

He briefly closed his eyes, recalling that moment in

the alcove when they'd kissed. It had been harsh and brutal, a manifestation of his fear. But he could still taste her, that unique cinnamon-spice that was forever Mac. As weak as he was, his body reacted, growing hard with need. He wanted to see her, *needed to* more than he needed his next breath.

But he wouldn't be able to touch Mac or hold her, or heaven help him, kiss her again. Not now, possibly not ever.

Despite the pain, despite the numbness that settled over his emotions like a heavy fog, he felt a kernel of anger spark to life. Welcoming it, needing it, he let it take root and grow.

He'd come to France to rescue her.

And she was sailing away as if he mattered not at all.

"But I did come to you." Unwillingly, he recalled her statement after he'd freed her from her cell. He'd accused her of fleeing Egypt without coming to him first.

"But I did come to you," she had insisted. What had she meant? Had she intended to tell him about Napoleon capturing Willie? And if she had, what had stopped her? Or was that another lie.

The *Nightingale,* now full of sail, sliced through the steel blue waves of the English Channel, taking him farther and farther away from Mac, until he lost sight of *Little Bess* completely.

The questions tormenting his mind didn't matter. Because one thing was perfectly clear.

She was going to Egypt. Not to England.

And not to him.

Turning from the rail, he realized he had only one thing to be grateful for. He hadn't told her how much he loved her.

Chapter 22

Gavin left the king's assembly room, his fists clenched, his booted footsteps resounding off the marble floor like blasts from a cannon. A fierce sound that suited his mood.

In record time, he reached the salon, where Connor leaned against a wall, arms folded over his broad chest as he studied the milling businessmen, lords and ladies hoping for an audience with the king.

"There's not a decent Scot among this lot," Connor murmured with disgust. "'Tis a wonder England has survived as long as she has."

"We're leaving." Ignoring the few people who called out in greeting, as well as the dozen pairs of curious gazes fastened on his back, he headed for the exit.

Connor fell into step beside Gavin, not speaking again until they'd reached the courtyard where their horses were tethered and waiting.

"I take it King George wasn'a pleased." At ease in a saddle, Connor spurred his mount down the gravel drive. Gavin followed, wincing when the wound in his shoulder protested.

A week had passed since he'd been shot. A week of pain and fever and endless doubts about the woman who had turned his life upside down.

Gavin shook thoughts of Mac away before they

could fully surface. He'd brooded long enough. Now it was time for action. "My sovereign was far from pleased."

"I've heard the king is a meek man, not given to shouting," Connor mused. "You wouldn'a think so from the way he bellowed."

"You heard?" Gavin swore under his breath. If Connor had overheard the king's furious reaction, then undoubtedly half the people in the castle had as well. Before the sun set, word would spread that the Earl of Blackwell had had King Menes' *pshent* in his hands, only to lose it to the very woman he'd hired to find it.

Nodding, Connor asked, "What path do we take, then?"

"The one leading to Egypt," Gavin said, torn between relief and anger.

The Scotsman huffed a miserable sigh. "That's what I was afraid of. Will Jake-o and Sarah be joinin' us?"

"When has Jake ever passed on going to Egypt?"

"Seems queer tae me. Napoleon has been driven out of Egypt."

"It doesn't matter. King George wants the *pshent*."

"Aye."

"And I want answers," Gavin added under his breath, shaken by how much he meant it. He'd never had the chance to ask Rachel why she'd turned to another man, why she'd fled. He didn't intend to make that same mistake with Mac.

"She made her choice and returned home," Connor said as if reading his mind. "What does it matter now?"

"Perhaps it doesn't. But I still want to know why she returned to Egypt without a word." He understood why she took the *pshent* without telling him. Or at least he thought he did.

She was stubborn, determined to take care of her family without help from others. But that didn't explain why she hadn't accompanied him to London. His brief glimpse of Willie had been enough for him to know the old man was ill; logically, Mac should have brought him to the city for medical care, not travel thousands of miles away from help. But something had caused her to run.

Was it because she was afraid of him, or was this another act of deception? He had to know.

And then what? a voice in the back of his mind asked. If she still loved him, what did he intend to do about it? Stay with her? Make love to her one last time and return to London? And what about his feelings for her? As much as he tried to forget her, or hold on to his anger for her leaving, he couldn't. There was a hole inside him, a gaping emptiness he had to fill, even if it was only with answers.

"Do ye love her, then?" Connor asked, snapping Gavin out of his thoughts.

He wanted to deny it, even started to say the words, but they stuck in his throat. "Yes, I love her. Though I tried like hell not to."

"Ah," the Scotsman said, shaking his head in sympathy. "Love ye canna deny is the hardest kind of love of all."

Gavin almost asked the man how he would know. Then he stopped to glare at Connor, demanding "Are you in love with her?"

A chuckle erupted from the Scotsman. "Mac? Aye, I suppose I am. But no the way ye mean."

"You talked about making her Lady of Bachuil Castle."

"Only tae make ye jealous. And it worked verra well, I'm thinkin'."

Gavin almost smiled. He should have known. Until Connor found the Staff of St. Moluag, he wouldn't allow any woman into his life.

Gavin had tried to have that same kind of control over his feelings for Mac, but he'd failed. Failed miserably. He loved her, and the thought that she might not love him in return, that she had coldly betrayed him, was a wound that wouldn't heal until he knew the truth.

"And once ye see her, what then?" the Scotsman asked.

Gavin couldn't answer; he didn't know how. Even if she loved him, and had a good reason for stealing the *pshent,* then sailing to Egypt instead of London after their escape, what did he want from her? What kind of life could they have?

"I hope ye know what yer doin'." Connor looked at Gavin as if he were a doomed man. "And that you're prepared tae hear facts that ye may not like."

"Such as she really doesn't love me?"

"That she does," the Scotsman said quietly. "But knows the two of ye must go your own way."

"How soon are ye leavin'?" Kippie asked as he set a heavy sack of potatoes on the floor next to the others.

Mac made a note in her ledger, adding the potatoes to the food she'd already gathered. Flour, rice, dried meat, salted fish and fresh water. Enough to last the three months she'd be gone.

"Tomorrow, if possible," she told him, and felt her stomach take a jittery roll. "Hollister and Frewin are making the final arrangements."

"Yer makin' a mistake, not takin' me with ye."

"I wish I could," she said truthfully. During the last

few weeks, her family had gathered around her, giving her strength to face what needed to be done. Now she had to leave some of them behind. "I need you here, Kippie. Try to understand."

"Tae sit with me," Willie complained as he slowly shuffled into the kitchen. "Who would believe it? Me own daughter treatin' me like a helpless babe!"

"Pop!" Mac leaped up from her stool and rushed to his side, guiding him to take her place. "What are you doing up? By the Gods, I'm going to chain you to your bed."

Slowly lowering himself onto the stool, he sighed and wiped the perspiration from his flushed face with a handkerchief. His hand shook more than it should have. "Someone 'as tae talk you out of this fool expedition."

"Foolish or not, it has to be done."

"But why you?"

Kneeling in front of him, she took his hands in hers. "You know why."

Pursing his lips, looking for all the world like a lad who hadn't gotten his way, he finally glanced at Kippie. "This is what we get for raising our girl tae think for herself."

She smiled despite the fear and worry that weighed on her shoulders like stones. They'd been home a month, and every one of those days had been as frightening as facing down a cobra. Instead of wondering when the asp would strike, she'd wondered when her father would finally take his last breath.

Until three days ago. He'd been feverish, as he had been since leaving Paris, muttering to Bess as if she were sitting beside him on his bed. Then suddenly one afternoon, he'd opened his eyes, looked directly at Mac and informed her that he'd discussed it over with his wife and they decided he should stay a while longer.

Since then, he'd recovered with remarkable speed, walking short distances, eating, using his boyish smile to coax her into giving him a cup of ale—which she refused time and again. She felt guilty for leaving him now, but believed the worst was over.

She wouldn't have considered leaving his side at all, if not for one thing. The *pshent*.

The red-and-white-gold double crown sat on a side table, gleaming like a magical talisman in the sunlight from a nearby window. A magical talisman? Mac wondered. Or a curse?

They should have left the crown in King Menes' tomb. She would take it there now, if she could. She wanted to. But she couldn't. There were things she had to settle. And returning the crown to Gavin DeFoe was at the top of her list.

No, she admitted, the first thing she had to do was find out if he had survived his wound. He had to be alive. Surely she would sense it if he weren't.

As much as she wanted to see Gavin, touch him, end the awful doubts that plagued her, she dreaded the moment she finally stood before him. How would he react? She doubted he would welcome her with open arms. He had cared about her, once, but he hadn't loved her. Hadn't even wanted to hear her admission that she loved him.

More than likely he would he be cold and distant, the way he'd been when he'd freed her from the cell. And he would undoubtedly be furious that she hadn't gone to London and explained her actions.

Her worst fear was that he would refuse to see her. So afraid that would be the case, that she'd never have the chance to say good-bye to him, she pushed thoughts of him to the back of her mind and focused on the present.

Standing, she crossed to the table and picked up the *pshent*. The weight pulled at her arms, just as life seemed to do now more than ever.

"I need to find Smedley, have him load the rest of our supplies." Glancing at the crown, she added, "This I'll take care of myself."

"You've taken care of it long enough, I think."

The booming male voice—a voice she recognized as it sliced through her soul—made her jump and turn toward the door. Her mouth gaped open and her knees threatened to buckle.

Gavin filled the doorway, his very presence stealing the air from the room. His glare was focused on her, intense and burning. Tension vibrated from him, reaching her like an oncoming wave, washing over her and dragging her under.

She couldn't move, couldn't speak. He was alive! By the Gods, he was alive. She wanted to rush to him, run her hands over his chest, make sure she wasn't dreaming. His eyes were dark and menacing, lethal spheres of black, the color matching the hair that was trimmed and brushed away from his face.

Wearing a white linen shirt with black pants and boots, she'd never seen him more breathtaking. She couldn't believe he was here . . . healed and standing within arm's reach!

Pop stood and broke the silence. "Lord Blackwell! 'Tis glad I am tae see ye, lad."

"Are you?" Gavin asked skeptically.

With uneven steps, Willie crossed to the scowling man and held out his hand, waiting until Gavin accepted it. "I never thought tae lay eyes on ye again." He glanced up at the ceiling and whispered, "See

Bess, my staying behind was the right thing tae do. Now I can thank Lord Blackwell for saving mine and Mac's life right and proper."

Gavin arched a brow, glanced at her, then at her father. "There's no need to thank me."

"But there is," Willie insisted, wavering on his feet. "If ye hadn't saved us, the street urchins of France would likely be usin' me head tae play kick the ball."

"Pop!" Mac said with a gasp.

"Sorry, sorry." Bending close to Gavin, he confided, "She can be a bit squeamish about such things."

Gavin started to say something, but just then Willie swayed and would have fallen over if Gavin hadn't caught him.

"Whoa, now," Willie said, his voice strained. "The floor's buckin' beneath me feet."

Mac was at his side in an instant. "You're going to bed. No arguing."

"I'll take 'im." Kippie shooed her aside so he could wrap his arm around Willie ample girth.

"That's not necessary," she said.

"Ye have things tae discuss, I'm thinkin'," the old cook said with a nod to Gavin. On his way out the door, he paused to say, "Glad tae 'ave ye back, my lord. You'll be savin' Mac a trip we didn't want her tae be takin'."

"I'm so glad I could be of help," Gavin said dryly.

The sarcasm wasn't lost on Kippie. "Remember, lad, I'm not far. If ye mistreat our Mac, ye'll 'ave tae deal with me."

"I'm sorry," Mac said when they were finally alone. *For everything*, she wanted to add. *For taking the crown, for not trusting you.*

"Your father. He's still ill."

Mac drew a shaky breath, her eyes tearing as they had

so often lately. "We almost lost him. But he's recovering now. The worst is over."

Gavin made a scoffing sound, as if he thought the worst was still ahead.

Unable to bear the wary look in his eyes, she glanced down. Running one hand over the crown, she held it out to him. "I suppose you want this."

"I do." He took the *pshent* from her, held it in the crook of his arm.

Is that why he came back? she wondered, feeling as if someone were squeezing her heart. To fulfill his duty to King George? Of course it was. Gavin was a man of his word. Considering everything she'd done, he had no reason to believe that she would bring it to him.

"It seems I arrived just in time." He nodded toward her supplies. "You're leaving?"

"Yes."

"What part of the desert this time? Or do I need to ask?"

She stared at him a moment, confused, but seeing the silent accusations in his fierce gaze, his meaning became clear. "You thought I was going to return the crown to King Menes' tomb?"

"You never wanted to remove it."

She shook her head in disbelief. "As tempting as that was, I had no intention of uncovering King Menes again."

"Then what were you planning to with this?" He nodded at the *pshent.*

"Give it to you."

"Of course you were, which is why you followed me to England." Gavin laughed, the sound bitter to his own ears. Seeing her standing there wearing her soft *galabiya*, her auburn hair loose about her shoulders, looking wild and beautiful and just as he remembered, he wanted to believe her, and that only made him angrier. "Being a sailor, I'd think you'd know Egypt is *not* on the way to London."

Her chin tilted in defense. "I'd had every intention of following you."

"Why didn't you?" he demanded, feeling as if everything, his life, his future hinged on her answer. He hated this, hated that he was angry with her, that he couldn't trust her, that he couldn't pull her into his arms and kiss her.

She hesitated for so long, he thought she wouldn't answer, but finally she said, "Pop. He was dying, or so we all thought. He pleaded with me to bring him home."

"It was obvious he needed to see a physician as soon as possible."

"Don't you think I know that?" she said, pressing one clenched fist to her chest. "I was frantic to help him. I had every intention of going to London. And not only because of him. You were . . ." She closed her eyes, bit down on her lip and turned away. "Pop could barely breathe. He was so sick. He knew how bad . . . He begged me to bring him home to . . ."

Gavin didn't need her to finish; he knew what she'd meant to say. Willie had begged to be brought home to die. He could easily envision the scene with Willie feverish and weak, knowing he was on the verge of death. And Mac, helpless to save him. With her worst fear coming true, she'd granted his last wish.

Gavin felt the anger he'd used to drive himself through the last weeks begin to crack. If she was telling the truth, and God help him, he wanted to believe she was, he could understand her not coming to London.

But that didn't justify her taking the *pshent* to begin with. She'd said she loved him, yet she hadn't trusted him enough to ask for his help.

Was Connor right, Gavin wondered for the hundredth time? After everything they'd been through together, were he and Mac destined to go their separate ways? Did he want to? Gavin had nursed that thought the entire trip to Rosetta.

"I'm sorry, Gavin." She wrapped her arms around her waist as if she were holding herself together.

"For what, Mac? Not trusting me? Stealing the *pshent*? Or nearly getting you and your father killed?"

She closed her eyes, bowed her head. "Yes. All of it."

"Why didn't you tell me Napoleon had captured Willie?"

Her head came up, and her eyes blazed with an emotion he couldn't name, an agonizing mixture of fear, longing and need. "I did go to the harbor to tell you."

"What stopped you?"

"You did."

"What the hell are you talking about?"

"I overheard you in the shipping office. You told the others that nothing would stop you from giving the crown to King George."

Gavin recalled that conversation clearly, and the despair he'd felt at having to leave Mac so soon. He also recalled what he'd said next, that what had been between him and Mac had belonged in the desert, not in London. Had she heard that as well? From the wounded look in her eyes, he knew she had.

"So you took the *pshent*," he said. "And faced Napoleon alone."

She shrugged. "Perhaps the most foolish thing I've ever done, but I honestly thought I had no choice. Saving Pop was all that mattered."

Because her family, the people she loved, came first. She'd loved him once; he had to know if she still did.

"What will you do now?" he asked.

She ran one hand through her hair, the gesture revealing the stress she'd been under. Shadows of exhaustion bruised her eyes; she seemed thinner, almost frail. Gavin tightened his hold on the crown, the urge to hold her overwhelming.

"I don't know. My only thought was to take the crown to you. After that . . . I don't know."

"Was returning the crown your only reason for coming to London?"

She looked at him, her eyes filling with tears. "I didn't know if you were alive. All this time . . ."

"My injury wasn't as bad as it first appeared. A bullet to the shoulder."

She reached out to touch him, but pulled back. "You wouldn't have been wounded if not for me."

He stood there, holding the *pshent,* uneasy with the emotions shifting through him. He understood why she'd taken the crown, and why she'd sailed for Egypt instead of coming with him. Her duty, first and foremost, had been to her family.

She'd admitted her love for him before, and if the anguished look in her eyes were any indication, she loved him still. Regardless that he'd never admitted his love for her.

Without any effort on his part, the anger he'd been harboring over the past weeks vanished. And though the depth of his love for her frightened him, made him feel vulnerable, it also made him feel alive.

He wanted to go to her, wrap her in his arms, but he didn't know how to cross the barrier between them. He glanced down at the *pshent,* and suddenly knew what he had to do.

"Since you have no plans," he said, looking at her. "I was wondering if you and your crew were for hire?"

Her eyes widened, the green darkening to jade. "What did you have in mind?"

"Napoleon has been forced out of Egypt, but that doesn't mean he won't return." He moved closer to her, and could smell her skin, cinnamon and sweet and warm. His heart hammered against his chest as he set the *pshent* on the table beside her. "After seeing the general wearing the crown, I want to make sure he never has the chance to do so again."

"It should be safe with King George."

Gavin nodded. "Undoubtedly. But I was thinking of giving it to someone who could protect it for years to come."

"Who?" she asked almost breathlessly.

"King Menes."

Her lips trembled with a sudden smile, and her eyes lit with something he never thought he'd see again. Love. "Are you sure?"

"There's only one other thing that I'm more sure of."

"And that is?"

"That I love you."

Her mouth gaped and a look of denial crossed her face. "You love me? But you said—"

"That what we had belonged in the desert. I was wrong, Mac," he said, still not giving in to the need to hold her, though it was nearly killing to keep his hands at his sides. "I belong wherever you are."

To his surprise, she shook her head. "It won't work. You hate Egypt."

"What I hate, Mac, is living without you."

Her breath caught. "Gavin . . ."

"Do you love me?"

"You know I do."

"Then I suppose you'll have no qualms about marrying me."

She looked at him as if she were afraid to believe what she was hearing. "We live completely different lives."

"Yes, you love the desert."

"And you love London."

"We'll obviously have to make some compromises."

"This is insane." She held back, her hands pressed against her stomach.

He took one step forward, coming so close the front of his shirt brushed hers. But still he didn't touch her. "I know I love you, Mac. And I know that wherever you are, that's where I want to be. In Egypt or England, on the deck of *Little Bess,* I don't care."

"Oh, Gavin," she whispered, smiling as tears ran down her cheeks. Then she launched herself into his arms, hers coming around his neck and holding him tight. He held her against him, the feel of her body, the heat of her skin, filling every empty place inside him.

"I was so afraid I'd never see you again, that you hadn't survived—"

He cut her off by kissing her, sweeping his tongue inside her mouth, tasting the honey-sweetness that made the world fall away. She was everything he wanted, and everything he needed. No matter what happened, or what problems they faced, he would never let her go.

Though he didn't want to, he pulled back slightly and looked down at her flushed face, her lips that were wet and swollen, and all his. "You didn't answer me. Will you be my wife?"

She smiled, the same mysterious smile he remembered from the first day they'd met. "You realize that you'll be getting more than just me. There's Pop and Kippie, Hollister and Frewin—"

"I wouldn't have it any other way."

She started to say something more but stopped when shouts of laughter rang out from the other room. Then they heard Kippie declare, "'Tis time for ale, men! The earl's part of the family now!"

Epilogue

Heat rose in shimmering waves across the desert floor, baking the sand so dry it whipped through the air with the slightest breeze. The mountains to the west seemed to quiver against the blazing white-blue sky, as if a fire raged from within. Gavin watched them every day, wondering when the jagged peaks would crack and shatter into rubble. Full summer was upon them, a time when no one but scorpions and cobras dared to venture into the sun.

But that didn't stop Gavin or Mac. Though it had taken twice as long to uncover King Menes' tomb as the first time they'd excavated it, they had agreed that the risks were worth taking. By digging during the hottest months of the year, there was little chance of anyone discovering what they were doing.

"We're ready, Gavin." Holding the *pshent* in her arms, Mac joined him on a rise that overlooked their camp. Wearing her *galabiya,* this set a soft petal blue, she looked as much a gypsy as ever, free and strong and beautiful.

He wrapped his arm around her waist, drew her close and pressed a kiss to her hair. "Mmmm, you smell good."

She barked an unladylike laugh. "I smell like sweat and dirt."

"You smell like cinnamon."

Frowning at him, she shook her head. "You've been in the sun too long."

"I take it everyone's waiting for me."

"You've been up here so long, Jake's beginning to hope that you've changed your mind about returning the *pshent* to King Menes' secret chamber."

"I suppose I'm going to have to disappoint him. Again."

"Have you decided what you'll tell King George? He's still expecting you to return with the *pshent*."

"I'm afraid King George will be disappointed, as well. As far as he will know, the crown is lost."

She glanced down at the scene below where Hollister, Frewin, Smedley and the others were milling about, carrying the last buckets of sand and taking torches into the open tomb. "I wish Pop and Kippie could have come."

"As do I."

"And Connor. It's a shame he couldn't stay long enough to see us return the crown."

"You can't be serious." He nuzzled her neck, felt his body respond and realized he needed to finish this last task so he could move on to things that were really important. Such as making love to his wife. "Connor was more than happy to leave Egypt. Especially now that he has a lead on finding the Staff of St. Moluag."

"Are you going to help him?" she asked, her voice a soft purr.

Though he didn't want to contemplate leaving Mac's side for any reason, he said, "I promised to do whatever I could."

Sighing, she said, "This is my last excavation."

"You've said so before."

"And you still don't believe me." She pulled away to

look up at him. "My family's too old for this. I wouldn't have brought them this time—"

"Except we couldn't trust hiring anyone else. If anyone learns where King Menes is buried, his tomb will be pillaged."

"I hope that never happens," she said, laying her head against his chest. "As much as my family loves the desert, they need an easier life."

So do you, Gavin thought. And he intended to give her one. She would never have to worry about how she would care for her family again. Whether they wanted to live in Egypt or England, he would provide for them now. Because they were his family, too.

His chest tightened as he took it all in. Rubbing his hand over his wife's flat stomach, he wondered if their family would grow, praying that it would. Wanting this moment to last, he whispered, "I love you, Mac."

Smiling, she ran her fingers over his rough-shaven face. "Gavin DeFoe, with everything that's going on, are you trying to seduce me?"

"You can't blame me for wanting to make love to my wife."

"Later," she said, her eyes flashing with silent laughter. Taking his hand, she tugged on it until he was forced to follow her down the slope. "At the moment we have things to do."

"You're right," he said, taking the red-and-white-gold double crown from her and holding it up to the light. The relic glowed with power and strength, hinting at the eons of mystery and secrets that were locked inside. If he had his way, they were secrets no one would ever know.

"It's time to visit King Menes one last time," he said. "And return him to the Afterlife."

Gavin was ready, because he had already started his life over again . . . and this time he knew he had it right, because this time he had Mac by his side.

AUTHOR'S NOTE

I love writing historical novels, the research, learning about the characters that defined our past and events that actually happened. But when writing the story I need to tell, history's timeline doesn't always cooperate. When this happens, it becomes necessary to alter certain facts. (Otherwise known as being creative!)

In BEYOND MY DREAMS, Jake and Mackenzie are able to read hieroglyphics, when in reality, it would have been impossible. The Rosetta Stone, a basalt slab containing a single text in three different languages—Demonic, hieroglyphics and Greek—wasn't discovered until July, 1799. And it wasn't until 1824 that Jean Francois Champollion successfully translated it.

I took the liberty to change certain dates involving Napoleon Bonaparte, as well. Though he was in Egypt on a campaign to oust the British and discover Egyptian artifacts, he didn't flee the country until October 1799 (five months after I have reported it happening). Also, the French general didn't move into Tuileries Palace until February 19, 1800.

At a pivotal part of the story, Mackenzie discovered the location of King Menes' tomb by solving the riddle involving Scorpio. In actuality, King Menes would not have used this sign because it had not been invented yet. It wasn't until 600 B.C. (2600 years after his death) that the Assyrians developed and named the twelve signs of the zodiac that we use today.

But there are elements of this story that are based on fact. King Menes, also known as the Scorpion King, actually existed. Egyptologists have determined that in 3200 B.C. he was the first king to unite Upper and Lower Egypt.

But it wasn't until recently that archaeologists discovered his tomb in Abydos. Unfortunately, it had been plundered during antiquity of all but a few items. Besides clay jars of wine, small tags (one-inch squares of bone and ivory) engraved with pictures of birds, trees, snakes, etc. were discovered. The similarities between the tags and hieroglyphics are so specific, scholars are convinced that King Menes is responsible for creating the first language. He was a remarkable man indeed.

I hope you've enjoyed BEYOND MY DREAMS, and can forgive me for taking liberties with history. But I think Gavin and Mackenzie's story was worth it.

Happy reading!
Tammy Hilz

About the Author

Raising three children and running a computer company with her husband left little time for pursuing anything else, especially the dream of becoming a writer. Then one day a miracle happened. Tammy and her husband sold their business.

Taking advantage of the free time on her hands, she began her new career. Since then, she has published seven historical, contemporary and paranormal novels and has won the prestigious RWA Golden Heart award. Tammy has no intention of returning to the corporate world. After all, who would trade a career based on love and happily-ever-after for one involving microchips and fiber optics! You can write Tammy at: *www.tammyhilz.com.*